Love and War 2

Love and War 2

Latoya Nicole

www.urbanbooks.net

Urban Books, LLC
300 Farmingdale Road, NY-Route 109
Farmingdale, NY 11735

ISBN 13: 978-1-64556-101-9
ISBN 10: 1-64556-101-1

First Trade Paperback Printing October 2020
Printed in the United States of America

10 9 8 7 6 5 4 3 2 1

*This is a work of fiction. Any references or similarities
to actual events, real people, living or dead, or to real
locales are intended to give the novel a sense of reality.
Any similarity in other names, characters, places, and
incidents is entirely coincidental.*

Distributed by Kensington Publishing Corp.
Submit Orders to:
Customer Service
400 Hahn Road
Westminster, MD 21157-4627
Phone: 1-800-733-3000
Fax: 1-800-659-2436

Love and War 2

Latoya Nicole

You led the way out of the darkness. You didn't go astray. You were ready to die for our sake, and that takes a soldier's heart.

—R. Kelly, "Soldier's Heart"

Normally, I start my dedication by expressing my love for my daughter. This time I'm going to start differently. My nephew is a proud member of the navy. He is leaving on deployment two days after my book is released, and I feel the need to let him know what he means to me.

When you were a baby, you stole my heart. Your big eyes and loving demeanor took over my world. We were inseparable. It was as if you were my child as well and Steph and I gave birth together. I couldn't get enough of you. You been my TT Baby since I laid eyes on you, and to this day, you allow me to call you that. We have been through so much together, and I want you to know I am extremely proud of the man you have become. And I am proud of everything you have accomplished, from having your own clothing line to serving this country. Know that your TT will always be your biggest fan. Be safe out there, and know that I will be waiting on you with tears in my eyes and my pom-poms. I love you always, Petty Officer Malik Daron McIntyre.

To the love of my life and the contents of my heart, Mommy is pushing herself so that I can be someone you are proud of. So that when you look at me, you don't see failure, struggle, hurt, or pain. All you see is the greatest mom in the world. I plan to be just that. You are my motivation, and I will continue to strive for you. Every day that I look into your eyes, you make me better. Don't ever change who you are because the world doesn't understand you. Be the one to make them understand. You're not different. You are *unique*, and I'm a proud autism mom. I love you, baby girl, and that will never change. My miracle, Monet Riley, you are the best.

ACKNOWLEDGMENTS

Curly B. Edwards, I'm still waiting on you to come home. You're in there fighting and hanging on. You have always been that person, so don't stop now. I love you, and I miss you.

To my publisher, Mz Lady P, the coldest in the game, thank you for giving me the tools I need to be that writer you believe me to be. You have pushed me to the limit like no one has ever done, and because of that, you have made me a better author. A better me. It's our time. MLPP, stand up. We taking over.

To pen sisters and bro, I am so proud of all of you. Don't ever give up on your dreams. Keep pushing. They see us. Now make them *see us*. Ashley Davidson, Paree Trenae, Manda P, thank you all for being there for me. From the moment I met you ladies, you took over my heart. I love you, and it's our time. Claim it.

Bookies Admin, you ladies keep me sane as hell. You believe in me even when I don't want to believe in myself. Thank you for being that extra push we need. You keep me smiling, and in you all, I have truly found some amazing friends. ZaTasha Shiffer, Ashley Davidson, KB Cole, Paree Trenae, Amber Shanel, Dawn Budgie, Manda Panda, I love you all from the bottom of my heart.

A special shout-out goes to ZaTasha "The Book Plug" Shiffer, my test reader. You make sure my shit's on point, and I appreciate you. Thank you for believing in me. I love you.

Acknowledgments

Lawrynn Brooks, hey, bestie. I love you and thank you for bringing the bitch squad together. Sasha, Victoria, Jaz, Faith, Keondria, Kadeene, Kenice, Monisha, Simone, ZaTasha, and Tommy (LOL), I appreciate all the laughs and encouragement.

To my readers, thank you for rocking with me. Book eight and I'm not done yet. You all have been really having my back, and I appreciate you all to the fullest. The past three books hit the top ten. Let's go for that number 1 spot. Tell everyone to download and grab that Hoover Gang. And please don't forget to leave a review. I love you.

PROLOGUE:

WHERE WE LEFT OFF . . .

DREA

"Why wouldn't you tell me he was coming over?" Ash was screaming at me like this shit was my fault. She was slamming pots all over the fucking stove. She was about to cook for Zavi, but her ass was a mess.

"I didn't know. He called and said he was outside. As soon as I got in the truck, you walked up. I didn't even see you until he got out and approached you. You should have told him. What the fuck you think was gone happen?" I was not about to let her play victim and blame me.

"I was going to tell him tomorrow. I can't believe this shit is happening." She was crying hard, and I walked over and hugged her. Even though she had brought this on herself, I felt bad for her.

"It's going to be okay. He loves you. He will be pissed and will maybe beat your ass, but he will forgive you."

She didn't respond; she just cried. After about twenty minutes of her crying and going off, she got it together.

"I'm about to take Zavi and go to a hotel," she said. "I don't want Quick coming over here and acting an ass in front of my son. I'll go and talk to him tomorrow, like I said."

I agreed. I didn't want that shit at my house. After she left, I lay in the bed, just shocked at everything that had happened today. I still didn't know what Face had wanted with me. He had got so mad, he had left without telling me. As I was lying there, trying to figure out what he could have wanted, my phone rang. I answered once I saw it was Mack calling.

"Hey, Mack."

"Hey. What you doing?" he said.

"Lying down. Shit got crazy over here."

"You want some company?"

"Yes, please."

"Open the door," he instructed.

I jumped up and ran to the front door like I was a kid. When I opened it, he was standing there, looking good as hell. I stepped aside so he could enter. We walked back to my bedroom, and I laid him on the bed. Then I took my robe off, exposing my naked, pregnant body.

"You so damn beautiful," he whispered.

Blushing, I leaned down to kiss him, but he stopped me.

"Shorty, I told you already, you don't have to do this. We can wait until you have the baby. I don't want you to have any regrets."

"I promise I won't. I need you," I said. "I had a rough day, and I need you to make it better."

I leaned down to kiss him again. This time, he didn't stop me. He pulled me gently down onto the bed, and then he started licking my pussy like it was his last meal. His head wasn't all that great, but that was okay. I could teach him what I liked. After he was there for about ten minutes, I was over it and was ready for him to be inside me. I climbed on top of him and ground against his dick. Then I lifted myself up and grabbed it. I was getting ready to slide it in when the smoke detectors went off.

"Fuck! Ash was cooking something for Zavi. She forgot to turn the fucking stove off." I jumped up and ran out of the room to try to fix the shit, but it was too late. Flames were everywhere.

"Mack!" I screamed.

He ran to the kitchen and saw the fire. Then he disappeared. I stood there in shock, as if I forgot the house was on fire, and then fell to the floor, crying. This day was supposed to be a happy one, and here I was, crying my heart out. This house was the last thing I had of my mom's, and Ash had set it on fire. In one fell swoop, because her life was fucked up, she had managed to take the last thing I had. Mack came running toward me, my robe in his hand.

"I know you're pissed, but we have to get out of here. Is Ash here?" he said.

"Nope. The bitch left and damn near killed our ass." I stood up and wrapped the robe around me. When the ceiling started falling in, he snatched my hand, and we ran to the front door. As we bolted outside, it dawned on me that all my money was in the house. I pulled my hand free, pivoted, and started running back toward the door as he screamed my name.

"Drea! The fuck is you doing?"

I stopped and turned around to face him, but for a few seconds, I didn't know what the fuck to say.

"Blaze," was all I could get out before I passed out.

CHAPTER 1

DREA

Sometimes when you passed out, people threw water on your face, and you felt like they were drowning you in your sleep. This was one time when I would have wanted to be awakened in that way. When I passed out, I kept telling myself it had to be a dream, but then I felt this heat on my face, and I knew Blaze was really here. It was he, not Ash, who had started the fire. I jumped up and looked him in his eyes, expecting to see nothing but love in those gray eyes of his, but all I saw was, "Ho, run!" and that was exactly what I did. I got my pregnant ass off the ground and hauled ass.

"Don't run now, Drea. Bring that ass here," Blaze yelled as he started after me. I could literally hear him flicking his Bic lighter as he chased me.

"Drea, what the fuck you running for? Fuck that nigga." The moment I heard Mack scream those words, I wanted to yell, "Save yourself. Run, Forrest. Run!"

Hearing Blaze's footsteps going away from me, I knew it was all over for that nigga. I knew I should go back, but I kept running until I made it to the gas station. That nigga was gone have to save his damn self. After I walked inside, I approached the clerk. I was out of breath like a motherfucker.

"Excuse me, may I please use your phone?" I asked, breathless.

Everyone was looking at me like I was crazy. I looked down. I had forgotten I had my robe on, and I saw that the shit had come untied. I was standing there in all my glory. After closing my robe, I looked back at the clerk, hoping he would allow me to use his phone. He obliged, and once he had handed it to me, I called Ash.

When she picked up, I blurted, "I need you to hurry up and come get me. I'm at the Shell gas station four blocks from the house."

"Why aren't you at the house?"

"Bitch, because it has burned down. I'll explain everything when you get here. Hurry your ass up." After I hung up the phone, I went and stood next to the chip rack and attempted to hide just in case Blaze came in here looking for my ass. This should be the happiest day of my life, but that nigga had just caught me with another nigga. This was not about to be a friendly visit. When Blaze thought I had set him up, he had had that same look in his eyes.

"Drea?" I could hear Ash whispering, and I came out of hiding.

"Why the fuck are you whispering?" I whispered back.

"Shit, I don't know. Why are you hiding, and how the hell did the house burn down?" Once we walked out the door and got in the car, I looked at her and finally spoke the words out loud.

"Bitch, Blaze is alive, and I think he burned down the house."

She shook her head as she squinted at me. "Okay, now you're starting to lose it."

"Girl, I'm not crazy. I thought I was dreaming about him when I passed out, but I woke up, and that nigga was setting my face on fire. I jumped up and ran. He was chasing me until Mack said, 'Fuck that nigga.'"

"What the fuck? Where is Mack?"

"Bitch, I don't know. I left his ass back at the house. That nigga Blaze was trying to kill me."

"He wasn't trying to kill you, but he did fuck you up," she muttered.

I looked at her like she was crazy, and then I pulled the visor down so I could look at myself in the mirror. What a sight I was. This nigga had burned my whole right eyebrow off. Something was wrong with him. Who would do that to somebody?

"Bitch, what the fuck am I going to do?" I cried as I pointed at my eyebrow. I thought about what me and Face had done, and I began panicking. "Oh God! He is going to kill me!"

"It ain't that serious. You thought he was dead, and you moved on with your life. I'm sure he will understand." She didn't realize the extent of what I'd done. "Bitch, okay, I need to know where we are going."

"Let's go back to your room. I need to think," I told her.

This shit was about to get real ugly, and a lot of people was going to be hurt. All I could do was pray that Blaze forgave me. The only problem was, I now had feelings for Mack. Who the fuck was I kidding? Blaze was back, and any feelings I felt for Mack were dead the moment I laid eyes on Blaze. Leaning my head back, I cried. This nigga had been alive all this time. This was a really sick joke, and now my dumb ass was about to pay for it.

Once we reached the hotel room, all kinds of thoughts went through my mind.

"This nigga was supposed to love me." I said as I sat on the edge of the bed.

"Who? Don't start that dumb shit, Drea."

"Blaze. How could he pretend to be dead all this time? Who the fuck would do that to someone they love?"

"I wonder if the brothers knew all this time," Ash mused as she paced the floor.

Thinking about what she had said, I got pissed all over again. "Fuck this shit! I'm not running from his ass. He better hope I don't kill him for the shit he has put me through. Give me something to throw on."

Ash stopped pacing and gazed at me intently. "Fuck is you going?"

"To find that nigga. I'm going to the main house," I said.

"Given the way Baby Face just dragged your ass by your neck, I'm coming too," Ash insisted.

"What if Quick's there?"

"I guess we gone be two dead bitches together," she declared.

Ash found me something to wear, and we both got ready to leave. I just hoped the stunt we were about to pull didn't get us sent to meet our Maker.

CHAPTER 2

BABY FACE

A nigga had been tossing and turning all night. That shit with Ash and Drea had me pissed off. I eased out of the bed so I wouldn't wake Juicy up, and then I went into the bathroom and pissed. Everybody thought it was okay to try us, and the shit was pushing me to my limit. Hearing my phone ring brought me out of my thoughts. Who the fuck would be calling me at this time of night? As soon as I walked back in the bedroom, Juicy was looking at me like she was about to go off. Not in the mood for her shit, I answered the call. If I didn't, I knew it would be even worse.

"Yeah?"

"You have a collect call from an inmate at the Cook County Jail. His name is Quick. Press zero if you accept these charges."

I hit zero. Quick came on the line.

"Face. These niggas done locked me up. Come get me."

"Who? And how much is the bond?"

"A million, and for Alaysia's dumb ass. I guess the bitch rolled up on the river."

"Quit talking like that on the phone. I'm on the way." I headed over to the dresser, opened a drawer, and grabbed some jogging pants.

"Baby, I have to go bond Quick out of jail," I informed Juicy.

"What the fuck? You need me to go with you?"

"The shit with Alaysia . . . And yeah, come along, just in case they lock my ass up with him."

After throwing our clothes on, we headed out the door. As I jumped in my truck, all kinds of shit went through my mind. Were we considered accomplices? How the fuck did they know Quick had done the shit? Had we covered all our tracks? I yanked my phone out of my pocket and called Shadow.

"Bro, you up?" I said the second he picked up.

"Yeah, I'm waiting on this back-page ho of mine to walk through the door." There was too much going on, so I decided not to ask what the fuck Shirree's ass had done.

"Meet me at the County. They locked Quick up about that Alaysia shit, and I'm on my way to bond him out."

"What the fuck? A'ight, I'm on the way," he said.

When I ended the call, I was pulling into my storage unit. I stopped the truck, turned off the motor, and opened my door. "I'll be back," I told Juicy. "It's usually empty in here, but if a motherfucker approaches you, point this and don't stop shooting." I handed Juicy one of my guns and got out. I knew she was gone have some shit to say, but with everything going on, I needed to start making better decisions. After unlocking my unit, I walked in and grabbed a suitcase. After walking out, I made sure I locked that shit back up and headed back to my truck. When I got back in, Juicy started going off.

"So, you don't trust me?"

"What are you talking about?" I mumbled.

"Why didn't you just drive to your unit?"

Thinking about it now, I could see why she was pissed. But she was right: with the shit that was going on, I didn't trust a soul. "I'm sorry. I wasn't thinking. Too much on my mind."

Hoping she was done, I cut the music on and headed to the Cook County Jail. There would be questions about the money I was putting up for bail, but our clubs were legit and would cover the amount I had to use. This was one place every street nigga hated to come. My ass was shaking like a stripper, but I walked in that bitch to get my brother out of this mess. Juicy was holding on to me like she was scared they was gone take her cat.

"You know we ain't going around any inmates, right?" I said.

Looking at me, she laughed. "Oh, a bitch was nervous as hell." She let my arm go, and we approached the counter.

"I'm here to bail out Zavier Hoover."

The officer typed his name into the computer, and his eyes got big. "You do know his bond is a million dollars, right?"

Laughing, I set the briefcase on the counter. "Obviously."

"Give me a minute." The officer stood up and walked away. When he returned, he came back with the captain.

"Anything over nine thousand will be audited," the captain announced. "You do know that, right?" He looked skeptical.

"Look, I got enough money to buy you and this mother-fucking place. I know how this shit go. Take this money, release my brother, and send whatever papers you have to. Now, if you don't mind, get the fuck out of my face and go do your job." I walked away and sat down on the bench. These niggas were mugging me like they wanted to lock my ass up. Shadow walked in the door just then, and it looked like he was the one who was coming out of lockup.

"Damn, nigga. You look like you ain't been to sleep in months. Fuck is wrong with you?" I said.

"This shitty-mouthed bitch been taking me through it. What they saying?" That was the second reference he had made to Shirree in less than an hour, but this wasn't the place to find out what the fuck he was talking about.

"I'm waiting on them to release him. I paid a mil to get him out."

"I'm glad he called your ass. That peanut butter mouth–ass bitch been cleaning my ass out." Me and Juicy looked at him like he was crazy.

"Bro, you pissed off, ain't you?" I said.

He shook his head, and I just laughed.

This shit usually took a few hours, so I thought we were in for a long night. I guessed money talked and bullshit walked, 'cause this nigga came walking out twenty minutes later. The sight of him made my skin crawl. They had beat him so bad, you could barely recognize him.

"Hey, niggas, we didn't pay y'all a million dollars for y'all to send out a nigga that might not be my brother. This nigga could be anybody," I told the officers. After slapping Shadow on the head, I walked up to Quick with tears in my eyes.

"You good?" I asked him.

He nodded. "Yeah. Let's go."

We all headed out and walked toward my truck.

"Shadow, meet us at the main house," I said. "I'm sure Quick don't want to go home, and your ass got some explaining to do."

Shadow shook his head. "A'ight."

When we got in the truck, Juicy had tears running down her face, and Quick was just silent. I knew he would tell us in his own time what had happened, but right now he just zoned out. He didn't say a word the entire way to the main house. As soon as we pulled up, he got out. I didn't know what to say to my nigga to make him feel better, so I said nothing. When we got to the door, you could tell it had been broken in.

"Juicy, stay right here," I said as I gave Quick my other gun.

We headed in. As soon as we walked in the front foyer, we could see someone standing in front of Blaze's shrine.

"You got ten seconds to tell me what the fuck you doing in our shit before you lose your hairline," I snarled. Me and Quick both had our guns pointed at him. When I heard the Bic flick, my heart started racing.

The guy didn't leave me in suspense for long. "Did you put this big, ugly-ass pic of me up before or after you fucked my bitch?" he said. I could recognize my brother's voice in my sleep. I walked over to the wall and cut the light on.

"Blaze, what the fuck?" I exclaimed.

He didn't speak; he just flicked his Bic again. I ain't never been scared of a nigga in my life, but right now a nigga was nervous. I couldn't even be happy he was alive, because I had to make sure this nigga wasn't about to set me on fire.

"I'm waiting to hear your answer," I said when about a minute had passed. For some reason, I was compelled to turn around. Juicy was standing behind me. *Fuck!* This shit was not about to go right for a nigga.

Quick walked toward Blaze, but I stayed back. "Blaze, how? Bro, I thought . . . I, man . . . You just don't know the weight you lifted off me." I was happy as fuck Quick had changed the subject.

Blaze frowned. "Hey, who the fuck is this ugly-ass motherfucker? Y'all better get this Kimbo Slice–looking nigga away from me before I light his ass up. And he can't afford to get no uglier."

Quick stopped in his tracks, but I laughed. It was good to hear my brother again.

Shadow came walking in just then and stopped dead in his tracks. "The fuck y'all niggas doing?" He looked over and saw Blaze and ran toward him. "How, bro? I prayed for this shit every night. Where the fuck you been?" Shadow was crying, and Quick walked up to hug him.

"Nigga, didn't I tell you to follow me?" Baby Face asked.

"Who the fuck is this nigga?" Blaze asked.

Shadow laughed and wiped his tears. "That's Quick, dumbass. The police beat his ass."

Blaze finally allowed Quick to approach him. As soon as they hugged, Quick broke down in tears. The shit made me cry too, but I wasn't going anywhere near that nigga.

"Face, you gone try to ignore what the fuck I asked you?" Juicy asked.

I hadn't heard her question. I turned toward her and prayed I could buy some more time. "We will talk about this when we get home. There's a lot I need to discuss with my brothers," I told her.

The tears started falling down her face, and it broke my heart.

"I knew you niggas were foul, but not this fucked up. Why the fuck would y'all let us think Blaze was dead?" Drea asked.

When I turned my head, I saw Drea, Ash, and her son standing there, and I swear, this couldn't be a more fucked-up time. Before anyone could respond, Juicy ran up on Drea and hit her so hard, my dick jumped.

"If you weren't pregnant, I would drag your ass," Juicy seethed. When Juicy slapped her again before she walked out, I knew this shit was about to be fucked up for me.

CHAPTER 3

QUICK

When Blaze asked whether Baby Face had put up that big-ass pic of him before he fucked his bitch, I almost passed out. I thought Blaze was just talking shit, but Baby Face didn't walk up on Blaze the entire time. All of this was going on, and I was in shock. It was like all the guilt was lifted off a nigga. My brother wasn't dead because of me, but now, as the thought sank in, I wondered where the fuck he had been.

All these emotions were running through me when Juicy punched Drea. That was the first time I took my *eye* off Blaze. I could see out of only one of them bitches since the police had Rodney Kinged my ass, but that one motherfucker was clear enough for me to see Ash standing there with a child who looked identical to me. My knees got weak as I walked toward her. She forgot she was standing there with her son once she looked at my face. She ran to me with a look of empathy and sadness on her face. Before she could make it to me, I drew my hand all the way back to Mississippi and slapped that bitch to sleep. The look on her face confirmed what I already knew.

"Is that my son, Ash?"

The tears flowed from her face, but I wasn't in the mood for no fucking tears. She seemed to be stuck, mute, so I slapped her ass again. Before anybody could do or say anything, I grabbed her by her neck and picked her up off her feet. I walked that bitch to the next room, because I didn't want to kill her in front of my son. When I released her, the bitch was acting like she couldn't breathe and had damn near died. Her dramatics didn't move me.

"I'm going to ask you again. Is that my son?" I said.

She had the nerve to look at me with hate in her eyes.

I ran toward her and slammed her into the wall. She fell to the floor. "Is that my fucking son?"

I guessed I must have slapped her tongue down her throat, because she sat there mute, not saying a word.

I grabbed the gun Baby Face had given me from my waist, then pointed it at her. "I promise if you don't answer me, I'm going to be a single fucking parent. You have ten fucking seconds to answer me, or you won't live long enough to blink."

Crying, she looked into my eyes, and she knew I was serious. "Yes, he is your son."

I couldn't even explain the emotions I was feeling. I had so many questions, and everything started running through my mind. The day she left . . . That was six years ago. He looked like he was about six now. All these years. All these fucking years, she had chosen to keep this from me. My knees felt weak, and I slowly sank to the floor. I couldn't stop the tears that fell from my eyes. My child didn't even know who I was. She got up off the floor and walked over to console me, and I gave her a hard stare.

"Don't fucking touch me," I growled. "I have never hated a person as much as I hate you right now. Get the fuck out of my house, but leave my son here. I don't care how you tell him, but you have ten minutes to bring him up to speed. I will call you when you can pick him up. If you come within two hundred feet of my fucking house and I didn't call you to come get him, I will blow your fucking brains out. Ten minutes. Now get the fuck out of my face."

She walked out of the room, and I broke down as I sat there on the floor. I thought I was a pretty decent person, but lately, all the shit that had been happening to me had me questioning that shit. What the fuck had a nigga done to deserve all of this? Getting myself together, I stood up and wiped the tears off my face. I was about to meet my son, and I needed him to see me for the nigga I was, not the nigga these bitches were trying to make me out to be. I heard the door open, and my heart started racing. She walked him over to me, and he looked at me and smiled.

"You look like me, just old," he said as he gazed up at me.

Laughing, with tears in my eyes, I grabbed him and hugged him. "Yeah, I think we might be twins," I told him.

"We can't be twins. You too old. Mommy said you're my dad. Is that true?"

"Yeah, I'm your dad. You are going to stay with me for a while so you can get to know me. Okay?"

"Are you going to leave like my other daddy, Jason?" Wanting to punch Ash in her pussy bone, I looked at her with death in my eyes.

"Mommy made a mistake," I said. "Jason wasn't really your dad. I am, and I will never leave you, son. You will always have me, okay?"

He nodded his head and hugged me again. I looked up, and this bitch Ash was standing there, grinning and shit, looking like a lifelong child molester. I snapped her ass back to reality quick.

"Why are you still standing here? Get the fuck out," I snapped.

She turned and walked out of the room. I looked down at my son and realized she had never told me his name.

"What's your name, son?"

"Zavier Hoover Jr. What's your name?"

"Zavier Hoover Sr. Come on. Let's go meet your uncles."

We walked back in the living room, and I saw that all hell had broken loose in my absence. Blaze had Baby Face on the floor, with a lighter to his face, and Shadow was trying to break them up, but he was laughing too hard.

What in the fuck had happened?

CHAPTER 4

BLAZE

When I walked in the door of the main house, I had so many emotions running through me. Drea had me fucked up if she thought it was okay to move on. Bitch was mine forever. Ain't no life after a nigga like me. I had expected her to be sitting around, looking like death in a wig, but she wasn't. She was beautiful, glowing, and pregnant. When I had seen the nigga go in her house earlier, I had known she was about to have a long night. No way I was letting that shit go down. When she had realized I was actually there, she had passed out. I had woken that ass up, though. I hadn't expected her ass to take off running like that. I had never seen a pregnant chick run that fucking fast.

When the nigga she was with had spoken up, I had chin checked his ass. Once I realized I wasn't catching Drea, I turned to his bitch ass. Fucked-up thing about it was, as soon as I hit that nigga, he hit the ground like a bitch. Before I could stomp his dreads off, the nigga jumped up and ran the other way. I knew I was too tired to try to chase him, but I would see that nigga again. I walked off, flicking my Bic, and headed to the main house.

Looking at my shrine now did something to me. I must say, my brothers went all out for a nigga, and looking at this memorial to me had me feeling like I was at somebody else's shit. I didn't expect these niggas to walk through the door. Getting my mind right and getting a good night's sleep were my intentions. I knew there was going to be some shit behind my return. Me revealing that I knew about Baby Face and Drea caught them by surprise. Everything that had happened since I was gone, I knew about it. A nigga seen the shit with Drea and Face with my own eyes. Quick dragging Ash out of the living room brought a lot of tension, and I was left to confront Drea and Baby Face.

"Don't get quiet now, bro. You thought it was okay to fuck my bitch?" I said. I could see the hurt in Baby Face's eyes. Drea was now crying and looking stupid as hell.

"Blaze, I promise that wasn't my intention. I would never do anything to hurt you." Looking into his eyes, I could see he meant it, but I wasn't about to let it go.

"Come over here and give me a hug. Why the fuck you all the way over there? A nigga come back from the dead, and you ain't gone show me no love?"

He walked toward me, and I could tell he was leery. As soon as he was close enough, I stole on his ass. Before he got the chance to react, I swept that nigga's legs out from under him and took him down to the floor. Not letting up, I pulled out my Bic and had the flame to his face before he could even think about getting away from me.

"Nigga, all the bitches in the world and you fucked *mine*? You think this shit sweet? Or did you forget who the fuck I am?"

He didn't even respond; he kept trying to get me off him. But I had my legs locked, and I was heavier than this skinny-ass nigga. Shadow's ass wouldn't stop laughing, and that only made Baby Face try harder to get away. I took the lighter to his hairline and lit that nigga up.

"Ah! What the fuck? Blaze, stop, nigga!"

I laughed as Baby Face realized his hairline was melting.

"What the fuck are you niggas doing?" Quick said when he walked back in the living room.

Ignoring Quick, I kept the fire on Baby Face. Once I saw his hair was on fire, I used my hand to pat out the flames.

"Damn. My bad, bro," I said as I stood up and let Baby Face off the floor. "Before you go look at your hair, I fucked up. I was only trying to get your hairline, but issa Lebron." He reached up to touch his hair and felt the bald spot.

"You play all your fucking life," he seethed. Shadow and Quick was dying laughing, and that only made Baby Face more upset. "Y'all think this shit funny. I hate this nigga."

"Nigga, you should be happy that's all he did. Look how he fucked up Quick's face over ZaTasha, and that wasn't even his bitch," Shadow told him.

When I thought about what Shadow had said, I realized that I had let this nigga off easy. Baby Face must have realized it, too, because he shut his ass up.

"All jokes aside, I get it, bro," I told Baby Face. "I know that you both were grieving, and that shit will have you doing fucked-up shit to feel close to the person that's gone, but if I even catch you looking at my bitch's hair wrong, that's your ass. The shit hurt me when I saw it, but I know y'all didn't intentionally hurt me. However, the fact remains that you did. Just know my, nigga, I'm gone get you back in some kind of way. It might not be today, and it might not be tomorrow, but I'm coming for your ass."

The look on his face was priceless. Baby Face knew I meant what I'd said too. We wouldn't be even until I felt we were.

"You motherfuckers carrying on and shit. Meanwhile, I'm the only person trying to figure out where the fuck this nigga been," Drea interjected.

Everyone turned and looked at her.

"Shut the fuck up. You don't have the right to ask shit," I told her. "A nigga was dead for six minutes, and you done fucked two niggas. You better be lucky you pregnant, or I would have lit your ass up. Out here acting like you got ads and shit on Craigslist. The fuck you do? Send out a memo?"

Everybody was laughing, but I was dead-ass serious. That pregnant pussy would have been loose as goose if I hadn't brought my ass back.

I went on. "But to answer everybody's question, that bitch-ass Rico had me locked away in a damn warehouse. Before the wedding, he came to me, and I told him to stay the fuck away from us. If I saw him anywhere around, I was gone murk his ass. When I got shot, the ambulance pulled up to the hospital, and they snatched my ass up. I'm guessing they sent another nigga in my place, but I woke up attached to machines and shit, but I wasn't in a hospital. They had a doctor there on call, taking care of me.

"The first thing that nigga did was show me the video of Baby Face and Drea. He been watching y'all's every move. I overheard him talking, and it seems he came back to get money from us. He owes a nigga in Puerto Rico a lot of money, and if he don't come up with it, they gone kill his ass. Since he knew I wasn't gone let him get close to y'all, he took me out of the equation.

"His bitch ass working with Tate and Slick. Them niggas was about to come for Baby Face next, and I knew I had to get out of there. I acted like my wounds were bothering me and I was in pain. When the doctor came to check me, I snapped that nigga's neck and took the gun he had. A nigga didn't have his Bic, but I shot my way up out of that motherfucker. First place I went was Drea's, and she was about to fuck some clown-ass nigga."

"Did you set his ass on fire?" Shadow asked.

"I tried to oven bake both of them bitches. She took off running, and I thought I had his ass, but that bitch-ass nigga took off running too."

They laughed, while Drea sat there with her head down. I would make it up to her later, but right now me and my brothers needed to come up with a plan. This shit was getting out of hand.

"We already handled Slick, and Quick's ass took care of Alaysia. We need to find that nigga Tate and Rico," Baby Face said.

I was glad Baby Face had been out here handling shit while I was gone.

Quick shook his head. "We definitely need to find Tate. He is the witness. He done went and told they ass all kinds of bullshit, and that's why they arrested me. They got a decorated cop telling them she confided in him about her relationship with me, and they got my nut in her throat. This shit ain't looking good."

"I can't believe you was still fucking that bitch," Shadow said.

I looked at Shadow, confused.

"Oh, I forgot your ass was dead, but she was in a wheelchair, paralyzed."

"Quick, you nasty as hell, bro," I said.

Quick replied, "She was blackmailing me. The shit felt like rape, and I was sick of it. I threw that strong-armed bitch in the lake."

This shit was too much for me. So much had happened since I left.

"Well, we may as well go tell y'all mama."

"Mama gone be pissed when she finds out Rico had you. She was fucking that nigga. Man, we walked in on that nigga and her going at it. Nastiest shit I ever seen," Shadow said.

I did not need that visual, and I was glad I hadn't been here for that shit. Shadow's nasty ass prolly had watched.

I walked over to Drea and grabbed her by the hand, and then we all walked out the door to head over to my mama's house. This shit was about to get real interesting. Rico's ass had to go, and I prayed my mama didn't try to stop us, or she was gone get her ass lit up too.

"Hey, is everybody strapped? Rico may be here," Baby Face said after we had climbed in my car.

Damn. Baby Face was right.

"I'm not," I said. "Drea, you and the shorty stay here, just in case shit go left. I'm gone run in and get some heat." We all got out of the car and walked back in the house.

"What if you don't come back?" Drea asked. I knew she was scared.

"I'll always come back," I assured her. "You just stay here and try not to slip on another dick. Love you."

I grabbed the guns from our stash and headed out.

CHAPTER 5

SHADOW

This nigga Blaze coming back done fucked my emotions all up. We had gone through hell, and this nigga had barely been asleep, let alone dead. I hadn't even got the chance to tell them about Shirree's skunk-mouth ass. Once Blaze got in the car, I decided to tell them what was going on.

"I had Shirree followed, and the bitch was cheating on me with Peter Pan and a fairy," I announced.

"What the fuck you talking about, nigga?" Blaze was confused.

"She was riding some nigga's face while another nigga was sucking his dick. Biggest part of it all is the ho was paying them. The nasty bitch tried to lick my ass, and I Mayweathered her ass."

"Where shitty at now?" Blaze asked.

I knew I shouldn't have told them that part. Blaze did the most.

"I don't know. I was waiting on her ass to come home when Baby Face called me and told me we had to go bond Quick out. I ain't seen the ho since I got the pictures." I replied.

"We will swing by Boystown when we leave from seeing Mama," Blaze declared.

I was confused. Looking at Blaze, I asked him what the fuck he meant. "Why we going to Boystown? Nigga, was you gay while you were dead?"

Blaze shook his head. "Naw, but your bitch like eating gay niggas' asses. She can find a bunch of shitty sissies in that motherfucker."

If this nigga hadn't played all his life, I would have knocked his ass out.

"Baby bro, when she licked your ass, did you have your ass tooted?" Now Baby Face was trying to throw shots.

"Fuck, y'all! This why I don't tell y'all shit," I muttered.

"This nigga been at home, twerking and shit. That's why his dick wasn't working. He needed that booty played in," Quick interjected.

I shot Quick a death look. He was the only one I had told that shit.

"Damn, nigga. Your shit already little. It's limp too? Here." Blaze passed me his gun.

"The fuck is this for?" I said.

"You may as well kill yourself, nigga. You walking around with a li'l limp dick, and your booty leaking. Issa suicide."

I slapped his ass with the gun, then gave it back to him. When he flicked his Bic, I tried to change the subject.

"Y'all think Mama gone be hurt when we kill Rico?" I asked.

"You know her ass gone be extra, but fuck her. She can get it too," Blaze replied.

"Damn. You gone kill your mama?" I looked at Blaze like he was crazy.

He shrugged. "I won't kill her, but I will shoot them old-ass knees up."

We all laughed as we pulled up to her house. We climbed out of the car and walked in the door in single file. The house was dark as hell. We had our guns raised just in case Rico was there. We walked all over the house, but we didn't find a soul in that motherfucker. The shit was weird, and it wasn't like our mama.

Baby Face pulled his phone out and started calling her. Finally, he turned, shook his head, and said, "No answer."

We walked back out the door and got back in the car.

"We not gone jump to conclusions just yet. We will keep trying and checking," Blaze declared.

Everyone agreed with Blaze, and we drove off.

"Hey, you ready to come back from the dead, nigga?" I asked as we drove along.

Blaze shot me a look. "What you mean? What the fuck am I now? Invisible?"

"Nigga, I mean to everyone else. Let's hit up Hoover Nights later. Y'all down? I'll call the DJ in advance and let him know all the brothers will be in attendance."

Quick nodded enthusiastically. "Hell yeah, I'm down. But if we can't find Mama, I'm gone need a sitter." Shit sounded funny hearing Quick say he needed someone to watch his son.

"Drea's ass can watch him," Blaze said. "Maybe it will keep her ass from slipping on a dick. I gotta watch my bitch. She got some ho tendencies in her ass." This nigga Blaze didn't give a fuck what came out of his mouth.

"So we good? Everybody down?" I asked.

Everybody agreed with the plan just as we pulled up to the main house.

"Blaze, you know you don't have to stay here. We didn't sell your house. All your shit is there. Phone and all," Baby Face said. "Just so you know, Drea didn't want a dime of your money."

We all agreed with Baby Face. She really just wanted him.

"She gone want that shit now. I burned her shit down, and her money was in that motherfucker," Blaze revealed.

I reached in my pocket for the key to his house and grabbed the keepsake urn. "Time out, Blaze. If your ass alive, who the fuck is the nigga Baby Face done gave us?" I said.

"I don't know. Toss that key, nigga."

"Blaze, you might wanna tell Drea to throw her necklace away. She walking around with another nigga's burnt dick around her neck."

I threw my lighter at Baby Face and got in my car and drove off. When I pulled up to the house and saw Shirree's car there, I got pissed. This bitch was trying me, and today I was here for the bullshit. After I walked in the door, I ran up the stairs. This bitch had the nerve to be in bed, all relaxed.

"Hey, babes. Why you have all my stuff out? You in one of your cleaning modes?" she said as I stalked into the bedroom.

"Naw, I'm in a 'Drag a bitch' mode. You got me fifty shades of fucked up." I walked over to the bed, then grabbed her ass by her hair and dragged her out of the room.

"Shadow, let me go! What the fuck is wrong with you?"

Making sure her ass hit each step, I dragged her down the stairs and out the front door. Then I let her go, pulled my gun out, and pointed it at her ass.

"Take your clothes off," I ordered.

She looked at me with so much confusion written on her face. The ho probably thought I wanted to fuck right there on the porch. She did as she was told, but continued to ask questions.

"Baby, why are you doing this? I thought we were working on us?"

"I thought we were too, until I found out your ass was paying to lick a nigga's ass. You were riding that nigga's face like it didn't just come out of a nigga's ass. Your pussy prolly got all kinds of shit crumbs in it. Issa infection. Get the fuck off my porch, and if I ever see your ass again, you a deceased bitch."

"I don't have my keys," she whimpered.

"That's my shit. I was gone let you keep it, but fuck that."

"How am I going to get to where I'm going?"

"I don't give a fuck, but you got ten seconds to get the fuck off my porch, or the ambulance gone be your cab."

She looked at me with tears running down her face. She thought that shit was gone move me.

"Eight seconds."

"Baby, I'm pregnant. Please don't do this."

"Bitch, my dick ain't worked in months. You better go find the daddy, and you got four seconds left to do it."

She walked off, defeated. I made sure she was completely gone before I went in my house and locked the door. I was fed up with her. *How the fuck you pregnant by me and my dick been dead with Blaze's ass?*

When I got upstairs, my phone rang. It was Quick.

"Hey, nigga. I just thought about it. I can't go to no fucking club. My face's fucked up. We gotta hold off on that shit."

"Didn't nobody tell your ass to get your dumb ass locked up, but a'ight," I said. "You should be good in a few days. We will go next weekend." I hung up and lay down on the bed.

This bitch Shirree had better not come back to my shit. I couldn't believe I had almost married a ho.

CHAPTER 6

BABY FACE

Nobody could ever understand the relief I felt from knowing that Blaze had forgiven me. Still, I knew him, and so I knew I would have to look over my shoulder at all times.

Convincing Juicy to forgive me would be harder. When I walked in my house, I could tell she wasn't there. Needing to see for myself, I checked anyway. Sure as shit stank, she was gone. Feeling defeated, I headed into the bedroom and sat down on the bed. I had wanted to tell Juicy myself. I would have left her ass at home if I had known Blaze's ass was gone rise up from the dead. *Fuck that*, I thought. I wasn't letting my girl get away that easy. I got up off the bed, left the house, and jumped back in my whip. I was going to Juicy's apartment. She was going to hear me out.

As soon as I drove off, my phone rang.

"What up, Quick?" I said when I answered the call.

"Hey, y'all niggas almost got me. I ain't going in the club looking like this."

"You are ugly as shit."

"Fuck you. We gone go next weekend."

"That's cool," I said.

We hung up, and I continued the drive to get my girl back. What me and Drea had done was fucked up, but if my brother could let it go, so could she. When I pulled up to her house, I was scared as hell. I jumped out of my whip and headed to her front door. My hands were sweating when I rang the doorbell. I heard her walk to the door, but she didn't open it. Knowing she was looking through the peephole, I knocked on the door. She still refused to open it.

"Juicy, open the fucking door! I know you in there." I took a look around to make sure she ain't have no nosy-ass neighbors watching. When I was convinced nobody was looking, I leaned back and kicked that bitch off the hinges. She jumped away from the door as it came crashing down. "Why the fuck you playing with me?" I muttered.

"Just leave. I don't play the types of games your family be on." She tried to walk away, but I grabbed her wrist.

"I'm sorry. It's not like you didn't know I cheated. I promise the shit just happened. I don't want Drea. I want you."

"You should have wanted me when you were dropping your dick all in your brother's girlfriend. Get the fuck out of my house," she yelled as she pulled away from me and freed her wrist.

I got as close as I could to her. "I don't give a fuck how mad you are. Don't you ever disrespect me," I growled.

"Nigga, are you slow? You disrespected me when you fucked that bitch, you disrespected me again when you came home to me and laid up under me like it wasn't shit, and then you disrespected me to the fullest when you had me around that bitch. Don't come over here and try to play the victim."

"I know I hurt you, but I swear I wasn't on that shit with Drea."

She glared at me. "I don't want to hear that grieving bullshit, either. Your brothers were grieving too, but they didn't fuck that ho. Now, if you don't mind, I don't feel good, and I want to lie down. Get the fuck out of my house, and get someone to come and fix my door." She walked away from me, and this time I allowed her to. I had no intentions of letting her go, but for now I'd leave her be.

As I walked out the door, I called someone to come by and fix her door. Then I got in my car and sat there, waiting for the handyman to arrive. Once the job was done, I paid the guy, then got back in my car. My ass was just going to sit there for a little while, but my dumb ass sat there for so long that I fell asleep. The banging on my window woke me up. I looked at the clock on the dashboard and saw that it was eleven in the morning. Juicy was hitting my shit hard as hell. I opened the door and stepped outside the car.

"What the fuck you getting out for? I'm just telling you to get away from in front of my house," she barked.

"I can sit where the fuck I want to sit. You doing the most, Juicy, straight up."

"I'm doing the most? Nigga, get the fuck on, before I tell the police somebody out here looking suspicious on the block."

"You about to turn this love into hate real quick, and that shit ain't gone go right for you."

"Then the feelings will be mutual. Get the fuck on." With that, she turned and walked off, and I swear, it took everything in me not to drop-kick that ho.

I got in my car and drove off. She was going to make this difficult as fuck, but I was a patient nigga. I decided to drive to my mama's house to see if she was back home and what she thought I should do about Juicy. I would leave out the person I had cheated with, though. When I pulled up, her car wasn't in the driveway, and that meant she wasn't home, but I got out and walked inside to see if I could ascertain whether she had at least stopped at home. As I walked around, I saw that everything looked exactly like it had last night, when we'd come by.

Suddenly it dawned on me that my mama might be in trouble. If Rico had had Blaze, then Rico knew Blaze would tell us what the fuck was up. Had this nigga kidnapped my mama, too, or was she somewhere on some bullshit? None of this was sitting right with me. I pulled my phone out and called my mama. No answer. I called again, and again, but the shit kept going to voicemail. I decided to send her a text.

Ma, you need to hit me back and let me know you good. Worried about you, and I need to know where you are.

After I sent the text, I jumped back in my car and drove off, with a lot on my mind. It was time to get rid of the rest of these niggas who were a threat to my family, and I had to figure out a way to get my girl back. Since I had nowhere to go, I went and grabbed me some food and then headed home. It was time for me to make some calls.

"Hey, Jermaine. What's good?"

"I can't complain. You calling to thank me for helping your brother?"

"Actually, I'm calling because I need you to do something else. I need an address."

"Okay. Give me a name."

"That's the thing. It's an official address. You feel me?"

"That will be double," he said.

"Money ain't an issue. Just get back to me as soon as possible." We allowed these niggas to go too far, and I was done playing games. These niggas had to go. I gave him the name. The moment I disconnected the call, my phone went off. I had a text from my mama.

Hey, baby. I'm fine. I went on vacation. It was last minute. Rico was getting on my nerves, and I needed some air. Sorry I didn't tell you all. Love you.

I texted her back. Don't do that shit no more. Hurry up and bring your ass back. We need to talk, and I have a surprise for you.

Okay. See you soon.

I laid my phone down. That shit made me feel better, knowing she was okay. Now all I had to do was get my girl back.

CHAPTER 7

BLAZE

When I made it back to the main house, Drea and the nephew was on the couch, asleep. Damn shame I didn't even know shorty's name. Quick picked him up, intending to carry him to his car.

"I'll holla at you later, bro, and thank you for coming back," Quick told me at the front door as he held shorty in his arms. "You just don't know how much that helped a nigga. I was losing it, Blaze." Tears started forming in his eyes, or at least that was what I thought it was. This nigga was ugly as fuck right now, and it could have been some eye boogers or some shit.

"I'm sorry y'all had to go through that, but, nigga, please don't cry. You already looking like that li'l nigga they had playing Bobby Brown. I can't take much more of this shit," I said.

"Fuck you, nigga, and damn, you right. I can't go to no fucking club. Y'all was trying to send a nigga off," Quick said.

"Naw, I was sending y'all ass off. I wasn't going nowhere with you looking like something I ate and shit out."

Quick laughed and headed out the door. "It's good to have you back," he threw over his shoulder.

"Shid, it's good to be back."

After he left, I walked over to the couch and woke up Drea.

"Come on, loose pussy. Let's go home," I whispered in her ear.

Smacking her lips, she stood up, and we headed out as well. I was glad we always keep a car at the main house, because I wanted to be home, in my own bed. As soon as we got in the car, Drea's ass started crying.

"I really am sorry. This wasn't supposed to happen. I was just so lost and broken, I didn't know what to do."

"Well, I don't think pussy popping for whoever walked in your door was it." When I saw the shame and guilt on her face, I got serious. "I mean what I said. I forgive you two, but only if that was it. A nigga knows it's hard to believe that shit, but I understand what kind of mind frame y'all was in, but it better have ended that night. I'm more concerned about that nigga Mack. You love that nigga?"

She dropped her head. "I'm not sure. I think I do. He helped me heal when my world came crashing down, but nobody could ever replace you. He was great, but there will never be another Blaze."

"Bitch, you talking like I'm still dead. You might wanna shut the fuck up while you still got one brow. That shit with his ass is over. I better not find out you still talking, texting, calling that nigga, or shit. Are we clear?"

"Yes."

We rode the rest of the way in silence. I placed my hand on her stomach at one point and left it there. When we got to the house, all I wanted to do was get in the fucking shower and then fuck my girl until her cervix fell out her ass. We walked in the door, and she stopped me.

"I don't know if you know it or not, but it's a girl," she said softly.

Tears formed in my eyes, and I pulled her close. "Thank you. I know this shit was hard for you, but you picked up the pieces and did what you needed to do for our daughter. I love you." I kissed her and then pulled her upstairs.

What she and Mack did was fucked up, and I knew some people would never understand how I could let something like that go, but I got it. Motherfuckers grieved in different ways. I knew my big bro would never do anything to hurt me, and I loved Drea. A nigga never been in love before. The six bullet wounds in my body should be enough for anybody to know how I felt about her.

When we got upstairs, I walked in the bathroom and cut on the water. When I went back into the bedroom, Drea was undressing. Seeing her step out of her clothes had my dick hard as fuck. This was about to be a ho bath, because I needed to get in them guts. After I washed myself as fast and as thoroughly as I could, I washed her up. As soon as we were done, I laid her on the bed. I placed kisses all over her body and stopped when I got to her feet. Taking each toe in my mouth, I sucked and licked slowly. Then I made my way up to her wet spot and placed soft tongue kisses on her clit. Listening to her moan from pleasure had my dick leaking pre-cum. Attacking her clit, I ate that shit like it was a nigga's last meal. As I twirled my tongue fast as fuck, I knew my shit had to feel like a vibrator. She grabbed my head and pushed it farther into her pussy.

"Damn, baby. I missed you so much," she said. A nigga could barely breathe, she was riding against my face so hard. As soon as she came, I jumped up.

"You about to bust a nigga's lip. Turn over," I told her.

She did as she was told. As much as I loved her, I still wanted to punish her for giving my pussy away. So I slammed my dick inside her, and she screamed out in pain. That only made me get harder. Spreading her ass cheeks apart, I made sure my entire dick was going inside her.

"You gone give my pussy away again?" I growled. Wanting to make my dick touch her throat through her pussy, I slammed inside her again.

"Nooo. I'm sorry." The more she begged for forgiveness, the farther I pushed my shit in. As soon as I felt her cream all on my dick. I pulled out and lay on my back.

"Come ride this dick," I said.

She climbed on top of me and slid down slowly. I knew she was trying to get used to the size, but I took over. I grabbed her around her waist and started pumping in and out of her hard and fast.

"I said ride this dick."

She leaned down and started bouncing her ass all on my shit. Her necklace slapped me in the face, and I went off.

"Get this shit off your neck," I muttered. "You got this dead-ass nigga in here watching me, and his dick done hit me all in the lip." I snatched her necklace and threw it. "Did I tell you to stop?" I slapped her on her ass, and she moaned and continued to bounce her ass. "Fuck right there, girl."

The moment I felt her cumming on my shit again, I couldn't hold it any longer. I released my nut all in her. When we were done, I lay back against the pillow, and she lay down against my chest. She never took my dick out of her. A few minutes later her ass was asleep. Knowing this position couldn't be good for the baby, I rolled her over and watched her sleep.

It fucked me up to know that she loved someone else, but that shit ain't gone last long. We had a few people to kill, and this nigga Mack had made the list. I wasn't gone give her the chance to choose. My ass was gone be the only nigga left standing. And so she wouldn't have any choice but to choose me. I was done taking L's.

CHAPTER 8

SHADOW

There was so much going on in our lives, and I was happy as fuck the weekend was here. Rico's ass had disappeared, and we hadn't found this nigga Tate yet. The good news was my mama was fine and was on vacation some damn where, and Shirree hadn't tried to bring her goat-mouth ass back around. Quick's face had finally healed, and the Hoover brothers were going out again for the first time in, like, eight months.

I grabbed my Ralph Lauren cardigan and completed my outfit. I had kept it simple with some jeans and Tims. I walked outside and jumped in my Phantom. It was wintertime, but I had this bitch shining like new money. When I pulled up to Hoover Nights, I was the second one to arrive. Baby Face was already there, and that was shocking as fuck. Looking at the crowd, you could tell they was waiting in anticipation. Nobody but the DJ knew Blaze was alive, but the flyers we had passed out mentioned a special guest. I wondered if they had figured it out. We hadn't done the brother line since he passed. All our Phantoms were tinted, so they wouldn't know until we actually got out of the cars.

When Quick pulled up behind me, you could see the crowd getting worked up. I thought they loved this shit more than we did. After five more minutes, Blaze finally pulled up. The crowd went crazy. They were pointing and shit, trying to figure out who was in the car. They were screaming, and we hadn't even stepped out yet. Letting the anticipation build up, we sat in the cars longer than we normally did. When Baby Face turned his lights off, each of us followed suit in what amounted to a domino effect. The crowd actually went silent.

We had decided to step out of our vehicles in unison, but as my feet hit the ground, I noticed Blaze didn't get out when the rest of us did. He was really milking this shit. We stepped to the other side of our cars and waited for this extra-ass nigga to get out. When his door opened, these bitches actually started holding hands and shit, like they were waiting for their name to be announced. When he climbed out from behind he wheel, you could hear a fucking pin drop. This nigga had a hood on his head and his sunglasses on, so the crowd really couldn't tell it was him. He walked with his head down until he got over to the side on which we stood. This clown-ass nigga stopped and just stood there like that, as if he could hear a drumroll in his head. Me, Quick, and Baby Face was dying of laughter. This nigga was making a performance out of this shit, like it wasn't colder than a motherfucker out here.

When I saw him reach in his pocket, I knew what he was about to do, so I reached in my pocket as well. I guessed all the brothers knew what he was about, 'cause I saw Quick and Baby Face do the same thing. Without any direction, all of us did the same thing at the same time. We flicked our motherfucking Bic. The crowd went nuts. You would think we were some celebrities in a fucking arena. We held our lighters up, and motherfuckers were digging through their purses and their pockets, looking for lighters. They started flicking they shit too.

I hoped this nigga raised his head and dropped his hoodie soon, 'cause my fucking fingertips were starting to burn. As if he could hear what I was thinking, he dropped his hood and looked up at the crowd. These motherfuckers started screaming and crying. His dramatic ass was loving every minute of it. After putting them hot-ass lighters back in our pockets, we waved at the crowd and headed inside the club. As soon as we walked in, we got the same reaction. Everybody was pointing, screaming, and going crazy. They tried to run up on us, but security stepped in.

"Let 'em through," one of the guards yelled.

This nigga Blaze sounded like Dresser from *The Five Heartbeats*, when Eddie was trying to get through the gates. He was on one tonight, and I wasn't mad at him. If I came back from the dead, I would act like an ass too. Once the DJ saw the commotion, he knew we were there.

"Aw shit! Hoover Gang is in the motherfucking building," he shouted into his mic. "You heard me right. The entire Hoover Gang is here! Your boy Blaze is back from the fucking dead. I need everybody in the fucking building to put your lighters in the fucking air."

The lights went out in the place, and all you could see was people flicking they Bics. When our song came on, we went crazy.

"*I think I'm Big Meech, Larry Hoover. Whipping work, Hallelujah. One nation, under God. Real niggas getting money from the fucking start.*" As Rick Ross's song "B.M.F." came through the speakers, the girls ran over to us and threw all kinds of ass on us. Li'l ass, big ass, funky ass. Bitches was everywhere. This was the first time we stayed downstairs and partied with everyone else. When Ross started rapping, me and my brothers started showing out.

"*My Rolls-Royce triple black, I'm geechee ho. Balling in the club, bottles like I'm Meech ho. Rozay, that's my nickname. Cocaine running in my big vein. Self made, you just affiliated. I build it ground up, you bought it renovated. Talking plenty capers nothing's been authenticated."* The crowd was turnt, and so were we. It felt good to be back in our shit, but it felt even better to know how our city felt about us. I noticed two girls kind of standing off to the side, while it seemed every other chick had their ass in our face. I waved them over when I caught the attention of the chick who was making my dick jump. She looked like she didn't really want to come, but her friend pushed her, and they walked over. I leaned down to her ear and tried to talk over the music.

"What's your name?"

"Kimberly, but everybody calls me Kimmie." I could tell she was shy, or the ho was pretending really well. The shit I been through lately, I was side-eyeing all bitches from now on. Especially since I had come to realize my ass was attracted to hoes, and with one incident, a yuck-mouthed ho.

"I'm Shadow. Who you here with?"

"My friend. I didn't want to come, but she dragged my ass here anyway."

"I'm glad you came."

Looking at her, if she was a ho, you couldn't tell. Everyone in the club, including her friend, was damn near naked. But Kimmie had on some jeans, a bodysuit, and some heels. She was thick as hell, but she carried her weight well. The thing I loved most was that she was naturally pretty.

"You wanna get out of here?" I asked her.

"I don't want to leave my friend."

I looked over at the girl she was with, and she was all over Quick. If I knew my brother, Kimmie was about to be left by her friend. I decided not to push it, though, and just see where the night led us. I could tell she was out of her comfort zone, and so I grabbed her hand. I left the dance floor and headed up to VIP. Everybody else was downstairs dancing and having a good time, but we sat upstairs and talked the night away. Until a fight broke out. Looking over the banister, I saw that Ash and her crew were in there, and from the looks of it, shit was about to go left.

"I need to go check on my friend," I said. I wanted so bad to tell her to stay up here, 'cause I knew they were no match for they ass, but I gave in when she insisted on accompanying me downstairs. "A'ight. Let's go."

We headed back to where everyone else was, and the shit was bad. Kimmie's friend was bleeding from her head. I assumed Ash had hit her ass with a bottle, since she was holding the end of it in her hand. Paris was stomping the girl now, and Blaze had the girl's wig and was setting it on fire. This nigga and his habit of burning wigs was funny as fuck. Kimmie tried to jump in, but I held her back the best way I could. I grabbed my phone out of my pocket and hit RECORD. I was hoping Kimmie didn't notice, but I had to get this shit on video. It was funny as hell. Quick pulled Paris off the girl, and Baby Face held them back.

"You think you about to cater to this ho? You got me fucked up." Ash yelled as she charged Quick and started punching the shit out of his ass. This nigga's face had just healed, so I knew he was about to go off. He grabbed Ash and body-slammed her to the floor.

All the brothers screamed at the same time.

"Damn," Quick muttered. He stood up straight, and Paris ran toward his ass while Panda helped Ash up off the floor. Blaze turned his lighter toward Paris and flicked his Bic. As soon as she saw that fire, she stopped dead in her tracks.

"This how you gone do me over some ho you just met?" Ash said to Quick. She was crying, but Quick was not moved.

"Bitch, please. You ain't even know who your baby daddy was. Issa Maury. Get the fuck out my face," Quick snapped.

Ash's eyes became slits. "Nigga, I will cut your ass. Don't play with me."

Quick laughed sarcastically. "Try it if you want to. Don't act like you don't know who the fuck I am. Matter of fact, security, escort this bum to the street. She infecting my space. If you ever let her in my shit again, your ass gone be missing. Bum hoes don't party with the Hoover Gang. Don't forget that shit."

Security started dragging Ash out of there, and Panda and Paris walked out behind her.

"You dead-ass wrong, my nigga," Paris spat over her shoulder.

Before she could say anything else, Blaze flicked his Bic again.

Paris did not back down. "I should have made your ass look like Ned the Wino on *Good Times*. Goofy ass." She talked her shit, but she kept it moving.

Once Ash, Paris, and Panda had been escorted out, Kimmie's friend walked back over to Quick. Ole girl was looking for her wig.

"My bad, baby girl. You may as well leave this here. This shit look like a muskrat," Blaze told her. He passed her the burned-up wig, and the bitch actually put it back on her head. I was done.

Quick whispered in her ear, and she turned to Kimmie.

"Do you mind if I leave with him?" she asked.

"Do you even know his name?" Kimmie answered. You could tell she was aggravated.

"Don't act like that. It looks like you straight," her friend said.

"It's good. I'll catch an Uber."

Her friend walked off with Quick, and I pulled her to me.

"You don't have to catch an Uber. I'll take you home. I ain't on no bullshit. I promise." For once, I was telling the truth. After the shit I had just gone through, I needed to get to know a bitch first.

When she nodded her head, I dapped my brothers up and headed out. When we got in my whip, she turned to me and started laughing.

"I just realized it was you who got out of this car. Y'all niggas dramatic as fuck. What is all that? Is this what y'all do every time y'all walk in the club?"

Laughing, I tried to explain it. "Tonight was different from most nights. This was our first time back since my brother died."

"Oh, my God. I'm so sorry."

"You don't have to be. That nigga was fake dead."

She looked at me like I was crazy.

"It's a long story, but we been doing the brother line since the grand opening of Hoover Nights. It was supposed to be for that occasion, but the way the crowd went nuts, we been doing it ever since," I explained.

"So, you own that club?"

"Among other things. You really don't know who we are?" I guessed a nigga was vain or conceited, because it kind of bothered me that she didn't know who I was. On the other hand, it was a turn-on.

"Should I know?" She actually looked sorry that she didn't.

"Naw, baby girl. It's cool. Now, where am I driving to? A nigga just going, and I have no idea where."

"Cermak and Wolf."

"Is that Westchester?"

"Yes." She was so polite and well mannered, the shit was scary.

"Where yo' man at?" I asked as we drove.

A sadness came over her face, and it made me want to hug her.

"We're done. He was cheating on me, and I don't tolerate that shit. We were together for six years, and this past year, it seems I didn't know him at all. I'm broken, and I really don't want to step into anything new. I just want to find myself."

"I can dig that. I just came out of something similar. So, what happened?"

I didn't take her for a talker, but this chick had a motor in her lungs. She didn't fucking stop talking. We made it all the way to her house, and she was still talking. I parked the car, and she was still talking. As we sat there, I must have nodded off about three times, and when I woke up each time, she was still talking. I caught the gist of the conversation, though. She had given him her all, and he had shit on her ass. Damn near my situation. I had given Shirree my all, and she was eating shit.

"We both done been through some things, and we don't know where we headed with this shit, but I do want to get to know you. No strings attached," I told her.

"We can do that. Just don't lie to me. Let me know what it is and allow me to decide."

"We all good, baby girl. I ain't fucking with nobody. We gone take this shit slow and see where it leads." I grabbed her phone and put my number in it. "Why don't you call me when you feel comfortable?"

"Okay. It was nice meeting you, Shadow."

"Likewise, Kimmie."

She got out of the car, and I watched her go in the house. When I drove away, I was smiling. This was the first time a chick ain't tried to throw the pussy at me because I was a Hoover. This one just might be different. She seemed free from drama and just what I was looking for. If she turned out to be who she said she was, I was gone make her mine. As I drove to my house, I prayed she wasn't a ho.

CHAPTER 9

KIMMIE

Shadow had me walking in the house, feeling hopeful. He was different from the thug niggas I was usually attracted to. He was a business owner and a gentleman. My ex was a hood nigga to the core. Realizing my ass was attracted to bad boys, I vowed to steer away from the shit from now on. I was so deep in thought that I didn't notice my ex sitting on the couch, and he scared the shit out of my ass when I finally spotted him.

"Mack, what the fuck are you doing in my house?"

"This is *our* house, and I can walk in when I fucking feel like it."

"This wasn't your house when your ass was out cheating on me, was it? I'm over this whole scene, and I want you to leave."

"You must have met a nigga. You have never thought about walking away from us before, but now your bitch ass wanna be free."

"I will not tolerate you calling me out of my name. You have turned into someone I don't recognize, and I would like you to leave my house."

"Kimmie, don't make me beat your ass. I'm not leaving, and you don't want me to, so stop fronting. Who else gone want your fat ass? They might fuck, but that's it."

With tears in my eyes, I walked over to him and slapped the thought out his ass. "I asked you to leave my

house. You have ten seconds before I call the police," I
said sternly.

I wasn't expecting him to draw his hand back and
smack my ass to sleep. I dropped to my knees and grabbed
my mouth, which stung. I was ready to curse his ass out.
But before I could say another word, he punched me so
hard, I farted.

"Have you lost your mind?" I screeched.

"Naw, but you must have lost yours. Ain't no out,
Kimmie. You know too much of my business, and I can't
have that. If I even think you are going to call the police,
I'm going to kill your ass. Don't forget who the fuck I am."

Crying, I tried to get up off the floor. He grabbed me by
my throat with one hand and unbuttoned my jeans with
the other.

"Please don't make me do this," I begged.

"Make you? This my pussy. You gone do it because you
want to." He threw me against the couch and pulled my
pants all the way off. When I felt him rub his dick against
my clit, the tears started flowing. The only good thing
about this was, I knew he wouldn't last long. He stuck
it in and did his same old tired stroke, moving his dick
in circles, like his ass was playing with a Hula-Hoop. I
counted the pumps in my head and knew he was seven
away from being done. Just as I counted down to two, he
started shaking and fell on top of me.

"Damn, that's some good-ass pussy. I love that shit, girl.
You always get me to nut fast," he said.

Once he climbed off me, I walked upstairs and jumped
in the shower. As the water fell over my body, I cried over
how I had got here.

My name was Kimberly Calloway, but everyone called
me Kimmie. My mother had raised me until she passed
away from cancer six years ago. I was sixteen years old
at the time. My grandmother had taken me in, and I

couldn't have been happier, until my uncle raped me. I ran away, but I had nowhere to go. My ass went to the park and fell asleep on a bench. When I woke up, the finest nigga ever stood in front of me, looking at me like I was crazy. His cat eyes pierced my soul. His dreads were so neat, and the sun was beaming off his yellow skin like he was a God.

"What your li'l ass doing out here?"

"Sleeping. What it looks like?"

He laughed. "Why your ass ain't at home, asleep?"

"I don't have a home." I tried to get comfortable on the bench.

"You know there's all kinds of predators out here?"

"Shid, they in the house too."

"Not at my house. You wanna go with me? I got an extra room."

"Why you wanna help me?"

"I don't know. It's just something about you."

I looked into his eyes and figured, Why not?

I'd been with his ass ever since. In the beginning, he'd been the sweetest thug I had ever met. He'd taken me on dates, picnics, and trips—without trying to sleep with me once. I realized later that he had just been trying to get me to fall in love with his ass before we had sex. When we finally did, my rape felt better than his ass. He couldn't eat pussy, and his stamina was terrible. On top of that, his dick size was just average. Maybe if it was big, he would rock my world in those five minutes. For six years now, I had stood by him and stayed faithful, even though he had never satisfied me sexually.

If I dismissed the sex, I could honestly say he had been a great boyfriend up until about a year ago. Shit had just started changing then. He had stopped hanging with Slick and the crew, but he'd left at all times of the day and night. The nigga started locking his phone, and he would come home smelling like a woman. I had put up with enough of his shit and had sacrificed too much. I was done. And now here he was, threatening me so that I stayed with him. As much as I wanted to talk to Shadow, I couldn't do this to him. If it was reversed, I wouldn't want to be brought into this kind of situation. I had to clean my life up before I started with someone new.

I stepped out of the shower and dried off. Then I lay down on the bed and cried myself to sleep.

CHAPTER 10

BABY FACE

Going to the club was exactly what I needed to get out of my funk. The laughs started with Blaze's ass. That nigga was being so extra, you couldn't do shit but join in with the foolishness. He was milking his fake death like he was Tupac. What made it even worse was how the crowd was acting. The feeling that we got when we did the brother line was like no other. This was the first time we had mingled with the crowd, and I had a fucking blast. When Ash and her crew came in, I couldn't stop laughing long enough to try to break that shit up. Quick was treating her bad, but I knew how my brother was when he was hurt. He had trusted her with everything, and she had been lying to him the entire time. That ain't a good feeling to nobody.

After I left the club, I stopped my ass at White Palace and got me some breakfast. Seeing all the drama at the club made me think of Juicy. Before I could talk myself out of it, I finished my breakfast and drove to her house. When I rang her doorbell, I almost didn't expect her to answer the door. When the door swung open and she appeared in this little-ass gown, me just wanting to talk went out the window.

"Can I come in?" I asked.

"What the fuck do you want? It's late, and I'm tired. My ass been sick, and all I want to do is sleep." Her red hair was wild as hell, and the shit looked sexy.

"It won't take long. Please."

She didn't respond, but she moved out of the way and let me in. When she sat on the couch, I caught a glimpse of her pussy, and all I wanted to do was taste her.

I sat down at the other end of the couch and remained silent.

"Talk, nigga," she barked. It hurt me to see the woman I had turned her into. They say, "You never miss your water until your well runs dry," and given how sexy she looked, my ass was thirstier than a motherfucker.

"I don't know what else to say, except I'm sorry. Baby, I swear I didn't mean for any of this to happen. Just tell me what I have to do to make this right."

Tears started falling down her face, and I felt like shit. Knowing she didn't want to hear what I had to say, I allowed my mouth to communicate in another way. I inched down the couch, then leaned toward her and kissed her. She tried to fight it, but I held her down. Then I picked her up and laid my head back against the couch.

"Ride my face," I told her.

She wouldn't climb on top, so I placed her against my mouth. Once I started licking, her body moved involuntarily. I grabbed her by her ass cheeks and pulled her against my mouth until she couldn't take it anymore and then did it on her own. When her pace picked up, Tsunami got hard as fuck. I reached down and freed his big ass. She was riding me so good, I got blue balls. My ass had to stroke him until she was ready to ride him. He was so hard, I had to give him some kind of attention.

I could tell she was really into it, because she started bouncing up and down on my face. I stuck my tongue out and allowed her to fuck that motherfucker. Her juices were so fucking good, I damn near came from anticipation. Once her body started shaking, I couldn't wait to slide up in her and feel that wet shit. When she sat on Tsunami, she slowly ground against him. She had me fucked up, though ain't no way we were about to juice like we were in grammar school and shit. I was a grown-ass man with a big-ass dick, and I wanted some pussy. So I lifted her up and tried to slide him in, but she stopped me.

"You got a condom?" she asked.

"What the fuck? We ain't never used a condom."

"That was before you cheated on my ass. Do you have a condom or not?"

Groaning, I laid my head back. "No, but I need to get this nut. Just let me put the tip in."

"You funny as hell. Go down the street and get one."

"My dick gone bust through my pants."

"Do you want some pussy or not?"

Just happy that she was about to let me in them guts, I said, "Fuck it." After pushing my dick in my pants the best way I could, I stood up and walked to the door.

"Hurry up. Shit," she said as she followed me. I walked out on the porch, and she looked at me and laughed. "Thanks for the nut, nigga. Now get the fuck off my porch."

"Juicy, don't play with me. My dick hard as hell right now."

"I don't give a fuck. Now go on, and if you outside my house when I wake up, the po po gone be knocking at your door." She slammed that bitch in my face and locked it.

I was so hard, my dick was in pain. A nigga wanted to kick this bitch in and beat her ass. If she wanted to play, I had something for her ass. I walked to my car, then leaned in, reached into the armrest, and grabbed some lotion. I went back to her porch and pulled my dick out. I poured lotion on my hand, made sure my dick was good and wet, and started jerking off right there. My shit was so hard, I knew it wouldn't take long. As soon as I felt my shit rising, I pointed Tsunami right at her door. My nut shot everywhere, including on her doorknob. I made sure I aimed that bitch all over as my nut flew out of that motherfucker. After putting my dick up, I walked back to my car, laughing. I climbed behind the wheel and drove away. A nigga didn't get the pussy, but her ass damn sure didn't win. I ain't taking no more L's.

As soon as I made it home, my phone started ringing.

"What's up, Jermaine? You got something for me?" I said when I picked up.

"Actually, I do. I have an address for you. I'll send it in a text."

"A'ight. I'll wire your money in the morning. Good looking out."

"Anytime."

I hung up the phone and sent a text to the brothers, telling them to meet me at the main house in the morning, and then I lay my ass down and went to sleep.

A nigga thought he was dreaming when I kept hearing clicking noises. The shit sounded like someone was continually turning my bedroom light on and off. When I finally realized I wasn't dreaming the shit, I kept my eyes closed while I tried to think of a plan. My gun wasn't by me, and I had no idea how many people were in my bedroom. How the fuck had I let a motherfucker catch me slipping like this? *Fuck it*, I thought as I opened my eyes so I could assess the situation.

"What the fuck?" I yelled.

This nigga Blaze was sitting on the edge of the bed, in my face, flicking his Bic. This gray-eyed nigga scared the shit out of me. He started laughing and stood up from the bed.

"It might not be today. It might not be tomorrow. Just know I'ma get your ass," he said. Then this nigga walked out the door, repeating that shit over and over.

I swear to God, this nigga had played all his fucking life. I touched my hairline and felt around to make sure he hadn't got my ass. A nigga was still wearing dye from the last time Blaze had left me with a patch of missing hair. Satisfied that he hadn't burned me tonight, I lay down on the bed and went back to sleep. All I could do was laugh. I hated that nigga.

CHAPTER 11

QUICK

Standing there with Blaze and doing our brother line gave me so much life. I had damn near hated myself from the guilt I had felt over his death. To have him back and pettier than ever was right up my alley. I loved every minute of this shit. The love that we received from everybody had all of us feeling ourselves. The shit was so turnt, we stayed downstairs with the crowd for the first time ever. The hoes were throwing that ass everywhere, and even the fellas were giving props.

Shadow had called two chicks over to us, and he had pulled one to the side. The other chick was all in my space now, so I knew she wanted to holla. When I pulled her to me, she wasted no time grinding on a nigga's dick. The waitress came over and brought bottles, and I knew there was no turning back. I turned to give Shadow a cup, only to discover that this nigga and ole girl had dipped off somewhere.

"Can I have that cup?" asked the chick who was with me. I saw she was a live one.

"It's good, Ma." I gave it to her, and she threw that shit back like a nigga would after looking at how much child support done took out of his check.

When Yo Gotti and Nicki Minaj's hit single "Rake It Up" came on, the chick went crazy. I had never had a chick bounce on my dick this hard, and we still had our clothes on. *"I made love to a stripper, first I had to tip her. Twenty thousand ones, she said, 'I'm that nigga.' I said, 'I'm that nigga, bitch,' I already know it."* A nigga was feeling that part, and I was digging my dick all in her ass through that li'l-ass dress she had on. When she turned around, she dropped down and started nibbling on my dick through my jeans. If we were up in VIP, I would have pulled this big motherfucker out and put it in her mouth.

When she heard Nicki's solo part of the song, she went crazy again. *"I tell all my niggas, cut the check. Buss it down, turn your goofy down. I'ma do splits on it, yes splits on it."* As soon as she rapped that part, li'l mama went all the way down in a split on this dirty-ass floor. Once I saw that ass come out from under that dress, I knew she was getting this dick tonight. I was so caught up in the tricks this chick was doing, I never saw the shit coming. Ash snatched a bottle from Baby Face's hand and went straight over the girl's head with it. Before I could stop her, Paris's ass had joined in, and they were stomping li'l mama back to hell, from whence she came. They stomped her out of her wig, and of course, Blaze picked the motherfucker up and set fire to the shit.

As bad as I wanted to help the girl, I ain't the type of nigga to get into chick fights. Shit looked sweet as fuck to me. But when I noticed Ash was about to cut her, I stepped in and grabbed her away from the girl. *What the fuck I do that for*? I wondered. I was concentrating so hard on making sure Ash didn't cut me, I forgot that Paris was still stomping the bitch. When I looked over to my brothers for help, I knew that shit was out the window, because they were laughing too hard. The girl who was with Shadow tried to run up and help my chick, but he grabbed her before she got very far, and held her back. I prayed she didn't get loose, 'cause Paris and Ash together, issa homicide. When one of my brothers finally grabbed Paris, I tried to help the girl up off the damn floor. A nigga was hoping she was okay. Ash snapping at me brought me out of my thoughts.

"You think you about to cater to this ho? You got me fucked up."

Before I could even respond, she charged my ass. Not taking a chance, since she had that bottle in her hand, I rock bottomed her ass. As soon as I slammed her to the floor, all you heard were my brothers screaming.

"Damn," I muttered as Paris ran toward me.

Blaze aimed his Bic in Paris's direction and flicked it. As soon as she saw that fire, she stopped dead in her tracks. A nigga was happy as fuck my brother was back. Niggas didn't play with Blaze and that lighter. Your ass was gone be a statistic if you thought he was playing.

"This how you gone do me over some ho you just met?" Ash tried to play the victim card, but I didn't give a fuck.

"Bitch, please. You ain't even know who your baby daddy was. Issa Maury. Get the fuck out my face," I snapped.

"Nigga, I will cut your ass. Don't play with me."

"Try it if you want to. Don't act like you don't know who the fuck I am. Matter of fact, security, escort this bum to the street. She infecting my space. If you ever let her in my shit again, your ass gone be missing. Bum hoes don't party with the Hoover Gang. Don't forget that shit."

Her girls were pissed when she got dragged out, but I didn't give a fuck. She had hurt me, and I was done taking L's.

"You dead-ass wrong, my nigga," Paris spat over her shoulder.

Blaze flicked his Bic at her again, and I was rolling. He was being extra, but I was glad he was putting these hoes in they place. All them bitches had known about my son, and none of them had said a word.

"I should have made your ass look like Ned the Wino on *Good Times*. Goofy ass." Paris talked her shit and kept it moving out the door.

I laughed until I saw that this simple bitch was actually looking for her wig. Ash and Paris had really fucked this girl up. I felt bad for her ass. The worst part of it was, a nigga still wanted to fuck.

"My bad, baby girl. You may as well leave this here. This shit look like a muskrat." Blaze passed her the wig, and she actually put it back on her head.

"Leave with me and let me make it up to you," I whispered in her ear. That was all a nigga needed to say, and she was game.

She leaned toward her friend, and I could tell they were having a heated discussion. I was guessing her friend didn't want her to go. But then she turned around and grabbed my hand. I steered her to the bar and got a new bottle. After we headed out the door, we jumped in my whip and was out. Tonight didn't go how I had wanted it to, but the shit was lit and I had a fucking blast. She grabbed the bottle from me and opened it. When I felt her unzip my pants, I knew I had picked the right one. A nigga didn't have time to try to convince a ho that she was a ho. *Let's get this shit done like we grown*, I thought. She drank some of the liquor straight from the bottle and went down to my dick as I kept driving.

"If you waste any of that shit on my fucking seats, we gone have a problem," I warned.

I didn't even know how she got my dick in her mouth without leaking anything, but she did. Needless to say, this chick was a pro. Hands down, she was the smartest bitch I knew. The head on her shoulders deserved some type of honors awards.

"Fuck, girl. Slow up. You gone make a nigga crash."

But she never slowed down. She kept right on sucking until she pulled my kids up out of my dick. She sucked so hard, it felt like she was pulling them motherfuckers from my ass. Not remembering if I had any condoms at the house, I pulled into a gas station. I jumped out and ran in to get what I needed. Once I was back in the car, she just sat there with lust in her eyes.

"Baby, you sober as hell. I'm trying to go all night, and I need you to be just as lit as me," she said. She poured me some liquor in a cup, and I drank the shit. A nigga didn't need liquor to go all night, but I didn't want her to feel like I was taking advantage of her, because she was the only one who was drinking. I was already fighting a case and had to go to court, and I didn't need a rape charge on top of that.

As soon as we pulled up, the expression on her face showed me the type of bitch she was.

"You *live* here?" she said. The bitch had the nerve to give me the "You the broke brother, and I picked the wrong one" look.

"Why?"

"I'm just saying . . . You a Hoover. How the fuck you live here?"

"Easy. Now, get your ratchet ass out my car and come suck this dick. That's the only thing you need to be concerned about."

She smacked her lips and did as she was told. When we walked in, and then she started wandering around the house, trying to find any evidence that I had money. But she found nothing.

"You brought me to your ho house," she said after her house tour was over. "This motherfucker way too empty to be your real house."

Ignoring her, I poured me another drink. She was blowing my high, and I was ten seconds away from putting her ass out.

"Why you bring me to your ho house?" she asked.

"You a ho, ain't you? Where else would I take you?"

She actually looked hurt. "I been wanting you for years now, and I finally had the chance to get your ass. That don't make me a ho. I'm just a girl that knew what she wanted."

Made sense, but everything about her screamed ratchet ho.

"Do you even know my name?" I responded.

"Quick. But you don't know mine. I'm Nala."

"Yet you're wondering why I think you a ho. You just used my dick as a breathing tube, and I didn't even know your name."

"When I saw you walk in, I started drinking more than I meant to, but I was trying to work up my nerve. I didn't mean to come across that way. You can just take me home, because you got me all fucked up."

I tried to walk to the front door, because I was the type of nigga who called bluffs, but my ass felt dizzy as fuck. "Look like you won't be going home until the morning. I'm more fucked up than I thought," I told her. "You can sleep down here."

The box of condoms I'd bought in my hand, I headed up the stairs the best way I could. By the time I got to my bed, I could barely walk. Nobody had better ever say our shit at the club was watered down. This shit was potent as fuck. Once I lay down, I threw the box of condoms on the dresser and removed my shoes. Before I closed my eyes, I got a text from Face.

Meet at the main house in the morning.

I texted him back. A'ight.

Then I closed my eyes, and my ass was out like a light.

When I opened my eyes, I had the worst headache ever. The sun had my shit hammering. I glanced over and saw that Nala was in the bed with me. Then I lifted the covers and saw that I was naked. The next thing I did was look at the condom box. It was exactly where it had landed on the dresser, and so I assumed it hadn't been touched.

Fuck. I hoped I hadn't done anything stupid. I hit her burnt-ass wig, and she turned over and smiled at me.

"Morning, baby. You want some breakfast?" she said.

"What the fuck happened last night?"

She looked offended that I didn't remember. "You begged me to come up here with you, and we made love. How you don't remember that?"

"Did we use a condom?"

"No. You told me you wanted to feel all of me."

"Fuck. Get up and get dressed. We gotta go."

As I got out of the bed, I still felt light headed. I jumped in the shower and then came back in the bedroom to get dressed. As I walked in, she was looking at a nigga's dick like she was ready to swallow that motherfucker again.

"Don't just stare at it. Come get this motherfucker if you want it," I said.

She walked toward me, smiling again, and then bent over the dresser. I guessed she thought we was about to fuck again.

"I ain't got time for all that, baby girl. Either you gone swallow this dick or we gotta go."

She walked over to me and then dropped to her knees. As soon as her mouth was wrapped around my shit, I knew it was going to be a quick one. Five minutes later, I was right. She massaged my balls as I shot my shit down her throat. She actually moaned, like she was loving the taste of my shit. As soon as she got up, I threw on my joggers and waited for her to fix herself up. Then we headed out, and I dropped her off. When she got out of the car, she leaned in the window.

"I hope you call me," she said. "If not, I know where to find you."

"You sounding like a stalker right now. Fuck off my window. That's some four-hundred-thousand-dollar glass. I'll call you." I wasn't trying to be mean, but something about her ass creeped me out. Still, she had some fye-ass dome, so I knew I would call her again.

I drove off and headed to the main house. When I walked in the door, I knew right away that my brothers were ready for war. I was the only one dressed regular; they were in all black, and they had their guns in their hands, ready to roll. Blaze had his can of gas good and full.

Baby Face glared at me. "Nigga, how you the only motherfucker didn't realize what the text meant?" I could tell Baby Face was aggravated.

I frowned. "I was drunk, and I don't even know how. A nigga could barely walk. Let me run upstairs and change."

"Hurry your pretty ass up." This nigga Shadow was back on this time shit.

This was the reason we kept clothes and cars here. Never knew what you might need. I ran up the stairs and changed my clothes. Five minutes later, I was downstairs, holding my AK-47.

"Y'all ready?" I said.

"Nigga, we *been* ready. We waiting on your Billy Dee Williams—looking ass," Blaze grumbled. "I bet you fixed your hair before you came down here, didn't you?"

Ignoring Blaze, I walked out the door. Everybody followed. We jumped in Baby Face's Infiniti truck and headed out. When we pulled up the block, I noticed something out of place.

"Ain't that mama's car?" I said.

Everybody looked over.

"It damn sure is," Baby Face agreed.

We parked on the opposite side of her shit and got out and looked inside the car. It was definitely her car, because her seats had her name engraved on them.

"Why the fuck would she be over here? Her ass better not be snitching, or she about to catch this fade with his ass," Blaze muttered.

We all looked at Blaze like he was crazy.

"Nigga, why you keep talking about killing Mama?" I said, incredulous.

"I told y'all, I ain't taking no more L's, and if her ass over here running them old-ass dick suckers, I'ma light her ass up like a Christmas tree. Fuck y'all thought."

I shook my head at him as we climbed back in the Infiniti. We headed down the street to the address we had, and hopped out again. As soon as we stepped on the porch, the smell smacked our ass in the forehead.

"The fuck this nigga got in here? A farm?" Blaze muttered. "Smell like this nigga change Pampers for a living, and he keep them to jerk off to later."

Usually, I said Blaze was being extra, but today I agreed with his ass. We tested the knob, and the door was open. When we walked in the door, the smell was worse.

"This nigga must got a dead body in here," Baby Face said between gags.

We could here movement upstairs, and we all raised our guns and waited for whoever was up there to come down. A minute later, Tate came running down the stairs with bags in his hands.

"Going somewhere?"

This nigga damn near shit on hisself when he saw us. I ran up on him and knocked his ass out with the gun. With his gas can in his hand, Blaze walked over to him and started pouring gasoline down his throat.

"Damn, nigga. You ain't gone wait until we kill him first?"

"Nigga, you got court in two weeks. I ain't got time to play with y'all," Blaze responded. "This nigga's time is up, and I'm not about to wait around for the cops to come. This a good neighborhood. We gotta get the fuck up out of here. This nigga gotta go." Blaze lit a match and threw it in the nigga's mouth. I had never seen someone burn from the inside before. Shit looked weird, and it was disturbing.

Blaze wandered out of the front room, still holding the gas can, and started pouring its contents all over the house. When he stepped in the kitchen, he screamed. "What the fuck! Ma, can you hear me? Ma!"

After hearing him say, "Ma," we took off to the kitchen. Tears welled up in all our eyes when we caught sight of her. She looked worse than I did after the police had beaten my ass. She looked dead and damn near unrecognizable, but I could tell that she was still breathing. Hearing Tate moaning and grunting, Shadow ran back in the front room. Then I heard a single gunshot, and I knew Shadow had handled business. I couldn't take my eyes off our mama. Blaze picked her up and then dropped her back down.

"Blaze, what the fuck, nigga?" Baby Face was pissed.

"Y'all got me fucked up. That's her ass smelling like death and booty. You can carry her ass."

Baby Face shook his head and picked up our mama.

"Check his pockets for mama's phone before he burns up. Somebody texted me from her number."

I ran back in the front room and saw that Tate's entire body was now on fire. There was no way I could touch him without burning myself. Looking for something to put the fire out, I saw a phone on the coffee table. I picked it up, clicked it on, and Ma's picture popped up.

"I got her phone," I yelled, and everyone ran back into the front room. "Blaze, light this bitch up. Let's go!"

Baby Face carried Ma out of the house as Blaze doused some of the furniture and the carpet with gas. Right before he threw a match, the rest of us got the fuck out of the house. Blaze ran out last and met up with us at the truck.

"Nigga, I know it's cold outside, but you gone either have to let these windows down or put her ass in the trunk," Blaze told Baby Face, who was still holding our mama.

Baby Face narrowed his eyes. "Blaze, this your fucking mama. You being aggy as fuck right now."

"Nigga, I know that's my mama, but her ass stank. The fuck! We all gone die in this motherfucker."

Baby Face checked mama's pockets and discovered that her car keys were in her jeans. "Here, nigga. Y'all take my truck, and I'll drive her in her car," He tossed the keys to the Infiniti to Blaze. "Let's go!"

Baby Face placed Ma in her car, then got behind the wheel. The rest of us jumped in the truck, and then we all pulled off and headed in the direction of the hospital.

"You always trying to ride with that nigga, but you know her ass was smelling like dead ass," Blaze told me.

I laughed, 'cause it was true.

CHAPTER 12

BLAZE

These niggas could talk that good shit, but they knew that shit was foul. The smell was stuck in my nose, my clothes, or something. After seeing my mama like that, I was glad I did that nigga the way I had. These motherfuckers had crossed the line. They didn't even have to do that shit to her. They were sending a message, and I sent one back loud and clear: *I'm coming.* All these motherfuckers had to go.

When we pulled up to the hospital, an eerie feeling came over me. The past flashed before my eyes. One minute, I was listening to my baby bro confess his love, and the next, my body was being riddled with bullets. My ass didn't even have a chance to think, but I knew I didn't want to live a life without Drea, and my protective instincts kicked in. Knowing I wasn't bulletproof, I didn't know what my ass was thinking when I slid across that pulpit in them ugly-ass dress shoes. Once I was hit, I didn't know if Drea had got shot or not. All the way to the hospital, I just kept hoping it wasn't in vain. We had so much more life ahead of us, and all a nigga wanted to do was get to live that shit with her ass.

When I got snatched up, fear overcame me once I saw who had me. I woke up and realized they had fucked up. This OG from the hood named Gangsta had always said that you never left the devil alive, because you didn't want to give him the chance to come back. I was nowhere near like that nigga, and Drea damn sure was no Paradise, but she was mine, and they had fucked up by giving me the chance to get free. When I killed the doctor and got his gun, I knew they didn't stand a chance. My gunplay was nothing like Quick's, but all of us were deadly with that bitch. I gave all head shots to anybody in sight.

The sight of the hospital brought all those emotions and memories back, but once we stepped inside and Baby Face started screaming for help, I snapped back to the present.

"Somebody help my mama! I don't know what happened to her. We found her like this," Baby Face yelled.

As the nurses rushed to him and put her on a stretcher, I wondered what they thought of that smell. Seeing that all my brothers were nervous wrecks, I wondered if this was how they were the night I was shot.

I listened to Baby Face go off. "I can't wait to body that nigga Rico."

"But y'all looked at me like I was crazy when I said I was gone body Mama's ass," I reminded as I watched the nurses wheel our mama away on the stretcher.

"Nigga, that's different," Quick interjected. "Matter of fact, shut up and call Drea and tell her what's going on and I want to talk to Zavi."

I grabbed my phone and called my girl to update her. As soon as she picked up, I blurted, "Hey, baby. Something happened to my mama. We up here at the hospital. It looks like someone tried to beat her to death."

"Oh, my God! Is she okay? Do you need me to come up there?"

"It's not looking good, but we don't need Zavi up here with all this. I'll call you once we know something. Quick wants to talk to him, though." I passed Quick the phone and went and sat by Shadow and Baby Face.

"Hey, is that nigga Slick still working with Tate?" I said in a low voice.

Shadow shook his head. "Nigga, we sent that nigga up there to keep you company, and you were down here with our ass."

I laughed at what Shadow had said. It was good to know they had been out there trying to avenge me.

"We only got one left to go, and that's Rico's bitch ass," Baby Face added.

I agreed with Baby Face, but that wasn't it entirely. "Naw, nigga, we got two."

"Who is the other nigga?" Baby Face quizzed.

"That nigga Mack. His ass gotta go," I said.

"When he came to the baby shower, I said there was something off about his ass. I don't trust that nigga, either," Baby Face responded.

"Good. We on the same page, but he was going no matter what. Drea's ass don't know how to avoid slipping on dicks, and I be damned if she sees him in the store or some shit and her ass falls on that motherfucker," I said.

"Nigga, you ign'ant. Get your dumb ass away from me." Baby Face smirked.

We burst out laughing, but soon the room got quiet. We were all in our own thoughts. After about two hours, a doctor finally came out into the waiting room.

"Family of Debra Hoover," he called.

We all stood up and walked over to the doctor.

"She is okay, but we have her sedated. She was beaten pretty bad. She suffers from broken ribs, a bruised windpipe, and a broken arm. Everything else is superficial."

"Can we see her?" I asked.

"You can, but she won't know you are there. We have her heavily sedated. If not, she would be in tons of pain. She will be that way for a few days. I promise, everything is fine. Go home and get some sleep."

"Thank you, Doc," we said in unison.

Then we left the hospital.

"This shit was too much for me. I'm going home to get some pussy," I said.

"I'm about to go *beg* for some pussy," Baby said.

We laughed at Baby Face. Juicy must be still mad.

Quick piped up. "I'm about to go get my son. Fuck a bitch."

"Ole girl from yesterday might be the one," Shadow said.

We looked at Shadow like he had lost his mind.

"Nigga, you know you a ho's keeper. Fuck out of here. She the one, all right. She the one that's gone suck ten dicks in one night." He punched me, and I reached in my pocket and got my lighter. That shit hurt, and if he did that shit again, he was gone be crispy.

"Don't make me burn your ass. You already one shade away from Cajun with your adopted ass," I warned him.

"Fuck you."

We jumped in the truck and headed back to the main house. When we pulled up, we all got ready to go our separate ways.

"We gone have to figure out where that nigga Rico hiding."

"That nigga lower than Bin Laden. His ass is in a cave somewhere." I thought about what Quick had said.

"Naw, he here. He was watching y'all every move. He sees us. He just don't know he about to *see us*. That nigga here. He can't go back to Puerto Rico. We just have to find his ass."

Baby Face nodded. "I agree. I'm gone holla at my nigga Jermaine. These other niggas ain't doing their job. He done found two motherfuckers in two weeks. He will find Rico."

We dapped it up, got in our vehicles, and drove off. I hoped Baby Face's nigga was able to find Rico, because I couldn't wait to kill that nigga.

As soon as I walked in the door, I went to the bedroom and grabbed Zavi. I knew Quick would be pulling up soon, so I carried Zavi downstairs.

"Uncle Blaze, my daddy coming to get me?"

"Yeah, li'l man. He about to pull up."

"Okay, I miss him, but I miss Mommy too."

"Tell your daddy you want to see your mommy. He will listen to you."

"Okay." He laid his head against my chest just as my phone rang.

I knew it was Quick, so I just walked out the front door. I put Zavi in Quick's car, dapped him off, and walked back in the house. I ran back upstairs and went and looked for my girl. She was lying in the bed, looking even more beautiful than she had when I left.

I took my clothes off and jumped in the shower, just in case my mama's smell was on me. When I walked back in the bedroom, I grabbed my dick and stroked it until it was hard. Then I walked over to Drea and slapped her on her forehead with it. "Baby, wake up."

She didn't move. When I slapped her the second time, she woke up. Her horny ass didn't even get mad; she just started sucking. While she was doing that shit, I almost came. I grabbed her off the bed and put her around my waist.

"I can't wait until your loose-pussy ass have this baby. Between the weight and your shit being open, my dick can't stay in."

"Stop playing all the fucking time, and fuck me."

We laughed as I slid her down on my dick. I had to fuck her in different positions since her stomach was so big. Leaning her upper body back, I started tearing that pussy up. My balls were slapping the shit out of her ass, I was fucking her so hard. I needed her, I needed this nut, and I was gone get it.

"Damn, baby. What the fuck? Slow down," she said.

"Ain't no slowing down. Take this dick." I continued to go as deep as I could. "Tell me whose pussy this is."

"It's yours, baby, but slow down. Fuck. I think you in my stomach."

"I got a big dick, baby. It's supposed to be in your stomach." I dug as far as I could in them guts, and for the first time ever, she squirted.

"Squirt on that dick again," I told her.

"Fool, I ain't squirt. You done burst my water bag. I'm about to beat your ass. I'm in labor."

CHAPTER 13

RICO

As soon as Shirree walked in the door, I went off on her ass.

"Where the fuck have you been, and where is Tate?"

"That's the only motherfucker you give a fuck about, and I just left his house."

"Y'all better not have fucked without me. Where the fuck is he?" I was pissed. He was supposed to be here by now. A nigga was starting to panic, and I was paranoid as fuck. I didn't trust anybody at this point.

"When I got there, the house was on fire, and they were trying to put it out. I stayed around as long as I could without looking suspicious. I don't know if he was in there, but that means Debra's ass is dead. Y'all done got me involved in some shit I didn't want any parts of. They are going to lose their minds when they find out y'all killed they mama."

"How the fuck are they going to find out? Are you saying you going to tell them?" I walked into her space, ready to kill her ass.

"You know damn well I ain't saying shit."

"If it ever comes down to it, I will tell they ass Tate did it." The shit was foul, but a nigga had to save hisself.

Still not having enough money to go back to Puerto Rico, I didn't know what I was going to do. Between all the money Debra and Shirree had given me, I had only a million dollars. That was enough for me to leave town and live forever, but I had to wait until the shit died down. I knew they had everybody looking for me. This shit was bad. When I had got the call the night Debra came over, I'd known my plan was fucked.

"Hey. Rico, man. Blaze is gone, and everybody is dead."

"What the fuck? How?"

"It looks like Blaze killed the doctor first and maybe got his gun from him. He killed everybody else by the door."

"Stay put. I'm on my way."

I left Debra to live another day and went to the warehouse. It was a fucking massacre. This nigga had done taken out an entire crew by hisself, and now I was fucked.

"That means you don't need me anymore, right?"

"Nigga, did I say I didn't? Just continue on as if everything is normal. I have to think."

I immediately left the warehouse and went to Debra's house to get my money. Then I headed to the apartment I had when I first got to Chicago. Hours later, I got a phone call.

"Shadow put me out. I need somewhere to stay."

"I'm going to text you an address. Make sure you are not being followed and come straight here."

I gave her the address down the street, just in case. Then I waited. A little while later, I looked out the window, and saw that she was parked down the street. I made sure she was alone, and then I left her ass out there for ten minutes more to ensure she hadn't been followed. Finally, I texted her the real address. A few minutes later she walked in the door, naked.

"Don't ask," she said.

Laughing, I thought to myself, I don't need to. *My son was definitely my child. That was some shit I would do. I lay down on the bed and fell asleep while trying to think of a plan.*

We'd been here ever since. At first, Tate would go check on Debra every once in a while, but most of the time, he'd been here. But then he'd gone to the house to get some more stuff, and he'd never come back. It had to be them, I decided, but had they got Debra out? If they had Debra, Shadow would be calling Shirree. I know she would tell him what she saw. Still, I couldn't be 100 percent sure if it was them or if someone else was fucking with me.

Looking over at Shirree now, I decided I may as well get some pussy. An empty nut sack always helped me think better.

"Get on your knees and come suck this dick," I ordered her.

"Do we have to do it now? I'm reading this book by KB Cole called *Kissed by a Young Savage*, and it's at the good part."

"Do you think I give a fuck about a book? I said, 'Come suck this dick.'"

She sat her Kindle down and walked over to me. After getting on her knees, she grabbed my shit with an attitude.

"Bitch, lose the attitude. Suck my dick like your last breath depended on it."

When she put her mouth on it, the shit felt much better. I could never get brick hard for Shirree, but she had learned how to get the job done. Her mouth felt nothing like Tate's, but she knew a couple of tricks that would make your knees shake. As soon as I felt my dick rise up, I knew I didn't have long. With Shirree, my dick would stay hard for only a little while. Tate had really fucked up my mental when it came to this sex shit. I pulled out of her mouth and walked over to the couch. I had an idea.

"Bend over the couch," I told her.

Once she did as she was told, I walked into the bathroom and got my clippers. She would be pissed, but I didn't give a fuck. If we were going to work out, I needed her to be able to satisfy me. I stood over her on the couch and held her down with one hand. when I turned on the clippers, she tried her best to get up, but I didn't let her. I ran the clippers over her head, and with each chunk of hair that fell, my dick got harder and harder. I knew this shit would work. By the time I had shaved her bald, my dick was harder than calculus. I let her go, then went and laid the clippers on the coffee table.

"Why would you do that, Rico? What the fuck?" she stormed.

"You don't get the right to question me. Now bend the fuck over, like I told you to."

I knew she was crying from how her body was shaking, but I didn't give a fuck. I stepped behind her and rubbed my dick up and down her asshole. Slamming it in, I almost came from the feeling alone. Looking at her bald head and the tightness from her ass had me feeling like I was fucking a nigga. I was turned on in the worst way. That only made me fuck her even harder. After getting a good grip around her waist, I tore the lining out her ass. Eventually, her shit got wet as hell. Shirree was a freak like that. No matter what you did, at some point, she would get turned on by it. When she started throwing her ass back, I was in heaven. My pace picked up and matched her speed. I could tell she was playing with her pussy, and I imagined she had a dick and was jerking it off. Once I got that visual going in my head, my veins started bulging, and I knew I was about to cum. Our bodies started shaking together, and I came all in her ass.

"Damn, baby. Now, that's how you get a nigga sprung."

She climbed off the couch and leaned down and started sucking my dick. Nasty shit like this always got me hard, and she was a nasty motherfucker. Looking at her bald head go up and down on my dick, I was hard in seconds. She turned her back to me and slid down on my dick. Realizing it was her asshole had me falling in love. She caught on quick and would do anything to please me.

CHAPTER 14

BABY FACE

As I was leaving the hospital, Juicy was heavy on my mind. She really wasn't fucking with a nigga. After that last stunt she had pulled, my ego had told me, *Fuck that bitch.* I hadn't attempted to hit her up or drop by, but seeing my mama like that and thinking about Blaze had me realizing life was too short. At the end of the day I had fucked up, and I would have to do whatever I could to get her back. Like my brother had said, we were not taking no more L's. One way or another, Juicy was going to take my ass back. As I drove to her house, I pulled my phone out and called my nigga up.

"What up, Jermaine? Did you get your payment?" I said as soon as he picked up.

"Yeah, I got it. I appreciate all the business you been throwing my way."

"I'm about to put your ass on the clock. I need you to find somebody else."

"Another official?"

"Naw. My father. He is here in Chicago somewhere, but we can't find that nigga."

"You sure he hasn't left?"

"I'm not sure, but we are going off our gut that he is still here," I replied.

"Okay. I got it. Well, just give me his name, and I'll get on it."

"A'ight, bet. Rico Hoover. Let me know when you find something out." I ended the call.

When I hung up, I was pulling up to Juicy's crib. I stopped the car and got out. As I walked to the door, I hoped she let me in, as a nigga was tired as fuck. When I knocked on her door, she opened it immediately, as if she was already standing down there, waiting on me. When she moved out of the way to let me in without a fight, I was shocked.

"How are you doing?" she said.

Not sure what she meant, I asked, "What you mean?"

I heard about your mom."

"From who?" Now she had me side-eyeing her ass.

"Drea called me to apologize. She was on the phone with me when Blaze called and told her. How is she doing?"

"She's fine. Wait, let me get this straight. You forgave Drea?"

"Yes, she didn't owe me shit, and even though we were cool, we weren't close. I get that y'all was grieving, but why her? What was so good about her that you were willing to say fuck us and your brother? Why wasn't I enough?" The tears started falling down her face, and I felt like shit, again.

"It wasn't anything about her. When I went over there, I was checking on her because I knew Blaze would want us to. We got to talking about him, and I started crying, and next thing I knew, we kissed. One thing led to another, and I fucked up. When I left, I could barely come home and face you. The guilt I was already carrying around for not protecting Blaze intensified. I don't know what else to say except I'm sorry."

"You came home and laid with me. Then you went out of your way to make up for the shit you did. You did everything but tell me the truth. You took my choice away. Making me fall deeper in love with you, knowing what you did, was fucked up and selfish."

"I just didn't want to lose you," I said in a low voice.

"But you lost me anyway. Had you told me and had I walked away, at least you would still have my respect. I love you, but I can't be with you. This shit hurts me more than it hurts you, but I can't let you think that shit was okay. I gave you all of me, and you chose to give it to someone else. That shit hurts." She was now doing the ugly cry, and I leaned over to hug her. Sex was no longer on my mind. All I wanted to do was heal the pain I had caused.

"Juicy, baby, I need you. Please don't leave me."

"I know that you are going through some things, but I can't be there to pick up the pieces for you this time. I have to pick up my own."

My phone rang just then, bringing us out of a stare off. I pulled the phone out of my pocket and saw that Blaze was calling. I picked up. "Blaze, let me call you back."

"Nigga, come to the hospital. Drea's in labor."

"I'm on the way." After hanging up, I looked at Juicy again.

"Just leave," she told me.

"They are about to have the baby. You want to come with me?"

"No, but you can send me pics. I need some time, Face."

I nodded my head, and then I kissed her and walked to the door.

"I'm not giving up," I said. Watching her cry broke my heart.

"You already gave up on us when you cheated."

Seeing that this was going nowhere, I left out of her house and jumped back in my car. I looked up, and she was screaming to me from the doorway. I let my window down to see what she was saying.

"What you say?" A nigga was hoping she had changed her mind.

"The next time your nasty ass nut on my door, I'm gone throw a shit bag on your porch."

Laughing, I rolled my window up and drove off. I grabbed my phone again and called my nigga back.

"I need you to find somebody else, Jermaine."

"Damn, bruh. What the fuck you and your brothers doing?"

"It ain't nothing like that. I need to find my girl's mom. My girl's name is Deana Banks. She lives here in the city."

"Okay, that should be easy. I'll have that for you either tomorrow or the next day for sure."

"A'ight, bet." Hanging up, I knew I was taking a chance going to Juicy's mother, but that was her best friend. If anybody knew what I had to do to get Juicy back, it would be her mom. Juicy was saying she was done, but those tears and the love she had for a nigga let me know I had some type of chance. I just had to do the right thing.

After I pulled up to the hospital, I walked in and found Shadow in the waiting room.

"Where is Quick?" I asked him.

"He got Zavi, and he didn't want to bring him up here."

"He could have called Ash. That nigga tripping."

"You know your brother. He holds grudges longer than Mama's coochie hair."

"Nigga, don't talk about your mama while she laid up in the hospital."

Laughing at this nigga, I realized they weren't gone let me get that image out of my head. Even though Blaze was back, alive and well, I didn't like sitting in waiting rooms anymore. A few minutes later, Blaze walked in the waiting room, and we got excited.

"The baby here yet?" I asked.

Blaze shook his head. "Naw. I was just letting y'all know they prepping her now. The baby's head is right there, so she ready. It won't be long. I would have let you niggas back there, but I didn't need your ass back there, looking at my girl's pussy and shit."

"You a fucking clown. You know I don't want her," I retorted.

Blaze stared at me. "And you a nigga that's lost his memory. I ain't forgot, nigga. I'm waiting on the perfect time to get your ass."

I shrugged. "I already know. Go deliver your baby so we can see her."

He walked off, and I couldn't wait until that baby was born. The first girl in the family.

Shadow looked over at me and said, "You know that nigga gone do some real fucked-up shit, right? I swear, that nigga ain't wrapped tight. Nigga's brain as loose as Drea's pussy."

"Here you go." I couldn't do shit but laugh.

Blaze's ass was special, and I knew he wasn't gone let this shit go until he got me back. I was gone give him that one, and then, after that, if he tried some shit, I was gone fuck him up.

Thirty minutes later, Blaze walked out with tears in his eyes.

"Everything okay, bro?" I asked.

"No man should have to witness that shit. It's beautiful, but it ruins you at the same time."

"What you mean?" I said.

"That baby stretched her shit out. That pussy is woe."

"What the fuck is *woe*?" I was glad Shadow was the one who asked the question.

"Wore the fuck out. Instead of saying *wore*, you just say *woe*. Ain't no coming back from that shit, and I got a big dick. My shit just gone be lost in there," Blaze said mournfully.

"Nigga, come on. Let me see the baby," I said.

We walked in the back and washed our hands. Drea was holding the newborn, and I swear I had never seen a baby this fucking cute in my life. She had grayish-green eyes and a headful of hair.

"What's her name?" Shadow asked as he reached for the baby.

"Zayna 'Sparkle' Hoover. Her nickname is Spark."

"Nigga, you special. So you Blaze and she Spark? Please don't teach my baby to play with fire," I said.

"As soon as she can hold a lighter, I'm gone teach her how to flick that motherfucker," Blaze replied.

I walked over to Shadow and grabbed the baby gently. "Your granny gone go crazy when she sees you. I promise you gone be so fucking spoiled. You the only girl, and the world gone know not to fuck with Spark."

Blaze shook his head. "The world ain't about to see her. Issa Blanket. I'm gone do her like Michael Jackson did his son."

Shadow rolled his eyes. "Drea, I don't know how you put up with this nigga. He ain't right up there."

The whole room laughed at Shadow, until that nigga Blaze flicked his Bic. I shut my ass up and grabbed my phone. I wanted to FaceTime with Quick. I wanted him to see his niece. As soon as he answered, I had the phone aimed at the baby.

"Aw, look at my niece. She looks just like Uncle Quick."

I hadn't even realized it, but she really did.

"You right, bro. She does. She just prettier," Blaze said, then looked over at Drea.

"Bitch, you slipped on his dick too?" Blaze asked with a straight face. Drea looked horrified, until Blaze started laughing. "When we were kids, everybody said me and Quick looked alike. We were the only one with those eyes. But Spark look like me. Y'all got me fucked up."

Everybody looked up when Ash, Panda, and Paris walked in the room.

"Where is my TT baby? We naming her Paris," Paris said.

As soon as Quick realized she was there, he hung up.

"Baby Face, give me the baby shit," Paris demanded.

"Wash your hands first. We don't know where the fuck you been." Blaze said.

Paris glared at him. "Nigga, I'm so sick of your ass talking shit. My hands clean as the fuck." Blaze and Paris argued more than anybody I knew.

Blaze glared back at her. "And you sound dumb as the fuck. Who says that shit?"

"*I* say it. You need to sit your ass down somewhere. You do too much," Paris retorted.

Before any of us saw it coming, Blaze ran up on Paris and grabbed her by her hair. He was about to set her shit on fire, but her wig came off in his hand.

"Damn, Paris. I was about to set your edges on fire, but them motherfuckers already see-through. Look like your shit been on oven bake for a while. Thin-ass edges. Motherfuckers looking anorexic and shit. Hungry-ass edges."

Paris took off running and hid under the table.

"Fuck is you doing, Paris?" I was lost.

Blaze leaned over and peered at her. "How you gone hide your ass under the table like we can't see you? Nigga, it's your edges that's invisible. Hide them motherfuckers."

She climbed out from under the table, and Blaze threw her wig back at her. Me and Shadow were crying tears.

This nigga Blaze been on one since he came back from the dead. When Ash tried to help Paris put the wig back on, I was done. I had to get the fuck out of there. Paris walked over to me and reached out to grab the baby.

"Fix your wig first, sis," I told her.

Paris put her hands on her hips. "I see all you niggas got jokes today. Fuck y'all. Just a group of li'l dick, ignorant motherfuckers."

I passed her the baby, with tears in my eyes. I couldn't stop laughing.

When I regained control of myself, I caught Blaze's eye. "Hey, bro, I'm out. I'll be back up here in the morning to check on Mama and the baby."

"I'm out too," Shadow said.

Me and Shadow walked out together, still laughing. They about to kill each other in that room.

CHAPTER 15

SHADOW

Seeing my niece had me rethinking shit. I'd always wanted to be the one with the family. My brothers had never really cared about a bitch or that family shit, unless it was us. After Baby Face handed Spark over to Paris and said he was leaving, I decided to head home.

I stepped up to Paris and stared down at Spark. "Okay, baby, Uncle is leaving now. Don't go to anybody else until I get back."

"Nigga, please, I have the baby now." I couldn't believe Paris was still at it.

"You would think that given the way you were just hiding under that table, you would shut the fuck up," I told her.

"I will talk shit forever." The baby in her arms, this crazy ho even spun around like Cardi B when she said it.

Just then Baby Face turned to Blaze and said, "Hey, bro, I'm out."

"I'm out too," I said.

Me and Baby Face left the room and then parted ways in the parking lot. As soon as I got in the car, I pulled out my phone and called Kimmie. She didn't answer, so I headed home. I guessed she wasn't feeling me like a nigga thought. It had been a long night, so as soon as I walked in the door, I hit the bed and I was out.

***

I woke up feeling like new money, and I was ready to go see my mama. She should be awake and good now. So I jumped in the shower, handled my business, and got dressed. I drove to the hospital, parked, and headed to baby Spark's room first. All the brothers were there and waiting on me.

"Let me find out your ass don't know the essence of time." I should have known Quick was gone throw that shit at me.

"Shut up and let's go see your mama. I can't wait to see her face when Blaze walk in."

"That's why my ass so early. I been waiting on this shit," Quick said.

After agreeing with Quick, we walked out of the room and headed upstairs to see our mama. We left Blaze in the hallway and walked in. She looked worse than she had when we found her, but she didn't smell like a goat's ass anymore.

"Hey, Ma. How you feeling?" I asked her.

She looked at me with death in her eyes. "How the fuck you think I'm feeling? That nigga beat my ass, and I can't wait to get out of here."

"Ma, he has been handled, and we still looking for your punk-ass husband, but we will find him," I revealed.

"Good. Fuck his fruity ass."

"It looks like you could use some good news. We have a surprise for you," Baby Face told her. He was about to reveal Blaze, and I pulled my phone out to record her reaction.

"It better be good, or I'm gone knock your ass out. I ain't got time for no dumb shit."

"You can come in now."

As soon as Quick said that, Mama turned toward the door. When Blaze walked in, it looked like she was about to have a heart attack.

"What the fuck is going on? How? Oh, my God! I'm about to beat your ass," she exclaimed.

Blaze squinted at her. "Damn, Mama. A nigga come back from the dead, and the first thing you want to do is hit me?"

"Naw, nigga. I'm beating your ass because I burned all my damn wigs."

I had tears in my ass.

"I was wondering why your ass in here looking like Grace Jones. Why would you burn your wigs?" Blaze said.

"That shit is irrelevant. Nigga, you gone replace all them motherfuckers."

"I got you, Ma. Now can I have a hug?" He leaned over, and she opened her arms and cried.

"Hold the fuck on!" Mama pushed away from Blaze. "Who the fuck is this nigga?" She snatched her necklace off and threw it at his ass. "You dumb motherfuckers had me walking around with another nigga's balls on my chest. Where the fuck you been?"

We laughed, and Blaze told her everything that had happened.

"When you niggas kill Rico, I want to be there. You will not do that shit without me," Ma said when he finished telling her the story.

"We got you, Ma. I'll be back. We got another surprise for you."

I knew Blaze was talking about the baby.

"Okay, son. Shadow and Quick, can y'all run by the mall and go get me a Kindle so I can read while I'm laid up in this motherfucker. I need to talk to Baby Face."

I nodded. "I got you, Ma. Quick, you need to go to the house and get that other surprise. I'll go get the Kindle." She still didn't know about Zavi, and we may as well do it all at one time.

I left the room. As I was heading to my car, I saw Kimmie. She hadn't hit me up, and I decided I was gone keep it moving on her phony ass, but I walked over to her anyway.

"Hey, stranger," I said.

She jumped when I spoke to her. That shit didn't sit right with me.

"Hey, Shadow. I'll call you later. I have to go."

"Did I do something to you, Ma? I'm confused."

"No, you didn't, and I'm sorry. I have a lot of shit going on right now."

"Let me take some of that load off you. Talk to me. What's going on?"

She sighed and removed her glasses to wipe her face.

"The fuck! Who hit you in your shit?" I said.

She tried to throw her glasses back on, but it was too late. I had already seen the shit. "I'm handling it. I'll call you later."

"Look, usually if a chick try to swerve me, I leave they ass in the wind, but there's something about you. I promise if you let me, I can help you. Let a nigga in."

She started crying, and all I wanted to do was hold her. "You remember when I was telling you about my ex? Well, he showed up at my house when I got home. He is basically trying to force me to be with him. I'm tired, and I just want out. Mack has changed, and I don't want to settle no more. I gave him my all when he didn't deserve it—" It dawned on me what she had just said, and I cut her off.

"Wait, what you say his name is?"

"Mack. I told you that the night we were talking."

Shit, she must have said his name during the time I took a nap on her ass.

She went on. "How do you know Mack? Is this the same person? He hangs with Slick and his boys." That was what this nigga's angle was.

"Do you love him?" I asked.

"What? No. At one point I did, but he is not the same person. Since the night I met you, he has been beating my ass and forcing me to sleep with him. I just want him gone."

"I told you I can help you and I got you, but I need to know that you are completely done with him."

"I just told you I am."

"When you get home, text me when he gets there."

"What are you going to do?"

"Don't ask questions you don't want to know the answers to. Just let me know when he is there."

I walked off and got in my car. I ran to the mall to grab this Kindle so I could get back and tell my brothers. Everything was falling into place, and the only nigga left to kill was Rico. Then we could get back to our lives. With this nigga out there, we wouldn't be able to rest. That nigga's time was coming, though, but Mack's time was up now.

CHAPTER 16

KIMMIE

I had had no idea I would run into Shadow at the hospital. After Mack beat my ass last night, I had to go. The pain was unbearable. I had no idea who this man was. Even with his flaws, he had never been like this before. You would think I had done something to his ass, the way he was treating me. When Shadow had said he would handle it, I had almost told him yes. He obviously had plans to kill Mack, and as much as I hated him, I didn't think that was something I wanted on my conscience. All I wanted was for Mack to leave me alone.

Even though Shadow had told me to text him when Mack came home, I had no intentions on doing that. I was not that person, even though that was what I was attracted to. Shadow offering to kill Mack had just let me know that I done did the shit again. Shadow was obviously more of a thug and more in the streets than I had thought. Businessmen just didn't go around killing people. So much was on my mind and heart when I pulled into my driveway after leaving the hospital. Mack's car was there, and I prayed he was in a better mood today. Those thoughts went out the window the moment I walked in the door.

"Where the fuck have you been?" he yelled.

"The hospital. I needed to be seen and to be given some pain pills." I walked in the kitchen, got some water, and took some pills.

"Bitch, what the fuck did you tell them?" He got so close to my face, I could smell the shit flakes he must have eaten.

"I didn't tell them anything. You know I wouldn't do that."

"I don't know what you will do, but you walking around here like I really did something to your ass. Bitch, I barely touched you, and now your ass a victim."

"I'm not about to argue about this. You know what you did, and the fact that you are sitting here trying to downplay it is fucking me up."

"You tough now, since you think them people got your back. What the police tell you? They gone check into it? Well, I'm gone give you something to tell since you want to act like a nigga beating you and shit. Get naked."

"I'm not doing that. My body hurts, and I'm tired."

He punched me in the same eye he already had on swoll, and that shit hurt worse than any pain I had ever felt in my life.

"I said get naked."

Trying my luck, I attempted to run past him so I could get out the door. Before I could pass him, he punched me in the throat and down went Frazier. Gasping for air, I prayed he stopped. Instead, he reached down and started ripping my clothes off me. I had no more fight in me to stop him. When he walked to the sink, I was confused as hell about what he was doing. After grabbing some water, he walked over to me and poured it all over my body. When this nigga took off his belt, I tried to get up and haul ass, but he was too fast for me. This nigga started beating me like I was a field nigga and had got caught in the house, stealing bread. The water made the shit hurt so bad, tears jumped out of my eyes involuntarily.

"Mack, please stop. I didn't tell them anything," I cried.

"You want to act like a nigga beat you, so I'm gone give you what you want!"

His belt broke just then, and I thanked God for that little blessing . . . until he grabbed a chair. Oh, this nigga was really trying to kill me. Balling myself up the best I could, I braced myself for the blows that would come next. On the third swing, he broke the chair. That was how hard he hit me with that shit. The good thing was, he stopped.

"Now fix me some fucking dinner, and it better not take you long! Get yourself cleaned up. After I eat, I want some pussy," he shouted.

He went upstairs, and I cried as I looked at all the blood. There were whip marks all over my body, and I knew then I couldn't take this anymore. I found my purse somehow and fished out my phone. Then I texted Shadow.

Please hurry. He is here now.

Shadow texted back right away. I'm on the way. Just in case, leave the door unlocked.

I punched in four letters in response. Okay.

I headed upstairs and then jumped in the shower to wash the blood off me. I cried as the water hit my body. Once I was out of the shower, I dried off and pulled my hair into a messy bun. Then I walked into the spare room, grabbed some clothes, and got dressed. When I walked back down the stairs, I found Shadow and his brothers standing in my house. One of his brothers had his gun drawn, one was flicking a Bic, and one was just standing still.

"He just fought you again? You didn't look like that earlier," Shadow said. He looked horrified.

I shook my head slowly, "*Fought* me? This nigga just beat me like a tranny getting caught with a dick between his legs."

"Kimmie, I'm going to need you to leave out of the house," Shadow said quietly. "I just texted you my address. Go wait for me there. Don't answer the door and don't leave. Just wait for me there, okay?"

I nodded my head, and tears running down my face, I walked out the door. This was not what I wanted, but I would have to live with the decision I had just made. This chapter of my life was closing, and I was going to pray for forgiveness. I jumped in my car and headed toward Shadow's house.

CHAPTER 17

QUICK

After leaving the hospital, I headed over to the hotel to pick up Zavi from Ash. He had been begging me to see her, and I couldn't keep telling him no. Everybody expected me to just forgive her ass, but the shit was deeper for me. I got why she hadn't told me years ago, but we had been together every day for months, and she had gone out of her way to make sure I didn't find out. That shit didn't sit right with me. *How can you say you love me but keep something like that from me?* I thought. That shit was as foul as my mama's ass was the other day.

After I pulled up to the hotel, I got out of the car and went upstairs. When I knocked on the door, Zavi answered it.

"What I tell you about opening doors? You go get an adult and tell them someone's at the door, okay?" I said sternly.

"Yes, Daddy. Are you here to pick me up?"

"Yeah. You're about to meet your grandma. Go get your coat and your bag."

He took off running, and I sat on the couch. When I looked up, Ash had walked out of the bathroom, naked. She must not have known I was there.

"Fuck, Quick! You scared me."

I tried my best to stop the moan that was escaping my mouth. She looked fucking sexy to me. Everything about her was making my dick jump. Before I could even stop myself, I was getting up off the couch and walking over to her. When I slid my hand between her legs, the juices started flowing. Her breathing increased, and I was ready to fuck her curls straight. I had leaned in to kiss her and was getting lost in her mouth when Zavi broke my trance.

"Daddy, I'm ready to go."

I stepped back from her, got my shit together, and walked away. "Yeah, let's go."

After I grabbed Zavi's hand, we headed out the door. I was happy he had interrupted and had stopped me from doing something I would regret. The entire way back to the hospital, Ash was on my mind. *How can you keep something like that from the person you claim to love the most? Fuck her.* I needed to get her out of my system, because what she had done was something I would never forgive. That was the shit I kept trying to convince myself of as I walked up to my mama's room, with Zavi right beside me. Everybody was there already, and she was holding Spark.

"I can't wait to teach my grandbaby everything. She gone be just like her nana."

"I hope not," I said. "Ma, this is your grandson, Zavi."

Her ass didn't even look up. "Nigga, what bitch done tricked you? Your ass ain't got no damn kids, and I ain't been out that damn long."

She was about to piss me off. He wasn't a baby, and he understood perfectly.

"Ma, I don't play about my child. Don't make me fuck your old ass up."

"Nigga, please. You been a daddy six seconds, and now it's you don't play about your child. Here, Blaze. Get Spark so Quick can bring me this baby he claiming."

"If you would look your ass up, you would see he ain't no damn baby," I muttered.

She finally looked my way. "Oh, shit. I can't hold that nigga. Damn, you couldn't deny him if you wanted to. That's your fucking twin."

I walked Zavi over to the bed, and I finally introduced them.

"Zavi, this is your grandma."

He reached down and hugged her.

"Hey, baby. You so handsome. I got me two babies to spoil. Who is his mama?"

I frowned. "Ash. She didn't tell me."

When her and Zavi started talking, Shadow called me over to where he, Baby Face, and Blaze were standing.

"I know where Mack is," Shadow revealed. "The nigga is Kimmie's ex, and he know Slick and them. I guess that's why this nigga was coming around. He was on some bullshit."

"What the fuck we waiting on, then?" Blaze asked. He was ready.

"I'm waiting on her to text me when he gets there," Shadow said.

"You sure she gone text you?" Baby Face said.

"I don't know. He beat her ass, and her eye was fucked up. She said she is, but if she doesn't, I know where she lives, and we gone have to do what we do."

"A'ight. Let us know as soon as she does," I said.

At first, we hadn't had a reason to kill Mack, other than the fact that Blaze wanted him dead. But now we did. This nigga was on some "get back" shit, and now he was about to get that wig knocked back.

"Let me take Spark back to flexi pussy," Blaze told us. "I need to get my mind right for this." Nobody in the world was more aggy than Blaze, and I didn't see how Drea put up with his shit.

Shadow took a seat in the chair near the bed, and he, Baby Face, and I talked shit with Mama until Blaze came back. As soon as he walked in the door, Shadow stood up.

"Let's go fellas. We got moves to make," he said. Kimmie must have texted him.

"Ma, can Zavi stay here with you until we get back?" I asked.

"Get your dumb ass out my face. You know damn well he can stay here. I swear, for your name to be Quick, you slow as hell sometimes."

I swore my mama's mouth was so bad, she made you want to talk bad to her. I almost called her a bitch after that.

Blaze, Shadow, Baby Face, and I walked out of the room, and our savagery instantly turned up.

"Who shit we in?" Blaze said.

"We can take my shit. I'm in the truck," Baby Face said. For some reason, it always seemed like we drove Baby Face's shit to a caper.

We went out to the parking lot, climbed in the truck, and headed out.

"We either have to be in and out, or quiet and precise. She lives in Westchester," Shadow announced.

Damn. Shadow done finally got him a bougee bitch.

"I say quiet and precise. She gone have to leave. We just met her, and I don't trust a soul right now."

Everybody nodded in agreement.

"No more L's," Blaze said as he flicked his Bic. He was unusually quiet, and that had me worried. He always had a joke or two, but not this time. This was personal for him, just like Alaysia.

We pulled up to the house and got out. We walked in, and nobody was downstairs.

"Let's wait a minute. I really don't want to do this while she is here," Shadow whispered.

We stood there for about ten minutes, and Kimmie finally walked down the stairs. After Shadow got her to leave, we crept up the stairs to the bedroom. This nigga was lying in the bed like he was that nigga. Blaze walked over to him and put his lighter to his nose. Mack must have had some nose hair, because that shit caught fire quick. He jumped up out of his sleep and grabbed his nose.

"Wake your bitch ass up, lucky charm."

When he saw all of us standing there, he knew his time was up.

"You pushed up on my brother's girl because you mad about your gutter-ass friends?"

"One of the niggas y'all killed in the bank was my baby brother. How the fuck would you feel if it was one of y'all?" Mack muttered.

Blaze crossed his arms. "It *was* one of us. The thing is, I wouldn't have tried to get in through a bitch. I would have stepped to the nigga and blown his fucking brains out. You feel me?"

I studied Blaze. I had never seen him like this before. I knew then, he was gone over Drea's ass.

"What if I had some information?" Mack said, desperation seeping into his voice.

Blaze tapped a foot. "I'm listening." We allowed Blaze to take the lead since this meant the most to him.

"I didn't even have any intentions on stepping to y'all. Rico paid me to. He even had me over the crew that had you at the warehouse."

I was so sick of this nigga Rico.

"Where is Rico?" Blaze said.

"I don't know. Since you got away, he been MIA."

Blaze walked closer to the bed and grabbed a pillow. "Here is where your problem lies. We already know Rico is a snake. Had you given me a location, I might have considered some shit. Your next problem is, it didn't take you no time to snitch. I don't like snitches. My brother got court in a week. We can't take that chance. Your last problem is . . ." He placed the pillow over Mack's dick. "You tried to fuck my girl. If I took a bullet for her, what do you think I would do about her?"

Blaze took out his gun and pulled the trigger. He done shot this nigga in the dick. "If you scream, I will end your shit right now," he snarled. There was nothing worse than hearing a grown-ass man screaming like a bitch.

"Blaze, let's wrap this shit up." Baby Face wanted to get the fuck out of this hot-ass neighborhood.

Blaze ignored him. "When I was growing up, this nigga named Gangsta cut a nigga's tongue off for talking shit to his girl." This nigga was being so dramatic, but I ain't lying, I wanted to see where he was going with this. He went in his jeans and grabbed a pocketknife. "You kissed my bitch, knowing she was mine. You fed her lies, knowing I was alive. You snitched out those same crusty-ass lips. Moral of the story, you won't be able to do that shit no more."

We raised our guns and aimed at Mack, just in case he tried to make a move on Blaze. This nigga sat on top of Mack and cut his lip off. Mack was a whole ho, because no way I would let a nigga do that to me. You gone have to kill my ass. When Blaze stood up, we lit Mack's ass up.

Blaze walked in the bathroom and came out with some rubbing alcohol. "It's time to go," he said as he poured the alcohol on Mack. And y'all know what happened next. He flicked his Bic. We took off running out the door.

As soon as we jumped in the truck, Shadow went off. "What the fuck, Blaze! That girl lived there. All her shit is in there!"

"Nigga, let her move in with you. Fuck out my face. You want the pussy anyway," Blaze barked.

When Baby Face opened his mouth to protest, Blaze shoved Mack's lip in Baby Face's mouth. "Nigga, shut the fuck up! It sounds like you about to say some stupid shit."

Baby Face started rubbing the shit out of his mouth. Tongue and all. My ass would have thrown up if it was me. Blaze's ass so disrespectful. That was why I didn't piss that nigga off. He was aggy as fuck. "Blaze, I swear on Hoover, you gone make me kill your ass!" Baby Face roared. "Why the fuck would you do that nasty-ass shit?"

"I told you, it might not be today, and it might not be tomorrow, but I'm gone get your ass back."

Baby Face glared at Blaze. "Nigga, we even! Fuck that."

"We even when I *say* we even. Your bitch ass will know when we are."

A moment ago I was thinking I would throw up if Blaze had done that lip thing to me. Now I was struck by the absurdity of the situation, and I burst out laughing. I couldn't stop. I had never laughed this hard in my life. This nigga had put a dead man's lip in Baby Face's mouth. My phone went off just then, and I saw that Nala had sent a text. I read it and saw she was asking me to come over to her house. After the brief thing that had happened with me and Ash, I could use some pussy. I texted her that I was on my way.

Seething, Baby Face put the key in the ignition and started the truck. Then he headed back to the hospital. When Baby Face pulled into the hospital parking lot and found a spot, I turned toward him.

"Hey, take Zavi with you. I'll pick him up later," I said. "Blaze, go home and change clothes, nigga. Don't go picking my niece up, and your ass got all that blood on you."

I stepped out of the truck, headed to my car, and pulled off.

When I walked in the door, she had the house smelling good. She was cooking, and her house was spotless. That was a plus in my book. As I looked at her now, when she was sober and at home, I realized she didn't really look like the ho I thought she was.

"Hey, baby. Make yourself at home. I'll make you a plate and bring it to you," she told me when I stepped into the kitchen.

I sat down on the couch and turned on ESPN. She had cooked some shrimp and chicken Alfredo. I must admit, when she brought me my plate, the shit looked good as fuck. I dug in, and it was fye. After I got done eating, we sat around and just talked, and I realized I really hadn't given her a chance. Maybe it was because I was only using her to get back at Ash, but after tonight I was willing to give her a fair chance.

Leaning over, I kissed her. For some reason, she seemed shy tonight. I guessed the liquor really had her turned up. I slid her tank top down, then put her nipple in my mouth.

"Damn, baby. That feels so good."

The way she moaned that out made my dick hard as hell. After pulling her boy shorts down, I slid my finger in her pussy as I kept sucking her breast. Then I slid my finger up to her clit and flicked that motherfucker like Blaze flicked his Bic.

"Come for me," she moaned and ground against my finger.

I picked up the pace, and her body started shaking uncontrollably.

"Damn, Daddy. I'm coming."

I kept stroking until my fingers were soaked. Then I reached in my pocket and pulled out a condom. I was not about to make the same mistake again. Sliding it over my dick, I looked up at her, and I could tell she had an attitude. I grabbed her by her hair and threw her against the couch.

"You mad?" I said.

She didn't respond, and I slammed my dick in her.

"You mad, baby? Tell Daddy why you mad."

"Because I want to feel all of you."

I slammed my dick inside her as hard as I could, and she screamed out in pain.

"You don't feel that dick?"

She didn't respond, and I really didn't need her too. I was gone show her who the fuck I was.

As soon as I picked up the pace and was tearing that pussy up, I slid my thumb in her ass. Fucking her with my finger as I tore her shit up, I was glad I was sober this time to feel it. Her shit felt good as fuck. After taking my finger out of her ass, I grabbed her by her legs and stood up. Making sure I had a good grip, I committed an assault on her pussy. She thought she wanted this shit until I got up in them guts. She couldn't even take it. She was trying her best to get away, but I had her ass on lock. When I felt her squirt all over my dick, I came instantly. I didn't even know the shit was about to cum. My knees shook, and I could no longer stand up.

"Damn, girl. I'm mad I didn't remember the pussy from last time. This shit was good as fuck." After pulling my condom off, I threw it in the trash and then lay down on the couch.

"Give me, like, twenty minutes, and I'll be ready for round two," I told her. Then I closed my eyes and drifted off, thinking about Ash.

CHAPTER 18

NALA

The minute I'd seen the brothers get out of their Phantoms at the club that night, I had had it in my mind I was gone get Quick's fine ass. He was that "I'll fuck him raw and let him beat me" kind of fine. When his brother had called us over, I'd been happy as fuck. I had been trying to get Quick's attention the whole night. Once I'd got in their circle, there was no turning back. Yeah, I had had to take an ass whupping for him, but I had got the nigga.

He had seen right through me that first night. My ass was the biggest ho Chicago had ever seen, and I didn't give no fucks. Quick didn't want that, and I needed that nigga like I needed a dick. When he'd got out of the car to go get a box of condoms after we left the club that night, I had slipped some Ecstasy in his drink. A bitch had only been trying to get him all the way turned up so he didn't think about a condom. Instead, that nigga had passed out on my ass. While he was out, I sucked his dick so long, I damn near got lockjaw. Needing him to be hard, I kept trying. But his dick would not stand up. I was going to ride his ass and have him cum in me, but that shit didn't work. The next morning, I told him we had had sex without a condom, since I thought he would do it again, but he didn't.

Since he had seen right through me and thought I was a ho, when he came over my house that first time, I put on the good girl act, and he bought it. We been messing around heavy for the past month now. Every time we had sex, he made sure he strapped up. When he went to sleep, I would go in the garbage and get the condom. A bitch been straight turkey basting his shit. Because he thought he had fucked me raw the first time, he would think that was when I got pregnant.

Today I was going to lie my ass off and tell him I was pregnant. Knowing how niggas were, I had got my home-girl to give me some piss, and I had it hid in my bathroom. I had used a little on one test, but I was keeping the rest just in case he told me to do the test again in front of him. Once he found out I was pregnant, he wouldn't use a condom anymore, and I could get pregnant for real. Yeah, a bitch had this all mapped out, and I didn't give a fuck who didn't like it. He was going to be my man, and a baby would solidify that.

I had placed the test on the kitchen table, and when he walked through the front door, I stood in the kitchen, smiling like a fool.

"The hell you so happy about?" he asked when he found me in the kitchen.

I nodded toward the table, and he walked over to it.

Then he said, "You know you can't keep that, right?"

Talk about a dream crusher, I thought.

"I know you not asking me to get an abortion. I don't believe in that shit, and I'm not killing my baby because you don't want to step up and handle your responsibilities. You can leave now," I told him.

"First of all, watch your fucking mouth. There's a lot of shit going on in my life. I just barely beat a murder charge. There's too much going on right now."

"If it's too much for you, then you don't have to be here. We will be straight no matter what. As I said before, you can leave." I followed him into the living room and could see him thinking it over as he went and sat down on the couch.

"I'm sorry. You right. I fucked up, and I don't have a choice but to be there. There will be a blood test done as soon as the baby is born."

Shid, I didn't give a fuck about a blood test. All I needed was for him to fuck me and get me pregnant for real.

I sat down next to him on the couch. "We can do that. I have no problems getting the baby tested. I haven't been with anybody. It may be hard to believe after the first encounter we had, but I really was drunk as hell. That ain't me."

"I'm glad we don't have to fight about that. If it's mine, I got you, Ma."

He kissed me, and I immediately took off my clothes. When he grabbed a condom out of his pocket, I almost smacked the life out of his ass. This nigga was doing too much. Who fucked they baby mama with a condom while she was pregnant? I guessed I was gone have to keep turkey basting until this shit worked. He was gone be my baby daddy whether he wanted to or not. I got this. Until I got pregnant, I was gone take drastic measures. Once I actually got pregnant, the timeline wouldn't matter. I would have the baby then. Fuck his ex. Quick was mine.

CHAPTER 19

BABY FACE

It had been over a month, and Jermaine still hadn't found this nigga Rico. The shit was pissing me off. How hard was it to find one clown-ass nigga? As long as that nigga was out there, my family was not safe.

My mother had told me some shit I couldn't believe. Her ass had given me the rundown on how she had ended up in the house and what she had seen that night. She didn't want me to tell Shadow, because she said her sons had been hurt enough. All she wanted was for us to make sure they died a slow death. At first it was down to one more person, but Shirree had just been added to that list. She wouldn't get away with that shit, and her nasty ass had to go. The bitch was okay with fucking some faggots, and the fairy was her man's father. Once you consorted with the enemy, you were now our enemy.

When my phone rang, I looked at the caller ID. *Speak of the devil.*

"Jermaine, tell me you have a location on Rico," I said after I picked up on the first ring.

"I'm sorry, Baby Face, not yet. But I do have that other address. I had some family issues, so it took me a little longer. I'm back now, and I will be on it. I promise I will have the other location soon."

"It's all good. I hope everything okay. Text me the address and make sure you get on that other one. His bitch ass thinks he done got away with some shit."

"I got you. I'm sending you the text now."

After hanging up, I retrieved Jermaine's text and looked at the address and saw that she wasn't that far. I jumped in my whip and headed over to Juicy's mother's house. She was gone help me get my girl back. As soon as I pulled up, I jumped out. Not wanting to waste any more time, I rushed to the front door and rang the doorbell.

"Who is it?" a woman's voice called.

"Zaire." Shit sounded weird when I said my name. I hardly ever said it or heard it. She must have known who I was, because she opened the door with no hesitation.

"Well, I can see why it was so hard for her to walk away. Come in."

"Thank you."

We walked into the front room and sat down.

"What brings you by here?" she asked as she peered at me.

"I need your help. Your daughter won't fuc . . . I mean, mess with me anymore, and I need to know what I can do to get her back."

She sat back and studied me some more. A minute ticked by, and then she said, "Nothing. Juicy is one of those people that can hold a grudge forever. It takes a lot to tear down her walls, but once you do, she will love you like no other. If you hurt her, she will use that same passion to hate you."

I took in everything she was saying, and the shit hurt. I would never get my girl back, and I didn't know how to deal with that.

Juicy's mother went on. "I will tell you this, though. She still loves you, but if you keep allowing time to pass, you will lose her forever. I don't know what you can do to make her forgive you—I don't know if that's something she is even willing to do—but I know that she still loves you. She cries every day, and it has been months. She is still hurting, and you need to find a way to heal her and fast."

"I've tried everything. She won't budge."

"If you have tried everything, I'm sorry, son, but you have lost her."

Standing up, I felt defeated. I wanted to cry, but I knew Juicy's mother would tell her, and I refused to give her ass the satisfaction.

"Thank you for your time, Ms. Banks. I appreciate it." I walked over to the front door and opened it to walk out.

"Zaire, I'm going against everything I believe in right now, but only because I don't agree with her actions. Juicy is pregnant, and she has no intentions of telling you. I raised her alone, and I don't want that for my grandchild. You can't get her back, but you should at least be given the chance to be a father."

Not giving a fuck, I let the tears fall down my face.

"Where can I find her?" I asked.

"She has a doctor's appointment today at two. She will be at UIC, on Cermak."

I hugged her and ran out of the house. As soon as I got in the car, all kinds of shit went through my mind. I looked at the clock on the dashboard. It was twelve thirty. I had enough time to reach UIC before Juicy's appointment. I called my brothers and told them to meet me there. I had a plan.

I stood in the waiting room of the doctor's office at UIC, surrounded by baby stuff. I had bought all kinds of shit. A nigga didn't even know the sex of the baby, and I had clothes, bouncers, shoes, and a crib sitting out there, waiting on her. My brothers stood behind me as I waited for her to come from the back. I didn't want her to know I was here until then.

The nurses had their phones out, right along with my brothers. The shit I was about to pull was sweet in my eyes, but Juicy was a mean motherfucker. She might laugh in my face and leave. One of the nurses gave me the signal that Juicy was about to walk out, and I cleared my throat. I hadn't done this shit in years, and no one knew this about me but my brothers. A nigga had never done this for a chick, and I was scared as hell. When the door opened, I began.

"I don't want to lose this relationship, so we gotta stay strong. . . ." As I sang "Did You Wrong" by Pleasure P, everyone in the room was crying, including me. The nurses were crying and recording the scene right along with my brothers. They knew what she meant to me, and this was my last chance to get her back. When I saw the tears flowing down her face, I knew she still loved me. A nigga just had to convince her that she still loved me.

I kept singing. " . . . 'Cause at the end of the day, I did you wrong. You did me wrong. I take you back. You take me back." When I finished singing the last verse, I dropped to my knees and pulled out a ring.

"Deana, I know a nigga fucked up, and I'm sorry," I said sincerely. "That fact doesn't change how I feel about you and how you feel about me. We created something beautiful out of love, and I think it's only right that we raise it out of love. Together."

Yeah, a nigga pulled the baby card on her ass, but so what?

I went on. "If you give me another chance, I promise you this. You will never have to wonder where I am or what I am doing. You will never have to question how I feel. All I want is you, and I need you in my life. A nigga can barely breathe with you gone. I just want my friend back. If you say yes, I will spend the rest of my life making you the happiest woman alive. Will you please piece my heart back together by becoming Mrs. Hoover?" There it was. I had put it all out on the table, and I was scared shitless. When I told her mother I had tried everything, that was a lie. The moment she'd told me about the baby, I knew what I had to do.

"You had me at hello." When she quoted that line from our favorite movie, *Jerry Maguire*, I almost passed out.

"That's a yes?"

She nodded her head. "That's a yes."

I got up off the floor and walked over to her and hugged her. I kissed that girl with my entire soul, and I hoped she felt that. I cried as I placed the eight-carat princess-cut diamond ring on her finger and then hugged her again.

"Damn, you just gone keep crying, ole sugar bear–looking nigga? Got the nerve to be doing the ugly cry at that. Who carrying all this shit out of here?" Blaze remarked. He couldn't have a serious moment to save his life.

"You brought all this stuff in here? I don't even know what I'm having," Juicy mused.

Looking around the room, I said fuck it. "Let's leave it here then. We can buy the stuff together."

I turned to the nurses and thanked them. "You can keep this stuff and donate it as you see fit. Thank you so much for allowing me this moment."

They cried even harder, and I walked out with my girl, hand and hand. My brothers followed us.

"Thank y'all for sharing this moment with your big bro. It means a lot to me," I told them once we were outside.

"What moment? All your ugly ass did was pull an R. Kelly. Nigga sang his way back into her life. Sweet-and sour-ass nigga," Quick declared. He was starting to act just like Blaze.

I rolled my eyes. "Whatever, nigga. I'll see y'all later."

When I walked Juicy to her car, I saw she had driven her old-ass Nissan.

"Where is the car I bought you?" I asked her.

"In your garage. When the last time you been in that motherfucker?"

"I been in and out of the house. Shit ain't felt the same since you left. You are coming home with me, right?"

"Yeah."

"To live?"

"Yeah, boy. I'll meet you there."

I jumped in my car and headed home. I was the happiest nigga alive right now. As soon as I pulled up, I saw that Juicy was standing in the doorway, naked. It was cold as fuck outside, but she was doing it for me, and that was why she was the one.

"You about to make me fuck you right here," I said after I climbed out of my car.

"What's stopping you? Tsunami can't keep me warm?" She was playing with me, but little did she know she was about to get this dick right here.

I pushed her face-first against the wall, then slid my fingers up and down her clit. As I leaned toward her ear, I took control. "Spread them legs."

She did as she was told, and I swear I couldn't wait to be inside her. Her skin was cold, and she shivered as I kissed her back.

"You wanna go inside?" I whispered.

"I'm okay."

I got down on my knees right there in the cold, then spread her ass cheeks apart and ate that pussy from the back.

"Fuck, Face. I missed you so much."

I showed her how much I had missed her with my tongue. I swirled my shit around her clit and then eased my way to her opening. I tongue fucked her until her juices coated my tongue. After sliding my tongue out, I licked up her ass and back down.

"Nigga. What the fuck! *Shit*," she sputtered.

After sucking on that thang for a few more minutes, I got up. We couldn't have a long-ass session outside in the cold. So I pulled Tsunami out and slid right in. I grabbed her by her breasts and used them as leverage as I went in and out of her.

"Fuck! This pussy so good, Ma."

She started throwing that shit back, and I knew it wasn't gone be long. After slamming inside her, I kept going until I nutted all in that pussy. I pulled out, and I was ready for round two.

"Go meet me in the shower," I told her.

"Okay, big daddy."

I laughed as she walked her ass in the house bowlegged. Fuck, I loved this girl.

CHAPTER 20

SHADOW

Looking at Baby Face profess his love to Juicy had me feeling some type of way. Just a while ago, I was the one that was supposed to be getting married, and that shit had got blown all to hell. How the fuck Shirree had turned to be that was beyond me, but I was glad her booty-sucking ass had shown her true colors. It had made room for Kimmie.

My feelings for Kimmie were stronger in the little time I had known her than they'd been for Shirree, and I'd been with her for years. Don't get me wrong. I loved the gutter rat, but I saw now that I didn't really know what love was. Everything about Kimmie had me rethinking everything I thought I knew about my life. She had brought things out of me I didn't even know was in there. She had a nigga going hiking, bowling, skating, all kinds of shit. I was a hood nigga; we didn't do shit like that.

She even had a nigga reading and shit. Reading books just didn't seem exciting to me, but she had me reading this book called *She Wanted the Streets, He Wanted Her Heart*, by A.J. Davidson, and there was all kinds of drama in that motherfucker. The nigga Weezy in the book was a drug dealer, and he didn't know his girl was a stripper and shit. I told Kimmie's ass that if this the kind of shit in books now, I was about to be reading all the time. It took me a while to get her to open up her heart to a nigga, but once she did, I knew then that all I needed was her. The night we killed Mack had turned out to be the best night of my life, after I had got her ass to calm down. I thought back on what had happened.

When I walked in the door, I knew she was about to panic. Blaze just couldn't be a simple nigga. He always had to do the most. She was sitting on my couch, waiting on me.

"Can I go home now? Did you all clean it out?" she quizzed.

"Look, about that . . . Blaze kind of, um, set your house on fire."

"He did what! How the fuck do you kind of set someone's house on fire?"

"Baby, how do you think he got his name? He has an obsession with fire. Him killing Mack was more than just about you. It was personal for him. There was no way he was leaving without leaving his signature mark."

"I don't give a fuck about his signature! Where the fuck am I going to live? This shit is fucked up. You said you were going to help me, but you made the shit worse!"

I threw my hands up in the air. "Look, we all do things our own way. That's his way. I'm sorry, but I got you. You can stay here with me, and I will replace anything you need me to."

"That's a waste of money. You know how much clothes and shoes I had?"

"I'm not trying to brag, because that ain't even how a nigga gets down, but one of my cars can cover the cost of your house and everything in it. Money ain't a problem, and I told you I got you. Whatever you want, it's yours."

She shook her head. "That's not the point."

"Well, what is the point? It's fucked up, I'll give you that, but are you gone be the one to go tell him that? I

promise you don't want to do that. The nigga thrives on fucking with people. He gets a nut off that shit. I'm telling you now, I ain't going with you. Did you see Quick's face? Who you think did that shit? And how about Baby Face's hairline? Who you think did that? If he could do that to his own brothers, what you think he will do to you? He crazy, and he don't care. Let me just replace the shit, and you stay here."

"So what you telling me is, all y'all scared of Blaze's ass?"

"Was that shade, nigga?"

"I don't throw shade, sweetie. I throws the entire tree," she retorted.

"Nobody scared of his ass . . . Hell, maybe we are . . . But the nigga ain't wrapped tight. You can go fuck with that nigga. I ain't."

She laughed at me, and I ran to her and threw her over my shoulder.

"Shadow, put me down! That shit hurt."

Ignoring her protests, I ran up the stairs with her over my shoulder. When I laid her in the bed, she had tears in her eyes.

"What's wrong?" I asked.

"I told you, it hurt. He hurt me so bad."

I removed her clothes, as I wanted to see what she meant. When I saw the swollen whip marks all over her body, that shit hit a nigga hard. Who the fuck could do that shit to a chick? Knowing my words wouldn't make her feel better, I placed soft kisses on her body. I kissed her on every single mark and bruise. By the time I got to her pussy, I had tears in my own eyes. Mack had fucked her up bad, and I was glad Blaze had done his ass the way he had. Even though the shit was disturbing as fuck, he had deserved that shit.

Knowing she needed me to be gentle, I sucked and licked on her as if I was making love to her. That was my intention, to make love to the pussy, and I did that shit with my tongue. By the time I was ready to give her the dick, she had cum twice. I grabbed a condom, put it on, and slid inside her. I gave her slow and deliberate strokes. I wanted her to feel what a nigga was trying to say every time I slid inside her. That curve was lying on her G-spot, and I took advantage of that shit. After she gave me three more orgasms, I finally released my seeds in the condom. She was lying there shaking when I got up and went over to the dresser. After grabbing the flowers out of the vase, I walked over to her and threw them on her.

She raised a quizzical brow. "What are you doing?"

"I just killed the pussy. I was giving it a proper burial."

She grabbed the flowers and threw them at me. "Asshole."

I went and grabbed some Vaseline, then walked over to the bed and took off the top to the container.

"Nigga, if you think you about to fuck me in the ass, you got me fucked up," she told me.

"Ain't nobody about to go in that big-ass booty, but that motherfucker sholl look like it can take the dick."

After scooping some Vaseline out, I rubbed it all over the bruises and whip marks on her body. I had never given of myself in this way before. As I looked in her eyes, I knew she was begging me to be the one. I was going to do everything in my power to show her that I was.

A nigga had never thought she would be the one teaching me. She was everything in a chick that I had never had. When I looked at her, my soul jumped with my dick. She was mine, and I was never letting her ass go.

***

As soon as a nigga got up, my phone was going off. My brothers had texted me, telling me to come to the main house. I hopped in the shower and handled my business. Kissing Kimmie, I woke her up.

"I'll be back. I got a meeting with my brothers. You need anything?"

She yawned. "Just that dick. Hurry back."

I rushed out of the house to get this shit over with. As soon as I walked in the main house, I knew I wasn't about to get a nut soon. They were dressed in all black.

"What's going on?" I asked.

"With us having kids and starting new families, we need to make sure we set," Baby Face informed me. "I know this last minute, but we about to hit a bank. If you not down, we won't do it. You know it's all of us or none of us. This will be the last one, and we are retired."

I listened to Baby Face tell me why we needed to hit it one more time, and I agreed. We needed to make sure we were set for life, but the last time we did a caper, I almost didn't make it out. That shit bothered me. What if I didn't make it back to Kimmie? She would be fucked. Everything she had, she had lost, and even though I had replaced her clothes and shit, financially, she would be fucked. She had no idea where nothing was, and I didn't know if my brothers would give her anything. After thinking it over, I decided to do this caper, but with stipulations.

"If I do this, I have conditions." I took a deep breath. "If I don't make it out that motherfucker, y'all have to make sure Kimmie is straight. Give her everything, and make sure Baby Face don't fuck her. He can't even go visit her."

Baby Face looked at me with death in his eyes, and then he looked over at Blaze, as if he was begging him not to feed into the bullshit.

"Deal. Let's do this. Shadow, go upstairs and change."

I looked at Baby Face and nodded for him to come upstairs with me.

Baby Face scowled at me as he followed me up the stairs. "Fuck you want, nigga? I ain't with that gay shit. You acting like you want a nigga to help you change."

"I just wanted to ask you, are you sure? I'm only doing this for you."

"I'm sure, baby bro. I got you. We coming out that motherfucker, I promise."

"A'ight."

Baby Face went back downstairs, and I changed my clothes as all kinds of thoughts went through my mind. This was how I knew she was the one. I'd never robbed a bank and thought about Shirree's ass and what would happen to her if I didn't come back. After I got my clothes on, I pulled my phone out sent a text to Kimmie.

I love you.

Seconds later she texted me back. I love you too. What's wrong?

Nothing. Just wanted you to know that.

Hurry home.

I'll be there soon.

Walking downstairs, I prayed Baby Face was right, and I promised myself that if I came home, I would make sure Kimmie knew how I felt.

We jumped in the beater and headed out. As soon as we got to the bank, we put our masks on and headed in.

"Everybody, get on the fucking floor! Don't try to be a hero, and you will be out of here in three minutes," Quick yelled as he jumped on the counter and pointed his guns around the room.

Blaze and Baby Face dragged the manager to the vault. As I pointed my gun, I kept having flashbacks from the last time I was in the bank. I could feel my body shaking from panic.

"Two minutes." As always, Quick yelled off the time.

I circled the room with so much on my mind. Happy this was the last caper, I couldn't wait to get the fuck out of this bank. This felt like the longest two minutes of my life. I walked to the window and checked to make sure no cops were outside. When I turned back around, a security guard had a gun to my face.

"Don't fucking move." He didn't have to say that, because I was frozen in place. All I could think about was Kimmie waiting for me to come home, but I would never come.

"Thirty seconds." Quick couldn't see me, and I wished he would come save me.

When the security guard took the safety off his gun, I knew I was about to die.

"I hate you niggers. You think you can just take, but you chose the wrong bank today, son. Say your prayers."

I closed my eyes and prayed God knew a nigga's heart. The gun went off, and my body fell to the floor.

"Nigga, what the fuck are you doing? Get your dramatic ass up before I leave your dumb ass here. Fainting and shit like a fucking sissy."

I opened my eyes, and Blaze was still cursing my ass out.

Baby Face was standing over the security guard, his gun still pointed at him. "I told you I got you, baby bro. Let's go."

We left the bank and jumped in the beater.

"Now, that's how you fucking retire. I'm gone miss the rush of this shit, though. I ain't even gone lie," Quick said. He was lit, and my ass was still shaking like a stripper.

"How much we get?" I asked.

"Baby bro, we just cleaned the vault. About fifty million, give or take a few," Baby Face replied.

I smiled. "Now that was worth almost getting shot over."

Laughing, we headed back to the main house. The money was divided, and we all went our separate ways. I ran to the mall and then home. As soon as I walked in the door, I ran upstairs to Kimmie. She was sitting in bed, watching TV. I dropped to my knees.

"It's scary to find someone that makes you happy. You start giving them all your attention because they are what makes you forget the bad shit that's going on in your life. The thought of them waking up one morning and leaving you makes you not want to take the next step. Today my life flashed before my eyes, and all my thoughts were of you. I know it hasn't been a long time, and you may think I'm crazy, but I need you in my life forever. Will you marry me?"

She rose from the bed, walked over to me, and got on her knees. "Yes."

I couldn't wait to make her Mrs. Hoover.

CHAPTER 21

KIMMIE

"Who the fuck thought of this white-ass shit? I'm telling y'all now, if I fall, I'm melting all this shit."

I laughed as Blaze talked shit. I had convinced them to go ice-skating with me, and he was acting up.

"It's not white shit. You just have to step out of your box. It's going to be fun," I said.

"Bro, you better tell your girl that if I fall, she gone be looking like fried salmon," Blaze said to Shadow.

"I agree with Blaze," his mama said. "Black people wasn't meant to do this shit, and my bones too fucking old for this shit. If my wig flies off when I fall, hurry up and slide that shit to me. Don't let these white people see me looking like Coolio."

I could see where these brothers got their crazy from. Mama Debra was a damn fool.

"Just take your time, and everybody should be fine. I'll show you," I assured them.

Shadow grinned. "That's right, baby. School they ass. Hold on. Let me get my camera."

I waited for Shadow to start recording, and then I took off. Some kind of way, I went left but the skates didn't follow, and I busted my shit.

"Aw, hell naw," Blaze muttered. "How you talk all that shit and you the first one fall? You too big to be hitting that ice. Bro, help her up. I bet it's a crack in it. Then I go skate my ass over the crack, and my shit get caught and I fall. Fuck that."

I really wanted to tell Blaze to shut up, but I had figured him out early on. These last couple of months, he had given me pure hell. I was nobody's fool.

"Shut up and get your scary ass out there," I blurted.

When he flicked his Bic, I got up and started skating again. This time I grabbed Shadow's hand, and we went together. When I looked around five minutes later, I saw that Juicy and Baby Face were holding hands and doing good. Quick, Nala, and Zavi were all holding hands and skating. Blaze and Drea were doing terrible. Their legs wobbled the entire way.

"Stop shaking," Blaze told Drea. "You gone make me fall. Your damn knees loose, like your pussy. Do it right. Shit."

"That's your big ass. I'm going by myself," Drea shot back.

"I'm just playing, baby. Don't leave me. I don't want to fall."

I laughed at Blaze and Drea; they were the cutest ever. It took a special kind of crazy to put up with Blaze's ass.

"Mama Debra, you not coming out here?" I called.

"Don't you see me sitting down? Get your dumb ass on, then. Always want somebody doing this Oreo shit."

I laughed and kept it moving. I promise, if you didn't have tough skin with this family, you wouldn't make it. They were always talking shit and cracking jokes. The moment Shadow had officially introduced me to them, I had fallen in love. I had never had a big family, and the family I had, we weren't close. After my mother had passed away, I had practically been on my own. Blaze's family talked a lot of shit, but they had welcomed me with open arms. That was after Blaze had talked about me looking like a cast member from *Django Unchained*.

I still had the whip marks on me, and he had gone in on my ass. Thinking about it now, all I could do was laugh. He was probably the most ignorant man I had ever met.

Right in the middle of my thoughts, Shadow grabbed me and lifted me in the air.

"Oh, hell no! You gone drop me. Put me down, baby!"

"If I drop you, I'll always catch you." He brought me down around his waist and started kissing me. To this day, every time he touched me, my ass shivered. This was my soul mate, and I was glad I didn't have to look any further.

"You are the best. I'm so thankful to have a man like you," I whispered.

"No, baby, I'm the thankful one. You changed a nigga, and that's the reason I'm able to be the man you need. I love you, girl."

"I love you too." When he bit my lip, my panties got wet.

"If y'all don't get y'all nasty asses from in front of me with all that bullshit . . . Who the fuck tries to fuck in front of their mama?" his mama screeched.

I hadn't even realized we were in front of Mama Debra.

Shadow rolled his eyes. "Ma, don't go there. We walked in on your old, nasty ass. Did you ever shave? Baby mama got a wolf pussy."

"That hair can catch all the niggas. Fuck you mean?"

"Ma, you real life nasty," Shadow told her.

As we skated away, all I could think was how lucky I was to have this man. I couldn't wait for the wedding.

CHAPTER 22

QUICK

Three months later . . .

It seemed like everybody was with the love of their life and I was settling. Me and Nala have been going heavy for the past five months, but I could tell it bothered her that I wouldn't go in her raw. She didn't realize a nigga been through too much shit, and I was doing things different this time. Since I wouldn't go in her raw, she wouldn't give me no pussy. She kept trying to tell me she was in pain, but I didn't believe that shit. Once I saw her baby bump, a nigga tried to do right by her. I moved her into my real place, and the shit had actually been working out.

Nala a damn good woman, but she ain't Ash. I guessed it just wasn't meant for me and Ash to be together. We co-parented now, and the shit been working out good. She didn't give me any problems about Nala living here, and Zavi and her got along great. Everybody kept telling me that in time I would learn to love Nala, but I felt like the shit should already be there. Regardless of my feelings, I was determined to do shit right this time around.

While I was lost in thought, my phone rang, and I saw it was Paris.

"What's up, P?" I said when I picked up.

"I want to talk to my nephew." That was one thing I loved about them: they always called to check on my son.

I walked into Zavi's room and passed him the phone, but not before I put it on speaker.

"Hello?" Zavi said into the receiver.

"Hey, TT baby. What you doing?"

"Playing the game. What you doing? Are you with my mommy?"

"No, I'm by myself, and I'm eating some gummies," Paris told him.

"Can I have some? I like those."

"Hell naw. I don't share my gummies with nobody."

"That's mean, Auntie Paris, and I don't like you no more."

Paris didn't respond.

I took the phone from Zavi. "Hello? Hello?" I looked at the phone and saw she wasn't on the line. I called her back, thinking the phone had disconnected by mistake. She picked up.

"Paris, the phone hung up. Hold on."

"I know. I hung it up. He was begging, and I ain't sharing. Now, get off my line." She hung up again. I swear, she aggy as fuck.

"Come on," I told Zavi. "We about to go to the mall. We need to get you fitted for your tux."

"Can Nala come?"

"Yeah, son. Let me go get her. Put your clothes on."

I went to my bedroom, and Nala was already getting dressed.

She jumped when she saw me staring at her. "You scared me. Hold on. I'm almost done."

Shit struck me as weird, but I wasn't staying anyway.

"Zavi wants you to come to the mall with us, so hurry up," I urged.

After I walked out of the bedroom, I went downstairs to wait on them. When they came down the stairs, I looked at my girl, and she looked good as hell carrying my baby. She had on a long fitted dress, and her hair was pulled up on top of her head. I rubbed her belly and kissed it, and then we headed out the door. My brothers were meeting us there, because they had to be fitted as well. The wedding was a few months away, and they ass was behind on getting they shit.

After pulling up to the mall, I waited for my brothers, and soon after they arrived, we headed in. It felt weird that I was the only one not getting married. Nala had kept dropping hints like we should do it to, but I wasn't ready for that. Hell, I didn't even love her ass, but I wouldn't lie and say I didn't like her a lot. At the end of the day, Ash had my heart, but I guessed it wasn't meant for us to be.

We got fitted and then walked around the mall, just checking out what they had. I bought Nala and Zavi some shit, and my brothers shopped for their girls. I stopped at the jewelry store, and Nala was about to pass out from excitement.

"Oh, my God, Quick. Are you about to do what I think? I can't believe this. I'm so happy."

"Chill out, Ma. I'm just grabbing a necklace and bracelet set for Spark. That shit will never happen."

Her eyes filled up with tears, but I didn't give a fuck. I wasn't allowing anybody to pressure me into shit.

Blaze walked up close to me as I stared down into a glass case. "Nigga, you just dragged her face all over this mall. You should have seen her face. Bro, you ain't shit," he muttered in my ear.

"Blaze, for once, can you shut the fuck up?"

"Nigga, don't be mad at me 'cause your girl thirsty."

Ignoring him, I kept looking for the set I wanted.

"You about to buy this bitch a ring?" I turned around, and Ash was standing there, with tears in her eyes.

"No, Ash, I'm not. Stop crying and shit, Ma."

Nala stepped in between us. "Just a minute ago, you didn't give a fuck I was about to cry, but now you sensitive and shit. You got me fucked up."

I glared at Nala. "First off, didn't nobody tell your ass to assume some shit. Second, watch your mouth. This is between me and my child's mother."

"I'm your baby mama too, if you haven't noticed," Nala retorted. "Fuck that bitch. She didn't even tell you about your son."

Before I could check Nala for getting in my business, Ash kicked her right in the stomach. I mean, she drew her leg back and kicked Nala halfway across the mall.

"Are you out of your fucking mind? She is pregnant," I yelled. Without even giving Ash a chance to explain, I grabbed her by her neck and slammed her into the wall. "Don't ever in your fucking life do anything to jeopardize the life of my child! You better pray my baby okay, or I promise you are one dead bitch."

Blaze stepped up to me. "Bro, I don't mean to interrupt y'all lovers' spat, but, um, your baby on her back."

"Nigga, what the fuck are you talking about?" I turned toward Nala. She had gotten up off the ground and was trying to catch her balance, but her baby bump was no longer in the front. The shit was literally on her back. Ash done kicked the bitch so hard, the shit had swung around. She didn't even realize it.

"Nala, come here," I said calmly.

She walked over, and she had a smug look on her face when she looked at Ash.

"You mind telling me how the fuck my baby is on your back?" I asked.

"What you talking about?" She didn't even realize Blaze had flicked his Bic and was behind her, setting fire to her shit. Her dress went up in flames, and she finally noticed. She pulled the dress over her head, not thinking, trying to avoid the fire.

Baby Face shook his head. "Aw, hell naw. I need to find out who to write about this shit. What the fuck is this shit called? Trick a nigga?"

I agreed with Baby Face; this shit was out of hand. Shadow's ass always had his phone out, recording, and he was on the ground now, capturing the scene and laughing so hard.

"This shit is pathetic."

"Bro, would you be mad if I set your baby on fire?" Blaze asked me.

"Fuck you, nigga." Pissed at how this ho had tried to play me, I turned to Ash. "Beat that bitch to sleep, and I swear, you better win."

Since Ash was mad at me, you would think she would have said fuck me. Her ass didn't need any encouraging. She walked over to Nala and hit her so hard in her mouth, one of her teeth flew out.

"Damn, Ash. Now she gone have fake teeth *and* a fake baby," Blaze noted.

We laughed at Blaze, but Ash was on a mission. She drop-kicked the girl again and then climbed on top of her. She was beating the girl so bad, I had to pull her off.

"Come on. That's enough. Let's go," I said, but she kept swinging her fists at the air. I literally had to pull her out of the mall.

"Fuck! We done left Zavi," I muttered. I pulled out my phone and called Blaze.

He answered on the first ring and beat to the punch. "Bruh, I know you just had a baby on a bitch's back, but you done left your real son here."

"I know, nigga. Walk him outside. I'm in the front." Ash and I waited until Blaze brought Zavi out to us, and I then walked her to her car.

"Meet me at my house," I instructed as I put Zavi in the car with her.

I walked over to my vehicle. This bitch Nala had me fucked up. I was so pissed. Who the fuck did shit like that? Now I knew why she had been trying to get me to go in her raw: she actually wanted me to get her pregnant. This bitch had lost her whole mind. Right now, I wanted to beat a bitch to sleep. *Why these hoes keep trying me*? I wondered. A nigga must got *goofy* written on his forehead or something. The shit always led back to Ash. I swear, I was two seconds away from dragging her ass. After I pulled up to the house, the first thing I did was run upstairs and grab all Nala's shit. When I heard Ash come through the door, I came back downstairs.

"Grab anything you think is hers and throw the shit outside," I said.

"Just throw it outside?"

"Ain't that what the fuck I said! Throw the shit out the door. Blaze will be by later to set the shit on fire. I want the shit out of my house." I walked back upstairs and continued to gather up Nala's shit.

"Bro, where you at?" I could hear Baby Face calling, and so I came down the stairs.

"What's up?" I said.

"Shit, we were coming over to keep you company. I know this shit was fucked up, so we wanted to come take your mind off it. We stopped and grabbed Mama and Spark. But when we pulled up, Nala was outside. Your mama has been trying to keep her from coming in, so you don't kill her."

I stormed past him and walked outside. My mama was talking to the bitch, but I wasn't in a forgiving mood today.

"Ma, drag that ho," I called.

My mama was worse than us, and that was all she needed to hear. As soon as I said that, my mama hit Nala's ass and knocked her to the ground. Not wanting to tussle, because she was old as fuck, she just stomped Nala's ass. I could tell when my mama was getting tired, and so I turned to Ash, who had come outside.

"Tag, baby. You're in," I said.

Shadow laughed as Ash walked over to my mama, and my mama actually held her hand out for Ash to tag her. As soon as they slapped hands, Ash started stomping on Nala. My mama walked over to us.

"Nigga, go get me some water, just in case this bitch try to tag me back in. A ho tired."

"It's okay, Ma. You don't have to. You did your part," I told her.

Shadow and I laughed as she sat down on a step.

"Thank you. 'Cause a bitch is wore the fuck out."

"Bae, get her off my shit," I called to Ash.

Ash grabbed Nala by her hair and dragged her down the driveway and out the gate. I walked down to the gate, made sure it was shut tight, and then changed my code.

I glared at Nala, who was picking herself up off the ground on the other side of the gate. "I was gone let you get your shit, but now you ain't getting a motherfucking thing. My mama told me never to hit a chick, but if you come back, I'm gone beat a bitch ass. Stay the fuck off my shit," I yelled. Then I grabbed Ash and pulled her back to the house. She was still mad and ready to fight.

"I'm gone take Zavi with me. It looks like y'all got some catching up to do," my mama said as she observed us. I went in the house to get Zavi, and Ash followed me in.

"Hey, li'l man, you want to stay at Grandma's house tonight?" I asked him when I found him in his bedroom.

"Yes, Daddy. We stay up all night talking and watching movies."

"Okay, but don't be up all night. I'll be by to get you in the morning." I walked him outside, and he left with everyone.

Once I got back inside the house, Ash was on the couch, looking scared as hell. My intentions were to choke her ass up, but to see that she actually feared me didn't sit well with a nigga.

"Come here," I said as I sat down on the opposite end of the couch.

She walked over to me, but you could tell she was leery about it. When she made it over to me, I pulled her down on my lap.

"Why would you keep my son from me, Ash? That really hurt a niggas's heart. With all the shit that was going on in my life and the way Alaysia lied to me, you knew that. You knew everything that was going on, and you chose to do the same exact thing. Why, Ma?"

"I didn't know how to tell you. The day I found out, I was coming to tell you, and I saw you with my best friend. I vowed never to see you again, and Jason stepped in, but he said I could never tell a soul that he wasn't the daddy. The only reason Drea and them knew is that the baby looks just like you. I had no intentions on seeing you again. Once I did, I didn't know how to tell you. When I saw what you did to Alaysia, that scared me, but I told you that day at breakfast we would talk. Baby Face found out before we could talk. None of what I did was right, and I swear, it was the worst mistake I have ever made. Please don't hate me."

"I don't hate you, and that's part of the reason I was so angry. I wanted to hate you so bad, but I knew that you had my heart," I told her. "The only reason I was with Nala was to piss you off. Once she told me she was pregnant, I wanted to step up and do shit the right way this time around. The fact that you felt you couldn't talk to me or you were scared to tell me hurts a nigga's heart. We are bigger than that. You stole my heart eight years ago, and I don't want the shit back. But this type of shit can't happen no more. I don't give a fuck what it is, you have to know you can come to me and tell me. I love you enough to work it out and get through it. Are we clear?"

"I am so sorry." She dropped her head and started crying. I knew she really had a nigga's heart, because I was no longer concerned about my own feelings. Hers were more important. I lifted her face up with my hand and looked into her eyes, and she looked so sad, the shit broke me.

"Take your clothes off," I said.

When she looked at me again, I could see the want take the place of the hurt. She stood up and started slowly removing her clothes. Not with the bullshit, I started snatching them off. Then I threw her against the coffee table, kissed her on her neck, and made my way down her back.

"Have you given anybody else my pussy?"

"No."

After snatching her legs apart, I continued my trail of kisses. When I got to her toes, I licked my way back up her body. When I got to her thighs, I slid my tongue from her clit straight up her ass. I kept going until I reached her neck. While I sucked on her neck, I removed my pants.

"Turn over," I ordered.

When she lay on her back, I slid her closer to the edge of the table so that her head was hanging over. I grabbed my dick and slid it in her mouth. It was as if she was sucking my dick upside down. Leaning forward, I sucked on her clit. She was losing her rhythm, so I started pumping in and out of her mouth. While I fucked her face, I sucked on her clit like I needed that shit in my life.

"Come for me, baby," I told her. As I flicked my tongue against her shit, it started throbbing, and so I covered it with my mouth. When I felt her body shaking, I picked up my pace, pushing my dick in and out of her mouth.

As soon as she came, I got up and got in position. After pulling her back down, I threw her legs back and pushed them as far as they would go over her head. I smacked my dick against her clit, then slid it up and down until I couldn't take the wetness anymore. Once I shoved it in, I held her legs back with one hand, and I played with her clit with my other. The louder she screamed, the harder I pumped. I wanted my dick to reach her soul. She tried to scoot back, but I wasn't having that shit.

"Take this dick, Ash."

"It's too fucking big."

I slammed it in harder. "I said, 'Take this dick.' Don't fucking move."

She lay still, and I pumped in and out of her until I couldn't take it anymore.

"Fuck! I'm about to cum!" I yelled. I shot my nut in her, and I lay there until it was all in.

"You know you don't have on a condom, right?"

"Girl, I been trying to get you pregnant since you came back into my life. Shut up and keep your legs in the air so my nut can make it to the top."

Catching my breath, I got ready for round two.

CHAPTER 23

BABY FACE

I didn't see how anybody could get married more than once. This shit was hectic as hell, and doing a wedding together with Blaze was the worst idea ever. This nigga was worse than a bride. Everything had to be a certain way, and the shit was becoming a headache. The men were in charge of the wedding because we wanted to do some boss shit, and the women would only have some girly-ass wedding. But keeping the shit a secret and working with Blaze was driving a nigga crazy. On top of that, Juicy's ass stayed sick all the time and was picking up weight. Don't get me wrong. The weight looked good as fuck on her, and I loved every curve, but it made it hard for her to get fitted for her dress.

Not wanting to do all that extra shit for the wedding, we had decided to learn the sex of our baby. And so now we were getting dressed to go to Juicy's doctor's appointment. She was in a lot of pain. The shit was scaring me, because they had said she would never be able to have kids.

"Baby, what's wrong?" I asked her.

"I can't bend down to put my shoes on. Every time I try, a pain shoot through me and the baby ball up in a knot."

I sat down on the floor, grabbed her shoes, and put them on one by one. She had tears in her eyes, and I felt bad for her. After moving closer to the bed, I put my hand on her stomach. You could literally feel where the baby was balled up on her side. The pain on her face was worrying a nigga, but I had to stay strong for her. Not knowing what to do, I decided to try anything.

So I sang the only nursery rhyme I knew. "The itsy bitsy spider went up the waterspout. Down came the rain and washed the spider out. Out came the sun and dried up all the rain. And the itsy bitsy spider went up the spout again." As I sang, I could feel the baby start to loosen up.

"Keep singing, baby." Not knowing any more kids' songs, I sang what the hell I knew.

"When the day turns into the last day of all time. I can say I hope you are in these arms of mine. . . ."

By the time I got through singing Prince's song "The Most Beautiful Girl in the World," the baby had completely loosened up. I kissed Juicy on the stomach and stood up.

"You okay now? You ready to go?" I asked her.

"Yeah, but how you figure it's a girl?"

"Because God wouldn't curse this family with any more boys."

We laughed and headed out the door to the doctor.

We walked in the doctor's office, and there were only a few people ahead of us. I continued to rub her stomach until they called our name. Once we were in the back, she jumped on the examination table, and I stood beside her, holding her hand. When the doctor came in, we were ready.

"Hey, Mommy and Daddy, you ready to see what your little one looks like today and hopefully find out the gender?"

"Yes." We said it at the same time.

The doctor put the gel on Juicy's stomach and started rubbing the monitor over it. We could hear the baby's heartbeat, and the shit had a nigga ready to cry already.

"There is your baby right there, and in this spot, you can see here that it is a baby girl. Is that what you wanted?"

"It doesn't matter, Doc. I'm just happy my baby doing okay," Juicy replied.

"With your history, I was a bit worried at first as well. This little girl wants to make it into this world and decided to beat the odds. Still, take it easy. And the closer you get to the delivery, I will have you coming in more frequently."

"Okay. Thank you, Doc," Juicy said.

She gave us copies of the sonogram pictures, and we were out.

"You have made me the happiest man alive. Thank you," I said to Juicy once we were heading to the car.

"I love you, baby daddy."

"You got me fucked up. I ain't no damn baby daddy. I'm about to be your husband."

"Yeah, but baby daddy sound better."

"These hands gone sound on your eye."

She hit me, and right when I was about to fuck her ass up, my phone rang.

"Saved by the bell," I teased.

Juicy grinned. "You wasn't gone do shit anyway."

Answering my phone, I gave her the finger with my free hand.

"Hey, Face," Jermaine said over the line. "What's up? I know it took a while, but I finally found out that information you wanted."

"On Rico?"

"Yes. I'll text you the address, and it's valid. He is there now, as we speak. He's been there the entire time."

"A'ight. Good looking out. I'll wire you the money," I said, then ended the call.

"Baby, I have to drop you off," I told Juicy.

"Whatever it is, can it wait until tomorrow?" she pleaded.

Knowing that Rico had been in the same spot all this time, I knew I could wait one more day. I had promised to show Juicy that no one and nothing would come before her, and I had meant it.

I smiled at her. "Yeah. Let's go home. I'll race you to the car." Knowing she couldn't run, I took off, leaving her chunky ass by herself. By the time she got to the car, I was already sitting inside it.

"You ain't shit. Take me home, baby daddy."

"You want me to put these paws on you, huh?"

"Naw, but you can give me that dick."

As soon as she said that, my shit was on brick, and I took off. I sped all the way home. I couldn't wait to get inside and get in my baby's guts.

We had a Netflix and chill night, but we barely watched a movie. Every time one would come on, she would attack my ass. This baby had her extra horny, and I was loving every bit of it. Niggas think it was weak to show your vulnerable side and apologize, but that was the best thing I could have ever done. I had laid the shit out all on the line and it had got me my girl back. My ass would never cheat on her again. This motherfucker held grudges too long. We fell asleep after about the tenth round. Yes, ten, and my dick was sorer than a motherfucker. If a nigga was standing up, I would probably be the one walking bowlegged.

Since she had been in so much pain lately, I had got in the habit of sleeping light. She would just moan and not tell me something was wrong. Tonight, as we were sleeping, I heard something sizzling and jumped up.

Blaze was standing over Juicy, trying to find something to put her hair out. The nigga actually had the nerve to put his finger to his mouth to shush me as he looked for something and tried not wake Juicy up. I ran to the bathroom and grabbed some water. When I threw it on her, she jumped up like her ass was drowning.

"Face, what the fuck! Nigga, did you just nut in my face?"

I nodded toward Blaze, and she leapt out of bed and ran in the bathroom.

"Nigga, what the fuck is wrong with you? I just got her back, and you pull this shit. I'm about to fuck your ass up!" I yelled at Blaze.

She walked out of the bathroom and half of her hair was burned damn near to the scalp. She only had about half an inch.

"You got me all kinds of fucked up, Blaze," she screeched. She ran toward him, and I had to catch her in midair. When I grabbed her, I realized more than half of her hair was gone. This nigga was bat-shit crazy.

Blaze hiked his shoulders. "Sis, I was only trying to do a little piece, and that shit caught flame fast as hell. You must use chemicals and shit in your hair. You know that shit ain't healthy for the baby, right?"

"Blaze, get the fuck out of my house!" I yelled. Juicy was about to kill him, and I swear, I wanted to knock his ass out, but I knew the reason he had done this. If I said it, Juicy might leave me again. This was his way of getting me back. We were now even.

"A'ight, sis, I'm gone," Blaze said calmly. "But for real, though, use some coconut oil or something. That shit you using flammable than a motherfucker."

I pushed him out the bedroom door. As I walked him downstairs, I went off. "Nigga, are you trying to get her to leave me again? Your beef is with me, not her."

"My beef ain't with you, either, but I told you I would get you back. You fucked my bitch, so I burned yours. Now we even. Go get some sleep. You look tired as hell."

"Fuck you, nigga, and we got business tomorrow. I have an address."

"Bet. See you tomorrow." He walked out the front door and left it open.

I closed the door and walked up the stairs slow as shit. I knew she was about to tear me a new asshole, but this was one L I knew I had to take. I just hated that he had chosen Juicy to get back at me. My baby was up there looking like Bootsy Collins, and I had to lie there and look at her while she went the fuck off.

Fuck my life and fuck Blaze too.

CHAPTER 24

RICO

Grabbing Shirree by her head, I was trying my best to get my nut. I was fucking the shit out of her face, but the shit was not working. I think it was because she was facing me or because we weren't having nasty sex. Either way, I needed her to do something different. My ass been hiding out in this house for months, and I had finally been given the green light to leave. I had hired an investigator to watch my sons' moves and to see when they were lacking and I could slip through the cracks. Shirree's dumb ass actually thought I was going to take her with me. She couldn't even keep my dick hard, so there was no reason to be bothered with her.

I damn near had to split her face apart just to get semi hard, and the shit was stressful as fuck. After slamming my shit into her mouth a few more times, I gave up on this position and walked over to the couch. As soon as I threw my legs up, she dropped to the floor and pushed my legs back damn near over my head. The way she attacked my ass, I think she liked this shit more than me.

"Suck that motherfucker," I told her.

And that was exactly what she did. She damn near sucked all my booty juice out of me, and when she thought that motherfucker was dry, she started tongue fucking me to get the shit back wet. Seeing her bald head face-first in my ass had my dick hard as fuck. She then began working her way up. She started sucking my balls and then went up and down on the motherfucker like she was trying to get an award.

"That's right, girl. Suck Daddy's dick."

She went to work on that motherfucker too. When I felt her slide her finger in my ass, I almost knocked her ass out, but she hit a spot, and my nut shot out of me into the back of her throat. She kept doing it, and my dick got hard as fuck instantly. When she put her mouth around my dick again, I grabbed her head and started fucking her mouth like it was the tightest asshole on planet earth. She just moaned and allowed the spit to run down my dick. When I released her, she leaned up and looked at me.

"I been thinking about the problem you been having to stay hard," she said to me.

"Bitch, I don't have a problem. Your pussy just weak as hell."

"Well, anyway, I snuck out of the house and went to the sex store, and I want to try something."

I looked at her like she was crazy. My ass didn't really trust her. How the fuck she get out without me knowing? And what did she want to try? She walked out of the room and came back, wearing a strap-on. This bitch had me fucked up, and I saw she wanted me to beat her ass. A finger was one thing, but she was not about to stick a dick in me.

"Bitch, are you high?"

"Just sit back and relax. It's not what you think."

I shut up and decided to see where she was going with this. I sat back on the couch and waited to see what she would do. She climbed on top of me and slid my dick in her ass. Once she started riding it, she reached for my hand and pulled it to her fake dick. She placed my hand on it, and then she guided my hand up and down on the dick. Looking at her from behind, with the dick she had on, actually did the trick. It gave me the illusion that I was fucking a man. Once I closed my eyes and thought about Tate, I started stroking the shit out of it. The pressure from the strap-on was brushing against her clit, and it caused her to start going crazy, but her moans were fucking with my illusion.

"Shut the fuck up and ride this dick."

She did as she was told, and the shit was almost perfect. Any dick would do, but I wanted it to feel like I was fucking Tate, so I would make her go back and get a different one, but for now, I was gone tear her booty hole up. This was the first time I had actually enjoyed fucking her since Tate had first put his mouth on me.

"Fuck, Tate. I'm about to cum, baby," I said. I knew it was Shirree, but I wanted to stay in character. She started bouncing her ass up and down on this dick, and I nutted good and hard. I was not sure if she came or not, but I really didn't care. I needed that nut, and this could actually work in her favor if she wanted to go with me.

"Thank you, baby. That shit was good as fuck. I need you to go back to the store later and get a smaller size. You know what Tate's dick was like. Get one to match his."

"Okay."

I couldn't wait for her to get the new dick. I could have my fantasy, and she wouldn't complain one bit.

"What the fuck are you doing?" I walked over to Shirree and slapped her Kindle out of her hand.

"I'm reading *Hood Dreams & Street Loving*, by Kia Meche', and the shit is getting good. Reminds me of your ass. The father is trying to set up his sons. He hates they ass too."

After slapping spit out of her mouth, I went off on her dumb ass.

"Bitch, I don't give a fuck about what no nigga is doing in a book. This is real fucking life, and I don't hate my sons. I came to them for help, and they turned me around like I wasn't shit. Fuck them and fuck they mama. If you keep talking shit, it's going to be, 'Fuck you,' too. You sitting here, reading this bullshit, and I asked you to do something."

"I know, and I was tired. All I wanted to do was relax. It's twenty-four hours. I can go later."

"If you don't want your eye knocked through your throat, you will go now."

She jumped up with an attitude, but she did what the fuck I said. Despite the nut she had given me earlier, I had started stressing again, and I was ready to get the fuck out of here. After she stormed out of the house, I started pacing back and forth. I had to be sure these niggas had moved on with their lives and wasn't thinking about my ass. After pulling my phone out, I called the guy I had paid to follow them.

"Hey, Jim. It's Rico. I just wanted to make sure it was still good to go."

"Yeah, they getting ready for a wedding, and it doesn't seem like you are on their radar. If you are going to do it, the shit needs to be quick. You need to get the fuck out of here."

"I'm going, but when I get to my new city, I'm going to find a way to bring they asses down. Especially Blaze. He got me fucked up. He killed my best men."

"Speak of the devil, and he will appear," said a familiar male voice behind me.

I turned around, and my sons were standing in my front room. How the fuck had they got in here? That dumbass bitch hadn't locked the door when she left.

"Come on, old man. Let's take a ride," Blaze said, motioning to me.

CHAPTER 25

BLAZE

"Speak of the devil, and he will appear," I said.

This nigga looked like he had seen Lucifer himself. I wasn't the devil, but I was definitely the grim reaper today. I had never wanted to kill someone so bad in my life.

I motioned to Rico. "Come on, old man. Let's take a ride."

"You think I'm going anywhere with y'all? Then you really got me fucked up."

"No, you got us fucked up, thinking you got a choice," Baby Face growled. "Shadow, you're up." Baby Face nodded at Shadow, and he did what he did best.

Shadow knocked that nigga out. I grabbed Rico's phone and ended the call, and then we carried his ass out the door. When we passed a sewer, I wiped the phone down and tossed it down that motherfucker. After throwing Rico in the trunk, we headed to the warehouse. Me, Baby Face, and Quick rode in the same car, and Shadow drove another. We were gone burn this motherfucker up once we were done.

As he drove, Baby Face said, "When we get there, I'm gone leave y'all there with the fuck nigga and go pick up Mama. I almost forgot that she said she wanted to be a part of it."

I looked at Baby Face like he was crazy.

"You sure about that, man? Mama a fighter. She ain't no damn killer. We don't want to give her old ass a heart attack," Quick said.

I agreed with Quick.

"Or have her shit on herself, like last time, 'cause she ain't riding with me smelling like that," I interjected.

Baby Face shook his head. "You don't know the things I know about Mama. Y'all were too young, but trust me, she will be okay."

If Baby Face said it was cool, then it was what it was. This shit was fucking with me more than I let on. Me and Quick had worshipped this nigga when we were kids. We had wanted to be just like his ass. Followed him around everywhere, and here he was, plotting on us every which a way. I was just glad the last piece of the puzzle was finally about to be tucked in. We could go on with our lives and live in peace. We were done with the street shit, and we were about to be family men.

After we pulled up to the warehouse, we waited for Shadow and then got out of the car. When I opened the trunk, Quick had his gun pointed at Rico just in case. The old-ass nigga was still knocked out, and we had to carry him inside. Then we strapped him to a chair. We had been out here that morning, and I had made sure I had a full can of gasoline, but only to torture him. We had a special kind of death for this fuck nigga.

"A'ight, y'all, I'll be right back with Mama," Baby Face said. "Blaze, don't burn this nigga up before I get back. We all want to see this happen, and I know your fire-happy ass will get on good bullshit."

I nodded. "I got you, bro, but hurry up."

After he left, we waited around for this nigga to wake up. He finally started moving around, and as soon as he opened his eyes, he started talking shit. Quick and Shadow were talking among themselves. I leaned against the wall as I flicked my Bic and watched our poor excuse of a father.

"I promise all you niggas gone die. You don't know who the fuck I am, but you will," he snarled.

I laughed at him making threats, knowing he was about to die.

Shadow started arguing with the nigga. "What the fuck you gone do to us from the grave? You sound real cocky for a nigga that's about to die."

I didn't care to waste my breath, so I just continued to flick my Bic and watch.

Rico harrumphed. "And you real cocky for a nigga that couldn't fuck his bitch right. Dick wasn't working, but I made sure I took care of that for you, son. I fucked and sucked that pussy real good. Fucked her so good, the bitch was paying me."

I just knew Shadow was about to break his jaw, but instead, he walked out the door. I continued to stare at this nigga, whom I used to look up to. I had never hated someone this much in all my life. A few minutes later, Shadow walked back in the door with an envelope in his hand.

"I can't believe it. Your nasty-ass fag," Shadow screamed at Rico. The conversation was interesting now.

"Fuck you talking about, bro?" I said. Shadow handed me the envelope, and I pulled out some pics and looked through them.

"I had Shirree followed. When I saw the first pic, I never looked at the rest, because I didn't want to see no fag shit. Until he just said that shit, I never knew it was him," Shadow explained.

Looking through the shit, I wanted to throw up. He had this nigga Tate sucking his dick, riding the motherfucker, and kissing him all in the mouth. In a lot of the pics, Shirree joined in on the bullshit.

"Nigga, you sitting here talking all this tough shit, and you a soft-ass fag." I started laughing so hard, I was crying. "This nigga a gay thug. I done heard it all. Instead of shooting bullets, you out here shooting nut up a nigga's ass. RIP. He just killed the ass. Let me find out you out here robbing niggas in skinny jeans and sandals. You a gay Oprah, my nigga. You get some booty. You get some booty. Everybody get some booty." I couldn't stop laughing, but he had hurt my brother, so I had to do something. I knew Baby Face wanted us to wait until he got back to kill him, but he hadn't said I couldn't have some fun. I grabbed the gasoline and poured some of it on his dick.

"What the fuck are you doing? Please, don't do this." Now the nigga was an R & B singer. His ass was begging worse than Keith Sweat.

"I didn't see a single condom in all those pics. Nigga, your dick probably already burning. I'm just rushing the process," I said. I flicked my Bic again and set the nigga's dick to 350 degrees. When he started screaming, Shadow bitched up.

"How long you gone burn this nigga? We don't want him dead yet."

"I'm gone cook the nigga until he well done." After letting him burn some more, I picked up the fire extinguisher and put out the flames. It felt good to be back lighting shit up. "Nigga, you about to have a long, hot night."

By the time Baby Face had walked in the door with my mama, this nigga Rico looked like fried bologna. His dick was curled up and burnt all the way around that motherfucker.

"Why the fuck it smells like burnt booty in this motherfucker?" my mama said. Then she checked out the scene and shook her head at me. "Here, Baby Face. Take my wig the fuck outside. This nigga on some other shit in here, and I'll be damned if he gets my ass again." She snatched her wig off and threw it at Baby Face. Doing as he was told, he ran outside, and we waited for him to come back in.

Mama cleared her throat. "Let's get down to business." My mama hit the nigga so hard, his chair flew back.

"Damn, Mama. You need to bust a nut. You're strong. You hit harder than Shadow," I told her.

We already knew she was crazy, but this just confirmed who we had got that shit from. We picked the nigga up off the floor, and Mama grabbed the gun from Quick.

"You had me fucked up twenty years ago, when you faked your death. You had me fucked up when you came back and tried to pimp me out some money. You really had me fucked up when you made me watch you fuck a man and tried to kill me. I'm a bitter bitch, and I'm scorned, but, bitch, you gone catch some of that heat too." She pulled the trigger and shot him in the stomach and what was left of his dick. We wanted him alive for what was gone happen, and that was why she had shot him where he would make it. We picked him up and laid him on the conveyor belt.

"Son." She turned to me and looked me dead in my eyes. "Light his bitch ass up."

After sprinkling just enough gasoline so that the flames didn't burn his ass too quick, I flicked my Bic and set fire to his ass. Quick hit the button to set the conveyor belt in motion, and we watched his ass burn all the way to the end of the belt.

"I bet you stay dead this time," I yelled right before his body started going through the meat grinder.

He was screaming bloody murder as his bones and flesh were ripped apart. He felt every bit of that shit before the grinder finally crushed his head.

"Let's get the fuck out of here. Y'all some nasty motherfuckers. I bet this was all your idea, Blaze," my mama said, shaking her head in disgust.

I grinned. "Naw, Ma, that was all your good son's idea. Baby Face a sick-ass nigga. Y'all think it's me, but it's his ass."

"He is definitely the worst one. Blaze just aggy as fuck."

I was agreeing with Shadow until the last part.

"Baby Face the calm one," my mama said. She was lost in the sauce.

"Mama, there is always a calm before the storm. Never forget that. He even calls his dick Tsunami," I countered as I poured gasoline everywhere, even in the car.

"You know what? You need your ass beat. You don't give a fuck what come out of your mouth," she told me. "Light the damn shit up, so I can go home. Dumbass nigga, I swear."

I laughed and lit the building and car on fire. We headed back to the main house, and everybody got in their cars. They headed home, but I headed back to Rico's place. That nigga had our money, and I wanted our shit back. As soon as I pulled up, I grabbed my gun, just in case. A nigga wasn't taking any more chances, and ain't no telling who he had working with him. When I walked in the door, Shirree was walking back and forth, pacing. This bitch thought we were gone let her be great, but she had me fucked up. Nobody that hurt my brothers would live to tell that story.

"Hey, shitty mouth. What you up to?" I said.

She wanted to take off running, but she had nowhere to go. "Let me explain. It was all Rico. They were blackmailing me. I didn't want to do it."

"Now, you telling me, you didn't want to eat his ass? Get your shitty ass in the car, and you better not breathe in my shit. If I smell one drop of booty scent in my shit, I'm gone blow your shit off. Are we clear?"

She nodded her head.

"You catch on quick. Get our money and walk your nasty ass out the door."

I couldn't wait to kill Shirree. Since it would be my last hurrah, it was going to be epic.

CHAPTER 26

QUICK

Today was our engagement party, and we were having a backyard barbecue at Blaze's house. I didn't understand how it was some shit for our wedding, but nobody would be there except the family. We didn't trust anybody else after the past year we had had. As my brother had said, we not taking no more L's, and to avoid that, we weren't allowing anybody else in our circles. The only thing I was trying to figure out was, why the fuck did Blaze want us there so early? The party didn't start until six, but he had texted us this morning, saying to be there at eleven and to leave our girls. He was sending Drea and Spark over here with Ash and Zavi. The women would all come later on.

"Baby, I'll see you later," I said to Ash as I tied my shoes.

"Okay, and there better not be no bitches over there, since y'all sending our ass away."

"The only bitch I want is you, girl."

She slapped me and took off running. As I chased her up the stairs, I slipped and fell down them bitches.

"Every time I chase you up the stairs, a nigga bust his shit," I moaned.

"That's because God don't like ugly."

"Well, He hates your ass. Come give me a kiss, so I can go."

She walked down the stairs and gave me a kiss that was so good, I almost stayed here and blew her back out.

"I have a surprise for you later," she told me.

I looked at her, trying to read her expression and couldn't. "Let me go. You know Blaze do the most. I don't want to be late."

I jumped in my car and drove to Blaze's house. When I got there, Shadow and Baby Face were pulling up at the same time. After getting out of the car, I questioned them to see if they knew what was going on.

"Y'all know what this nigga wants?"

Shadow shook his head. "Nope, but knowing Blaze, it's about to be some bullshit."

I agreed with Shadow; this nigga couldn't act right to save his life.

"Well, let's head in to see what it is. Be prepared for anything," I said. I gazed over at Baby Face and saw that he almost looked scared. I laughed, and then I thought about who we were talking about. I looked straight ahead as we walked in Blaze's house, making sure nothing was out of place. Once inside, we saw immediately that the patio door was open, and so we headed out back.

"Damn, nigga. What the fuck you cooking? Ass?" I muttered. The shit smelled like he had ass on the grill.

When we rounded the corner, this ignorant nigga was sitting in a lawn chair and had three empty ones next to him for us. He was smoking a cigar as he watched Shirree spinning around on a rotisserie stick. He had this ho tied up, cooking, like they did pigs at a luau. He had completely lost his mind.

"Y'all hungry? I got a special meal just for you, Shadow. Shit à la mode," he said gleefully.

"Where the fuck you find this bitch?" Shadow was looking at her with disgust.

"I went back to Rico's house to get our money, and she was there. Have a seat, fellas. She just now warming up, and she got a long way to go."

We sat down, and the bitch was actually looking at us with pleading eyes. We didn't give a fuck, though. We sat around having a normal conversation, as if this bitch wasn't cooking right in front of us. This nigga Blaze played all day, but I swear, this shit here was giving me life.

If you gone retire some shit, go out with a mother-fucking bang, I thought to myself.

The girls were finally arriving, and we had everything cleaned up and the real food on the grill. When Juicy walked in, everybody paused and looked at her like she was crazy. She had cut all her hair off and was rocking a fade.

Blaze turned to Baby Face. "Damn, bro. Let me find out you just like your daddy and you really want to fuck a nigga."

Juicy rolled her eyes at him so hard, I thought them bitches was gone get stuck.

Baby Face scowled at Blaze. "Nigga, don't play with me. You the reason she had to cut it. I still want to beat your ass, but my baby looks good regardless."

I agreed with Baby Face. She definitely was still fine as fuck.

"If that's what you have to say to convince yourself to fuck with Shaft, go right ahead," Blaze retorted.

Laughing, I had to ask. "What the fuck did this nigga do?"

"This is how he decided to get even. He set Juicy's hair on fire while we were asleep."

I looked at Baby Face to see if he was serious, and the nigga didn't crack a smile.

I gave Blaze a dirty look. "Wait a minute. Blaze, your ass need help. She ain't have shit to do with that. You petty as hell."

Blaze gave me a hard stare. "I mean, you talking a lot of shit, Quick. A nigga can easily come out of retirement and go holla at Ash. Her shit blowing mighty hard in the wind. Shit will catch on like a forest fire."

Knowing he meant it, I sat my ass down on a lawn chair and shut the fuck up. That was Baby Face's battle. I wondered how he had convinced Juicy not to kill Blaze, since her ass was bat-shit crazy too. Looking over at Ash, I thought about everything we been through. As if she was reading my thoughts, she walked over to me. She reached in her purse, pulled out something, and handed it to me. When I looked down at it, I jumped up.

"Are you serious?" I asked.

She nodded her head yes, and I grabbed her and kissed her.

"You niggas got it bad, trying to fuck in public. Damn, get y'all a life. Nobody wants to see that shit." My mama had finally arrived, and she walked in talking shit.

"Well, my baby just told me she is pregnant," I announced. Then I kissed her again. I was happy as fuck.

Blaze flashed an evil grin. "We not gone get excited until we sure the baby don't end up on her back. Your chicks be creative as hell."

"Shut up, Blaze," we all said in unison.

But Blaze kept right on talking. "Fuck y'all. This is *my* house. I got a question, though. Ash, you just walking around with piss in your purse. Now this dumbass nigga holding it in his hand, like you ain't pissed on that shit."

Thinking about what he said, I threw the shit down. I hadn't even thought about that shit. Earlier I hadn't been sure if I was gone actually do it here, but I was glad I had brought the ring just in case.

I took a knee, the ring in my clenched fist. "Ash, you were the first girl I fell in love with, and I want you to be the last. You were there for me through my darkest hours, and when shit got rough, you waited for a nigga until he was ready. You stood by me, and most importantly, you're the mother of my kids. I don't want to wake up another day, and you don't share my name. Will you marry me?"

With tears in her eyes, she walked over to me. "Yes. Yes, I will marry you."

She was finally mine. I slid the rock on her finger, and then I stood up, with tears in my eyes.

Shadow broke the silence that had fallen over the backyard. "Damn. That means we having a four-way wedding."

Shadow was right, but I loved that shit. To others, that may seem a bit extreme, but I wouldn't have it any other way. Me and my brothers had done everything together. No matter what it was, we were right there by each other's side. Why not declare our love to our soul mates while standing side by side?

"Damn right, and we gone do that shit the Hoover way."

"On that note, let's make a toast," Baby Face proposed. Then he raised his glass, and we all followed suit. "To the Hoover Gang! Anything else is un-fucking-civilized."

We laughed and toasted to the shit anyway. As corny as it was, the shit was the truth.

CHAPTER 27

BABY FACE

Blaze had fucked my baby's head up, and she'd had to cut all her shit off, but I swear, she was still fine as fuck. I had always said I wouldn't date a chick with a fade better than mine, but here I was, staring at the sexiest bitch alive. We were getting ready for our bachelor and bachelorette parties. The girls' theme was Moulin Rouge, and she had on a black bustier, black panties, black fishnets, and some red Christian Louboutins. Her short hair was dyed red, and I swear, as we stood in the foyer, I almost told her, "Let's stay in."

"Damn, baby. You got Tsunami ready to knock your pregnant ass up. How the fuck do you look sexy as fuck with a pregnant belly?"

"Because I can make anything look fly."

"That shit ain't hurting the baby? It looks tight as hell," I said.

"No, crazy. I got it bigger so it could fit over my stomach. There's lots of room in it."

"A'ight. Have fun, but don't get a nigga killed."

We walked out the door, and she jumped in her red Maserati, and I jumped in the Maybach. We were having our shit at Diamond in the Rough. Why spend money when you had your own strip club? When I pulled up to the club, I saw that Shadow was first in line. I pulled behind him, and we waited for Quick and Blaze to arrive.

Once they did, it was time to do our normal routine. Once we stepped out of the car, we walked to the other side and stood next to each other. As we waved to the crowd, I turned to my brothers.

"Do y'all think this is the last time we will do the brother line, since we getting married and having kids and shit?" I asked.

"It may be the last time we do it at the club, but the Hoover Gang will still live on. We can do that shit at the main house and make our girls stand they asses outside and wave," Blaze replied.

Laughing at Blaze, I knew he was saying it, but I didn't think none of us believed that. This may be the very last time we did this shit, and it felt like I was giving up a piece of myself. Though I was usually not one to be with the dramatic shit, tonight I needed to feel the love from the crowd, since this was it. I started waving my hand up and down, and the crowd started mimicking me. I knew they would, and that was what I would miss the most. They loved the fuck out of us, and it would be hard to let this shit go, but we all had good women, and they were worth it.

As I waved my hand up and down, I started chanting, "Hoover. Hoover. Hoover." My brothers chimed in, and then the crowd. It was like they could feel we would never do this again. They were going crazy, and the shit was getting emotional. Not caring how they would look at me, I let the tears roll down my face. They didn't know us, but they loved us. They had shown me that the day Blaze came back. They had cried that day as if they had known him their entire lives, and they were doing the same thing now. When they noticed my tears, they started crying with me. When I looked over at my brothers, I noticed they were crying with me too. Emotions were running high, and as we turned to walk in the club, even over the music, all we heard was them chanting, "Hoover. Hoover. Hoover."

As we stepped into the corridor, we wiped our faces and got ready to party like it was 1999. With security close on our heels, we headed farther into the club and got ready to turn up.

Right away the DJ spotted us, and then he announced our arrival. "Y'all know what time it is. Hoover Gang is in the motherfucking building. I don't know if y'all heard or not, but tonight is their bachelor party. You heard me right. All they asses is off the market. Tonight may be the last night you ever get to shake your ass on a boss. Make that shit count. I love you niggas, and congratulations."

We waved our hands and nodded our heads, letting the DJ know the feeling was mutual. As we walked to our VIP booth, the DJ threw on the females' number one anthem, "Bodak Yellow," by Cardi B, and the song flooded the speakers. Ass was being thrown everywhere. I knew this song was for the chicks, but that bitch went hard. The dancers were fucking that beat up, and I was loving the view. I poured all of us a shot, and we held up our glasses.

I gave the first toast. "To the motherfucking Hoover Gang. I love you niggas, and I wouldn't want to see this shit any other way." We clinked glasses.

Shadow said his toast. "Growing up, I looked up to you niggas. You were everything I wanted to be. Now that I'm grown, I'm still trying to live up to that shit. Y'all the best big brothers a nigga could have. Thank you for being the father I never had." We clinked glasses.

Blaze went next. "Nobody really got me when we were growing up. My obsession with fire had motherfuckers thinking I was weird, but y'all never judged me, and you allowed me to be who I was. That shit meant a lot to me. I never had to be anybody but Blaze, and I love y'all niggas." We clinked glasses.

It was Quick's turn. "This past year was rough on a nigga. I fucked up big-time, and not once did you judge me or question my motives. You stood beside me and helped me clean up my mess. Even when guilt consumed me, you carried me when I lost the will to do it myself. I love you niggas, and I wouldn't have it any other way. Fuck a friend." We clinked glasses.

"Hoover over everything," we yelled in unison. Then we tossed our shots back.

"Okay, now that y'all boy bonding is over, can we come in here and show y'all a good time?" said a female voice. There were strippers standing outside our rope, and we motioned for security to let them in. It was our bachelor party. We got a pass tonight.

"Hey, take that liquor from Shadow," Blaze told me. "Last time that nigga got drunk, he fucked the shit out of a ho raw as hell. We not going through that shit again."

Blaze was right, and I grabbed the bottle in Shadow's hand.

"Well, shid, if that's the case, pour that nigga some more," one of the strippers said.

Blaze got in her face. "See, bitch? Now your ass gotta go. Get the fuck out of our shit with your bamboo feet–having ass. How the fuck you dancing with them big motherfuckers anyway? Toes twerking against the floor and shit."

We laughed as Blaze put her out. It was time to enjoy our last night before we became married men.

CHAPTER 28

FOUR BROTHERS AT A WEDDING

Four brothers stood on a white sandy beach in Jamaica, awaiting their brides. The only other people in attendance were the pastor, Juicy's mom, Debra, Paris, and Panda. It was a small and intimate ceremony. "Thinking Out Loud," by Ed Sheeran, played as Zavi made his way down the aisle.

Zavi was dressed in an all-white linen short set, just like the groom, but with no socks, and he was holding in one hand a pillow bearing three rings. With his other, he pulled Spark in a twenty-four-karat wagon that was filled with flowers. She couldn't throw them, but she still deserved to be the flower girl. She was dressed in a white dress with a train attached. Zavi continued to make his way to the front as the song continued to play.

"And I'm thinking 'bout how people fall in love in mysterious ways. Maybe just the touch of a hand. Well, me, I fall in love with you every single day, and I just wanna tell you I am." Even when Zavi had made it to the front, the song continued to play. Once it ended, the projector screen that had been set up beside the men filled with images. They were videos and pictures of the couples, showing the journey they had embarked on to

get here. Then, as the videos and pictures played, R. Kelly got up and stood in front as the ladies began to make their descent down the beach.

Then he began to sing. "Hey, beloved, we are gathered here, to join each other hand and hand. . . ." As Kells sang the lyrics to his song "Forever," the girls came into view. Then they joined the brothers.

As each couple stared into each other's eyes, they all knew they had made the right decision.

Kimmie . . .

A year ago, no one could have convinced me that I would be here, that I would have the man of my dreams and a fairy-tale wedding. Shadow was everything I needed and more. He gave me the strength to love myself, and I was able to pour that love into him. The women in his past had hurt him, but I was there to heal him and show him what true love was. Once I made it to the front, R. Kelly leaned down to kiss me on the cheek, and he handed me to Shadow. Staring into Shadow's eyes, I knew my soul had found my true love. I grabbed his hand as we vowed our love to one another.

Shadow . . .

As I watched Kimmie walking toward me, my heart was beating out of control. Not because I was feeling scared or having second thoughts, but because the love I held inside for her was overwhelming. She was wearing a flowing, see-through white dress with gold undergarments. So bold and confident, my baby had me wanting her right then and there. She was so beautiful with all her curves, and she was mine. The woman of my dreams had ended up being a woman I normally wouldn't have looked at twice. Shirree hurting me the way she did had opened my eyes, enabled me to step out of my box and try something different. Kimmie had taught me so much, but she also knew how to let me lead. She trusted me with her soul, and I trusted her with mine. There was nothing in this world that could make a nigga like me ever walk away from her.

As Kimmie and I stood together, the pastor began to speak. "Dearly beloved, we are gathered together here in the sight of God, and in the face of this company, to join together this man and this woman in holy matrimony, which is commended to be honorable among all men, And therefore is not by any to be entered into unadvisedly and lightly. Into this holy estate, these two persons present come now to be joined. If any person can show just cause why they may not be joined together, let them speak now or forever hold their peace."

When no one spoke up, the pastor continued. "Marriage is the union of husband and wife in heart, body, and mind. It is intended for their mutual joy and for the help and comfort given on another in prosperity and adversity. But more importantly, it is a means through which a stable and loving environment may be attained." He gazed over at me and paused.

Then the pastor began anew. "Do you, Zavien Hoover, take Kimberly Calloway to be your wife, to live together after God's ordinance in the holy estate of matrimony? Will you love her and comfort her, honor and keep her in sickness and in health? For richer, for poorer, for better, for worse? In sadness and in joy, to cherish and continually bestow upon her your heart's deepest devotion, forsaking all others? Keep yourself only unto her as long as you both shall live?"

I didn't know half of what that motherfucker had said, but I responded, "I do."

He went through the same confusing-ass questions for Kimmie, and she said the same words. We placed our rings on each other's fingers, and then we stepped back and waited for the pastor to do the same for each brother and bride. As Kimmie wiped her eyes, Ash and Quick stepped forward, since it was now their turn.

Ash . . .

It felt as if I was gliding toward this man, and I swear, it was the best feeling ever. There was no other place I would rather be than right here with this man. We had been through so much, and now I knew that what they said was true. I was once told, "If you love something, set it free. If it comes back to you, it is yours. If it does not, it was never meant to be." As I stared into this man's eyes and saw tears forming, I knew he was made just for me. Every part of his being made my heart skip a beat, and I couldn't wait to marry this man and give him all the love we had been missing out on and then some. He was my forever, and R. Kelly's song fit perfectly. When I reached the front, Kells leaned down and kissed me on my cheek. Then he handed me to Quick.

Quick . . .

Lucky couldn't even begin to describe how I felt in this moment. This girl was sexy as fuck, smart, funny, and mine. Watching her walk toward me, I couldn't stop the tears that were forming in my eyes. Her long white dress was flowing perfectly. She had chosen to wear a flared one that turned into a long train. The way the wind was blowing it made it look perfect. She had stood by a nigga at his weakest point, and I was not ashamed to say she had helped build me back up. A nigga had been losing it, but she had willed me back. Now I was able to laugh and be Quick again. Even when I had turned her away, she hadn't left. She'd given me my space to find my way back. There was no other person I would have chosen to give my heart to.

After we stepped forward and stood before the pastor, I kissed her, and then we stood there solemnly. The pastor went through the same thing he had said to Shadow and Kimmie. Me and Ash said our "I do's." And then we stepped back and turned to Baby Face and Juicy, because it was now their turn.

Juicy . . .

How a man could tear you down to your lowest point and then build you back up to where you came back stronger than ever was beyond me. That was exactly what Baby Face had done. We had been through so much, and there had been times I didn't think we would make it. He had come in like a storm and stolen my heart, and I didn't think I wanted it back. As I looked at my stomach bulging through my dress, I knew he was a blessing sent to me in disguise.

When the doctors had told me I would never be able to bear children, I had accepted it. Not once had he judged me or held that over my head. He had loved me as I was, and that had made me love him in return. He had torn down the walls I had taken years to build up. The moment he sang to me, I knew my heart would be his forever. He was mine, and I was his. There was nothing anybody could say to me that would make me leave this man. As I walked toward Baby Face, R. Kelly sang, then kissed me on my cheek and handed me to Face. I was ready to be his forever.

Baby Face . . .
A nigga didn't even deserve to be standing here right now, but God had answered my prayers and had given me my baby back. When Juicy walked away from me, a nigga had been lost. I knew I had fucked up, and a part of me felt I deserved to live with that hurt. Me and Drea's actions could have damaged so much, and I was grateful for the forgiveness they had shown us. Juicy not taking my shit had taught me a hard lesson. *Never do something if you aren't willing to risk it all behind that action.* She had stood her ground and hadn't taken me back because I was sorry. My baby had taught me to appreciate and not take advantage of the ones I loved. That was a lesson I would carry with me forever.

As I watched her walk toward me, the tears fell down my face. Juicy was beautiful as fuck, and her fire-red hair made her stand out from the others. She was wearing a white chiffon dress, and my baby girl in her stomach gave her a glow. Her skin was shining, and the red hair only intensified it.

Blaze leaned over to me and whispered, "All I know is your ass better be watching Juicy and not Drea. I'm retired, but I still got that Bic, my nigga."

Looking over at Blaze, I laughed. This nigga just couldn't act right. When Juicy made it to me, Kells kissed her cheek and handed her to me. I stared at her with nothing but pure love in my eyes. She was mine, and I was never letting her go. The pastor repeated the ceremonial words he had delivered twice now, and we said our "I do's." Then we turned to Blaze and Drea, because it was now their turn.

Drea . . .

Walking toward my man, I cried tears of joy. Just a year ago I'd cried because I had lost him. He had been taken from me, and I'd thought I would never be able to feel this type of love again. He'd come back to me, and even though I had hurt him, the love he had for me had allowed him to forgive me and love me more. That showed his true character, and I would forever be grateful to have him in my life. He was my everything, and I would be his all.

Spark was a blessing to us both, and I was filled with so much joy that she would get to know her father. As I gazed at this man, I knew he was flawed, but he was *so* perfect. No one understood our connection, and they didn't have to. The first time I laid eyes on him, I knew he was meant to be in my life. He had melted the hurt from my heart, and I had allowed him to heal me. The love he had for me and his brothers was rare. I would never let that go, and I couldn't wait to become his wife. When I made it to the front, R. Kelly was singing his ass off. He kissed me on the cheek and handed me to Blaze.

Blaze . . .

As I stared at each woman individually, love took over a nigga's heart. Me and my brothers were hell, and it was hard to deal with us, but these women loved us. My brothers and Mama were the only people who understood me—until I met Drea. She accepted a nigga for who he was, and that did something to me. She was different from the start, and therefore I showed her different. The fact that she was the mother of my child only made me love her more. She was the epitome of a woman. Nothing I could do would make her look at me differently. We laughed together, and she laughed at the shit I said and did. Accepting me for who I was, she never got upset or offended. That shit always made a nigga's dick hard. She never nagged or complained. She trusted in the love she knew I had for her.

As she walked toward me with her dress flying in the wind, all I wanted to do was make her mine. R. Kelly leaned down and kissed her cheek. When he handed her to me, I grabbed her hand.

"Kells, I fucks with you the long way, my nigga, but this one here is loose as a goose, and your smooth ass can probably steal her from me. I'm gone need you to keep them lips off my girl. You don't want these problems."

He laughed—until I flicked my Bic.

"Don't pay him no mind. He the special one," Baby Face declared. Face had just saved that nigga, 'cause he was about to be lit up. He ain't have no hair, but the nigga was gone have burnt patches from fucking with me.

When I turned to Drea, she laughed at me, and I wiped her tears away. I couldn't wait to spend the rest of my life with this woman.

The pastor went through his speech again, and Drea said, "I do."

Then it was my turn. "I don't know half the shit you said, Rev, but I'm gone trust you didn't just send me off. I know you friends with Jesus, but I don't think you ready to go meet him yet. Oh, and I do."

Everyone laughed, but I was serious.

The pastor waited until we were silent, and then he announced, "I now pronounce you all husband and wife. You may kiss your brides."

My brothers and I all leaned down and kissed the women we were about to spend the rest of our lives with. We brothers had a bond no one would ever understand, but all we needed was each other. The Hoover Gang wasn't breaking up; the women in our lives had just helped us grow up.

Since there was only a handful of people at the ceremony, we mingled with each other for a short time, and then we headed off on our honeymoon. Mama talked to the pastor as all of the married couples talked shit to each other. Kells got the fuck out of there. I guessed he didn't want problems. Out of nowhere, we heard our mama snap off.

"Rev, you out your damn mind! Nigga, I can't date you. How in the fuck am I gone be somebody's first lady? A bitch probably can't even wear her wigs. No thank you. Y'all can keep that shit."

We stared at her in shock. She was worse than me.

"Baby Face, get your damn mama," I groaned.

CHAPTER 29

BLAZE

One year later . . .

"Come here, Daddy's baby. Walk to Daddy." Spark made it halfway and then dropped down to crawl. As soon as she got over to me, she reached for the lighter in my hand. "Let it go. I told you not to play with Daddy's toy."

"Why the hell are you walking around carrying that shit anyway? We have a toddler. You can't have that shit around," Drea said.

"Girl, if you don't get your ass out my face and take your ass somewhere and wash that pussy . . . You done had that shit on since yesterday, so I know that cat hot. I mean, if you want a hot pussy, I can help you out." I started flicking my Bic, and she rolled her eyes and walked away. "Your ass better be getting in that shower."

"Blaze, don't do that. You know damn well I been getting shit ready for this get-together. You ain't helped me with shit."

"So you saying because you been cooking, you couldn't wash that hot pocket? Girl, if you don't get your nasty ass out my face and go wash your ass . . ."

"Whatever, asshole. I'm going."

I put my lighter away and continued to play with my angel. I couldn't believe baby girl was one. A nigga ain't felt real love until they had a child.

"Da Da, juice."

"You thirsty, Ma Ma? Hold on." I walked in the kitchen, grabbed her cup, and poured her some juice. When I got back in the front room, there was a big-ass flame in the fireplace.

"Drea! Come here. Hurry up!"

Drea came running down the stairs, and she damn near bust her shit, she was running so fast. "Oh, my God. What happened?"

Tearing up, I had to gather my thoughts. "She threw her blanket in the fireplace," I finally said. "That shit touched a nigga's heart. She gone be just like a nigga."

"Have you lost your damn mind? Your ass happy because our one-year-old in here playing with fire?"

"You damn right. At least now I know she mine. Don't look at me like that. You know that pussy got some miles on it while I was dead."

"You have issues. Give me my damn baby. She gone done set the whole house on fire, and your dumb ass will stand there, proud and happy." She grabbed Spark, and I slapped her on the ass.

"Your lips getting looser than your pussy. I retired, baby, but I still got my Bic. I'm trying to let you be great, but your ass determined to feel this heat."

"You set me on fire again, you gone feel a divorce."

"Divorce deez nuts."

Smacking her lips, she went back upstairs. I headed into the kitchen and started grabbing the food and taking it outside. She did all the sides, and I was supposed to do the meat. I poured the charcoal into the grill, then covered it in lighter fluid. As soon as I flicked my Bic, I started thinking about all the good times I had had over my lifetime with this motherfucker. It had been hard for me to walk away, but I'd done it for my family. I did not realize I was standing there, just looking at the flame in my hand, until Drea brought me out of my thoughts.

"Baby, are you happy? Do you miss the streets?"

When I turned to face her, I could see the worry in her eyes. "Sometimes. The rush we got from hitting those banks or killing people was like no other. Some nights I think about sneaking out and finding somebody and setting they ass on fire. That 'fire on flesh' smell, man, I miss that shit. But I would walk away ten thousand times for my family. I'm happy. A nigga just miss the shit sometime."

"That's some sick shit, baby." She shook her head at me as she laughed.

"The fact that I had to tell your ass more than once to go wash your ass is sick. The fucked-up part is, you still ain't got in that motherfucker. Let me find out you done tricked me, and I done married a motherfucker that take ho baths with her leg kicked up on the sink."

"I hate your ass."

Laughing, I turned around and flicked my Bic again. When I placed the fire to the charcoal, flames shot up and damn near took a nigga's fade clean off. I could smell burning, so I knew that shit had got me. My dumb ass had tried to light the grill with a li'l-ass lighter.

"That's what the fuck you get. God don't like ugly," Drea remarked.

"I bet he hate funky bitches more. For real, bae, this is starting to get weird. You got ten seconds to get your ass in the house and wash your ass, or I'm gone sterilize that motherfucker."

"Sterilize it?"

"You know, when you boil something, it's sterilized. I'm about to cook your shit. My dick hard as fuck, and I can't even ask for no damn pussy. Shit smelling like do not disturb."

"Bye, Blaze."

She walked off, and I lit the grill the right way and started the meat. Minutes later I heard the doorbell ring, so I walked through the house and opened the front door.

"Hello, sir. I have something for you." This dude held out an envelope. I looked at it, but I knew I hadn't ordered shit. When I saw the envelope had no name or address on it, I turned that shit down.

"Naw, bruh, I'm straight. Take that shit back where you got it."

"It's just a—"

"Nigga, are you deaf or slow? I said I don't want that shit." Seeing he still had no intention to leave, I reached in my pocket and grabbed my lighter. "I know you don't know me, 'cause if you did, you wouldn't be standing in front of me, looking like Lionel Richie. You got so many chemicals in your hair that fire would spread quick. Now, I asked you to get the fuck off my porch. You need to leave before I forget I'm retired."

He looked at me as if he was trying to ascertain if I was serious. As soon as I flicked my Bic, he took off down the driveway. *Smart man.* I closed the door. I was heading back toward the kitchen when the doorbell rang again. This nigga had me fucked up. When I swung the door open again, I went the fuck off.

"What the fuck did I say?" I seethed. But then I saw my mama and the pastor standing there, and I calmed down.

Mama wagged her finger at me. "Nigga, if you don't watch your damn mouth . . . Who raised your ass? You so damn disrespectful."

Me and the pastor looked at each other and burst out laughing. My mama didn't even realize she cursed worse than I did.

"Pastor, when you step in here, just know I ain't shit, and as you already know, my mama ain't, either. Just pray for me."

"Son, be careful what you ask for. I believe God has a plan for your life."

"Hold the fuck on. Ain't gone be no preaching in my shit. I had to listen to your long-winded ass at the wedding. Not today, motherfucker, not today. Ma, what the fuck you doing with him anyway?"

"Nigga, I said, 'Watch your mouth.' Damn. You trying to run my damn man away."

The pastor started blushing, and I was ready to knock his ass out.

"What's your name, Pastor?" I asked.

"Devon."

"Devon, if you hurt my mama, I'm gone burn you so bad, you gone think your ass done went to hell. Are we clear?"

Clearing his throat, he started to look nervous. "Yes, we are clear."

"Good. Now, leave all that holy shit on the porch. We about to turn the fuck up and act a whole ass out here today. I don't need you trying to pray for our souls.".

"Nigga, move out the damn way and let us in. Shit, I'm hungry. Is the food done?"

"Naw, Ma. I just started the meat." I moved out of the way and finally let them in the house.

"Go change your clothes," Mama ordered me. "I got it. The shit better not be burnt, either."

"You know what the fuck my name is. If I don't know shit else, I know fire."

"Then why the fuck you standing here, looking like a damn rapist with alopecia in the eyebrows?" she fired back.

I ran to the foyer mirror and looked. The damn fire had taken my eyebrows off. "Ain't this a bitch."

Mama shooed me away with her hand. "Get your blank ass on. I got the meat. Nigga standing there, looking like nothing. Ain't shit on this nigga's face." Her and Devon laughed loudly, until I looked at his ass. He shut up quick.

"You catch on fast, Devon. I'll set your damn throat on fire and have your ass preaching smoke on Sunday. Y'all got me fucked up," I said.

Heading up the stairs, I prayed Drea could help me. My brothers was gone let my ass have it if they saw me like this. My mama had called my ass blank. I was gone get her ass back. She had got me fucked up.

CHAPTER 30

BABY FACE

"Baby, Tsunami need some attention. Where the fuck you at?"

When she didn't respond, I got up and walked around the house, looking for her. When I stepped in baby Zaria's room, I found Juicy was lying next to the crib, knocked out. This baby was wearing our asses out. We hardly ever had time for each other anymore. I swear, I loved my girl to death, but all her spoiled ass did was cry. Her li'l ass gone be an attention seeker. If she even thought a motherfucker not paying her attention, she started crying and shit. She wouldn't sleep at night, and she cried all during the damn day.

I didn't know how Juicy got her ass asleep now, but I was about to use that shit to my advantage to get my dick sucked. I walked over to Juicy, pulled Tsunami out, and pushed against her lips. When she didn't wake up, I slapped her ass in the face with that big motherfucker.

"What the fuck!" As soon as she screamed that shit, the baby started crying.

"Damn, Juicy. This was our first moment to ourselves."

"Nigga, you the one came in here, slapping a bitch with your third leg." She bent down to get the baby, lifted her out of the crib, and then started rocking her.

I tried to speak in a calm tone. "When the baby went to sleep, why the fuck didn't you come find me? You know we don't got time for shit."

"Your hand works. Use that shit."

"I shouldn't have to when I got a wife at home. This is starting to get ridiculous. A nigga ain't had no sex in three fucking months."

She shrugged her shoulders and walked into our bedroom. Rubbing my hand down my face, I was getting frustrated. Don't get me wrong. Being a father was the best thing in the fucking world. But the shit that came with it was stressing a nigga out. It was like the old Juicy was gone. My ass trying to be faithful, but she making this shit hard. How long did she expect a nigga like me to go without sex? I walked out of the nursery, went in our bedroom, and prayed the baby would fall back asleep. When the baby's crying stopped, I got excited as hell.

I waited until Juicy had put the baby back in the crib. Then I whispered, "Come on. Let's get a quickie in before she wakes up."

"I don't feel like it. Damn. Can a bitch get a break?" She walked back into our bedroom, and I followed.

"This ain't no fucking break. This a damn retirement. What the fuck you need a break from? I'm not understanding."

"From you. All you do is crowd me and beg for sex. Damn! Can a bitch breathe?"

"This is why niggas cheat. I ain't never seen a motherfucker have to beg for sex from his own damn wife."

"Go cheat, then. It ain't like you never done it before. Get the fuck out of my face." I walked up to her and grabbed her around her throat.

"You feeling yourself too much. Don't forget who the fuck I am." I let her neck go, then walked into the bathroom to get a shower. She started crying, and I had no fucks to give. Slamming the bathroom door, I hoped the baby woke up on her goofy ass.

"I fucking hate you."

"Touché, bitch. Touché," I yelled through the door.

I ran the shower, and as I stepped under the water, I started to think I had made a mistake. This was not how my life was supposed to be going. Retiring from the streets was a decision me and my brothers had made because we were trying to be family men. Outside of my daughter, I was feeling like this bitch could leave. I grabbed my body wash, and I started stroking my dick. Seeing him come to life, all I wanted to do was put him in some pussy. Slowly stroking my shit, I closed my eyes and imagined me being balls deep.

Since it had been so long since I had had some pussy, my nut started rising up quick. *Fuck.* This motherfucker was cumming hard and strong. The shit shot out of me so hard, my knees got weak. When the feeling came back in my legs, I washed my ass and got the fuck out of the shower. When I walked out of the bathroom, I saw her lying in the bed, asleep. I started to slap the shit out of her ass. Nigga was thirty years old and beating his meat. I looked at the clock and saw that it was time to start getting ready for the cookout. Deciding to be petty, I got dressed and left her ass. I jumped in my Hummer and headed over to Blaze's house.

As soon as I walked in the door, all my troubles left my mind. I loved being around my brothers. We had a bond like no other. These niggas kept me laughing. Shadow and Quick hadn't made it yet, but I saw that my mama was here. Leaning down to give her a kiss, I side-eyed the pastor. The fuck was he doing here?

"Ma, I thought you said you wasn't on that shit?"

"Nigga, don't question me. A bitch need some dick. Why not get some holy penis dipped off in me? Shit, I get a nut and a blessing at the same time," she replied.

"You nasty as hell, and that ain't how that shit work. I hope your ass shaved," I said.

"Don't worry about it, bitch. I know somebody that like it." She laughed as she tried to mimic Ms. Pearly, and I walked away and grabbed me a drink.

Blazed headed my way. "What up, nigga? Where my niece at?" Something about Blaze looked different, but I couldn't put my finger on it.

"I left her ass with her depressing-ass mama," I said as I took a seat.

He poured a drink, then sat down next to me. "What's going on? You done cheated again?" He caught sight of Drea and shouted, "Drea, if I find out your ass been slipping on dicks again, I'm gone sew that bitch up." When he yelled that shit across the yard, the pastor damn near choked.

I shook my head. "Can you ever be serious? Naw, I ain't cheated, but I'm damn sure thinking about that shit. She won't give me no pussy, and her ass just different. I ain't sign up for this dumb shit."

"Nigga, she did just have a fucking baby."

"Three fucking months ago."

"Yeah you right. Me and Drea didn't even wait until her six weeks was up. Man, I stuck my dick in and fell all in that pussy. I cried real tears. A nigga thought the baby had fucked her shit up."

"You dumb as fuck."

"Nigga, I'm dead ass. Shit felt weird as fuck. Told her ass I could wait. She was horny, though, so I fucked her with my fist."

"I'm telling you, Mama should have got a check for your slow ass."

"You think I'm playing, but her shit was wide as hell. One night, I was rocking the baby to sleep, right? This motherfucker wanted it so bad, she started grinding against my foot. I kicked her ass dead in the pussy. The nasty bitch moaned."

This nigga had me laughing so hard, I was holding my stomach. "Tell me you playing, my nigga."

"Ask her. I swear. Matter of fact, don't ask her shit about her pussy. You ain't getting none, either, so your bitch ass might try to fuck again."

"Fuck you. And, nigga, what the fuck is wrong with your fucking face? I keep trying to figure out what the fuck is different."

"Mind your fucking business," he snapped.

I was staring at him, trying to figure it out, until he flicked his Bic.

"I said, 'Change the fucking subject.'"

Laughing, I watched as Paris and Panda walked in. They were in their swimsuits, and my dick got brick hard. Juicy needed to give me some pussy. A nigga was ready to bend Paris over the grill. Hell, or Panda. At this point it really didn't matter.

Blaze caught me looking. "Nigga, you need some for real. Since you staring at Paris so hard, nut in her edges. I heard that shit grow your hair."

Laughing, I swore I hated his ass.

CHAPTER 31

SHADOW

After grabbing our bags from the luggage claim, me and Kimmie walked hand in hand. We were hoping that this trip was a success. First, my dick wasn't working, and now it seemed like my damn soldiers ain't marching. I had been trying to get her pregnant since our wedding night, and ain't shit shaking but my balls. She didn't speak on it, but I could tell it bothered her. All these dick problems was fucking with a nigga's mental. I done did a lot of shit in my life, but I didn't think a broke dick needed to be a nigga's karma. How the hell I was attracted to hoes, but my dick didn't work, right? God had a funny sense of humor, and I ain't laughing.

Kimmie glanced over at me. "You okay, baby?"

"Yeah, I'm just thinking this one has to be the one."

"I hope so."

We walked to the parking lot, and then we jumped in my whip and headed out. This girl was everything to a nigga, and all she wanted was my seed. If I hadn't wasted all my shit going down a bitch's throat, I may have had some working nut to give her. Every time I saw the disappointment on her face, I be wanting to go grab an ex-ho and snatch my shit out they stomach like, "Here. Try these." If all they asses wasn't dead, I would try anything at this point.

We stopped at home. We wanted to freshen up and shit before we headed to the cookout. As close as me and my brothers were, everybody been doing the family thing, and we hadn't been around each other too much lately. We had managers working the club, and business was still booming. Overall, we were living the good life. Even though I had married the perfect woman, it seemed like I was the only nigga that didn't get their happy ending. All they asses had kids or their girl was pregnant. That was why a nigga had planned this trip: a change of scenery might make my eggs move different. It had been the perfect trip, even though a motherfucker had tried to fuck my shit up. I thought back on it.

As we sat on a white sandy beach in Puerto Rico, I fed Kimmie strawberries and we drank champagne. A nigga was trying to set the mood, and I wanted to be lit. Many motherfuckers had got a bitch pregnant when they were drunk. I knew I should be able to pop my wife off. I was drinking this soft shit now, but when we got ready to fuck, she was getting that Henny dick.

"Baby, I wish we could live here forever. It's so fucking beautiful," Kimmie sad softly.

"It is, but a nigga need them Chicago streets. I done already retired, and now you want a nigga living like a lame-ass motherfucker, eating beans all day."

"I'm gone need you to broaden yourself. Puerto Ricans don't eat beans all day, retard."

"Bottom line, the shit ain't happening. I'll bring your ass whenever you want to come, but that's it. Issa hood rat."

"Fuck you. I'm not a damn hood rat." She hit me in the arm as she laughed.

"I'm talking about my ass. You think you too good for them streets, but I see your ass got left off bad and boujie."

As we laughed, a man walked our way. I thought he would keep going, but he stopped in front of us.

"My boss would like for you to have a word with him at his compound," he announced.

"Compound deez nuts. Don't you see me with my girl?" I said.

"It's to discuss a very important matter," he insisted.

"Nigga, ain't shit more important than my wife, and I don't know you niggas. Here. Take these beans and get the fuck out my face."

"Baby, I told you they don't eat beans like that," Kimmie interjected.

"I forgot. The nigga pissed me off."

Kimmie frowned at me. "You have to learn to control your anger. There are different ways to handle things."

"Didn't I just tell you I'm a hood rat?"

"Excuse me, sir."

Realizing this nigga was still standing there, I looked over at Kimmie and took a deep breath.

I gave him a hard stare. "Sir, can you please tell your boss I respectfully decline? I'm on vacation with my wife, and you have about ten seconds to get the fuck out of my face before I slap your ass to sleep. You ever fall asleep on the sand? I could only imagine that shit gets hot in the morning." I turned back to Kimmie, it felt good to see her smiling at me again.

"I'm so proud of you. That's a step. Now all you have to do is leave off the threats," she told me.

When I saw this nigga still standing here, I wondered if his ass was a mute, like the nigga Quick had killed. As I jumped to my feet, he realized I was serious, and took off running.

"Let's go, before I fuck around and go to jail out here. I'm too pretty for that shit. My ass will be fighting all night, trying not to become somebody's burrito," I told Kimmie.

"Yeah, let's go, so I can get your ass a nap."

Once we got inside the hotel room, we fucked all night. We didn't leave the room until it was time to go back home. I didn't see the nigga again, but curiosity did have me wondering who the fuck his boss was and how the fuck he knew me. Shit was strange as fuck if you asked me.

Kimmie pulled me from my thoughts when she told me it was time to get ready. After getting dressed, we headed over to Blaze's crib. As soon as we walked in the yard, the shit felt good. I was so happy to see my brothers, I damn near knocked Kimmie over when I tried to get over there to them.

"What up, fam?" I said, a wide grin on my face.

Blaze did a fake second take when he saw me. "Bro, I thought you wasn't gone make it. Did you go see a doctor about your weak-ass sperm?"

"Nigga, damn. Do you joke about everything?"

Blaze shrugged his shoulders and kept flipping the meat. "Don't get mad at me because you walking around with kiddie sperm."

"Fuck you." Leaving that nigga laughing at my expense, I headed over to Baby Face.

"I don't even know why I be excited to see that nigga. He don't even make it a minute before I be ready to knock his ass out," I confessed.

Baby Face shook his head. "Stop fronting, bro. You know damn well your ass ain't gone do shit. That nigga itching to set something on fire. Go speak to your mama and her new man."

Looking over, I saw Mama sitting on the lap of the pastor who had married us. "You know what's fucked up? That nigga did our wedding, and I don't even know his name."

"Me either. Fuck him."

I laughed with Face, then went to say hi to my mama and the pastor.

"Hey, beautiful." I nodded at the pastor before I bent down to kiss my mama.

Ma screwed up her face. "Nigga, I don't know where your lips been. Get the fuck on."

"Ma, that's how you talk around the pastor?"

"Nigga, please! I cursed his ass out at church on Sunday. He was all in this lady's face and passing her notes and shit. Almost got that ho a spot on the 'sick and shut in' list."

The pastor came to his own defense. "Debra, I told you she is the secretary. All I was doing was giving her the church announcements."

Mama shook her head. "You was about to be announcing her funeral. Fuck you mean?"

"Ma, they got a special place in hell for you. I'm gone pray for you," I said.

"You better pray for Devon. He the one gone need it."

"Who is Devon?" I asked.

"The pastor. Nigga, you about dumb as hell. How you gone let somebody marry you, and you don't know they name? How you know you and Kimmie really married? Matter of fact, don't answer that. Get your slow ass out my face. Who the fuck raised you niggas?" Ma actually got up and walked away as she shook her head. Any nigga that dealt with her had my respect. That motherfucking lady was bat-shit crazy.

Blaze and Kimmie was arguing, as usual, and I grabbed Kimmie away and took her to sit down. I didn't know why she insisted on playing with this nigga. Especially around fire. If I told her ass what he did to Shirree, maybe she would leave his ass alone.

"Baby, why you pull me away?"

I rolled my eyes. "Shut the fuck up. I just saved your life."

"I'm sick of y'all." She got up and walked over to Paris and Panda. She could keep playing, but I swear, she on her own.

Leaning back in my chair, I just smiled. Our lives was great, and it felt good as fuck to be around my family.

CHAPTER 32

QUICK

"Where the fuck you coming from, Ma?"

Ash's ass been leaving a lot lately, and the only reason I didn't think she was cheating was that she had Zavi with her all the time. A nigga didn't want to turn his son into a snitch, so this motherfucker was gone tell me what's up.

"We just ran to the mall."

"When I took you back, what did I tell you?"

"What are you talking about, Quick?"

"I asked you to never keep anything from me, but that's what you doing right now. You disappearing and shit every damn day. Now you standing in my face, lying. Don't make me fuck you up, Ashanti. Now, where the fuck you been?"

"I'm not keeping anything from you baby. Please just let me handle it." She got me fucked up, and she was really trying me.

Grabbing her by her neck, I was ready to choke a booga out her ass. "What the fuck you mean, you gone handle it? I'm your fucking husband, and I'm asking you what the fuck is going on."

After letting her neck go, I walked away from her before I hurt her ass. She was eight months pregnant, and I was trying not to lay hands on her, but she was making the shit hard.

"If you don't trust me enough to understand or handle what the fuck is going on, then I'ma leave and give us some space," I warned.

"Baby, please. Don't leave. I'm sorry." After sitting down on the couch, she dropped her head in her hands. "I don't think you will understand, and I don't want you going off."

"It don't matter how you think I will react. I'm your husband, and I ain't doing that sneaky shit. Now, what the fuck is going on?"

"Jason been wanting to see Zavi. That's it. He misses him, and I didn't think you would get it." When she realized my eyes had turned from hazel to smoke gray, she knew she had fucked up. "Quick, he doesn't understand."

I walked to the closet, opened my safe, and grabbed my gun. Pointing it at her, I let her know where she had me fucked up at. "Help me understand how you thought I would be okay with you taking my son to see that bitch-ass nigga."

She stood up and walked up to me, throwing me off guard.

"Make this your last time pulling a gun on me and don't use it," she yelled. "You're pissed. I get that. But you better figure out how to use your fucking words before you lose your life. I'm not going through this shit again for nobody. If you feel the only way to get your point across is to put your hands on me, then you can leave."

"Bitch, first of all, this my shit. Secondly, don't think I want light your ass up over my child. Thirdly, I see this nigga done gave you some fucking balls. I ain't never disrespected you, yet you keep thinking it's okay to play me like a bitch-ass nigga. All I have been is a hunnid with you, but you stay keeping secrets. You can have that shit, Ash." I put my gun away, then stalked into the kitchen to pour me a shot of Julio. Ash followed me into the kitchen.

"I'm not trying to keep secrets from you, but he is a child. All he knew was Jason, and he misses him. I didn't see nothing wrong with allowing Zavi to visit him."

"Let me ask you something. When you take Zavi to see him, what does he call him?"

When she started looking stupid, I knew the answer. "Daddy Jason. Look, before you snap off—"

"Get the fuck out of my face, Ash. Matter of fact, give me your phone."

"Why do you want my phone?"

"Because you obviously don't know how to tell a nigga to fuck off, and I'm gone help you out before I have to kill you."

She reached in her pocket, retrieved her phone, and passed it to me. And then she stormed off.

I figured it was time for a talk with Zavi, so I walked up to his room.

"Hey, son," I said as I gazed at him from the open doorway. "What you doing?"

"Playing the game."

"Turn it off. Come talk to me for a second." I sat down on his bed, and when he walked over, I pulled him to me. I wanted him to understand what I was about to say, but I didn't want him to think he was in trouble. "I know you grew up with Jason and you miss him, but you hurt Daddy's feelings when you go to see him. It hurts even more when you call him Daddy. Do you want to hurt my feelings, li'l man?"

"No, Daddy, I don't."

"Then you can't do that anymore, okay? I'm your only daddy, and when you leave to see him, I miss you."

"Okay, Daddy, I won't. I only want you. Just don't leave me too, okay?" That shit hurt my heart, and I saw that Jason putting them out had really fucked my li'l man's head up.

"I told you, I'm not going anywhere. Now get ready, so we can go see your granny, uncles, and cousins."

"Okay, Daddy. Just one more turn, okay?"

Laughing, I stood up. "Okay, just one more." When I walked out of the room, Ash's dumb ass was standing outside the door. I walked past her like I didn't even see her creep ass. I jumped in the shower so I could start getting ready. Just as I was starting to wash up, she got in the shower with me.

"I know you are mad at me, but I wasn't trying to keep anything from you. You get so upset, and I'm afraid to tell you some things."

"Look, I know I got a temper. That still don't give you the right to keep something like that from me. I'm your fucking husband, and if I can't trust you, the shit won't work, Ash. Do better, my nigga, or you gone lose me."

"Why do you always do that? Every time shit don't go your way, you threaten to leave. That shit ain't cool, and it makes me feel like you want me walking on eggshells."

"With the dumb shit you be pulling, you need to tiptoe on them motherfuckers. You like to play the victim, but you be doing some foul shit. We have to go at this shit together or not at all." After rinsing off, I got out of the shower. I realized as I dried off that she wasn't getting this shit. If she hadn't thought the shit was wrong, she wouldn't have hid it and lied to me. I was not about to play these games with her ass.

Once we were done dressing, we headed over to Blaze's house. The ride in the car was quiet except for the noise from Zavi's iPad. This motherfucker had the nerve to be sitting over there pouting like somebody had stolen her fucking bike. When we pulled up to the house, I jumped out of the car fast as hell. A nigga wasn't with all that depressing shit. Even though she was eight months pregnant, I left her ass to waddle on her own. She had done the stupid shit, and now she needed to own it. When I walked in the backyard, everybody was laughing and having a good time. A nigga got excited as hell.

"Hoover Gang in the motherfucking building," I yelled.

They all turned and looked at me. My brothers got excited, and I decided to get shit cracking.

"Hoovers, front and center," I ordered.

They dumb asses walked over to me and didn't have to question what I was on. We threw our shades on, and then we stood in front of the family, doing the brother line. Our dumb asses stood there waving and shit, and even though we weren't at the club, it felt good as hell.

Ma yelled, "Sit y'all dumb asses down, looking like a gay version of *The Five Heartbeats*." Our mama sholl had a way of crushing a nigga's spirit.

"You been real slick at the mouth now that you done found a new man," Blaze told her. "Don't forget your old ass was just getting stretched out by our gay-ass daddy. Motherfuckers get some human hair and don't know how to act."

"Fuck you, Blaze." Mama got up and went in the house, with the pastor on her heels.

"Please tell me the pastor is not her new man."

"Yup, and his nasty ass going to hell," Baby Face said, confirming that bullshit.

"Mama about to turn his ass out."

"Y'all be going in on Mama like she ain't supposed to find love," Shadow said.

Blaze rolled his eyes. "Shadow, shut yo' dumb ass up and help your mama find a cute wig, since you wanna do something."

I stared at Blaze. "Nigga, what the fuck wrong with your face?"

He didn't even respond to me; the nigga just flicked his Bic. His ass wasn't gone ever change.

CHAPTER 33

BLAZE

When I heard the doorbell ring, I walked away from the family and went to open the door. Everybody was here but Juicy, so I assumed it was her. But as soon as I opened the door, I found a nigga and his security standing there.

"The fuck your big ass want?" I muttered. "You came to my door strong ass fuck my nigga. I'll sell your ass a plate this time, but I ain't with that friendly neighbor shit. And yo' big ass gone get some string beans. You look like the type that want all the meat and shit."

"I've been trying to set up a meeting with you and your brothers. Since you won't accept any of my messages, I came personally to talk to you."

"It would have been easier for you to ask for extra meat. We don't know you, and therefore you don't have business with us. Now, do you want this plate or not, fam?"

"You talk a lot of shit for a nigga with only one trick." Before he could even blink, I had my lighter up to his eye, ready to deep-fry that motherfucker. His men raised their guns at me, and I guessed they thought I was worried.

"Even if they shoot me, my nigga, you won't use this motherfucker no more," I growled. Looking over at one of his men, I asked a question. "You ever seen a fat-ass pirate?"

"That one trick gone get you dead real quick," the man snarled.

"Try your luck, bitch," I shot back. When I turned around, my brothers were behind me with guns drawn. Quick passed me my strap, and I pointed it at the fat-ass nigga. "Now, what was you saying?"

After motioning for his men to drop their weapons, he turned back to us. "I came here only to talk. Your father owed my boss ten million dollars. I'm here to collect on that debt."

Baby Face stepped up, and I knew he was ready to end this shit. "How the fuck you thought that shit?" he said.

"The moment you killed him, that became your debt."

I shook my head. "You got us fucked up. Look, do you still want this plate? Because I ain't got time for this dumb shit."

"If you don't have the money, you can work off your debt. Just know, the debt will be paid. Voluntarily or involuntarily. We would prefer you guys to work for us. You each possess a skill that is useful to our organization. We will give you a week to think about it. Someone will come by here and get your answer. It is in your best interest to accept our offer."

"You got ten seconds to make your exit," Baby Face growled. Him and Baby Face had a stare down.

"One week," the fat motherfucker said in a flat voice. Then he walked off, and his men followed.

I turned to my brothers. "Why the fuck didn't we just handle that shit right now? We gone give this nigga time to come back?"

"Because he is not the boss. If we kill him, it still doesn't solve our problem. We need to figure out who the fuck this nigga owed. We have to know what we are up against before we make a decision," Face explained.

Looking at Baby Face, I snapped, "What you mean, a decision? The answer is fuck no. Blaze don't work for no motherfucker, and if we give they ass ten million, we have to get back in the business."

Baby Face spread his hands in front of him. "I know all of that. Which is why we need to figure out who it is. If we are going to war, we need to know who we are up against. In the meantime, we need to be careful. These motherfuckers know where we live and can pop up at any time."

"When I was in Puerto Rico, a motherfucker came up to us on the beach, telling me his boss wanted a meeting with me. I know the vicinity, but I still don't know who it is," Shadow interjected.

I eased my lighter up to Shadow's lip, and then I flicked that motherfucker.

Shadow jumped back. "What the fuck, Blaze! Now ain't the time to be playing."

"Nigga, I ain't playing. You stood your dumb ass in my yard for about an hour and ain't told us shit. You sat your ass back there and didn't say a word. I should leave your ass on the porch."

"Leave this dick in your mouth, clown ass," Shadow shot back.

I got in Shadow's face. "First off, you gay. Second, nigga, your dick never work. Get your flaccid ass on. Nigga's shit can't even say hi, let alone stand up, and he talking shit."

Baby Face got in between Shadow and me. "Enough. Damn, can you niggas ever be serious? Everything always a joke to y'all. We retired and walked away from this shit, and a nigga on your doorstep, threatening to take away everything we worked for, and you niggas out here joking." This nigga Baby Face was pissed.

"Nigga, you just need some pussy. Shut the fuck up. You ready to shoot anything since you can't shoot your shit in your girl."

Shaking his head, Baby Face walked back in the house. Before he disappeared, he muttered, "I should have let them shoot your ass. You aggy as fuck."

I shrugged my shoulders, and we headed toward the kitchen. On the way, I heard moaning from the bathroom, and I got pissed. "Drea, I know your bitch ass ain't slipped on another dick, right?"

After kicking the bathroom door in, me and my brothers stood there in disbelief as the pastor hit our mama from the back. When Baby Face snatched our mama up, I grabbed the pastor by his dick, and you already know what happened next. I flicked my motherfucking Bic. They nasty asses had me fucked up.

"Oh, my God. Please stop!" the pastor pleaded. He wanted to scream and call on God now.

"Blaze, let him go," Mama ordered. "I need that dick. I don't want no scabby penis in my pussy."

"Get the fuck on, before that wolf pussy be howling pussy," I told her. Then I turned away from her and looked at the pastor. "There's kids in my fucking house, so don't you ever disrespect my shit again. I will cook your shit and serve it to the fucking masses. Issa flame broil. Now get your fraud ass out my fucking shit."

He fixed his clothes and ran out of the bathroom. "Come on, Debra. I think we should go." He had caught on quick.

Mama made it known that she wasn't going anywhere. "Nigga, you better put some butter on that shit. I'm hungry as fuck, and I want to see my grandbabies. He just helped you feel what hell is like. Now you got something to preach about on Sunday. That's some juicy-ass shit. I might even stay woke. Come on, hot dick. Let me get the butter."

Shadow shook his head. "Your mama just gone make that man sit back there with a bubbling dick. Something is wrong with all y'all."

Laughing at Shadow, we headed outside to finish the party. I couldn't get no pussy; his ass couldn't, either. As soon as we stepped outside, we found Kimmie flipping the meat on the grill.

"Go on, girl," I told her. "We don't want no white people's barbecue."

Kimmie put her hands on her hips. "You always talking shit. I'm not scared of your ass."

Everybody got quiet. We were family, and we all talked shit, but I saw Kimmie thought it was sweet. She the only one out here who ain't really felt this motherfucker. I grabbed my Bic, but she slapped it out of my hand.

"What you gone do now, brother? You ain't shit without your lighter," she taunted.

Everybody started laughing, until I reached in my pocket and retrieved another Bic. When she saw it, she turned to Shadow, looking for help.

"Run, bae, run!" he urged her.

"Nigga, you gone let him get your girl?" Quick asked. Then he was laughing at Shadow's scary ass.

"I told her I wouldn't have her back," Shadow said. "Girl, why the fuck you still standing there? Run."

Realizing that her husband wasn't coming to her rescue, she looked at me and then took off running. As I went after her, I was shocked. She was hauling ass. Literally. This big girl was gone, jumping over chairs and all. A nigga was keeping up with her and almost got her, until we got to the last chair. My mama's dirty ass stuck her foot out and down went Frazier. I went flying into the pool, and I couldn't do shit to stop it. When I swam up to the surface, I leaned on the edge of the pool and let my mama know it was on.

"You know I'm gone get your ass back, right?" I barked.

Baby Face stepped closer to the edge of the pool and stared at my face. "Nigga, your eyebrows crying."

Looking up at Baby Face, I didn't realize what he meant right away. Then it hit me. Drea's ass had watched a YouTube video and had drawn me some eyebrows on me since I had burned mine off. The shit must be coming off in the water. Baby Face and Mama were laughing so hard, I couldn't even get pissed. As I climbed out of the pool, I shot Drea's ass a look.

"All this fucking money we got and my wife using cheap-ass make-up," I muttered.

"Nigga, where the fuck are your eyebrows?" Quick was laughing so hard, he was crying tears.

"Fuck, y'all, I made a mistake and burnt them off," I revealed.

Shadow gave me a squinty smile. "How you burn your own shit? Nigga, them motherfuckers done made an *M* on your face."

I threw my middle finger up at Shadow.

"Da Da cry?" When Spark said that shit, the whole damn yard started crying tears, they were laughing so hard. I damn near threw her li'l ass in the pool. They had got me fucked up.

"Drea, bring your ass in the house and come fix my eyebrows," I said. Then I turned and glared at the person who had caused my trouble. "Kimmie, this ain't over."

"Fuck with me if you want to," she told me. "All I gotta do is lick my thumb." Now she had the upper hand on me. I couldn't wait until my shit grew back.

I laughed as I went in the house, but then I couldn't do shit but wonder if the war had really come to an end. My family had made it out of all that bullshit, only to be dragged back in now. A nigga couldn't go to war with fake eyebrows. What if it got hot? Laughing at myself again, I sat down, and then Drea hooked me up.

"We going to MAC tomorrow. Y'all got me fucked up," I told her.

CHAPTER 34

BABY FACE

Leaving Blaze's house, a nigga was feeling good. My savage was about to be released, and I couldn't be happier. Motherfuckers would never understand how much I missed that shit, and I would never admit it. I was the one that had wanted to walk away from it all, but I hadn't known it would have me feeling incomplete. Maybe if I wasn't going through so much shit with Juicy, a nigga could feel good about leaving the life. But sitting at home, arguing all damn day, wasn't the life I had pictured.

I dragged my ass home, and it took everything in me to get out my truck and walk in that motherfucker. As soon as I entered the house, I knew something was off. I ran upstairs and couldn't find Juicy and the baby anywhere. They were gone. After the visit we had got today, I started to panic and feel like shit for leaving her the way that I had. In my defense, I hadn't known we had enemies out there.

As I grabbed my phone to call my brothers, I glanced in the closet and saw that it was empty. There was no way a motherfucker had taken her and let her grab clothes. This bitch had left. Running my hands down my face, I walked down the stairs and jumped in my car. How the fuck she walking out, and she the motherfucking problem? I knew I had done some shit in my past that had put a strain on our shit, but a nigga been making up for that shit ever since. Juicy couldn't be nowhere but at her mama's crib. I didn't have time for the stupid shit. I took the ride across town, and when I pulled up, her mama was sitting on the porch, holding Zaria. I climbed out of my ride and walked up the porch steps.

"Hey, Ma. What's your daughter's problem now?"

"Honestly, I don't know. She came by here and dropped off the baby. Said she was leaving and how she need a break. Gave me all the baby's stuff and was gone. I tried to convince her not to leave the baby, but something in her eyes wasn't right. Her ass didn't even look back, and she took off."

Sitting down next to her mama, I felt defeated. "I've tried everything to make that girl happy, but nothing has worked. How the fuck could she leave our baby like that?"

"I don't know. Zaria is fine here. I know that you're her father, and I'm not taking that from you. But Zaria needs a lot of attention, and I know that as much as you would like to give it to her, you can't. Not all day. She will be here whenever you want her, and that way if Juicy stop by, she can see her too."

I was not feeling right about leaving my baby, but I thought about what she had said. I decided that with the war that was coming, maybe it was for the best.

"Okay, Ma. I'm going to take her tonight, and I'll bring her back tomorrow. You can keep all the stuff you have, and I'll get her all new stuff. That way I don't have to keep dragging the stuff back and forth."

"It's going to be okay, son. Juicy just needs time."

"To be honest, I don't know if I have it in me to wait. She been treating me like shit for months, and I continue to kiss her ass. It ain't in a nigga, Ma. I have given that girl all of me, and it's still not enough. I'll be by here tomorrow." After grabbing Zaria, I strapped her in her car seat in the back, got behind the wheel, and drove off.

Juicy had me fucked up if she thought she could keep putting our shit on hold whenever she felt like it. I loved Juicy with everything in me, but I was still me. As I drove, I grabbed my phone, then called my mama to see what kind of store I needed to go to.

"What you want, boy? Y'all showed the fuck out today. Now y'all got my ass over here sucking burnt dick. The fuck I'm gone do with that hard-ass, crispy shit? I like my shit medium well, and you niggas done gave me Cajun."

"First off, Ma, I don't wanna here that shit. Second, that was your favorite child, Blaze, that did that shit. I was gone shoot his ass, but I let him be great once Blaze got hold of his ass."

"You could have stopped his ass."

"Ma, you forgot what that nigga did to me. How the fuck was I gone stop him? I see your ass didn't help, either."

"Fuck no, I didn't. That wig just look like good hair, but the shit was synthetic. A spark would have had my ass looking like a blowtorch."

"Ma, I didn't call you to talk about this. Where can I get some milk from for the baby?"

"Where the slow-ass mama at? How the fuck she don't know that? What the hell y'all been feeding that baby?"

"She left and call herself not coming back. The baby with me now, and I need to know where to go."

"Go to Walmart. They will have everything you need. Clothes and all."

"You fucking tried it. I'm going to the mall tomorrow. You won't have my baby out here looking like buy one, get one free."

"Whatever, nigga. Jerk chicken over here trying to get some. Call me if you need me."

As I hung up, I shook my head in disgust. That lady ought to be ashamed of her damn self.

After pulling into Walmart's parking lot, I got Zaria out of the backseat and walked in the store. As soon as we walked in the door, she started crying.

"Come on, baby. Don't start that shit right now." She ignored my pleas and kept screaming at the top of her lungs. I rushed to the baby aisle and looked at the milk, and the shit was giving me a headache. They had powder, liquid, and different brands. Confused about what I was supposed to get and nearly hard of hearing from the baby screaming, I was ready to say fuck this shit and take her to McDonald's.

"You need some help?" said a female voice behind me.

I turned around and noticed right away that the girl didn't work there. I guessed she was tired of Zaria's screaming.

"Please. I'm lost as hell," I told her.

She reached for Zaria, and I side-eyed the shit out of her ass.

"Just trust me," she said. I let her have Zaria, and she started singing. When Zaria calmed down, I wanted to kick my ass for never trying that. When Juicy was pregnant and having complications, I had sung to her and she had settled down.

Once this girl realized Zaria was good, she passed her back to me. As soon as the baby got in my arms, she started crying again. For the second time in my life, I began to sing in public. "When I see your face, there's not a thing that I would change. 'Cause, girl, you're amazing just the way you are. . . ."

As I continued to sing Bruno Mars's song "Just the Way You Are," the girl started grabbing the milk and water I needed. She walked with me to the register so I could continue to sing to my baby girl. I reached in my pocket, pulled out some bills, paid for my stuff, and walked out the door. The girl carried my grocery bag for me. After I put Zaria in the car seat, the girl passed me the bag. Finally, I got a chance to take a good look at her. She was a different kind of beautiful. She looked exotic but had this innocence about her. Tsunami was ready to attack.

"You're a lifesaver. What's your name?" I said as we stood there.

"Royalty."

"That's your real name?"

She laughed at my question. I guessed she had heard that a lot. "Yeah it is. Are you going to tell me your name?"

"Baby Face, and no, it's not."

"Your baby is gorgeous. Her mother didn't tell you what you needed to get at the store?"

"Her mother is no longer with us."

"Oh, my God. I'm sorry for your loss."

"She ain't dead. Yet." I mumbled the last part.

"This may be bold of me, but take my number, just in case you need me."

I handed her my phone, let her put in her digits, and then she called her number to make sure it worked.

"I'll call you soon," I told her, and then we said our goodbyes.

As I got in my truck, I started to feel guilty. *Fuck that,* I thought. *Juicy is the one who left me. I'm a fucking Hoover. You don't put us on hold when you feel like it.*

Bitch had me fucked up. I was that nigga. She was gone learn that shit quick.

CHAPTER 35

SHADOW

"Bae, what is wrong with your brother? That fool done burnt his own shit off. He is so fucking funny. He thought he had my ass," Kimmie said.

"You don't even know what you started. That nigga not gone stop until he gets the last laugh."

"He ain't gone do shit. His ass don't want these problems."

"I'm just letting you know, when he gets your ass back, it's gone be fucked up. You ever wondered what the hell happened to Mack?"

Looking at me crazy, she got quiet. After many seconds had passed, she said, "No. I didn't want to know."

"All you need to know is he put that nigga's lip in Baby Face's mouth, and they still wasn't even. He don't like for people to have an advantage over him. I promise he won't quit until he gets the last laugh. You better sleep with your eye open."

"*Eye*? Nigga, you acting like I ain't got two."

"Baby, you know damn well one of them motherfuckers is sleepy. You be talking and your shit dead ass take a nap."

"Fuck you and your brothers."

I grabbed her around her waist and picked her up. "You know you just want to fuck Daddy."

"All I know is your ass better not drop me."

Putting her down, I laughed. "You right. Motherfuckers be talking about issa snack. Your ass a whole meal."

She tried to hit me, and I ran up the stairs. As soon as we got to the bedroom, I slammed her on the bed.

"You know I love you, right? No matter what happens as far as the baby goes, it won't change how I feel about you," I told her sincerely.

"Thank you, but I want to be a mother. I want to give you your first child."

"If I can help it, you will. But you have to quit swallowing, though. You can't get pregnant that way."

"Get your dumb ass off me. All you motherfuckers ignorant. Starting with your mama."

"I'm telling on your ass." As I kissed her, I slid my tongue in her mouth, and just like that, playtime was over. I sat up, grabbed her by her ankles, and slid her to the floor.

"Damn, nigga. You done hurt my whole damn back," she complained.

"That bitch got some cushion. Now shut the fuck up. I'm trying to get in them guts." After pulling her pants off, I got her panties off and threw them to the side. Her body was perfect, and I loved every last curve. I leaned her legs back over her head, and then I lay on top of them and started doing sit-ups in her pussy. I needed my nut to go straight to the egg.

"Damn, baby. I don't think I can take this position," she said.

"You gone take this dick, and you gone love it." Going faster, I made sure my dick was reaching the bottom. When I felt her body shaking, I jumped up and put my mouth over her pussy.

"Cum in Daddy's mouth."

And just like that, she did. After catching all her juices, I sat up and slid my dick back in while her body was still going through it.

"Cum on Daddy's dick."

When she started grinding back, I knew my nut was about to make an appearance.

"Cum with me, Daddy."

"Fuck, girl. I'm cumming." Spreading her legs as far as I could, I started slamming my dick hard as hell in that pussy. My curve caused me to lay on her spot.

"Fuck!" she yelled. As she rubbed her clit, her body started shaking, and I came all in that pussy.

Rolling over on my side, I prayed this was our baby. Kimmie got up and went to get in the shower, and I looked at all that ass shaking, and I couldn't believe this was my first BBW. She was so fucking sexy to me. As I was trying to gather my thoughts so I could get in the shower with her, I heard her scream.

"Nigga, you gave me carpet burn. I should beat your ass."

"Girl, it only took off one layer. You got plenty more, so quit crying."

I could hear her talking shit, and I decided to wait to shower by my damn self. She got petty when she was mad, and I was too tired for that shit. When she walked out of the bathroom, I got my ass in, and I couldn't wait to get my ass in the bed. We been fucking nonstop, trying to get her pregnant. We had fucked in Puerto Rico before we jumped on the plane and went straight to Blaze's house. A nigga was tired. I was just happy my shit was working. My ass didn't ever want to go through that shit again. Not even bothering to put on clothes, I lay down on the bed. Kimmie was already sleep before my head hit the pillow. Shortly after, my ass was knocked out.

Hearing a motherfucker laughing, I jumped out of my sleep. This nigga Blaze was standing over Kimmie in the dark. Cutting the light on, I could only imagine what the fuck he was up to. This nigga had a Pampers and was spreading baby shit all over Kimmie.

"Nigga, what the fuck are you doing?" I squawked.

"She thought she was hot shit earlier, when she knocked my lighter out my hand, but now she about to literally be hot shit." Before I could stop him, this nigga flicked his Bic and the shit caught fire. It was the worst smell ever.

"Kimmie, get the fuck up! Get up, before that shit start melting in my bed!" I yelled.

She jumped up out of her sleep and saw the flames.

"How the fuck you didn't feel that shit?" I shouted at her.

She ran her big ass to the shower so fast, the baby shit was flying off her arm.

"Man, your ass getting these shit chunks up before you lay your ass back down," I called after her. I hated this nigga Blaze. I swear, his ass had played all his fucking life. *Who thinks of nasty-ass shit like this?*

Blaze gave me an evil grin. "Hey, nigga, I know why you can't get your girl pregnant."

"Don't start that shit," I snapped.

"Nigga, your damn dick broke. That motherfucker pointing too far to the left. The nut hitting her walls. How the fuck is it gone go up if the motherfucker blind? Nigga, you just out here all wrong, running into walls and shit. Fix that shit. Don't nobody want no hanger in they pussy."

"Get the fuck out of my house, bro."

"Gladly. Y'all need to clean up in here. Your girl's nasty as fuck. It smells like straight shit in this motherfucker, and your ass just in here, asleep."

"Blaze, get out."

"A'ight, nigga. There's a couple of chunks by her pillow, though. You might wanna get that, just in case she sleeps with her mouth open. Then again, maybe you don't care.

You like bitches that eat shit and suck booty holes. Nigga, seriously, though, it's a booty hole."

When he saw me rub my hand down my face, he threw his hands up and walked out. I tried to get the smell out of the room by opening a window. That shit wasn't working, and I wondered what the fuck Spark had eaten for lunch. Her ass smelled like a grown-ass nigga. Kimmie walked out of the bathroom just then, and you could see the steam coming from her ass, she was so mad.

I shook my head. "Don't look at me like that. I told your ass."

"That nigga need to be admitted. He only do this shit because y'all let him."

"You're more than welcome to try to stop him. Oh, and he said you got shit on your pillow. I'm going to the guest room. I can't sleep in here."

"You not gone help me clean this up?"

"Hell naw. I told you, 'Don't start a war with him.' You ain't ready for his kind of petty."

"Fuck your scary ass, then."

"Good night, shitty."

Laughing, I went into the guest bedroom and laid my ass down to get some sleep.

CHAPTER 36

QUICK

"You really not gone give me my phone back? I told you that I wouldn't keep shit else from you."

"Ash, you told me that when I took your ass back, and here we are again. You can quit asking. I'm not giving it back just yet."

"You not slick. You just waiting to see if Jason gone message me."

"Well, duh, dummy. It took you that long to figure the shit out? You know I ain't letting that shit fly. This nigga on his way."

"On his way where?"

"The upper room." When I sang the shit like Eddie Murphy, she sucked her lips and got mad. "You sucking them lips. Come suck on something else."

Her eyes lit up, like she thought that could get her phone back. She could think I was playing if she wanted to, but as soon as I found out where this nigga at, he dead as Paris's edges. Leaning down, she pulled my dick out and started caressing it. Shit felt good as fuck, and I couldn't wait for her to get this big motherfucker in her mouth. As if she could hear my thoughts, she deep throated my shit. Her ass wasn't even playing around with this motherfucker. Before she started getting a good stroke going, her phone beeped, indicating she had a new text message, and I damn near broke her neck when I tried to get up to get the phone.

"I'm sorry, baby," I told her as I grabbed her phone.

"Damn, nigga. Be careful. How the fuck I'm gone tell the doctor I got whiplash from dick?"

"I'll just pull this motherfucker out, and they will understand."

"Shut up."

When I looked down at the phone, I got happy as hell when I saw it was that nigga who had texted.

Can I see my son today?

I texted back, pretending I was Ash. Yeah. Where you want to meet?

Come by the house about nine tonight.

Okay.

When I gazed over at Ash's ass, I got pissed all over again. "Why the fuck this nigga want you to come so late?"

"I don't know. Ask him," she told me.

"It don't matter. You won't be meeting his ass no more. You better pray your ass ain't fucked him."

"Quick, don't play with me like that. I would never cheat on you. This shit is getting out of hand, all because he wanted to see Zavi."

"You should have told the nigga no. Now the nigga can go visit all the kids of mine that didn't make it when you swallowed they ass. He not living to see tomorrow. I'm about to go handle this shit right now."

I threw my Air Max 95s on, and then I headed out the door. As I went, I sent a message to my brothers, telling them to meet me at the main house.

We all damn near pulled up together, and I got out and unlocked the front door. After stepping inside, I cut the lights on and waited for them to come in.

"What's up, Quick?" You could tell Shadow's ass was ready to get back to his girl. He was the only one who didn't miss the life. All he thought about was what if he didn't make it back to Kimmie.

"Ash been going to see that nigga Jason," I explained.

"Damn, bro. Your girl got slip-an- slide pussy too?" This nigga Blaze was actually looking like we had something in common.

"I don't know, my nigga. She said Jason wanted to see Zavi. Her ass been taking my son to see this clown-ass nigga."

"You want to kill him for visiting with your son?" This motherfucker Baby Face acting like we ain't killed for less.

"I'm with you, bro," Blaze said. "You see, Mack's ass had to go. Only nigga fucking my bitch and live to tell about it is me."

"And Baby Face," Shadow added.

That nigga Baby Face turned around and looked at Shadow so fast when he said his name. They were determined to get his ass fucked up. Nigga's hair had just grown back in, and they kicking it back off. When Blaze flicked his Bic, I got back on the subject.

"Look, that nigga don't have claims to my son. He playing on Ash because he wants her back. Nigga told her to meet him tonight. Who wants to play with a kid this late? Not me. Only kids I'm playing with at that time is the nut I'm shooting down her throat. Them bitches be playing hopscotch."

Baby Face shook his head. "She ain't fucking that nigga. Her ass eight months pregnant."

I agreed with Baby Face, but still.

"Nigga, Drea was eight months," Shadow noted.

Me and Baby Face turned and looked at Shadow at the same time. This nigga was on good bullshit. Blaze walked up to Shadow and rubbed his lighter across his lip.

"It's all good, y'all," Blaze assured us. "He just pissed because I rubbed Spark's shit on his girl and set that shit on fire. Now they can be mad together. That's the lighter that had the shit on it."

Shadow took off running, and we fell out laughing. "Nigga, you need a check."

"When you trying to do this? I gotta go get the baby."

"Now, nigga."

I looked at Baby Face like he was crazy. We never let a nigga make it.

When Shadow walked back in the room, we strapped up and headed out. It wasn't close to nine, but I wanted to catch the nigga off guard. After parking down the street, we crept up the block and tried the door to Jason's house. It was unlocked.

"Motherfuckers gone get enough of leaving their doors unlocked," Blaze muttered under his breath.

We crept inside the house and headed upstairs. He had to be up there, because all the lights were off. We eased the bedroom doors open until we found the right room. He was lying in front of a bitch's pussy and was wearing her shit out.

"Nigga, you keep eating the pussy like that, her shit gone be woe," I said in a low voice.

Not giving him the chance to get up, I shot his ass up. Nigga's head didn't even get off the pussy. When the chick started screaming, I shut her up quick. My ass had done got rusty, as I hit her in the eye, though I was aiming for her forehead.

"Damn, nigga. You ain't give us a chance to do shit. We didn't get to have fun with they ass," Blaze groused.

"Nigga, all you wanted to do was burn they ass. Just set the house on fire and let's go," Shadow told him.

We let Blaze do his thing and got the fuck up out of there. I dropped them niggas off and rushed my ass back home. Ash was about to finish sucking this dick.

When I walked in the door, this retarded motherfucker was sitting on the couch, holding Zavi, and they were crying. My dick went soft, and my pimp hand got hard. She was really trying me and pushing me to my limit.

"Son, go get ready for bed. I'll be up in a minute to make sure you good," I told Zavi. I waited until he had walked off, and then I turned to Ash and snapped, "I really pray that it's the baby that got you losing your motherfucking mind."

"Baby, I don't give a fuck about Jason, but he was a part of my life for years. He was the only father your son knew up until recently. We have a right to grieve him."

"You about to have the right to get put to sleep. He was the only father Zavi knew because of your bullshit. You decided to keep my son from me. Don't act like I was a deadbeat and wouldn't be there."

"Whatever the reason is, it don't matter. At the end of the day, he was still there."

"And now he not, so what you saying?"

She shook her head. "You just don't get it."

"And you pushing me to my fucking limit."

I walked off and headed to Zavi's room, with a lot on my mind. Shit was crazy.

CHAPTER 37

DEBRA

I knew everybody trying to figure out how the hell my ratchet ass ended up with a pastor. The day at the wedding, I cursed his ass clean out, but he still wanted me. For some reason, that shit turned me on. A man that could want you how you were and didn't try to change you was a winner in my book. After leaving the wedding, I still had no intentions to mess with Devon.

My kids had their own lives going on, and even though I knew they loved me, they didn't come around that often now. They ass didn't even bother to see if I was okay after the shit with Rico. They made decisions for all of us, and it felt as if you had to deal with it. Don't get me wrong. Rico's ass had to go. That nigga was foul as fuck, but he was the only man I had known. I loved that man with every part of me, and not once had they asked me how I was doing. All they ass did was drop my badass grandkids off, eat, and go back home. Being the G that I was, my ass played shit off cool, but I was hurting bad.

Tired of sitting in the house, crying, looking like the ugly son at the end of *The Color Purple* going, "Hey, Mama," I decided to take my ass to bingo. That was when I ran back into Devon.

As I stepped in the room at the church, I thought, I hope they ass don't be in here cheating. I will tear this church up over my coins. *I took my seat, and then I got aggravated when two old bitches came and sat next to me.*

"Damn all these seats in here and y'all choose to sit by me. You got walkers and shit. Take that mess over there. A bitch ain't got room to stamp her damn card," I snapped.

One lady told me, "You are in a church." She had the nerve to look appalled.

"Good. You can die and have your funeral in the same night. Get the fuck out my face." Knowing I wasn't with the shits, she got her old ass up and left. When I glanced over, I realized she called herself telling. Laughing to myself, I set up my cards and chips at my table.

"Miss, we had some complaints." When Devon realized who I was, he stopped in his tracks. "We meet again, Miss Hoover."

"Just call me Debra. You ain't gotta try to be fancy and shit. We too old to be trying to play games."

"Okay, Debra. It's good to see you again. I see you don't cut people a break even when they in church. Just try to keep it down."

"If y'all leave me the fuck alone, I'll be silent. I'm just trying to play my game in peace."

"Okay, gone 'head. I'll talk to you after, if you don't mind."

I nodded my head so he would leave. The real reason I wanted they ass gone was so I could pull out my cheat cards. Motherfuckers was trying to fuck up my win. As soon as the caller started doing the numbers, I started racking up. My ass cleaned that church clean out. I got all the money. Ain't nowhere for me to go, but, hell, after this shit, I'd rob the devil of his fire if my ass got cold. Laughing at myself, I tucked my money in my purse. The old ladies eased they ass toward me on their walkers, talking shit. When they got to me, I tripped one of them, and she almost had a heart attack while trying to catch herself from falling.

"You don't want these problems. Keep it moving, Blanch," I warned.

"You are something else," said a male voice.

When I turned around, Devon was standing there, and for some reason, he looked sexy.

"Been that way all my life," I assured him. "What do you want with me? We live in two different worlds, and as you can see, my ass ain't gone even be able to look in heaven's window."

"You never know. People change."

"I'll never change. I'm gone die a shit-talking sinner with good pussy. You don't want this in your life. The more you deal with me, the farther heaven gone get from your ass."

"Let me judge that for myself."

Liking his style, my tiger started purring. My shit was too old to be a cat. After grabbing him by his hand, I walked him out to my car.

"Come talk to me, Pastor," I said as I unlocked the car doors.

He got in the car, not knowing I was about to snatch his religion. As soon as he sat down, I grabbed his dick and pulled it out. I sucked that man's soul in four minutes, and he been following my ass around since.

Being with Devon was totally different than being with Rico. He was attentive, and no matter what I said or did to him, he tried to make me happy. We went on dates, took walks, and we read to each other. Granted, I be reading him shit like *She Wanted the Streets, He Wanted Her Heart*, by A.J. Davidson. And I be asleep while he be reading me the bible, but it was the thought that counted. His sex was good as hell too. Never thought a pastor could lay it down like that, but he be taming my ass. Even though I had more money than him, I never spent a dime of my own shit. The only thing I hated was that he was the pastor. Nigga be wanting me at church every Sunday and throughout the week. I done told him I was not fit to be no damn first lady.

"Baby, are you ready?"

Looking at him like he was crazy, I hoped he wasn't talking about church. "For what?"

"I told you I have revival this week. It's a service every day."

"*You* have revival. Who in their right mind would sit in church every damn day, Devon? My grandbaby on her way over here, and my ass is tired. You just fucked my booty hole loose, and you want me to go sit in somebody church. What if the Holy Ghost hit me? Shit juice gone be everywhere."

"You know dang on well the Holy Ghost ain't coming near you. Just do it for me."

"Not today. I'm tired, and we literally just got through fucking. You gone be in church, smelling like burnt coochie. This tiger is woe. I need some rest. Go on now and have a good time. Pray for me, baby."

He just shook his head and left out. God knew I wasn't shit. He had made me. I just hoped He remembered He did this shit when it was time for me to try to get in them gates. I walked to the tub, then ran me some water. A bitch needed to soak after that last session. I was getting too old for this shit.

CHAPTER 38

BABY FACE

With so much on my mind, I headed over to Juicy's mom's house to pick up Zaria. It was crazy how just months ago, a nigga was walking down the aisle and vowing his love forever. Now my bitch gone, and I had no idea what the fuck her problem was. The shit hurt, but I would never admit it to her ass. It had been three weeks now, and she hadn't even called my phone once. As I was pulling up to her mom's house, I saw her car parked in the driveway, and I felt hopeful. When I rang the bell, Juicy answered the door. She rolled her eyes as soon as she saw it was me. You would think I had done something to her bald-headed ass.

"You not gone speak to your husband?" I asked as I stepped inside.

"Hi." She threw her hand up and walked off.

"Juicy, let me talk to you outside for a minute."

"Damn, nigga. All the fuck you want to do is talk. What?" She had an attitude and stomped all the way out the door.

It took everything in me not to lay hands on her ass. When I got out the door, I sat down next to her and just looked at the girl I had given my heart to. She was not the same, and the shit was baffling me.

"What's wrong, baby? Something is obviously bothering you, and I want to know what it is. What can I do to fix it, to fix us?"

"You ain't did nothing. I just need some space. Can't a bitch get a break?"

"Parents don't get to take a break. Married couples don't get to take a break, Juicy. We figure it out and do what we can to get back on track, but I can't do the shit by myself."

"Get a divorce, then, Face. I'm tired, and if you don't want me to get some rest, then leave. I'm not trying to hold you back. As of right now, I'm done. You can have it."

Even though a nigga would kill niggas for less, she had hurt a nigga. I got up, walked in the house, and got Zaria.

"She'll come around, son. Give her time," Juicy's mom said when she met me by the front door.

"She don't have to. Her ass wants space, she got it. With all due respect, fuck Juicy."

When I walked out the door, I saw Juicy was still sitting in the same spot, just staring into space. She didn't even get up to say bye to our daughter. She finally turned her head and looked me in my eyes. I never broke my stare.

I started to sing. "There's never a right time to say goodbye, but we know that we gotta go our separate ways. And I know it's hard, but I gotta do it, and it's killing me. 'Cause there's never a right time, right time to say goodbye." As I sang "Say Goodbye" by Chris Brown, I let a couple tears fall and Juicy cried. Never moving, she just stared at me, with her face soaked in tears.

Finally, I turned away, walked down the stairs, tucked my daughter in her car seat, and got in my car. I couldn't do this with Juicy. If she wanted out, that was what I was going to give her. Driving home, I felt like less than a man. As soon as we got in the house, Zaria started with her normal routine. The screams were piercing my soul, because I shouldn't be here, doing this by myself. My ringing phone brought me out of my trance.

"Hey, is everything okay over there?" It was Royalty, and her voice calmed me.

"Yeah, it's good."

"It don't sound like it's good over there. What's your address? I'm coming over. That baby gone be sick the way you are letting her scream like that."

"I'm not really in the mood for company."

"That's fine. I'm not coming to see you anyway. Text me your address." She hung up the phone, and after thinking it over, I said fuck it. This was what Juicy wanted, right? Why the fuck was I over here, sad and depressed and shit, because my wife had chosen to leave me and my baby for no fucking reason? After texting Royalty the address, I got up and got my baby girl.

"Daddy will never leave you. I got you, Za." Singing to her, I rocked her to sleep and laid her in the playpen. Royalty must have been close by, because my bell rang five minutes later. When I opened the door, I had to tell my dick to sit down. She was in some booty shorts, and that ass was sitting nice. With her hair pulled off her face, you could see her features more.

"I brought dinner. Have you eaten?" she said as she stepped through the door.

"Naw. What you got?"

"Tour of Italy from Olive Garden."

I showed her the kitchen, and we sat down and ate. It was easy to talk to her, and I liked that about her. Before I knew it, I had told her everything about me and Juicy.

"Well, just give her some time. You don't know what's going on with her. Just see if she comes around," Royalty advised.

"Naw, I'm not that nigga. She wanted out, and she got it."

"Good. At least now I don't feel like a home wrecker."

At first, I was not sure what she meant, but I understood clearly when she got up and sat on my lap. Once her mouth touched mine, Juicy was the furthest thing from my mind.

"Tell me you want me," she whispered.

What the fuck? That was my line. Her ass was sitting here, sounding like a whole nigga right now. My mouth betrayed me and made me a straight bitch.

"I want you."

"Take this shit off," she ordered as she removed her own clothes.

Her aggression was turning me on, but it was scaring me at the same time. I was the nigga, and she was in here treating me like a whole ho. My ass damn near felt violated, but I got up and took my clothes off.

"Mmm, perfect," she remarked. She dropped down to her knees and took my entire dick in her mouth. She was sucking my shit so good, my ass felt dizzy. When she stood up and dropped her shorts, I was mesmerized, until she tried to sit on my dick.

"Hold on, Ma. You got a condom?" Being married, I didn't need them motherfuckers no more.

"Naw, but we good." She tried to slide down, but I grabbed her by her waist and stopped her.

"We not good, Ma. I fuck around and fuck you raw today, and then in four months, you got a baby on your back. I'm straight."

"What you mean?"

"It's irrelevant, Ma. The shit ain't happening without a rubber."

"Fuck it, then."

This crazy bitch jumped up, threw her clothes on, and walked out the door. She actually slammed that motherfucker, and I sat there speechless, until Zaria started screaming. I should catch her and beat her ass. These hoes ain't got no manners. I got up, locked my door, and grabbed the baby. I headed upstairs and sang to her until she fell asleep. Then I jumped in the shower, handled my business, and lay down. My mind drifted back to Royalty. She was crazy as fuck, but that shit just had turned me on. I grabbed my phone and called her, and she picked up.

"What's up?" she said.

"You don't have to act like that. You shouldn't want to fuck me without a rubber. My ass could have anything. You don't know me."

"Whatever. Look, is that all you wanted? I'm about to go handle some business." This bitch was hell.

"A'ight. I'll hit you up tomorrow." Looking at the phone, I realized she had already hung up.

Laughing, I closed my eyes. Royalty didn't know who the fuck I was, but she was gone find out soon. I was gone tame the shit out that ass.

CHAPTER 39

DREA

This was the only thing about being a parent that was hard. These kids kept your ass on your toes. I was embarrassed as hell when my baby walked in on Mommy and Daddy being freaky. Blaze's nasty ass had wanted to keep going. People asked me all the time how the hell I dealt with him, but I loved him just as he was. That nigga gave me so much life, and he kept me laughing. That was how I knew we were meant to be. This aggy-ass nigga was my soul mate.

After strapping Spark down, I jumped in the car and headed to Jewel. Walking through the grocery store, I thought about how far we had come. Everything was going great in all our lives. Looking down at Spark, I smiled as she reached for the lighter fluid.

"No, baby, we don't play with that."

Looking up at me with her bright gray eyes, Spark smiled. I swear, this baby was only a year old, and I could tell she was going to be just like her daddy. She was attracted to anything with a flame, and I tried my best to keep her away from the shit. Since she was sitting in the cart, I stepped a couple of feet away to get her some grapes. Thinking she needed to eat more fruit, I grabbed some bananas. I turned around and went to place the items in the cart. Spark wasn't there.

"What the fuck? Spark? Spark, baby, where are you?"

Not wanting to think the worst, I walked around the store, praying she had climbed out of the cart. Starting to panic, I stopped anybody walking by. Nobody had seen. I tried one last time.

"Excuse me, have you seen a little girl?" I asked an elderly man. "She has gray eyes, curly hair, and she has on all pink."

"No, I'm sorry."

Fuck. Blaze was about to kill me.

I ran to the front and had the manager make an announcement over the loudspeaker. "If anybody sees a little girl wearing all pink by herself, please bring her to the front desk."

"Can you give them her description?"

"Ma'am, I'm sure that there is only one baby walking around by herself."

Ready to slap his ass, I let him be great and took off running around the store to look for her. The more time that passed, the more tears fell down my face. Reality was starting to set in: my baby was not in this store.

"Can the mother of the missing child please come to the front desk?" When I heard that over the loudspeaker, I took off running toward the front. Thank God they had found her.

When I got to the desk, I didn't see her, and I didn't understand what the fuck was going on.

"One of our staff members said they saw a man carrying her out of the store and putting her into a van. Was it her father? Do you need us to call the police?"

Ignoring his questions, I took off running to the parking lot. Her shoe was lying by the curb, and I broke down. I grabbed my phone, and then I made the call I never thought I would have to make.

"Baby, get to Jewel right now!" I shouted when he picked up.

"What's wrong, Drea?"

"Somebody kidnapped Spark."

"If my baby not there by the time I make it, you gone be one dead ho." Knowing I didn't want to face Blaze's wrath, I went back in the store and prayed the man had seen the wrong baby.

As soon as Blaze walked in the grocery store, I knew it was about to be all bad. His facial expression showed me he was coming with the bullshit. I didn't expect him to blame me, though. I told him this was on him and his Hoover Gang lifestyle. That was when he choked me and slammed me into the wall. I thought a ho was gone need CPR. It wasn't his normal bullshit as he choked me; he was actually trying to take my ass out. But then he backed off when Baby Face suddenly appeared in front of us.

After reviewing the store's security tape, we left and headed home to get some belongings. Staying at the main house was a good idea, but I wished they had thought of it before these motherfuckers had taken my baby. Wondering if they were feeding her or if she was crying for us was breaking my heart. Why the fuck would they take our child? Our baby girl? She was only one year old.

When we pulled up to the house, I got out, crying. Blaze was trying to look like he had it figured out, but you could tell he was going through it. I didn't mean to blame him, but he was putting the shit on me. He knew damn well the person who had taken Spark was after the damn Hoover Gang. The shit was surreal when I walked in her room and looked at her stuff. I sank down on the floor and broke down.

Blaze appeared in the doorway minutes later. "Baby, I'm gone get her back. Have faith in your man. You're right. This is on me, and I'm going to fix it. I promise to get her back, even if I have to give my own life."

"Nigga, both of y'all better come back. I can't make it without you, baby. I won't go through that again. That was the worst year of my life."

"Bitch, please. You slid on two dicks, and I was gone only six months."

Hitting him in his arm, I started laughing. "Your ass can't stay serious for shit. Come on. Let's pack."

"I'm just saying," he replied before he walked out of the room.

I grabbed some of Spark's belongings and placed them in a duffel, just in case they got her back and we still had to stay at the main house.

Blaze reappeared in the doorway. "Baby, you seen my lighters? I can't find none of them motherfuckers. You hiding my shit?"

As soon as he said it, I grabbed Spark's shoes, and a bunch of Bics fell out. "This shit don't make no sense," I exclaimed.

"That's right. She Daddy's baby. You can't fight that shit."

Shaking my head, I couldn't believe that the harder I tried to keep her from fire, the more she was drawn to it.

"Hurry up. We gotta go," Blaze called.

After taking one last look at her room, I walked out, the duffel in my hand. Praying, I made my way downstairs. I needed my baby to come home, but I didn't want Blaze to give his life, either. I needed both of them, like I needed air to breathe. They were my life, and all I had was them. I couldn't believe this shit was happening now, after everything had been going perfectly.

God, please protect my baby and bring both of them home safe.

CHAPTER 40

BLAZE

"Drea, draw my shit on right. Don't have me walking in the barbershop with my eyebrows leaking and shit."

"You bought the good kind, so it ain't gone do that," she insisted.

"A'ight, 'cause them niggas will clown me for life, and I'll have to burn that bitch to the fucking ground."

"One day your Bic ain't gone work, and your ass gone be in trouble."

"I been thinking about how motherfuckers been trying me lately. I hit up my homie, and I got some shit coming in. Niggas gone walk in silence when they see that bitch."

"Oh, Lord. I thought you retired?"

"From the life, baby. I'm Blaze until I die. Well, when I die for real this time."

She laughed, and it felt like my shit went crooked.

"Stop laughing and shit. Man, if your ass have me walking around looking like I'm asking niggas, 'Hmm?' all day, I'm gone fuck you up."

"Shut up. I got this."

I pulled her down on my lap and started kissing her, and she kept on drawing. My bitch was so fucking fine, no chick out here was touching her. When I pushed her against my dick, she stopped drawing and leaned down to kiss me. I slid her shorts to the side, and then I pulled my dick out and slid it in.

"Girl, I can sleep in this pussy. Damn, baby."

When she started winding her hips, my dick got brick hard. Cupping her ass, I started bouncing her up and down on my dick.

"That's right, girl. Ride that dick." I slapped her ass, and she went harder on a nigga's dick, and I knew I was about to nut. Her pussy was so wet and tight, it was like she was pulling my nut out with her walls.

"Horsie. Horsie." This badass baby had done crept up on our ass.

"Spark, get your ass out of here," I ordered.

"Me horsie."

Damn it. Now her ass thought I was about to play and shit, and I was trying to get a nut.

"Daddy will play with you in a minute. I'm trying to play in Mommy's."

"You better not." Drea slapped me, and I turned my body so she could climb off.

As I slid my blue-ass dick back in my pants, she grabbed Spark's cock-blocking ass. Now, all of a sudden, her ass ain't thinking about no damn horse, and my dick about to bust and shit. When I saw Drea bent over, playing with Spark, I walked up behind her and started grinding my dick against her big ass.

"Baby, stop. I got your child."

"And I got some kids you can swallow. Don't leave me like this please."

"I got you later on. We about to go to the store so I can cook. You can hold off until tonight."

Pissed, I walked off on her ass. Soon as she left the house, Jen the deep throater was getting this nut. My ass was gone watch some porn and nut all on her MacBook.

When her and Spark left, I headed upstairs. I was just getting settled when the doorbell rang. *Fuck*. After putting my dick up, I ran down the stairs and opened the door. Two big, greasy-ass men was on my porch.

"Our boss wants to know if you have an answer," one of them barked.

"The answer is, get your big ass off my damn porch."

"I'll take that as a no."

"Take it as a 'You gone be getting my porch fixed if that motherfucker crack when you move.'"

He smirked at me and walked off the porch. "Sleep light, Mr. Blaze," he called over his massive shoulder.

"Nigga, eat light. The fuck," I yelled back.

Slamming the door, I came to terms with the fact that this nut was gone have to be put on hold, and I hit my brothers up. Whoever these clowns were, they getting real friendly, just showing up at my shit. After I told Baby Face to hit his boy up and find out where these motherfuckers laid their heads, I went upstairs to get dressed. Too pissed to jerk my dick off, I decided to go on and head to the barbershop. I headed out, jumped in the Maybach, and drove off. I hadn't even made it to the city when my phone rang. After seeing it was Drea, I started to let that motherfucker go to voicemail, since she wanted to play with a nigga's nut. But then I thought twice and picked up.

"What, girl?"

"Baby, get to Jewel right now!"

"What's wrong, Drea?"

"Somebody kidnapped Spark." This motherfucker done let somebody take my baby. It was a nigga out here that didn't value their life.

"If my baby not there by the time I make it, you gone be one dead ho." I ended the call, then dialed Baby Face.

When he picked up, I talked fast. "Nigga, tell everybody to meet me at the Jewel down the street from my house. Somebody kidnapped Spark. We need an address on these motherfuckers, like, yesterday."

"I'm on it. We gone get her back, bro."

After I hung up, all kinds of shit went through my mind. When I pulled into the Jewel parking lot, I had murder on my mind. As soon as I walked up on Drea, I grabbed her ass around her neck.

"How the fuck did they get my baby? Where the fuck was you?" I bellowed as I grabbed her.

"I turned away to get her some bananas. She was in the cart. Baby, I'm sorry. I don't know what happened."

Letting her go, I tried to calm down so I could get the story. "Then how the fuck do you know she was kidnapped?"

"Because the guy that works here said someone told him a man walked out of here with her. When I went outside, her shoe was on the ground."

As I punched my hand through the wall behind her, it took everything in me not to fuck her up. "You carried her ass for nine months with a loose-ass pussy and didn't lose her one time. How the fuck did you lose her in a fucking grocery store?"

"Her being kidnapped is because of your lifestyle, not mine. Don't try to turn this shit around on me."

I choke slammed her ass against the wall. I was about to fuck her up. Not because she was talking shit, but because I knew she was right. This shit was all my fault. Knowing what was going on, I shouldn't have let them out of my sight.

Baby Face appeared just then. "Bro, let her go. This ain't the place."

With tears in my eyes, I turned to Baby Face, and I let her down. I knew I was losing it, but this was my seed.

My baby girl. She ain't have nothing to do with this shit. I walked toward customer service, then approached the man at the counter.

"Let me see your surveillance tapes," I ordered.

"You're not authorized to look at them, sir."

I grabbed his fat ass across the counter and put my lighter to his face. "Nigga, I will burn this bitch down. I asked you to show me the tapes, and I won't ask again."

When I let him go, he reached for the phone. Quick, who had dashed into the store minutes ago, pulled his gun and pointed it at him. "I promise you don't wanna do that, my nigga. Just take us to the back and show us the tapes. You get to go home and sleep tonight. Don't try to be the hero."

The man at the counter knew what Quick was saying and motioned for us to come to the back.

"Don't think about calling this in after we leave, either. I will find you, and I will melt your fucking skin off your body," I informed him.

The man nodded and showed us the footage. Out of nowhere, Shadow gave his ass a one-two combo that put the nigga to sleep. I glared at him.

Shadow held up his hands. "Don't look at me like that. When he wakes up, our black asses and the tapes will be gone."

As I focused back on the tapes, I noticed the guy behind Drea on the screen.

"He was following her from the time she walked in the store." I turned to Drea. "How the fuck you didn't realize someone was behind you?"

"Nigga, it's a grocery store. Somebody always behind you."

Everything she said kept making sense, but I didn't want it to. I needed somebody to blame, and I didn't want it to be me. I looked back at the footage. As soon as Drea turned her back, the guy on the screen grabbed Spark and headed out of the store.

I put the pieces of the puzzle together. "So we know it was one of the niggas that came to the house. When Drea left to come here, some other niggas showed up at the door, looking for an answer. When I turned them down, they must have given him the okay to snatch Spark. How long did dude say he needed to find them?"

"He told me he would get back to me as soon as possible. I'm gone hit him up and let him know what the fuck just went down."

"In the meantime, I think we all need to move into the main house," Quick proposed. "We need everybody to be around each other. That's the only way to protect everybody at the same time."

I agreed with Quick, because being in my house would only drive me crazy.

Shadow held up a hand, as if trying to stop us. "Hold the fuck up. Only way I will agree to this shit is if Blaze promise to leave the bullshit at his house." Shadow must be still pissed.

"He been cool lately. He should be straight," Baby Face commented.

A deep frown formed on Shadow's face. "Baby Face, are you smoking dog food? This nigga just threw shit on my wife and set it on fire. This nigga is aggy as ever."

They looked at me in disbelief.

I threw my hands up in the air. "A'ight, damn. I promise to leave y'all weak ass alone. Now let's go. We gotta find my daughter."

As I headed to my car, Drea walked at my side, looking stupid. "Did you really do that girl like that?" she asked.

"Fuck yeah, and you need to be worried about your damn self. You two seconds away from getting your ass fucked up. Meet me at the fucking house, so we can grab some clothes."

Once I was away from everybody, I broke the fuck down. My baby girl was missing because I had let my ego get in the way. All the playing and talking shit done got my baby kidnapped. One thing I knew, there was gone be hell to pay when I found them kidnappers.

CHAPTER 41

BABY FACE

This shit was getting crazier by the minute, but I refused to let motherfuckers come in and hurt my family. I'd put myself on the front line before that shit went down. As I headed to my crib, I called my boy to make some shit happen.

"Jermaine, what it do, nigga?"

"I'm still working on it. My guys are busting they ass to find these niggas. You didn't give me much to go on. There can't be that many cartels being run in Puerto Rico."

"Put a rush on it. I'll pay extra. Listen, when we go out there, we gone need a spot to stay. I need you to buy us some property there. Can you handle that for me?"

"I got you. You called me because you know I can make it happen. Just give me a couple days, at the max. I'm gone try to get it to you sooner, though. Stay out of sight until then. I can't have my friend getting into some shit."

"We got that handled. I'm waiting on your call." After hanging up the phone, I called Juicy's mom and told her that I wouldn't be coming to get Zaria until I handled some shit. The last thing I needed was my baby getting caught up in this bullshit. I could only imagine how the fuck Blaze was feeling. The nigga was like me in a lot of ways, and I knew he over there blaming hisself.

After running in the house, I grabbed some shit, but I didn't need much, because me and my brothers always kept shit at the main house. I jumped in my Hummer and headed over, prepared to calm my family down. I knew they needed me to keep them strong in this situation. Everybody would be panicking, and me being the oldest, I needed to keep shit in order.

When I pulled up, I saw my brother's cars were there, and I climbed out of the Hummer. As much as I hated the situation, it was gone feel good to be around they ass. With the shit I had going on with Juicy, I needed to be around family. When I walked in the house, it was total chaos.

"What the fuck is going on?" I yelled so I would be heard above the din.

"The girls feel like Blaze shouldn't be allowed to bring his lighters in here, and you know what he saying."

I got where the girls were coming from, but at the end of the day, that was who Blaze was. "Look, that nigga been the same for twenty-six years," I said. "He ain't gone ever change, and y'all gone have to get over it. Everybody in this room has been burned by this nigga. Just don't do shit to piss him off. We not here for the bullshit, and we got real life shit going on."

I went on. "This man's daughter has been kidnapped, and y'all sitting here arguing about some fucking lighters. Let his ass be great. Fire calms him. If you take the lighters, you are creating a monster. This nigga done had a lighter since he could hold one. No bitch on this earth gone change my brother. If you that scared, call up your families and go stay there. This is his house, and you will not disrespect him in it. Get the fuck over it, or get the fuck gone."

Blaze nodded vigorously. "That's what the fuck I'm talking about, nigga. Boss up on they ass. Fuck they think this is?"

Shadow scoffed. "Blaze, shut up. The only reason Baby Face taking up for your ass is that he praying you don't light *his* ass up."

I looked over at Shadow, and the look I gave him let him know I was dead ass.

"You know when I'm serious, nigga. Get your girl in check and leave him alone," I said, doubling down. "He needs us right now, and I won't allow anyone to make him feel a certain kind of way in his shit."

"I appreciate the fuck out of you, Face, but don't be talking like they got a nigga shook or some shit. If they know what's best, they would shut the fuck up," Blaze said.

A nigga couldn't even take up for this simple mother-fucker, I thought.

Kimmie got up and rolled her eyes at Blaze. She was gone be a problem if she didn't fix her attitude. Nothing I could do would keep him from cremating her ass.

Blaze's eyes turned to slits. "Walk past me again and roll your eyes. I promise I will set your big-ass calves on fire. You probably want me to. They say heat and sweat makes you lose weight. You want me to melt them bitches in half, sis?"

Kimmie glared back. "Fuck you."

He laughed, and everybody went their separate ways. This mansion was big as fuck and had four different wings. I was sure they could make it without being under each other. I walked out back and stood there, with so much on my mind.

Blaze approached. "Bro, we gotta get her back. That's my world, man."

"I know. We gone get her. You have to trust me. Even if I have to give my life to save hers, she coming home."

"I said the same shit to Drea. No matter what, my baby girl was gone be straight."

"Y'all niggas out here holding hands and shit. Fuck y'all doing?" I heard behind me. I turned around and saw that Shadow and Quick had come outside as well.

"Nigga, you better get Kimmie's ass under control," I told Shadow. "Blaze gone fuck that girl up. I don't know why people insist on trying him. This the pettiest nigga in the fucking world. You would think she knows that by now."

"I be trying to tell her ass. If she wanna poke the bear, that's on her. Bro, just know I ain't in that shit. A nigga got perfect eyebrows. I ain't trying to lose my shit." This nigga Shadow was terrified of Blaze.

"She lucky I gave my word, or I would be thinking of some shit to do as we speak. Too much on my mind. Oh, let me show y'all my new toy I got. Hold on." We looked at this nigga Blaze like he was crazy, but he ran off, and we just stood there in our own thoughts. This nigga came back out the door with a motherfucking flamethrower. He had that shit on his back, looking like he was ready for war.

"Nigga, where the fuck you carrying that big-ass motherfucker?" Quick was laughing, but he looked scared as hell.

"I'm about to try this motherfucker out."

When he turned and aimed it, I moved the fuck back. This nigga Blaze with a flamethrower, issa Cajun. As soon as he pulled the trigger, that fire shot out so fast, it caught Quick in the ass. Shadow pulled out his phone and started recording while Quick ran his dumb ass toward the pool and jumped in.

Blaze squelched a smile. "My bad, bro. I didn't know it shoot that far. For your name to be Quick, you move slow as hell, my nigga."

"Nigga, you set my ass cheeks on fire. The fuck?" Quick screeched.

Me and Shadow had tears in our eyes, we were laughing so hard.

"Y'all gotta see the video. This nigga's whole ass was really on fire." When Shadow hit PLAY on his phone, I looked down at the little screen. I couldn't breathe, I was laughing so hard.

"I'm glad y'all think this shit funny. How the fuck I'm supposed to lay down with crispy cheeks?"

"Nigga, you better lay down on your side," I advised. "For real, though, we all gotta get some sleep. We don't know when this nigga gone call us with the info. We have to be ready."

They all nodded in agreement, and we walked back in the house.

Mama was there waiting for us. "I'm trying to figure out why the fuck I had to climb off my dick to come sleep with y'all raggedy asses?"

"Ma, straight up, we don't wanna hear that shit," I told her. "Go lay your old ass down somewhere. And why the hell you got Devon here when you knew what the hell was going on?"

"Ain't shit old on me, and I'm your mama, so I can say what the fuck I want."

We didn't respond to her bullshit. I looked over at the pastor and waited for him to answer the question I had posed. When he didn't, I asked again.

"Devon, can you explain to me why you are here? At this point, I don't trust no motherfucker, and you dating my mama. She ain't shit, and you a pastor, so what's your motive?"

Ma got in my face. "Nigga, you tried it. Don't play pussy and get fucked. He here because I want him here," she said.

After moving her to the side, I looked at Devon again. "Now that you mention it, his old ass do look like he could be mixed or some shit." Blaze's ass pointed his flamethrower at the pastor, and I didn't stop him. I needed answers.

"Your mama told me what was going on, and I wanted to pray for you all," Devon finally confessed.

Blaze lowered the flamethrower. "Nigga, I wish your ass would bring that churchy shit in here. You won't make it out of here. I talk to God on my own. That's my nigga."

"Blaze, your ass going to hell," Shadow said.

I agreed with Shadow; he didn't give a shit what he said.

Blaze shrugged his shoulders. "It's okay. You know how much fire in that motherfucker."

Shaking my head, I started to walked away. "See y'all in the morning. This too much."

I was gone let Devon make it tonight, but he better pray he legit. When I got upstairs, I lay down, but I was restless. Too much shit was on my mind, and the only thing that would fix that was some pussy. After grabbing my phone, I called Royalty.

"What you on?" I said when she picked up.

"Shit, lying down. What you want?"

"Some of that pussy. Now bring it here."

"I'm on the way."

"I'll meet you there." After hanging up the phone, I eased out of the house without anybody noticing. Royalty was fine, but we didn't bring strangers to the main house.

That was why I was pissed at my mama. I was gone have my guy look into this pastor. I didn't trust his ass, but in the meantime, I was about to go balls deep in some much-needed pussy. On my way, I stopped by the store and made sure I grabbed a box of condoms.

CHAPTER 42

QUICK

When I walked to the pool, I was finally able to do some shit. When Blaze set my ass on fire a few days ago, I could barely sit my ass down. The shit wasn't funny, but every time I walked past these simple motherfuckers, they were laughing and cracking jokes. The water felt good hitting my ass, and I was enjoying the peace by myself.

"Baby, why didn't you tell me you were getting in the pool?" Ash was standing there, looking good as hell. She had barely gained any weight during this pregnancy. Zavi had already jumped in the water, so Ash came in as well. For some reason, the way she walked over to me was sexy as hell. We hadn't been on good terms since I killed that nigga Jason, which meant a nigga ain't been getting pussy. As soon as she was close enough, I grabbed her and pulled her to me. I looked over her shoulder and made sure Zavi wasn't paying us any attention. Then I picked her up, situated her around my waist, and moved her swimsuit to the side.

"Baby, what are you doing? My stomach too big for this, and our son is in the pool with us."

"Did I ask you for permission?"

She shook her head no.

"This my pussy, right?"

She bit her lip and nodded yes.

"Then ride this dick." Before she could respond, I slid inside her. She couldn't avoid the moan that came out of her mouth. I eased her body up and down on my dick slowly, as I was trying not to make it look obvious. She leaned down and bit my lip, and I lost it. I started pushing harder. My dick was brick hard, and this shit wasn't working.

"Zavi, do your pops a favor and go in the house and make me some Kool-Aid."

"Okay, Daddy. I'll do it all by myself."

As soon as he was out of the pool and in the house, I let her down and pushed her against the wall of the pool. After spreading her legs, I slammed my dick back inside her. The water and her juices were giving my dick a vibration, and the shit felt good as fuck.

"Damn, girl. I love this pussy." The louder she moaned, the harder my dick got. After grabbing her by her ass, I rammed my shit in as far as it could go, and we both screamed out at the same time.

"Daddy, I'm cumming."

"Me too, Ma. Fuck." My nut shot out of me, and my knees got weak. This was why my ass was so sprung on her ass. She had the best pussy in the world.

"You motherfuckers nasty as fuck." When we looked up, my brothers were standing there, looking at us.

I splashed some water at them. "Shut up. Why the fuck y'all watching anyway?"

"Nigga, that shit was looking good as hell, and the sounds had me ready to go knock Drea's back out," Blaze commented.

"You ain't got no home training, nigga," Baby Face scolded.

Agreeing with Baby Face, I put my dick up and kissed my girl. I was not ashamed for being on some exotic shit and fucking my wife.

"Bring your bleached-dick ass on. We got a location."

When I heard Shadow say that, I jumped out of the pool quick as hell. After running upstairs, I showered and got dressed. As soon as I walked back into the bedroom, Ash was there, crying.

"I don't want you to go," she blurted.

"Baby, you know I have to. It's either all four of us or none of us. You know how we roll. If it was Zavi, they would be there for me. Don't put me in the position to choose."

"Don't worry. I'll never do that. You would never pick me over your brothers."

"That's the thing. My brothers would never ask me to. You're my wife and the mother of my child. Your well-being will always come first. Just know that this affects us all."

"Just come back safely. We need you."

"I got you, baby. You know I'm coming back. I need some more of that fye-ass pussy." After kissing her, I walked out the bedroom door and went to give Zavi a hug.

After everyone had said their goodbyes, we headed to the airport.

"Face, did you make sure the plane was fueled up? A nigga ain't trying to go down in that bitch before we get there."

"Nigga, we good. We even got a place to stay. I bought us some property. When have you ever known me not to be thorough?"

"Man, I'm just trying to make sure we come back in one piece. What about weapons?" I asked.

Baby Face nodded. "Already taken care of. Nigga, just be ready. You were rusty the last time you pulled the trigger. We can't have any mistakes out here."

"Fuck you, nigga. I'm good," I said.

By the time we got to the airport, everyone was quiet and in their own thoughts. This would be fucked up if we made it through all that shit back home and got here, only for it all to end. We could not let this go bad.

After walking into the new house, we got situated, then met back downstairs to come up with a plan. We couldn't just go in there and get our asses lit up.

"Jermaine gave us a layout of the estate, but a nigga going off memory," Baby Face explained. "We don't know where they are holding Spark, so we have to proceed with caution until we have her. Once we get her, nothing else matters. Get the fuck out of there and make sure we all make it out. Kill anybody that gets in your way. Are we clear?"

"Yeah, nigga. You could have kept that 'We didn't land on Plymouth Rock'–ass speech. We familiar, my nigga," I said. Baby Face was always going into some long, drawn-out-ass speeches.

"Blaze, your ass better take some guns, and not that li'l-ass lighter," I told him.

"Light these nuts. Let's go get my baby girl and get the fuck out of here," Blaze said.

We strapped up and headed out. I'm not gone lie. A nigga was nervous as fuck. We had never taken on an entire cartel before, and it was only the four of us. Trying not to think negatively about the situation, I started playing with my nine. Out of all the guns I used, it was my favorite.

Shadow had been quiet since we left the main house, and it was bothering me.

"Baby bro, what's on your mind?" I asked him.

"This shit just don't feel right," he answered. "We going to their shit, and we walking in there four deep. We supposed to be out of this life, and here we are again, with our life on the line."

"I feel you, li'l nigga, but you a motherfucking Hoover," Blaze declared. "You may never be completely out this shit, and you have to be okay with that. We lived a life and did some things that created some enemies along the way. Just because we done, don't mean they are. We have always come out on top, and we always will. Our bloodline won't let us lose."

I nodded in agreement with Blaze, then went back to cleaning my shit. When we pulled up, I looked at the only niggas in the world that had my back, and I knew we would be okay. Plus, nobody was colder at this gunplay than me. I knew only one other nigga, and he had retired. After stepping out of the car, we looked at each other and then headed into what could possibly be our last hurrah.

CHAPTER 43

BLAZE

The entire time, I tried to play this shit cool. To be honest, this was the first time I was actually scared of something. Don't get shit twisted. I was not scared of no nigga that walked this motherfucker like I did, but I didn't know if my baby was still alive or if I would make it out with her. She didn't deserve this shit, and it was fucking with me.

Everybody kept making these cracks, like my lighter ain't shit, but niggas have feared me for twenty years behind this Bic. My gunplay was serious, but the things I could do with fire was ridiculous. They could talk that shit, but my lighter could do just as much damage. Even though I wanted to burn they fucking flesh off, this was not that type of situation. A nigga needed to be on point and to remember that I couldn't use fire this time.

Too many thoughts were running rampant in my mind, and a nigga was trying to keep busy. Everybody always looked at me as the strong one, the one that didn't give a fuck, so nobody really checked to see how I was actually doing behind this shit. A nigga was hurting bad, but I promised I would die before I left my baby with these fuckers. Only thing I was scared of was Baby Face easing his pretty ass back to the States and fucking my bitch again. When the car stopped, I knew I had to get my shit together in order to pull this shit off. As I stepped out, I looked at this big-ass estate and got discouraged.

"Nigga, how in the fuck are we supposed to know where to look in this big-ass house?" I said, keeping my voice low. Baby Face hadn't said we were coming to a mini fucking island.

"I told you Jermaine said he didn't know where she was. We just have to look," Baby Face answered.

"If we make it past the gate and into the fucking house, we don't know where to look. We have no idea what part of the house my baby girl is in." As soon as I said that, a room on the lower floor caught fire. "Niggas, let's go! If Spark is my child and ready pussy didn't play my ass, my baby girl set that room on fire."

"Let's go!" Quick and Shadow said in unison.

After making sure our silencers were on, we hopped the gate and took out the first line of security. Actually, Quick did. By the time I raised my gun, those guys were already hitting the ground. As we headed into the house, Shadow and Baby Face took out the next set of guards. I ran straight for the room that was on fire. When I walked in the door, Spark was choking from the smoke and a candle was knocked over. Who the fuck lit candles in a room with a toddler?

I grabbed her, and then I walked out of the room and down the hall with tears in my eyes. I gazed down at her. She was okay, and I could take her home. When I looked up, I saw a man across what appeared to be the living room. He was standing there, smirking, with his gun pointed at me. I kissed my baby girl, and then I turned my back and held her as tight as I could. There was no way I was letting one of the bullets hit her. I would take them all for my baby.

"Never forget that Daddy loves you, baby."

"Me love Da."

Smiling, with tears falling down my face, I closed my eyes. Hearing his gun go off, I braced myself for the hit. A body fell against me, and I turned to see what had happened. Baby Face was lying there, choking on his own blood. *Fuck.* He must have jumped in front of the gunfire to save me and Spark. Quick came through the front door and aired the man out. Shot him at least ten times. He was dead and no longer a threat.

"Face, what the fuck, man! Why did you do that?" I cried.

"Y'all get out of here. Make sure she gets home safe. I had to protect you. I love you niggas."

"Nigga, naw! Get up. Face, you have to get up!" I told him. When his eyes closed, my heart shattered. I passed the baby to Shadow, and then I grabbed Face and threw him over my shoulder.

"Quick, shoot anything that moves. No nigga can outshoot you. I need you to be all of us right now and lay they ass down," I said.

"You know I got you, bro. Let's go."

As he ran toward the door, Quick was shooting niggas left and right, but they were still coming. I shot out of there like a bat out of hell and barely made it to the car. After Quick and Shadow jumped in, I put the closest hospital in the GPS and headed there.

"Call our doctor and tell him to get on the next plane out. If Face pull through, we can't let him stay at their hospital. He will be dead by morning," I said.

Quick grabbed his phone and made the call. As soon as we pulled up at the hospital's emergency entrance, I grabbed Face and rushed him inside. The nurses came running toward us, and they put him on a stretcher. They checked him over and started spitting out orders.

"No pulse. Get him to the OR stat. Let's go, people. We have a code blue."

I walked over to Shadow, who was holding Spark, and I grabbed my baby girl and cried as I held her. My brother might die because he had saved us, and that shit was hurting a nigga's soul. We headed into the waiting room and sat down. Sitting there silently, I was consumed by my own guilt, until a doctor came out four hours later to talk to us.

"It was touch and go for a while. He coded a few times, but we were able to get the bullet out that was impinging on an artery. We repaired it, and he is stable. He will be in a lot of pain and probably out of it until tomorrow, but he is fine."

"Thank you for saving my brother, Doc," I said.

Finally able to breathe, I sat down and thanked God for keeping my brother. This war was far from over, and this was the first time I felt like we wouldn't make it out.

After sneaking Face out of the hospital, we took him to the house, and our doctor was there, waiting on him. After the doctor hooked him up to the IV and a heart monitor we had stolen from the hospital, he monitored Face and told us he just needed to heal. When Face opened his eyes the next day, I could fully relax my mind.

I edged closer to the side of his bed. "Bro, you good?"

"Yeah, but the shit hurt like hell."

"Don't ever do that shit again. You have a baby at home, and she needs you. I know you were looking out for me, but that shit would have ended a nigga. You the only father we know, and we need your ass."

"Your baby girl need you too, Blaze. Plus, you already died once. Nobody would have believed your ass was gone for real this time. You can't be around here faking deaths and shit."

Shadow stepped up. "I'm just glad you okay. We the fucking Hoover Gang. It's all of us or none of us."

I looked at Shadow like he had lost his mind.

"Nigga, y'all ain't die with me. Fuck out of here," I said. "That only work when we robbing banks and shit. I'm not killing myself if one of y'all go. You got me fucked up. Ain't no pussy in hell. I died before, and the shit wasn't that great."

Quick wagged a finger at us. "Why you niggas can't be serious for once? This shit is fucked up."

Quick had a point, but hell, laughing was good for the soul when everything in your life was going fucked up.

"Y'all know this shit is far from over, right?" I said, getting serious. Everybody got silent, and I knew they agreed. "There's too many of them, and this is a war we may not win."

"It's a war I'm not willing to lose. These niggas tried to kill you while you were holding your daughter. I damn near died, and I'm not stopping until somebody dead." Baby Face was dead set on going to war.

"Nigga, that *somebody* gone be our ass. We can't go up against they ass. We not deep enough. We barely made it out."

"We just gone have to keep breaking they ass down. They lost some soldiers today, and if we keep hitting them, they will lose more and more," Baby Face insisted.

"Your decision is to go to war?" Shadow asked.

Baby Face nodded, and I could see the fear on Shadow's face.

"You know what that means, then, right?"

"What's that?"

"We have to make a call. We need to call Lucifer."

CHAPTER 44

GANGSTA

"I can't wait to get you upstairs. From the print in your pants, I can tell you have a big, long black dick."

Smirking, I picked her up and placed her around my waist. "You have no idea. Now shut the fuck up. You doing too much talking."

"Damn, Daddy. I like that rough shit."

I grabbed her around her neck and squeezed as hard as I could without snapping it. "What the fuck did I say? If you say another fucking word, you're gonna piss me off, and trust me, you don't want that."

I walked up the stairs, then into the bedroom, and laid her down on the bed. "Since you like it rough, give me something to tie you up with."

She reached in her drawer and gave me three neckties. I was guessing they were her husband's.

"Damn! I forgot my condoms. Give me a second." I ran out to my car, grabbed my bag, and headed back in. She was still lying in the same spot, but now she was playing in her pussy.

"Did I tell you to start without me? I see you think you can do what the fuck you want, but that shit about to change," I told her.

Taking her hands, I tied her wrists to the headboard with two neckties. I took the last tie and gagged her with it. The anticipation in her eyes was obvious. She wanted a nigga bad, but I wanted her more. Sitting on top of her, I licked my lips, and her eyes begged me to stop teasing her. I raised my hand, and I stroked her face with the back of it.

In one swift motion, I punched her in her throat. Her eyes bulged out of her head, and a look of confusion filled her eyes. After placing my hand over her mouth and nose, I took the remaining air that she had, and watched as she took her last breath. Once I was satisfied she was gone and wouldn't be able to scream, I got up and grabbed my pocketknife. After slicing entry points all over her body, I took the knife and started peeling her skin off.

When I had her entire face off and had removed the skin on her body, I grabbed my pliers. I pulled each tooth out of her mouth, then packed up all the remains and left just as quietly as I had come. After I jumped in my rental, I drove off, feeling satisfied. When I was about ten miles away from the scene, I let my window down and removed my gelled fingerprints. Then I tossed her remains out the window, and I was ready to go. I headed back to the private plane, jumped on, and reflected on the day's events. Paradise had no idea where I was, and I intended to keep it that way. A nigga supposed to be retired, but every now and then I took on a job. Going from being the highest-paid hit man and the most feared killer to a husband and father had been a hard transition for me.

I had promised my wife and brother I would stay out the game, but I couldn't. This shit was in my DNA, and I felt like life was passing me by. Something about peeling the flesh off a motherfucker gave me a rush like no other. After the shit with Journey, I had promised never to cheat on my girl again. When a nigga took on a hit, I made sure I didn't actually give these bitches the dick, but I sold them a dream in order to get in their world.

Just in case motherfuckers didn't know who I was, I had no problems letting them know. I was Kenneth "Gangsta" Jamison. Known to most people as the Devil or Lucifer. I had picked up that name after the world had realized the way I preferred to kill. My brother Suave had that same monster inside him, and he could be sick when he wanted to be. The difference was he killed only when he had to, I did it for sport.

Well, we used to. Nowadays, all we did was have playdates with the kids or trips with our wives. I needed to kill like I needed to breathe. I was not gone sit here and reflect on my entire life or how I had got this way. That was why I had agreed to let Latoya Nicole write my story. I thought it was dope how she had titled it *Gangsta's Paradise*. Her ass did such a great job that Suave allowed her to do his and Tank's story. I didn't know why she picked that dumbass title *No Way Out*, but the story came out dope as fuck. She mastered that shit and covered every part of our life, but I didn't like how people walked up to me and thought they knew me.

I was a different type of nigga than people were used to. I was wicked with a gun. It would take me only seconds to lay down a roomful of niggas, but I preferred to torture people. My thrill came from cutting niggas up and removing tongues and shit. Realizing that life was behind me now, I looked forward to the random jobs I got. I didn't know what this bitch had done to her husband, but he had paid me a million dollars to make sure they couldn't identify her.

The plane ride was quick since I had come from Miami. My brother had convinced me to come out to Hawaii and live near him and his family. When he'd retired from the drug game, he had relocated there. I still didn't see how he had given all that shit up. He was the biggest kingpin Chicago had ever seen, and he had walked away from it all. Whenever I asked him if he missed it, he would always give me some politically correct–ass answer. He could tell that shit to somebody else, but I knew him, and I knew that he wouldn't have chosen this new life if it wasn't for his family.

After I landed at the airport, I jumped into my Maserati GT and headed home. As I stepped through the door, I made it my business to be quiet as hell. I snuck into the bathroom and took a shower without waking my wife. But as I was climbing into bed with her, I woke her up because I needed some pussy. No one could get my dick harder than a dead body. The rush I felt after a kill took me to different heights.

I slid in between her legs and sucked hard enough to wake her up completely. My sex was always aggressive after a kill. The best thing about Paradise was, she never turned me down when it came to sex. After flipping her legs back, I slapped her hard as hell on her ass. Then I slapped her across her pussy, and she moaned and reached for my dick. I snatched her up by her hair, flipped her over again, and then pushed her head down in the bed.

"Spread your ass cheeks open," I ordered.

As usual, she did as she was asked. As I watched my dick slide in her pussy, a nigga couldn't help but moan. I'd had my share of bitches, but my wife had the best pussy in the world. I slammed my dick into her nonstop, and she took that shit and threw that ass back. Feeling my nut rise, I pulled out.

"Come catch this nut," I said.

Barely able to turn around after the punishment I had just put on her pussy, she opened her mouth. I grabbed her by her head and fucked her face until my nut shot down her throat. I pulled back, and then I lay down.

"I love you, girl," I told her.

"I love you more, G." And her ass was back asleep within minutes.

"Baby, wake up. Suave is here and wants to talk to you."

Groaning, I rolled over and looked at the time. It was one in the afternoon, so I got my ass up and handled my hygiene. When I walked downstairs, Suave was sitting in my office.

"What's up, big bro?" I said as I entered the room.

"Where have you been going in the plane?"

"Damn, nigga. At least greet me when you walk in my house."

"What's up, baby bro? Now tell me where the fuck you been going."

I shrugged. "On trips for my business. Why? What the fuck is the problem?"

"The problem is your ass is lying. Nigga, you been doing jobs, and I told you that shit is dead. You said you were leaving that life behind. We almost didn't make it out the last time."

Him and Paradise both used that over my head when they wanted to keep me on board. Paradise was the heiress to the Garzon Cartel, and we had had to take out her punk-ass father. They kept saying we had barely made it, but we had. We'd taken out their entire organization, and the only motherfucker we had left behind was her mama and the dog. This nigga acted like we still got enemies out here and shit.

"Look, that's a part of me. In order for me to stay out of that life, I have to indulge in it here and there. I be needing a fix," I explained.

"I'm gone fix the plane on your ass, and you ain't gone make it back next time. Keep playing with me, nigga."

"That was almost convincing. A nigga damn near believe your ass." We both burst out laughing when I said that.

Our laughing was cut short when my phone rang. As I looked at the number, I knew something had to be wrong. He hadn't called me in years. I looked at Suave and gave him the "Something is up" face.

"The fucking world must be ending if this nigga Blaze calling me." I picked up on the third ring. What up, boi?" I said into the receiver.

"Nigga, you don't fuck with me. Baby Face your nigga."

"Yeah, you right. Your ass play too much, and I'll be done fucked your ass up. What's up, though? You hitting me up for a reason?"

"Long story short, my daughter was kidnapped, and Baby Face got shot up trying to save us. We all made it out, and we good, but the war ain't over. There's too many of them to go up against, and we need your help. We need Lucifer. I know you retired and all, but we need you."

"I'm on the way," I assured him.

CHAPTER 45

SUAVE

This nigga Gangsta thought he was slick. The log at the airport showed that he was leaving in the plane once a month. He knew we had given that shit up. The way the shit had been going, our ass would have been dead if we had kept moving in the same way. I was a calm, subtle nigga, and I wasn't into wars and shit. My name spoke volumes, and all that rah-rah shit wasn't for me. My world had literally got flipped upside down when I met my wife, Tank.

Not only had she got a nigga to settle down, but she had also come with a lot of baggage and a war that wasn't mine. I was retired when G had needed my help with the cartel, but I was done. Almost losing my wife had changed my perspective. Since I had more money than I could count, a nigga didn't need to still be out here in these streets. Not to mention my girl and her crew thought they hittas like us.

I climbed out of bed now so I could go holla at my brother. I needed to know what he was into and if it could affect us all.

"Where you going, baby?" Tank asked me.

"I'm going to holla at Gangsta for a minute. I'll be back in a few. Have me some food done, and be naked when I get back."

"You don't give this pussy a break."

"You want me to give this dick to somebody else?"

"I gave up the street shit because you asked me to, but I still got my heat. Don't make me use it," she countered.

"What did I tell you about threatening me? Check your tone before I check it for you."

She looked at me crazy, but she shut her ass up. I was Kendyl "Suave" Jamison. The biggest kingpin the Chi had ever seen, but I had left it behind for her. Even when I'd been in the streets, I'd never raised my voice. I didn't have to do all that. When I spoke, motherfuckers knew I meant business.

After throwing on my clothes, I headed out and went to my brother's spot. He stayed only five minutes from me, so I did my daily jog over there. Paradise let me in and made my way to Gangsta's home office. When he walked in a few minutes later, I knew he was about to lie to me. After finally getting him to tell me the truth, I got where he was coming from. Hell, I missed the shit all the time, but it was about priorities. That ain't our scene anymore. I had left it all to my nigga Smalls, and I made money while sitting back and relaxing. It had been a couple of years since I had even fired a gun.

Realizing it was Blaze on the phone with my brother, I knew it couldn't be good. Face had run with us back in the day, but he had his own crew then and now. They didn't have friends. It was just his brothers, the Hoover Gang. Not being able to hear what Blaze was saying, I hoped Gangsta put the call on speaker, but he didn't.

"I'm on the way." When my brother hung up the phone, he turned to me, and I knew in that moment, we were going back into the life.

"Where you going, G?" I asked him.

"You mean *we*, nigga. If I go to war, I need to know the person I trust most is on the battlefield with me."

"You trying to get me divorced? Hell, are you trying to piss off Paradise?" She was the only person I knew who was sick like my brother. He would never admit it, but he was scared of her ass.

"You know damn well we don't have a choice in the matter. They like family, and we can't leave them out there like that. They kidnapped Blaze's daughter and shot up Face. They still coming for the Hoover Gang, and Blaze and his brothers need us."

"Who is 'they'?"

"Nigga, I don't know shit. He said 'they,' so I'm saying 'they.' All I know is it's a cartel in Puerto Rico. We will get all the details when we get there. We at least have to go to hear them out and find out what the fuck is going on."

I ran my hand over my face, thinking. As much as I wanted to say no, we couldn't. We didn't live by that code. They knew we were retired, and the fact that they had still called meant it had to be bad.

"If we do this, we can't leave for a couple of days," I said.

"They could be dead in a couple of days."

I raised my hands in front of me. "Nigga, we could be dead if we don't try to butter our wives up first. I'll call Smalls and have him and his crew keep an eye on them until we get there."

"You scared of Tank's ass, huh?"

"Don't get beat the fuck up. You know damn well I ain't scared of shit. Get fucked up if you want to," I muttered.

"We ain't kids no more. I will lay your ass out."

"Lay on deez nuts."

"I don't play that gay shit, bro. Pull that shit out if you want to. I'll cut that shit off and feed them bitches to your wife and tell her it's hard-boiled eggs." I stood up and walked in his face. "What you saying, nigga? All this talking you doing ain't moving me."

"Sit your old ass down. Fuck around and have a stroke if I sneeze on your ass." He laughed, but G knew not to fuck with me. He had learned everything he knew from me. That nigga knew what it was and didn't want these problems.

"Do something special for your girl before she beat your ass."

"A'ight, bro. Holla at me with the specific time," I said.

After I left his house, I decided to make my call before I got home. Tank was going to go the fuck off when she heard the plan, and most importantly, she was gone try to go with me. But she wasn't going this time around. I didn't know what we were up against, and I wasn't having that shit. I dialed Smalls, as I needed him to look out for the fam in my absence.

He picked up on the first ring. "What up, nigga? Is something wrong with the payment? I counted that shit myself, so it should be good."

"Naw, it's straight. I know you legit. I need you to do me a favor. You know the Hoover Gang, right?"

"Yeah, I remember them from back in the day. You were close to the oldest brother."

"Yeah, he needs my help, and it looks like me and G are back in the game until we help them out of this situation," I explained. "I need to smooth this shit over with Tank, so I need you to make sure they straight until I get there."

"Say no more. You know I got your back, and when you get here, count me and my crew in. Whatever it is, it don't matter. Shit been boring around here anyway."

"You sound like G's ass. This nigga been sneaking and doing hits," I revealed.

"I don't think you thought about the real problem you gone have."

"What's that?" I asked.

"Nigga, Blaze and Gangsta in the same room. I don't even know Blaze all that well, but he disrespectful and ignorant as fuck. Nigga will set anybody on fire."

"That's his nigga, so they gone be straight, but it is gone be funny as fuck to see. On some serious shit, though, make sure you have the crew ready. We trying to be in and out that bitch. I don't need Tank's ass coming down there on no rah-rah shit," I said.

"Y'all talk that good shit, but she done saved your life a couple of times. My bitch the one that can't fight. Bald-headed ass can't even fight the perm on her edges right. I ain't never seen a motherfucker with hair that nap up a few hours after they get a perm. I be begging her ass to get a sew in. She talking about she going natural. Look like I married a fucking sea monkey."

"Nigga, you ignorant. I can't wait to see your ass."

"Enough with that soft shit. Shoot me the info, and I'll see you in a couple of days," Smalls said.

After hanging up the phone, I walked in the door and prepared to do some major ass-kissing. This was gone take some finessing, but at the end of the day, Tank had no choice but to roll with it. For some reason, now that I knew I was going to war, I was excited. Murder always got my blood moving.

CHAPTER 46

TANK

Rolling over in my bed, I thanked God for another day. He had brought us out of some shit, and I was grateful for being given the chance to be with my family. Knowing Suave wanted food ready when he got home, I got my ass up and jumped in the shower. I knew not to play with him. He was one of those silent threats and killers. He was one of the sweetest people ever until you crossed him. In the beginning, we had bumped heads a lot, because he wanted me to quit acting like a street thug and be the mother to our child. That was who I was, though. Lashay Wright, a bitch from the streets. But to keep a happy home, we had both agreed to leave that shit in the past and raise our son. His name was Kendyl Jamison, Jr., but we call him Deuce. Our big boy was now two years old.

When Gangsta had moved here, I had thought it was going to be hell. That man had scared me so bad that if he walked in the room, I had goose bumps. Over time, we had grown close, but he still had ways about him that shook my ass to the core. Having a baby had changed him and Paradise. I'd never met a couple that was equally sick in the head. Laughing at my own joke, I went in the kitchen and started making some steak, potatoes, and asparagus. Feeling my pussy jump, I knew Suave had walked up behind me. I turned around, then kissed him and sucked on his bottom lip.

"The food will be ready in a minute, baby."

"Fuck that food. Go get dressed. I want to take you out," he told me.

Looking in his eyes, I knew there was some bullshit in the game. "You're not going back," I said quietly. If I didn't know anything else, I knew my husband. Even though he was calm and laid back all the time, he had a certain look in his eyes when he was about to kill somebody. Knowing he had no enemies here, that could only mean one thing.

"What did I tell you about demanding some shit with me? I'm the nigga, and you my wife. Act like it."

"No, *you* act like it. How could you make that decision without talking to me first? You just said I'm your wife. Then, I should have a say-so."

"It's not for good. I just have to go help my people. It won't take long," he said, almost pleading.

"How many times have we been through this? We barely made it out the last two times. You have a child to live for, and I'm not about to let you go and possibly get hurt over somebody else's shit."

"Loyalty means everything to me, and I need you to understand that there are some people in my life that I have to be there for no matter what. If something happened to Smalls or Nik, do you think I would sit here and not do shit?"

"I get what you are saying, but the minute you said, 'I do,' and had a child, we became your top priority," she pointed out.

"Lashay, you are wasting your breath. This is not negotiable, baby. I'll be back soon." When he walked up to my face, I knew he was about to threaten me. His eyes went cold. "Hear me well. If you even think about showing up, you won't have a husband when it's over. Stay here with our son and make sure he is good. I'll be back."

"You think I'm letting you go without me?" I replied.

"You heard what the fuck I said, and I have never been in the business of repeating myself. Stay your ass here, or lose me."

I stalked away from him, went in the bedroom, and slammed my door. This was the Suave that I didn't like. A bitch and her crew was just as cold with the gunplay as him and his boys. Hell, I had saved his fucking life more than once. How could he even think about making me stay here? I grabbed my phone and called Paradise.

"Hey, sis. Can you meet me at Starbucks? We need to talk," I said before she had a chance to speak.

"When?"

"Right now. And don't tell Gangsta where you are going."

"A'ight, but it better be good. If you have this crazy motherfucker ready to fight me, it better be worth my while."

After hanging up the phone, I put on my running gear and acted like I was going for a jog to clear my mind.

"Baby, keep an eye on Deuce. I need to clear my head, so I'm going for a run," I told Suave.

"I got him, but don't play with me, Lashay. Try me if you want to, but I'm gone hurt your fucking feelings."

"Yes, massa, I heard you. I'll be back."

As soon as I got out the door, I took off running. I didn't want him trying to follow me, and I didn't trust that he wouldn't. When I walked in Starbucks, Paradise was already sitting at a table, sipping on a Frappuccino. I headed to the counter and ordered me a Vanilla Frappuccino and sat down.

Paradise frowned at me. "Why you got me lying to Lucifer and sneaking out of the house and shit?"

"Has he said anything to you about going somewhere?"

"Naw, he ain't said shit. Where the fuck he going?"

"Somebody need their help in Chicago, and they going back to their old ways to help a motherfucker I don't even know. Then the nigga said if I try to pop up, he leaving me."

Paradise leaned back in her chair. "Let me guess. You want me to go with you."

"Yes. The last time he went on his own, without me, I almost lost him. I'm not going through that again."

"I'm a rogue bitch, so you know I don't mind going with you. All I ask is you really think this over and figure out if it's worth you losing your husband over. Suave is not the type of nigga that give idle threats. He the craziest of us all, because he is the quiet before the storm. If you're willing to lose it all to save his life, then I'm down."

"If he leaves me for making sure he good, then so be it. At least he will be alive to help raise our child," I responded.

"We have another problem. If they leave in the plane, how the fuck we gone get there, and how we gone get our weapons through baggage?"

"Bitch, we can fly commercial. We just gone go first class. My crew in the Chi will have weapons for us there. Let me worry about that, but please don't say anything to Gangsta. The only thing I need you to figure out is where they are going."

She stood up from the table. "I got you, but I gotta get out of here. A bitch might have to suck some toes or something for this info. You gone owe me, bitch. Babysitting duties for six months."

"Damn, bitch, and your baby bad as hell. I never seen a one-year-old li'l girl get into the shit that she does," I said, grinning.

"Not my problem." Laughing, she left the table and walked out the door.

I grabbed my phone and called my crew.

"Guess what, bitches? I'm coming home."

CHAPTER 47

PARADISE

After all me and my man had been through, married life was great. Me and G had been through the unthinkable, but it had made our shit stronger. We were made for each other and had a bond like no other. Name another couple that enjoyed decapitating a nigga together. We were one and the same when it came to that stuff, but we had given all that up to be parents. Our daughter, Kenya, was one, and I swear, she was bad as hell. You could tell she had our genes, and I prayed for whatever nigga was gone be her man.

When I walked back in the house, it looked like a tornado had hit it. My ass had been gone only fifteen minutes, so how the hell G had let Kenya do this shit that quick was beyond me. When I made it to the bedroom, I could see how. His ass was knocked out, and she was using a marker to write on my red bottoms. Somebody was about to die. This nigga had done lost his damn mind. He knew our baby was bad as fuck, so why would he go to sleep on her?

He was already in the doghouse. His ass thought he slick, because I ain't said shit, but I knew he had killed somebody last night. The only time G had sex like he trying to rip me open was after a hit. I wanted to give him a chance to tell me hisself, but the nigga walking around like it was sweet. Most of the time, I let shit slide, because of the guilt I always felt. See, G was already a monster, but I had turned him into Lucifer. Literally had trained him to be the hit man he was today. And he threw this in my face anytime I wanted him to be normal. Back then, I had been a young bitch that wanted a nigga as crazy as me, and I had seen the potential in him.

I was Paradise Garzon, the daughter of Louis and Mary Garzon, and head of the Garzon Cartel. Growing up, I had been trained by the best, and I had needed a nigga as crazy as me. When I'd seen the monster that G possessed, I'd known I could mold him into the most feared nigga to walk the streets, teach him to cut off his feelings and kill in such a way that motherfuckers would be scared to sleep at night. He was Gangsta, but I had turned that nigga into Lucifer himself. When I'd got older, I'd wanted that nigga to show feelings and emotions, and he ain't have shit for a bitch. He had been working hard to show me, now that we were married, but I could tell it was still a struggle for him.

We had both agreed to turn in our machetes for bottles and diapers. Now his ass done reneged on that agreement. Now his ass planning on going back without me, and he got me fucked up. Tank was pissed, but I had played it cool at Starbucks. Little did she know, I was ready to kill his ass. Not for going back, but for leaving me behind. How the fuck you gone be having a good time, slicing niggas up, and I was stuck at home, changing shit diapers?

I didn't want G to slip back to the nigga he once was and completely turn into the devil, as I would rather have the family life. A bitch would be lying if I said I didn't miss the power, though. The feeling I got when I rode a nigga's dick and sliced his throat was like no other. When people looked at us, they automatically thought he was the worst one. That was far as fuck from the truth. G ain't have shit on me, and he knew it.

After grabbing my red bottoms that Kenya was writing on, I slung them at his ass.

"Wake your ass up, nigga," I shouted.

He blinked up at me. "What the fuck, Paradise? You be doing the most. A nigga been letting you make it, and you pushing me."

"Look at my fucking shoes! Why the hell would you go to sleep on her, knowing how bad she is?"

"Because I was fucking tired. Damn. You should have taken her with you."

"Tell me why you tired, G," I taunted.

He got the dumbest look on his face and acted like he ain't hear me. He got out of bed, reached down to pick Kenya up off the floor, and tried to play with her, like we weren't in the middle of a conversation.

"You heard me. Why the fuck is you tired, G?"

"Shut the fuck up sometimes. Damn. Your ass talk too fucking much. I'm tired because I am. Get the fuck out of my face."

As soon as he placed Kenya back down on the floor, I ran up on him so fast, he didn't have a chance to react. As I charged his ass, he flew onto the bed, and I climbed on top of his ass in one swift motion. Before he could say anything else, I had my knife to his neck.

"What you not gone do is disrespect me, because you don't want to tell your wife the fucking truth," I growled. "We done been down this road, and I be damned if I go back. If you ever disrespect me like that again, I will send your ass to your mama. Fuck with me if you want to."

The adrenaline that was rushing through me quickly faded when I saw his eyes change over. As I looked into them bitches, it felt like I was looking right at the devil. All his emotions were turned off now, and I knew I was in for a fight. No matter how crazy and tough I was, this G scared me. Hell, he scared everybody. Before I could try to calm the situation, he grabbed the knife from me. I didn't even get the chance to fight to get it back. As soon as he snatched it, my ass was on my back, and he was on top of me.

"I told you before if you ever pull another weapon on me, you better kill me." He grabbed me around my neck, then started choking all kinds of snot out my ass. My ass was getting dizzy, and looking at him, I knew he wasn't going to let go. G was no longer here, and Lucifer had now taken over.

Knowing my fate if my ass just lay here, I reached back and punched his ass so hard in his face, his head snapped back. When he looked back into my eyes, I saw that his lip was bleeding. That nigga licked the blood and smirked, and I prayed to Jesus to take the wheel. We were about to fight like two niggas in the street, but G was back. He had a spark in his eyes, and they no longer looked dead.

He tossed the knife aside and punched my ass in the forehead. *Who in the fuck does some shit like that*? I wondered. Feeling a knot rising on my head, I leaned up and bit his lip. I tried to pull that motherfucker off, until he pimp slapped my ass to the floor. I looked over at Kenya when I landed, and I saw this bad motherfucker was now biting my shoes. If she wasn't one year old, I would have squared up with her ass. I got up off the floor, and G was standing there, waiting for me in his fighting stance. Swinging my arm at him to make him think I was trying to punch him, I brought my leg up and kicked his balls into his stomach. As soon as his ass bent over, I gave him an uppercut like that bus driver had delivered to that girl. I rocked his ass to the moon.

Doing a victory dance, I jumped up and down in a circle. By the time my ass turned back around, however, this nigga roundhoused my ass. It was a wax on wax off Karate Kid ass kick, and I went soaring through the air. Thank God I landed on the bed.

Looking at him come at me, I tried to say, "Gina, I don't wanna fight no more," in my Martin voice, but I think the nigga had kicked my throat out. When I felt him snatch my pants off, the flood gates came open, and he hadn't even touched me yet. As soon as his mouth hit my clit, I was cumming.

"Damn, G. Suck that pussy, baby." I tried to grab his hands, but he snatched them back and then pinned me down. He was winning the end of the fight by punishing my pussy with his tongue. A bitch came three times before he got up. When he put me in the doggy-style position, I knew he was about to beat my shit up. After grabbing my ass cheeks, he pulled them so far apart, I felt the tip of my ass crack like chapped lips. Knowing I couldn't do shit but enjoy this ride, I let him attack my pussy until I felt his body shaking.

"I love you, girl."

"I love you too, G."

I rolled over and kissed him. Then I grabbed our badass baby, put her in her playpen, and got in the bed. Both of our asses was out in seconds.

When I woke up, I looked over and saw that G was packing. My ass tried to stand up, but it felt like my body had been run over by a train. How this nigga was moving around like it was nothing was beyond me. I flopped back down on the bed.

"Where you going, G?" I knew the answer, but he hadn't told me yet what was going on.

"Me and Suave gotta go back to Chicago. Don't trip. I should be back in a few days."

"What are y'all going to do?" I asked, feigning innocence.

His body tensed up, and I knew he didn't want to tell me that part.

"Look, I know we agreed to leave that part behind us, but my people need me, and I can't tell them no," he confessed.

I sat straighter up in bed. "Okay, so why can't I go, then? If it's as simple as you're trying to make it out to be, let's go handle this shit together."

"Not this time, baby. I need you to stay here and keep an eye on Tank. Not to mention we have a child that you need to be here for."

"There's only one way I will agree to you leaving without me. You have to give me your exact location. If something happens and you don't return, I need to know where to come looking."

"I'm waiting on him to send me the location, and I will give it to you. Thank you for not doing the most. Let a nigga be stress free, so I can come back and tear that pussy up."

"You know I'll be here waiting," I told him, feigning innocence no more. "I'll sleep with my legs open. Make sure you lick it first."

"Nasty ass. Let me get out of here. I'll text you the info in a few. If I'm not back in three days, come through that bitch, killing anybody that's breathing. If my ass didn't make it, they ain't, either."

"Be safe, baby, and let me know when you make it."

He leaned down and kissed me and walked out the door. That was easier than I had thought it was gone be.

I got up out of bed, walked around the house, and cleaned up the mess Kenya had made. Thinking about the shit I was about to pull gave me goose bumps. I couldn't wait to feel that rush again. The thought of cutting a nigga up had me excited. A bitch needed this shit.

CHAPTER 48

GANGSTA

Niggas didn't get the connection me and Paradise had. Fighting with her had my dick so hard, I thought the shit was gone bust. I was not gone lie. When she pulled the knife on me, her ass was about to go have a father-daughter dance in the upper room. She knew I didn't play that shit. Her crazy was what turned me on the most. What other chick you know, you could have a fight like that and she ain't trying to call the police on your ass?

She wasn't weak, and her ass was gone make sure the shit was an all-out battle. When she uppercut my ass, that motherfucker almost knocked me to the moon. Seeing her do her happy dance pissed me off. My ass was standing there in my Karate Kid stance, waiting on her to turn her ass around. That shit turned me on like a motherfucker.

As I left the house, I knew my girl thought she had done played my ass. I knew her ass better than she knew herself. Paradise was my other half, and I knew what she was thinking even when she didn't say it. Her ass wanted the address I was headed to because she coming there. I knew Suave would be pissed when Paradise showed up at our location, because Tank's ass gone be mad as fuck about being left out, but I would just play along. Truth was, my bitch was more ruthless than damn near every thug-ass nigga I knew. I trusted her to have my back and to make sure I got my ass out alive. We had killed together for ten years, and I trusted her with my life. When Suave found out Paradise was there, I was gone play dumb as shit and act like I didn't know her ass was coming.

Blaze sent me the info to his house in Chicago. They didn't want the women to know that Baby Face had been shot, and they wanted him to heal before they went back. Everybody thought they still in Puerto Rico. We would try to get this handled as quickly as possible, before they figured anything out.

After sending the address to Paradise, I walked in Suave's shit so we could get there and go handle business. He was nowhere on the first floor.

"Bro, where you at? You ready?" I called from the base of the stairs. When I ain't hear shit, I pulled my gun out and walked quietly up the stairs.

As I crept down the hallway, I heard a muffled sound coming from one of the rooms. It was like someone was gagged and was trying to speak. I stopped outside the door and waited a beat. As I twisted the knob slowly, I knew my ass had only a split second to assess the situation. When I opened the door, I saw this nigga had Tank in some type of swing shit that hung from the ceiling, and her ass was tied up and gagged. Nothing about my sister turned me on, but this shit looked interesting as hell. After watching for a couple of minutes, I had had enough.

"If you don't get your fifty shades of I can't fuck right ass on and let's go," I said.

"Nigga, get the fuck out!" Suave yelled.

Tank was screaming something, but I couldn't understand her, since she was gagged.

I met Tank's eyes. "That's the best gift he ever gave your ass. Been telling his ass since I met you that you talk too fucking much," I joked. Then I burst out laughing.

"G, give me ten minutes. Damn," Suave grumbled, his irritation showing.

Laughing, I walked out and let them finish they freak session. She must have been really acting up for her to agree to let him do that shit. When he finally came out of the room, I could tell he was still irritated.

"Why the fuck you bust in my room like that?" he snapped.

"Nigga, I called out your name, and I heard muffled screams, so I thought somebody got your ass. A nigga was trying to save your life. Next time, I'll let them kill your old ass."

"Fuck you. You got the address?"

I nodded. "Yeah. We need to be in and out. I'm not trying to be there long, or my ass ain't gone wanna leave."

"The streets have a way of sucking you back in. Let's go, before she brings her ass out here, crying again."

As we walked out the door, I wondered if he was just as excited as me.

"Big bro, you not a little excited about this shit? It's been a while since you had to fade a nigga," I said once we were in the car.

This nigga looked over his shoulder, like Tank's ass was in the car with us. "Man, I miss this shit every day. A nigga getting too old to be out here dealing with all the problems the streets bring, though. We got millions, and I have no reason to still be out here taking risks, but I swear, I miss the thrill of it all. I love my family, but I need this excitement."

"That's why I take jobs here and there," I told him. "This family life isn't for me, but I'm doing it. I ain't gone lie, though. It feels like a part of me is missing. Like I ain't being me, like I'm pretending to be somebody else. My ass be dreaming about killing niggas and shit. My ass can be at the store, and the person standing in front of me . . . I would stand there and think of ways to kill them. The shit driving my ass crazy."

"You sound like your ass ready to say, 'Fuck the family life.' I'm proud of the nigga you became, but I get where you coming from. It's hard, but you have to let that shit go. That ain't our life no more, G."

We both fell silent. I drifted away in my own thoughts, and it dawned on me that it seemed like everybody got it, but nobody understood. It felt like my ass was drowning or suffocating or some shit. I needed to kill like I needed to breathe, and motherfuckers was asking me to let the shit go. How did you get something like that out of your system? My entire identity was based around me being the coldest killer niggas had ever seen. Feeling myself going into a depressed state, I thought about the task at hand and immediately got excited again.

Half an hour later we reached the airport. As we loaded the plane, I couldn't wait to land in Chicago. Once we were seated, I sent Smalls a text to let him know to meet us at the airport.

Looking at the house in front of us, I realized these niggas had come a long way. Blaze's house was big as shit. and the cars lined up in the driveway let me know they had made it. We all had done good, and it made a nigga proud to see how far we had come. Young black millionaires alive to tell the story.

"These niggas living like the rich and famous out this motherfucker," Smalls commented. He was admiring the house like I was. My shit was probably a little bigger, but this shit was nice.

"All of us went way out with our houses. You the only nigga that got his shit built in the middle of the hood. I gave your ass the keys to the whole city, and you out here living like you got a nine to five," Suave said.

Smalls squinted at him. "Nigga, I was born a hood rat, and I'm gone die one. Fuck you mean? Don't front like you don't know what's in a nigga's pockets."

"We know what's in them motherfuckers," Suave retorted. "That's why we can't believe your ass trying to live ghetto fabulous. Get your ass out of the hood. You don't eat where you shit, nigga." Suave ass was always in lecture mode.

Smalls was getting fed up. "Look, Malcolm X, a nigga gone do what he wants. You picked your life and how you want to live, and I chose mine. We both out here eating. I just choose to eat in the ghetto."

"Are we really gone stand out here and argue over houses? Bring y'all dumb ass on," I said, having heard enough. They about to get worked up over where a nigga choosing to lay his head.

I rang the bell, and a dark-skinned nigga answered the door. *It must be they youngest brother*, I thought. He the only one I ain't know like that. When he just stood there, blocking the door, it irritated me.

"Move the fuck out the way, nigga," I ordered.

"Who the fuck are you niggas, and why are you here?" This nigga was lucky he they brother, or he would have caught a fade quick.

I crossed my arm over my chest and exhaled loudly. "First off, nigga, put a shirt on. You out here, oily as shit, in the middle of a fucking war. You ain't got time to take no pictures. Second, get the fuck on with all them fucking questions. You should already know who the fuck I am. My rep speaks for itself. Now you can play pussy and get fucked if you want to."

Suave spoke up. "G, calm down. He was too young to know who you are. Give the nigga a break."

Suave was trying to calm the situation, while Smalls's ass just watched, eating a bag of chips. Even after Suave said that shit, this nigga stared me down. He was about to learn a lesson today. In one swift motion, I had him pinned to the ground, with my gun pointed at his head.

"Your attitude gone get your life cut short, my nigga. Off the strength of your brothers, I'm gone let you make it. But I promise, your ass better check your attitude quick or I'm gone forget who the fuck you are. Are we clear?" I snarled. He was struggling under me, but I had his ass on lock. I knew he was pissed, but I didn't allow any nigga to disrespect me.

Blaze appeared in the doorway just then. "Gangsta, what the fuck is you doing, nigga? This my little brother. Shadow's his name."

Never taking my eyes off his little brother's ass, I responded to Blaze. "Your brother feeling tough today. I'm gone need you to explain to him who the fuck I am, because this is the last time I'm gone let his ass be great." I heard a lighter and then saw the flame at my face.

"Nigga, it's hard to be scared of a motherfucker with no eyebrows. Let his ass up, before I leave your ass with a patchy eye, my nigga."

"Blaze, get that lighter out of my face, before I make you swallow that bitch," I growled. When I felt the heat hit my face, and heard my hairs sizzling, I pulled my gun away from Shadow's head. "A'ight, damn. Get your lighter-happy ass on, Blaze, before you have my shit looking like roasted peanuts."

"Get your dumb ass up and stop playing. He sensitive. He ain't like us," Blaze said.

Laughing, I stood up and reached my hand out to the li'l nigga. When he didn't take it and tried to stand up on his own, I swooped his legs, and he hit the ground again. "By the time I leave, we gone have your attitude in check. Get out your feelings before I hurt them bitches," I warned him. Smalls, Suave, and me stepped over him, and then we walked up the stairs to go holla at Baby Face.

"When you speak of the devil, he will appear. What the fuck took you so long, nigga?" Face said when he saw us. He looked weak, but other than that, I could tell he was good. I was glad they ain't fucked my nigga up.

"Man, y'all sent y'all purse dog downstairs to open the door, and I had to teach his ass some manners," I said. "This our nigga Smalls. Smalls, this is Face, Blaze, Quick, and Purse Dog." I could tell the nigga Shadow wanted to say something smart, but he ain't wanna get embarrassed again.

"Now that everybody here, what's the move? How are we gone do this shit?" Quick asked. Even though me and Quick didn't really hang like that, he was more like me. He was nice with his gunplay as well, but nobody was nicer than me.

"We know where the headquarters are, but we don't know if that's it. We went in there and took out at least thirty niggas and still barely made it out. They know where we live, but I don't think they know about the main house. That's where we have everybody," Baby Face explained. "We can wait until they come here, but if we do that, we won't know if we got them all. Our asses will be like sitting ducks, waiting to see if more will come. So I say we take the war to them. In Puerto Rico."

After thinking it over, I agreed with Baby Face.

I glared at Shadow. "First off, fix your face, li'l nigga. You standing there in your feelings, and we here to save your fucking life. We gone all need to work together, and if I can't trust you to have my brother's back, you considered an enemy. Now, we done been down this road before, and it's hard to penetrate an estate from the outside unless we have the place surrounded."

Suave took over from there. "My nigga Smalls will have his team with us, but they are not trained like us. We gone have to mix the crowd in order to make sure we don't have a weak side. Face, are you gone be good to go?" Suave was the only nigga I knew that could shake your soul without raising his voice. The li'l nigga actually fixed his face after that.

"Whether I'm good or not, I'll be there," Baby Face answered. "Me and my brothers never go without the other. It's either all of us or none of us. I know Shadow was too young, and y'all didn't hang around him, but at the end of the day, that's my brother. Whatever happened downstairs, y'all need to deaden that shit. Just like you protect yours, I'ma protect mine."

Baby Face looked over at Shadow. "Now, Purse Dog, get out your feelings. As Gangsta said, we needed them and they came out of retirement to help us. You may not know them personally, but you've heard the stories of Lucifer and Suave. You are in the presence of legends. No man is going to take disrespect. We didn't bring them here to end up at war with they asses."

Smalls was getting antsy. "Damn, nigga. You talk more than Suave's ass. You can tell you the old nigga out of the bunch. Y'all got some food in this motherfucker? I can go eat a meal until y'all niggas ready to talk about what we gone do. All this 'Kumbaya' shit done made me hungry."

Quick pointed in the direction of the stairs. "The kitchen's downstairs."

Smalls left after Quick told him where to go, and we continued the conversation. We would catch him up later.

"Face, you just got shot days ago. How we gone go back right now?" Shadow said. I guessed Purse Dog was out his feelings.

Quick spoke up. "Because if we wait, we giving them the opportunity to come to us, and that puts our family at risk. We were laying they ass out, and there was only four of us and a baby. There's more of us now, so we should be able to end this shit with no problem." I knew Quick laid most of them out by hisself.

"Quick is the best nigga you know with a gun, but I'm better," I said. "I can lay out at least ten in five seconds. We got this, but we need a secure plan on how we are going in and who we are going after."

"That's the thing. The nigga kept talking about his boss, but we don't know who that is. Our guy led us to the cartel, but we don't know who is actually in charge of it," Quick commented.

Listening to everything Quick was saying, I realized that going to war now may not be a good idea.

"That can pose as a problem. If we go in and take everybody out, but we don't know who we looking for, they can always get a new crew and come back. The shit will never be over," Suave said, voicing exactly what I was thinking.

"Damn, did y'all friend go down there and cook an entire meal?" Face asked.

Realizing Smalls had never come back up, Suave gave me a look, and I knew what that meant.

"Purse Dog, you and Blaze stay here with Face and light anybody up that come in this motherfucker and it ain't us. Quick, come with me and Suave," I said in a low voice.

They looked at us like we were crazy, but they weren't like us. Even though they were street niggas, they were a different kind. We knew when shit wasn't right, and we knew Smalls. He looked for snacks or already cooked food. That nigga ain't about to cook shit hisself.

We eased down the stairs, and Suave reached the bottom first but didn't continue. He pointed at the mirror on the wall, and you could see Smalls in it. He was holding a baby, and five niggas had they guns pointed at him. He dropped his weapon, and they grabbed the baby from him and tied him to a chair. I knew Smalls, and he kept quiet because he didn't want them to know someone else was in the house. This was the reason I always needed Suave with me: he was the thinker. Had it been me, I would have gone around the corner blazing.

When Suave looked back at us, we raised our guns, and me and Quick knew we had to be fast and precise. On Suave's count, we rounded the corner so fast, they didn't have a chance to react. After taking down four of them, neither of us hit the last one, because he was holding the baby.

"If you let the baby down, I won't kill you," Quick said.

After looking at his crew, this dude decided to put the baby down. Once Quick had her, I knocked dude's ass out. As I untied Smalls, I noticed the fire on the stove was on and there was a body in the kitchen.

"Nigga, you was actually about to cook a meal in their house?" I said, confused.

"Hell naw. When I made it down the stairs, her badass was cutting the stove on. Before I could get to her, a nigga grabbed her. He didn't see me, so I laid his ass out. As soon as I picked her up, the others came in."

Suave motioned at the stairs. "Quick, go get your brothers. It's time to get some info out this motherfucker Lucifer's way."

When Suave said that, my heart started racing. This was the shit I lived for. I was back.

CHAPTER 49

BABY FACE

When Quick came in and told us what had gone down, Blaze went crazy, and I knew it wasn't gone be good for the nigga who was alive downstairs.

"Why they keep fucking with my daughter? You would think these nigga's beef was with me. I'm done playing, bro. Y'all can keep sitting around, letting these niggas plot and just walk in our shit like they live here, but not me. I'm not sitting around, waiting for them to hurt my child."

Understanding where Blaze was coming from, I knew we had to do something quick.

Shadow started pacing. "I'm with Blaze on this shit. We not even safe in our own shit. They walking in and out her house at will. They want a war, they got one."

"Calm down, Purse Dog," Blaze muttered. "You let a motherfucker walk all in our shit and beat your ass. How the fuck you gone stop a cartel?"

Laughing at Blaze's comment, I knew Shadow's ass wasn't gone find that shit funny.

"That nigga a contracted killer. How the hell was I gone win against that motherfucker?" Shadow countered.

"You won't, and that's why your ass need to fix your attitude. He was about to skin your ass until you were our color."

"At least you wouldn't look adopted no more," Blaze quipped.

When Blaze said the last joke, Shadow walked out of the room, and we left out behind him. "Fuck, y'all," he threw over his shoulder. By him being the youngest, we had to fuck with him. The shit would make him stronger.

Blaze put Spark back in her room and closed the door. "I don't even know how her li'l ass got out of there anyway. She doing too much," he wondered aloud.

Heading downstairs, we were all laughs and giggles until we rounded the corner and saw the setup Gangsta had. I had hung around the nigga, so I knew what he was about and had seen it firsthand. I didn't think my brothers were ready for what was about to come.

Looking at all the knives he had on the table, I knew this was about to get ugly. The dude was knocked out cold, and they were standing around, waiting for him to wake up. I decided to help them out.

"Shadow," I said. I nodded toward the guy, and Shadow walked over and knocked his eyes open.

"Damn, Purse Dog. I'm glad I didn't give you the chance to swing first. That right hook nasty," Gangsta said.

Knowing G's rep, I knew it made Shadow feel good to hear that coming from an OG.

Suave pulled up a chair and sat in front of the guy. "I'm going to ask you some questions, and how you answer them will determine what happens next. Are we clear?"

The guy nodded his head.

"Good. Now, who do you work for?"

The guy's eyes got big, and he looked scared as hell. He was more afraid of the people he worked for.

"I can see in your eyes that you fear your boss more than us, and that is a very big mistake." Suave stood up and moved his chair out of the way. "In this room we have a hit man, a fire starter, two niggas that can shoot you in seconds and you won't even see the gun, a nigga that could have been a heavyweight, and two of us that are quiet storms. Do you know what that means?"

The guy shook his head no, and I felt bad for him.

Suave turned on his heels and said, "Gangsta, you're up."

This nigga actually smiled as Gangsta walked over to the table and grabbed a knife. Smalls had to be used to this shit as well, because he stood there eating cookies and chips. G started carving one of the nigga's eyes out, and he screamed so loud, I thought he shook the house. When Gangsta got the eye out, Suave walked up again, and I had no idea what was about to happen.

"Blaze, you're up," Suave said.

I thought my brother was gone say, "Hell naw, you got me fucked up," but he walked up to G and took the eyeball. Standing in the man's face, Blaze set the eyeball on fire. When it fully caught fire, he dropped it to the floor and stepped on it. The sound of that shit smashing turned my stomach. Shadow started throwing up, and I knew he wouldn't be able to take much more of this. Blaze walked up to the bleeding eye socket and flicked his Bic.

As he held the fire to it, the man finally screamed out. "Okay, I'll tell you whatever you want to know! Please stop!" After a few more seconds, Blaze finally pulled back and walked away. Suave grabbed his chair again and sat back down.

"Who do you work for?" Suave asked, his voice calm as could be.

"His name is Felipe. He is in charge of the entire Puerto Rico operation."

"How many estates do he have there?"

"Just the one."

"You said the Puerto Rico operation. What other countries do they have a faction in?"

"I don't know."

Suave stood up again and moved his chair. "Gangsta, you're up," he said.

This time G chose a different knife, then walked over to the man and grabbed his hand.

"I don't know. I promise I don't know," the guy repeated.

Suave wasn't moved, and that let me know the man was lying. Suave could read anybody; this nigga's gut was never wrong.

Gangsta started peeling the skin from the guy's fingers, and then he worked his way up to his wrist.

"Oh God, please help me! Somebody help me! Oh God," the guy screamed.

"Don't pray to God. Pray to Lucifer," Gangsta told him. Then, in one swift motion, he chopped off his hand.

"Blaze, you're up," Suave called.

My brother walked over and flicked his Bic, then put fire to the man's wrist. It wasn't until then that I realized what Suave was doing. He was making Blaze burn the guy to stop the bleeding. He didn't want the guy to die before he got all the information. When Blaze was done, Suave grabbed his chair again and sat down.

"How many other factions are there, and where are they?"

"Two more. Cuba and Colombia."

"Who is in charge of Felipe? Who is the head of all the factions?"

The man started crying. Hell, I wanted to cry for him. We all knew what was about to happen next.

Suave stood up and moved the chair again. "Gangsta, you're up."

This time G grabbed a bottle and walked over to the guy. He poured the liquid inside the bottle on the side of the guy's face that wasn't messed up, and his shit started smoking and melting off. G was pouring acid on him. Seeing the meat slide off his face had me ready to get the fuck out of there.

"It's a woman," the guy sputtered.

Gangsta stopped pouring. Suave walked over to the guy, grabbed the chair, and sat down.

"Hold the fuck on. I ain't get my turn." Blaze was actually pissed.

"What is her name?" Suave asked, ignoring Blaze.

"Nobody knows, only Felipe. If you find Felipe, he can take you to her."

Suave stood up, grabbed the chair, and stepped away from the guy. Then he spoke again. "Shadow, Quick, Blaze, Face, Smalls, and G, you're up."

We all grabbed our guns and fired. The guy should be happy. There was no way I would have wanted to live life after that shit.

"Smalls, call the cleanup crew. Hoover Gang, get ready. We heading to Puerto Rico tomorrow," Suave instructed.

"Y'all niggas is sick," Smalls said. He laughed as he grabbed his phone to make the call.

When I looked at my brothers, I saw that we all had the same expression on our face. We had called the right niggas for the job.

CHAPTER 50

QUICK

Growing up, we had all heard stories about Lucifer. Baby Face was the only one old enough to have hung with G, but him and Blaze had always connected. I think it was their "I don't give a fuck" attitude that had drawn them together. Even after all the stories Face and Blaze had told us, nothing could prepare me to see the shit up close and personal.

Not wanting to look like a bitch, I had summoned everything in me earlier not to throw the fuck up. When Shadow had, I'd been glad to know I wasn't the only one who was bothered by the shit. But at the end of the day, no matter how fucked up the shit had been, I was glad they were there. If we couldn't get the job done with they asses, it was meant for the Hoover Gang to get laid down.

That thought alone scared the fuck out of me. When the cleanup crew arrived, I walked outside to get some air. Heading down the driveway, I tried to clear my mind, but I couldn't. These niggas were coming at us hard over our father's debt. A nigga we hadn't even fucked with. This shit needed to be over soon. My wife was about to have our baby, and we couldn't be at war when that happened. These niggas got us hiding out in our own shit, like we some bitch-ass niggas.

"You good, nigga?" When I looked up, Blaze was standing there, looking at me crazy.

"Naw, I'm not good. I'm not with this 'laying low' shit. When we go to Puerto Rico tomorrow, this shit has to end. We the fucking Hoover Gang. We don't duck no nigga, and I ain't trying to start that shit today."

"I'm ready too. These niggas keep coming for my baby, and I ain't having that shit. It's time to show them who the fuck they dealing with."

I noticed Blaze's dirty hands then. "Damn, nigga. You ain't wash your hands after touching that nigga's eyeball? I always knew you were crazy, but I ain't know your shit was twisted."

"You got me fucked up, nigga. I almost fed that nigga my breakfast. When Suave said I was up, I almost flicked my ass out of the fucking house and said, 'Fuck that Bic.' Shit was nasty as hell, but I couldn't let them show us up in our house. I ain't getting left off bad and boujie."

"Shut your dumb ass up."

"No lie, though. Once I did it, the shit gave me a rush like no other. Y'all think G is bad, but Suave is worse. It just don't seem that way, because he so quiet," Blaze said.

"I can't imagine it being worse than that."

"Now, y'all done fucked up and let me like the shit. I'm gone be cutting up body parts and setting them on fire. I wonder if they can make a lighter with acid in it. Nigga, y'all eyebrows will never come back if I had that shit." I was glad he had come out here and had me laughing.

"Let's get back in there before they asses done killed Shadow," I told him.

He agreed. As we were turning around to walk back to the house, we heard gunfire. We ducked down and tried to run toward the house.

"You strapped, Blaze?" I was pissed that I had left my shit in the house.

"Fuck no. All I got is this motherfucking lighter. I'm about to throw this shit at a nigga."

"The fuck is that gone do?"

"Nothing, but at least I'm fighting back. Your ugly ass ain't doing shit but dripping curl juice."

"We gotta make a run for it. We can't stay out here, or we dead," I said, ignoring the insult.

Blaze counted down, and we took off running. That nigga forgot about my ass and took off so fast. As soon as I ran a few steps, I got hit. My entire body shook, and I hit the ground. The last thing I heard before my heart stopped was the gunfire getting closer. All I could do was pray that Blaze made it in the house safe. Closing my eyes, I knew it was over for me. My brothers would avenge me and take care of my seed. My work here was done.

CHAPTER 51

TANK

Getting off the plane, I was excited and scared at the same time. The stunt I was about to pull was going to have my marriage in jeopardy, but I didn't care. He would never go to war without me being there to have his back. If he left me for that, then so be it. When I looked over at Paradise, she had this look on her face that I had never seen before. I knew that her and Gangsta had killed together, but I had never seen it with my own eyes. The look on her face scared me, and in that moment I knew she was just like him. She looked soulless right now, and if I didn't know her, I would fear for my life right now.

I caught her eye as we entered the terminal. "Hey, bitch. You good?"

"Yeah, I'm straight. I'm just happy to be home." She downplayed that shit, but I could see it in her face that she was ready to kill some damn body. The bitch had better wait until we dropped these damn kids off.

My friend Nik was here to pick us up, and I was happy. A bitch was ready to go make sure my man was straight, and I ain't have time to be waiting at a damn rental car counter. As soon as we got in the car, Nik started in.

"You know I don't mind keeping the kids, 'cause Poo Poo will have somebody to play with, but Suave is going to kill you. Why do you insist on fighting him about this, Tank?"

"First off, you nicknamed your daughter a pile of shit? Secondly, I'm not fighting him. *He* is the one making this hard. I'm not trying to be out here in these streets, but if that's where my man is, then that's where I am."

Nik didn't give up. "I'm just saying . . . You know how he is, and you steady playing with fire."

"Look, I ain't trying to hear that shit. Where is the old Nik? We come from the same crew, and now you done turned into a scary bitch."

"I got a family. You have to give shit up in order to make shit work," she countered.

Paradise had heard enough preaching. "What the fuck has Smalls given up? You sounding like a weak bitch right now, and anybody that know me knows I don't do that weak shit," she remarked. "You want to be a bitch, fine. Just leave that shit where you at. She choosing to ride for her man and you choosing to sit at home while your man out there at war. To each its own, but chill with all the fucking lectures and drive. Because if something happens to mine while you trying to preach, I'm coming back for your ass, and I promise you not gone live to speak another fucking word. Now drive."

I could tell there was some shit Nik wanted to say back to Paradise, but her scary ass knew better. This the bitch that had created Lucifer, and Nik knew she better choose her battles wisely.

After pulling up to her house, Nik jumped out of the car, mad as hell. The shit was about to be awkward, because Paradise still needed her to keep her badass daughter. How you gone curse out the bitch that was babysitting your kid? Laughing at the thought of Paradise having to play nice, I grabbed Deuce and headed inside.

"I appreciate you being concerned, but I got this, sis. You just have to trust me," I told Nik. She hugged me and realized that Paradise hadn't come in the house.

"Girl, go tell Paradise to bring me that damn baby. I'm not letting her go to war with her damn child in her arms."

Paradise walked in the room just then and said, "Oh, I wasn't going to. This bad motherfucker took off down the damn street. I was bringing her in here, and you was gone take her with a smile. Here."

As Paradise passed Nik the baby, I looked at her in disbelief. Who in the fuck talked to somebody like that and then made them watch they baby? Only Paradise. I mouthed, "Thank you," to Nik, and then Paradise and I walked outside. After pulling my phone out, I was ready to call my cousins to see where they were. They were supposed to pick us up. Before I could dial the number, however, they pulled up.

"What's up, bitch?" my cousin Shay yelled through an open window.

Me and Paradise walked up to the truck and got in.

"Shay and Bay Bay, this is Paradise. Paradise, these are my cousins and the other half of my crew. Did y'all bring the heat?" I said.

"You know it. The bag is in the truck. You hoes ready?" Bay Bay was always in go mode.

"Let's ride. This is the address. I'm not sure if anything is going on right now, but when they leave to go to war, we are going with them," I said.

"I'm down. Gerald's ass is getting on my nerves anyway. I wish he'd get the fuck on."

I shook my head. "I'm still in disbelief that you went back to that nigga."

"Don't worry about me. Worry about this nigga Suave, who is about to go upside your head."

Everybody laughed, and I saw they all got jokes today. This was one ass whupping I was willing to take. Almost losing him had broken me, and I'd be damned if I'd go through the shit again.

When we pulled up to the house, I didn't know if this was where they were coming to take a motherfucker out or if this was where they were staying.

"Paradise, do you know whose house this is?" I asked.

"Naw. He just said this was where they were going. Let's just sit here a minute and see what happens."

Everyone agreed, and we kept our asses in the truck and watched. After about ten minutes, a guy walked out.

"Damn. That nigga fine. *Shit*. Y'all brought my ass to the right place," Bay Bay exclaimed, and she and Shay high-fived. I silently agreed. When the next nigga walked out, my panties got wet.

"Okay, y'all better not ever repeat this shit, but I'll let them niggas run a train on me. The fuck. It's a houseful of fine-ass niggas. It better not be the niggas we gotta lay out, because I swear, I'm not gone be able to do it. They too damn fine to be in somebody damn grave."

"We here to help them. The last one to walk out is Blaze. He used to be around G and them," Paradise said. "Y'all think he cute now, but the nigga ignorant as fuck, and he will set your ass on fire in a minute."

"He can set this pussy on fire. Damn, that nigga is everything." Shay's nasty ass was getting worked up.

"Hold up, y'all. You see them niggas right there?" I pointed down the street, and some niggas was coming fast as hell toward the house, but they were bent down low. The fine niggas in the driveway didn't see them coming.

"We don't know if G and them are here yet, so we stay put," Paradise advised.

I didn't agree with what Paradise was saying, so I kept my heat in my hands, ready to jump out at any minute. When the unknown niggas started shooting in Blaze and them's direction, we had to wait. If we got out now, they would air our asses out. When those unknown dudes walked toward the driveway, Blaze went running past and the other nigga hit the ground. I was done waiting.

After jumping out of the truck, I started blasting at they asses. Shay and Bay Bay followed suit, and Paradise had no choice but to join us. In thirty seconds, we had laid all they asses out. When Blaze came out the door, he had his gun pointed at us.

"What the fuck? Paradise?" he said in disbelief.

Paradise grinned. "Yeah, nigga, and you welcome."

I ran over to the other guy, and he was laid out, looking deader than a motherfucker. But when I got up close, I saw that the only hole on him was in his arm. "Macee, get your faking ass up. You was hit in the arm, nigga."

By then Blaze was there. "Who the fuck are you, and who the hell is Macee? That faking-ass nigga's name is Quick."

"I'm Tank, Suave's wife, and Quick's ass was moving slow as fuck. Macee is this gay nigga in KB Cole book's *He Ain't Perfect, But He's Worth It*, and his ass did the same dumbass shit. Only thing Quick forgot to say was, 'And scene.'"

"Girl, shut the fuck up," Blaze barked. "Nobody know who that nigga is. If he faking, why this nigga ain't got up yet?" This nigga Blaze was a rough one. I liked aggressive.

I squinted. "I don't know. Maybe he hit his head."

Blaze leaned down and put a lighter to Quick's face. As soon as he flicked that motherfucker, that nigga Quick shot up fast as hell.

"What happened?" Quick looked around like he was lost.

Blaze rolled his eyes. "Nigga, your ass fainted like a sissy in a book. Get up."

Everybody started laughing, but then, out of nowhere, I was lifted in the air and slammed against the ground so hard, a bitch couldn't breathe. For the first time since

I had met Suave, he looked soulless, like Gangsta. His eyes had turned black, and I saw no love there.

"Damn!" It seemed like every nigga said it at the same damn time.

The nigga never let my throat go. "What the fuck did I tell you?" he growled. When I didn't respond, he pulled me up off the ground and slammed my ass again. "What the fuck did I tell you!"

"Nigga, she can't talk. You done knocked her vocal cords out her ass," Blaze noted.

Suave shot Blaze a look, and the crazy nigga flicked his lighter. When Blaze gave Suave a look like, "Nigga, try it," I wanted to laugh, but I couldn't. Finally, Suave released my neck and walked off. He may leave me after this, but at least I knew he was safe. This was worth it to me, and nobody else might ever understand that shit.

"Tina. Hey, Tina. You wanna borrow my lighter? You know Ike keep them good juices in his hair. I ain't never seen a nigga check a motherfucker that calm. You scared? You should be scared. Hell, I'm scared."

Somebody had better get this nigga, I thought. He fine as fuck, but this ain't the time to be joking. He played too damn much already.

Gangsta walked over to Paradise and kissed her. Why the fuck my man couldn't be happy to see me? Sitting up, I wanted to yell that this was some bullshit, but I thought my ass was still in my back.

Gangsta had a concerned look on his face. "Sis, you good?"

Rolling my eyes at G, I stood up and went to go find my man.

"You got some leaves in your hair," Blaze told me. This nigga was aggy as hell.

"Fuck you," I told him. Then I walked toward the house, praying my husband wasn't done with me.

CHAPTER 52

SUAVE

When we heard the gunshots, we all had to take cover. None of us had our weapons on us, and that was a bad move on our part. Baby Face made his way through the gunfire and up the stairs to make sure the baby was good. As weak as they thought Shadow was, that nigga played no games. When he was trying to get outside to his brothers, I had to hold him down until the gunfire ceased. He was in protect mode, but what he was doing wasn't smart. All we could do was pray that Quick and Blaze was straight.

The shooting stopped for a brief second and then started back up. Once it had completely stopped, we waited a minute before we moved, just in case they were trying to trap us. After finally easing off the floor, Smalls made his way to the window and started laughing. Me and Shadow looked at him like he was crazy.

"You niggas in here, on the floor, hiding and shit, but you got reinforcements out here," Smalls reported.

"Fuck you talking about?" I said.

"All I'ma say is them niggas dead as shit out there. You think they will care if I grab some more snacks?"

"Nigga, all your ass care about is eating. Who the fuck out there?" I said.

"Come see for yourself."

When I got to the window and saw Tank and her crew with guns drawn, making sure they were all dead, I saw red. This motherfucker had deliberately said, "Fuck me." Punching the wall, I tried to calm down. I looked back out the window and saw that she was all he he, ha ha with Blaze, and that shit pissed me off. Not because I was jealous, but because she thought the shit was sweet.

"G, you told Paradise where we were going?" I said over my shoulder.

"Yeah, so just in case our ass didn't come home, she would know where to start looking. Why? What happened?" This nigga was lying, and you would think he would know not to lie to me after all these years.

"Quit lying, nigga," I spat. "I'll deal with you later. Right now I'm about to beat the jet lag out her ass."

As I walked out the door, I was trying to tell myself to calm down, but the more she talked and laughed, the madder I got. She was so deep in her conversation, she didn't even see me walking up on her. After grabbing her by her neck, I lifted her ass in the air and tried to take her ass through the concrete. When she wouldn't answer me, I wanted to knock her ass out, but the fear in her eyes stopped me. I was not the type of nigga that hit on females, but I swear, she the only one that ever made me come close.

She was always pushing her limits, and I didn't like the way she made me stoop to this level. Not wanting to kill her, I walked off. Seeing all the bodies laid out, I smiled on the inside. Not wanting my chick in these streets had nothing to do with me not wanting her to get hurt, but she ain't no damn nigga, and I wanted her to be a wife and a mother to my child.

Every time I tried to be mad at her for doing shit like this, I ended up proud or happy as fuck. Her hardheaded ass be putting in work, and you couldn't be mad at that.

I was sure Blaze and Quick were happy as hell, because those women had saved their lives, but I wanted to be mad. Knowing we all could possibly be dead, I decided to give her another pass. I wouldn't let her know that I was happy as fuck that they had shown up when they did, but I was. When I reached the kitchen, Smalls's ass was in there making a sandwich.

"Nigga, call the cleanup crew back and tell they ass to come quick," I told Smalls. "These niggas outside, and we don't want them to be out there long. Even though nobody lives on this block, we don't want a motherfucker to end up driving past." I headed outside, then stood in the yard and tried to collect my thoughts. The streets had a way of sucking a nigga back in. This was the most excitement I had had in a minute, and I didn't want to admit that I was loving this shit.

My family was more important than this shit, but the streets ran through my blood. Once this was over, it was back to my life as a retired kingpin. While I was here, I would enjoy this shit.

"Kendyl, can I talk to you please?"

When I turned around, Tank was standing there, with tears in her eyes. Everything about her turned me on, and knowing she had just put in work had my dick hard. When I walked up to her fast, she closed her eyes and flinched, not knowing what I was about to do. After grabbing her by her neck, I lifted her off her feet all the way in the air and slammed her against the back wall of the house. Using my free hand, I snatched her leggings down and started sucking on her clit. My wife never wore panties, and that always gave a nigga easy access. When she realized what I was doing, she wrapped her legs around my neck, and I continued to suck the soul out of her ass.

She couldn't take the assault I was putting on her pussy, and she started shaking. Sticking my tongue inside her, I caught all her nut and went right back to her clit. She tried to grab my head, and I slammed her back against the wall. Never taking my hand from around her neck, I applied just enough pressure.

After cumming a second time, she was ready for the dick, I knew. I dropped my jogging pants down, then slammed her down on my dick without warning or prepping her. Using her neck as grip, I brought her up and down on my dick hard as hell. Knowing I didn't want to hit her, I beat her pussy up instead. Every time she tried to moan or scream out, I squeezed harder and slammed her against the wall.

She was gone take this dick and shut the fuck up. Feeling my nut rising, I slid her off my dick and pushed her down to her knees. I pushed my dick in her mouth, and she tried to take all of me in slow. I grabbed her by her head and fucked her face until I was cumming down her throat.

"Fuck!" I yelled.

Knowing I was weak, she started going crazy on my dick, making sure she got every last drop. When my knees started shaking, I knew I couldn't take no more. She pulled her head back, then stood up and pulled her clothes up.

When I looked past her, I saw Blaze just a few feet away.

"Damn, Tina, you took that ass whupping like a G," he said, grinning. "Hey, Suave, I fucks with you and all, but don't be fucking in my yard, nutting on my walls and shit. I started to burn your ass hairs off. Nigga, why you got hair back there any damn way? You think you in Nutbush city for real, huh?" This nigga Blaze didn't give a fuck what he said out his mouth.

"Nigga, get the fuck on before I think you saw my girl naked, and if I think that shit, I'm not gone let you live to tell it," I growled.

"Chill out, my nigga. I ain't seen shit. Her shit look intact, though. My wife's shit looser than a Jheri curl."

He walked off before I could slap the shit out of his ass. This nigga played too much. After fixing ourselves up, we walked back in the house, and everybody was in the kitchen.

"This house not safe, and I'm not staying here, waiting on these niggas to keep coming back, so what's the plan?"

Baby Face said, "Our family at the main house. We can all go there. It's big enough for everybody. Tomorrow we leave for Puerto Rico, as planned. If most of they niggas here, it should be easy to penetrate they shit."

Baby Face had made a point, and I agreed.

"Paradise already took care of my bullet wound, so I'm good to go," Quick said. "We need to get the fuck up out of this motherfucker right now. A nigga thought he was gone."

"How Sway? You got shot in the arm and passed out like a ran-through sissy," Blaze joked.

Everybody laughed at Blaze and got ready to head out.

Shadow held up a hand. "Wait, everybody staying at the main house? We never bring people to the main house."

"Damn, Purse Dog, I thought we got past that shit. Nigga, your ass will sleep on the porch before me," Gangsta said.

"Shut the fuck up. Damn, I was talking about them." Shadow pointed.

We looked over and saw he was talking about Shay and Bay Bay.

Gangsta shook his head. "Damn. Purse nigga toughening up. I like that, li'l nigga, but don't bark if you not gone bite. They cool. They with us." Gangsta liked fucking with Shadow, and it was funny to see them going back and forth.

"Then it's settled. Let's roll," I said. I thought G liked Shadow. He got a lot of heart to be that young.

"Hey, can I have one of these Lunchables?"

Everybody looked at Smalls and laughed.

"Damn, nigga," Baby Face said. "You gone owe us some money in a minute. Your hungry ass better go eat some pussy or something."

Baby Face was joking, but I swear, Smalls would eat all your shit.

We headed out of the house and drove over to the main house.

CHAPTER 53

BABY FACE

Juicy picked a helluva time to leave. These chicks who came with Suave's wife was fine as fuck, and I was ready to put Tsunami in somebody's life. Getting ready to head to the main house, I shook my head at all the shit going on. It was gone be hell being under the same roof. Add all of us and my mama to the mix, and this was a recipe for disaster. When I headed to my Hummer, one of the fine chicks walked over with me.

"Can I ride with you?" she asked.

I knew this was not a good idea, but I let my dick answer for me. "Yeah," I said. Trying my best not to look thirsty, I played the shit off cool and just jumped in the Hummer. I turned up my radio, to avoid any conversation, but she deadened that shit.

"What's your name?" she asked me.

"Baby Face. And yours?"

"I'm Shay. I'm Tank's cousin. Where your girl at?"

Even though Juicy had left, and I wanted to say, "I ain't have a girl," I knew I should keep this situation under wraps. This shit could get complicated, and a nigga didn't need that shit. "I'm married, and we on a break."

"Can you fuck another chick on this break?"

Tsunami damn near jumped out of my pants when she said that shit. My ass wanted to scream, "Fuck yeah!" but I tried my best to keep this shit cool.

"We never talked about that. I see you a live one, huh? Straight to the fucking point. You trying to fuck, Shay?" Why the fuck did I ask that?

She slid her hand in her pants and started fingering herself. Her shit was gushy as fuck, and I damn near crashed when I tried to look. When she slid her hand out and tried to stick it in my mouth, I straightened up quick as fuck.

"Hold on, Ma. I don't eat random pussy. You fine as fuck, but I ain't going there." Seeing the disappointment on her face, I tried to redirect this scene. My ass wanted to see the rest of the show. "Let me see how you suck it. This dick big as fuck, and I need to know if I'm gone be wasting my time."

When she slid her fingers in her mouth, I almost leaned over and sucked them motherfuckers with her. She was doing that shit so sexy, it took everything in me not to fuck her right now. Needed to slow this shit down, so I tried to talk with her.

"Why your fine ass ain't got a nigga?"

"Who said I didn't?"

"My bad. I assumed you didn't, because your ass in here, ready to fuck, and you don't know me like that."

"He fucking up right now, and I need some dick. Are we really gone sit here and talk about my nigga when you got all this good pussy right here?"

"I would talk about my dick, but, man, that shit would be a long story."

She laughed, as I had quoted Lil Wayne. "Let me see," she said.

"Let you see what? My dick?"

When she nodded her head, I could see it was gone be hard to turn her ass down.

"There ain't enough room in this motherfucker to pull this bitch out," I told her.

Out of nowhere, she straightened up, and her demeanor changed. Thinking she must have an attitude, I turned the music up. The shit was for the best anyway. When we pulled up to the house, I had barely parked the motherfucker before she jumped her li'l ass out. Since I was used to feisty chicks, the shit didn't bother me.

Everybody else pulled up, and Gangsta got out, holding Spark. If I didn't know he had a baby, I could never picture him with a child. This nigga looked like he ate children and shit. As we headed toward the house, everybody was already in the front, like they knew we were coming.

Drea saw Spark and took off running toward Gangsta.

Blaze was right behind Gangsta and said, "You can slip on his dick if you want to, Drea. I'll have your pussy looking like burnt Italian beef. Back your ass up. No disrespect to you, Gangsta, but my wife likes to bust it open. That pussy like an eighty-nine Cutlass. Motherfucker got some mileage." Blaze was never gone let Drea live that shit down.

"Shut up, Blaze. I was going to get Spark." Reaching for the baby, Drea had tears in her eyes. Once Spark was in her arms, she kissed her a million times.

"I'm just saying, you was running kind of fast in those socks, and your ass might have slipped," Blaze mused.

We all shook our head at the nigga and walked all the way in the house. Zavi and Ash ran to Quick, while Shadow picked Kimmie's big ass up in the air and hugged her. Everybody but me had somebody welcoming them back, and the shit pissed me off.

Mama made her grand entrance, the pastor at her side. "Y'all got me fucked up, leaving me with these worrying-ass bitches. Y'all need to toughen they ass up. Every time I tried to get this thang ate, one of them was knocking on the door, trying to talk and shit. A bitch ain't got no dick since y'all asses been gone."

Gangsta, Suave, and they crew looked on in horror as my mama showed her ass.

"Is this Ma Dukes? Nigga, I'm criiinnee." Smalls was dying from laughter, and my mama finally noticed the new crew.

"Devon, you can go home now," Mama said, grinning devilishly. "They done brought Mama a houseful of young dick. Damn, y'all fine. Which one of y'all wanna sample this tiger pussy?"

Before I could warn Mama, Paradise damn near made my mama's wig fly off, she ran up on her so fast. "That one there is mine. Keep your teeth in your mouth and stay away from him," Paradise warned Mama. I knew Paradise was crazy, but she didn't know my mama was just as loony.

"Hold on, Devon. Don't leave yet. Hold my wig," Mama said. "This motherfucker got me fucked up. Sons, I'm about to whup her ass, but make sure you break it up in five minutes. After that, a ho won't be able to breathe, and y'all better not let her beat y'all mama's ass. Shadow, go get me some water, and have it on standby. Now you, what you wanna do, li'l bitch? 'Cause you got me fucked up. If I wanna suck his dick, I'm gone suck the skin off that motherfucker." My mama actually handed her wig to Devon, and his slow ass just stood there and held it.

"Ma, go sit your old ass down somewhere," Quick said. "Nobody fucking that old-ass wolf pussy. You do the most."

Mama looked at Quick like she wanted to beat his ass.

"Don't worry about it, bitch. I know somebody that like it," Mama told Paradise.

Laughing, I prayed the tension would die down. Paradise was still staring my mama down, but I would give her a fade so fast if she touched my mama.

A glint in his eye, Blaze decided to do the introductions. "Everybody, this is Gangsta, aka Lucifer, and his wife, Paradise. And this is Suave and his wife, Tank. And that's Shay, Bay Bay, and Smalls. Ma, Smalls's girl ain't here, so he up for grabs."

Blaze wasn't shit for throwing Smalls under the bus like that.

Mama frowned. "Lucifer? Oh, hell no, I heard all the stories. You won't get this tiger. Motherfucker might pour acid on my shit, and my hair long. Acid gone catch hold of that shit and burn this pussy up." She looked at Paradise. "Girl, you can pick your face up and stop mugging. I don't want his ass. Nigga might kill my poor tiger dead. The motherfucker already old." She turned and held her hand out. "Come on, Devon. Give me my shit and let me show you this new trick I saw on Porn Hub." She grabbed her wig and threw it on her head and was gone.

Smalls started laughing even before he spoke. "Nigga, that's a damn shame. If Paradise leave your ass, you ain't never gone be able to get no pussy."

Everybody laughed at Smalls. Then they started to relax and mingle. On my way to the kitchen, I overheard Shay talking to her sister.

"Girl, yeah, he too fine to have a big-ass dick."

"He showed it to you?"

"Nope. As soon as I asked, he bitched up and wouldn't let me see. That mean that motherfucker gotta be small."

Now, I could have let Shay have that shit, because I knew my dick size, but I wanted to shut her the fuck up. I turned around, walked over to them, and grabbed her by the arm. Then I damn near dragged her ass up the stairs.

"What the fuck you doing? Let me go!" Shay yelled.

Not responding, I dragged her all the way to my bedroom. I pushed her down to the floor. I didn't even let her get on the bed.

"Take that shit off," I demanded.

"Nigga, please. I don't give away sympathy pussy. I'm sorry if I bruised your ego, but you not hitting this."

"I'm not gone ask you again."

When she looked into my eyes, she slid her pants off and lay there, looking ready. She was gone get the dick, but not yet.

"Play with that pussy." I needed her to get it ready, since I was gone fuck, but I wasn't eating no pussy to get it wet. Since she wanted to talk all that shit, I should have gone in her shit before it got wet, but a nigga didn't want a murder charge.

Hearing that motherfucker talking to me, I was ready to shut her the fuck up. When I walked over to her, she spread her legs like she thought it was time for that. But I grabbed her by her hair and pulled her up to her knees.

"Damn, nigga, that hurt."

I dropped my pants, and I freed Tsunami, and her eyes damn near fell out of her head. My dick was damn near bigger than her body, and she was talking shit. Without warning, I pushed my dick in her mouth and made her head go all the way to my balls. She was gagging out of control, and spit was flying everywhere. *Go figure. Talk all that shit and can't even suck this big motherfucker*, I thought. Guiding her head up and down my dick slowly, I let her throat relax before I slammed it all the way in again. Her eyes got watery, and I eased up. As I moved it slowly, she tried to go crazy, and I slammed it back down again.

She was gone think about shit the next time she tried to talk about a nigga. Realizing she wasn't gone be able to take much more of Tsunami being in her throat, I pulled out and walked to the dresser and grabbed a condom. After strapping up, I walked over to her and picked her up. I put her on the bed and made her do a headstand.

With her being so short, it wouldn't have worked with her on the floor. Hands on the mattress, face down, and ass up, I slid my dick in her, and she immediately screamed out.

"Fuck, wait! Your shit too big."

"Naw, you said my dick was little, and now you gone take this shit." I grabbed her by her waist, then rocked her back and forth on this motherfucker until I got it all in. I had picked this position because she couldn't do shit but take all of it. She kept trying to run, but I started slamming this dick all in her pussy. My ass was so deep, I thought I felt her heartbeat. I slapped her ass so hard, my handprint was left on that yellow motherfucker.

"Don't get quiet now," I told her. I slapped her ass again, and she screamed.

"Fuck, I'm sorry. Fuck. This shit so big." She tried to get away again, but I had her ass on lock.

"Take this dick. Quit running." Tired of fighting with her ass, I grabbed her legs and put them around my waist. Then I grabbed her hips and slammed her on this dick until I felt my nut rising. Filling the condom with my nut, my body shook, and I lay on top of her. After I caught my breath, I rolled over, and she was unable to move.

"Go get your bag, so you can take a shower. You staying in here with me tonight. I'm gone fuck you until you able to take it."

She groaned and got up and did what I asked.

When she came back up, we showered together and then headed downstairs to mingle with everybody else. Her sister saw how she was walking, and tried to whisper in her ear.

"I'm guessing his dick wasn't little. Bitch, he fucked you bowlegged."

I heard what she had said, and I started laughing. I walked over to the fellas to talk shit.

"Hey, quick question," Smalls said. "Why y'all got this big-ass picture of Blaze in here, like this nigga dead or something?" Smalls was looking confused, and I tried to explain it to him.

I shrugged, like the answer was obvious. "The nigga died, and we got it done." Before I could finish explaining what had happened, Smalls pulled his gun out and pointed it at Blaze.

"Y'all telling me this nigga a ghost? Suave, y'all know I don't play that ghost shit. Why the fuck y'all ain't tell me this nigga was dead? Nigga, I swear to God, if you come through my walls tonight, I'm gone air your ass out."

Everybody looked at Smalls like he was crazy, and fell out laughing.

"Nigga, what the fuck are you talking about? I fake died, but they didn't know it when they got this pic," Blaze explained.

Slowly, Smalls put his gun away, and then he reached out and touched Blaze. "Aw, okay, you did that shit Suave did. Y'all niggas gone quit playing with me with the dead. That shit creeps me the fuck out." He relaxed some, but he still never took his eyes off Blaze.

I couldn't do shit but laugh. These niggas was crazy as fuck, and I was gone be pissed when they left. We all needed this last hurrah.

CHAPTER 54

GANGSTA

Paradise was ready to kill they mama, but I wasn't gone let that shit go down like that. These my niggas, and that was their OG, and Paradise was acting like I would really fuck her old ass. My baby still got jealous, and I thought the shit was cute. It had been a long time since she had felt intimidated.

From their mama talking shit and my niggas cutting up, a nigga barely wanted to go back home. A nigga was already missing the kill, but this shit was life. We were having a fucking ball, and I hated that tomorrow there was a chance that one of us might not come back. That was always a risk we took when we went to war. That shit wasn't gone be easy to take us down, but it was always a possibility. Deep in my own thoughts, I didn't see Purse Dog's wife, Kimmie, walk up on me.

"They over there telling stories about you, and I'm intrigued. How the hell did you turn into the devil?" She looked like she was actually excited, but I wasn't a friendly nigga. But since I had already fucked her nigga up, I decided to be nice.

"The streets named me Lucifer. They said when you look in my eyes, you didn't see shit but death. When I killed, people felt only a nigga with no soul could do the shit I did. Suave started it, and the name kind of stuck."

"I get that, but what did you do that made them say that? Murder is murder, right?"

Damn, this girl talked a lot. She was asking a million questions, and she was so into it, her ass didn't even know she in danger. Paradise was burning a hole through her head.

"Because me and my girl cut my parents up and made a game out of it," I informed her.

"Wait, what?" The excitement was replaced by disgust, and it took everything in me not to laugh in her face. "Who in the hell would do something like that?"

"Lucifer." As I stared at her, my eyes went cold. I didn't like the judgment in her eyes. "Would you like to meet him?"

"What the fuck is that supposed to mean? Are you threatening me?" She was getting loud and starting to piss me off.

"I don't throw threats, but I can tell you this. You close to bringing him out."

"I'm not sure who the fuck you're used to dealing with, but—"

That was all she got out before I had her off her feet, in the air, by her neck. She was pushing my buttons, and I didn't like that shit. "You got one more time and your ass gone regret ever meeting me," I told her.

Out of nowhere, my head snapped back, and I dropped her big ass. This nigga Shadow had socked the shit out my ass. Paradise ran up on Kimmie, and they started rumbling. I was turning toward Shadow, about to react, when Blaze went over to Paradise and lit her ear on fire. *Who in the fuck burns an ear?* I thought. The house was about to go crazy, and I wasn't for the dumb shit.

"Enough," I shouted as loud as I could.

Everybody stopped and looked at me like they were scared. The entire house was ready to meet Lucifer.

Turning to Shadow, I licked the blood in my mouth. The nigga stood his ground, and I walked up on him. You could hear a pin drop in that bitch.

"It's about time, Purse Dog," I rasped. "Who knew all I had to do was go at your girl to bring the beast out your ass? Make sure you have that motherfucking monster in your ass tomorrow." I walked toward the fellas, then turned back around. "Oh, and, Purse Dog, if you ever hit me like that again, I'll cut your hand off and feed it to your wife—"

"Nigga, shut your sick ass up and go check on your wife," Blaze interrupted. "I don't think her ass can hear you."

Laughing at Blaze, I wanted to slap his ass. This nigga played so much, he lucky I fucked with his ass.

"Blaze, I swear, your ass ain't shit. Why would you burn me, nigga?" Paradise muttered.

"Sis, I been looking at that motherfucker all day. You got pretty ears, and a nigga been waiting to get them motherfuckers."

Everybody laughed and went back to mingling. Shadow didn't know it, but I was proud of him. His brothers were a different kind of monster, but he was still reserved. I been trying to get that beast out of him all day. First time I'd looked in his eyes, I had seen potential. In another day and time, I would have made him my protégé. He had it in him to be worse than all of us, and a motherfucker just needed to bring it out of him.

Baby walked over. "You gone have my baby brother thinking you don't like him." Baby Face knew me, and he knew I had taken a liking to Purse Dog.

"That's because he don't know me," I answered.

"A'ight, y'all, we out. I'm about to go fuck my girl before she get horny and you niggas run a train on her ass," Blaze announced.

Everyone laughed at Blaze as he and his family headed upstairs. Then we all sat around, talking shit and having a good time. This was the life, and I prayed tomorrow we all made it out.

After about an hour of us all sitting around and kicking it, Paradise got up and went upstairs. Knowing I needed to get in them guts, I thought it was best that everybody laid it down. We had a long day ahead of us.

"A'ight, y'all, go be with your families and get some rest. Tomorrow we go to war. See y'all in the a.m.," I said.

Everybody finished up and headed upstairs. When I got to the room, Paradise wasn't there. She came in five minutes after me. I was about to ask her what the hell she was doing, but I just wanted some pussy and sleep. After taking my clothes off, I motioned for her to come over to me.

"Come suck this dick."

Her eyes lit up, and I knew this was about to be a good nut.

The next morning we were all downstairs, waiting on Blaze to grace us with his presence so we could go handle business. Everybody was just sitting around talking when Blaze came running down the stairs, screaming.

"Who the fuck did it? Which one of you motherfuckers wants to play these games? I'm about that fire life, and one of you motherfuckers just kicked off a war!"

We all looked up at him, and this nigga had one eyebrow, and half of his mustache was gone. We laughed so fucking hard, my side was killing me.

"This shit ain't funny! My shit just grew back," he yelled.

"At least you not blank, son. Now we can call you half assed." They mama was hell, and she kept my ass laughing.

When everybody kept laughing but nobody would say anything, he started snapping. "Okay. All right. I'm taking eyebrows off all you bitches. You think you can do this shit to me? You motherfuckers will be walking around hairless in Pelican Bay when I get finished with you. Shoe program, nigga! Twenty-three-hour lockdown. I'm the fucking man up in this piece."

When we realized this nigga was doing his version of Denzel Washington in *Training Day*, there wasn't a dry eye in the room, we were laughing so hard.

He went on. "I run shit here. You just live here. You better walk away. I'm gone burn this motherfucker down. King Kong ain't got shit on me. I'm winning anyway. I can't lose. I'm fine as fuck, and that eyebrow ain't gone make me." This nigga was doing the hand movements, laughs and all.

I was fucking done. I didn't think I had laughed that hard in my life.

"Nigga, shut up and go let that girl go draw you an eyebrow on, so y'all can hurry up and go handle this shit. I'm ready to go home and fuck in my own bed. I'm in a house full of Jeffrey Dahmers, John Wayne Gacys, and O. J. Simpsons and shit. Too many sick motherfuckers in here for me. My damn tiger won't get wet, because I'm too nervous. Motherfucker might come in and try to take my shit." Debra's ass was hell.

"Ma, don't nobody want that dry-ass pussy. Shit probably sound like corduroy pants rubbing together. Get yo' life. You can call me half assed, but I'm gone call your ass Sandman," Blaze declared, and then he walked off to go get his brows done.

"I hate you motherfuckers. Who raised y'all ass?"

We all looked at Debra and laughed.

Ten minutes later, Blaze finally came downstairs with his new brows and shit.

"Nigga, you look like an Instagram model." Smalls's ass stayed trying to go in on a nigga.

We grabbed our weapons and got ready to head to this plane.

"We don't have to go to Puerto Rico, y'all," Shadow announced, his expression grim.

Looking over at Shadow, I got disappointed. "Damn, Purse Dog. I thought you found your backbone last night."

"Back deez nuts. We don't have to go to Puerto Rico, because they are here. The entire house is surrounded."

Jumping from joke mode, we all went into killer mode instantly. We crept to the windows and looked out, and they definitely had us surrounded.

"Drea, go get all the kids, Mama, and the pastor and take them in the basement. Don't bring y'all ass out until I come get you," Blaze ordered. The funny Blaze was gone, and we got ready to go to war. Even the girls were in go mode.

"We gone have to split up in order to cover the entire grounds," Baby Face told us. "The girls can't be by themselves, so we mix it up. Gangsta, Blaze, me, and Smalls will take the front. Shadow, Paradise, and Shay, y'all take the east. Tank, Quick, Bay Bay, and Suave, y'all take the back. We will all work our way to the west. Everybody good?"

"Suave, go with Shadow. Quick got the back on lock, and now we good."

Everybody nodded and went to their designated place. Within seconds, all you heard was gunfire. We were dropping the niggas in the front like flies, and it felt good to be back. Wherever I heard the wind blow, I was letting my shit rip. Turning to get a nigga that was on the roof, I didn't see a nigga creep up on me. My instincts kicked in, and I felt him behind me, but by the time I turned, it was too late. Paradise ran in front of me, and he lit her up. Her body was jerking left and right. I went crazy, and I didn't stop shooting until every gun of mine was empty. His face was gone, and I kept shooting. I was so pissed, I didn't even realize all the other gunfire had stopped.

Suave ran up to me. "Baby bro, he dead. Let's get Paradise to the hospital."

I was so stuck looking at the holes in her body, I broke down.

"Come on, baby bro. We have to go," Suave urged. "If we want to save her, we have to leave now."

After picking her up, I cradled her and carried her to the car.

"Blaze and Shadow, come with us," Suave called. "The rest of y'all stay here. Smalls, call the cleanup crew. I'll keep y'all updated."

Suave was barking orders, but I didn't care about shit but my wife. Why the fuck would she jump in front of me like that? If anybody deserved to die, it was me. A nigga had done so much in his life, it was only right that I went to meet the real Lucifer. Seeing her body jerk like that . . . Man, I couldn't get that image out my head.

As soon as we got to the hospital, they took her in the back, and we were left to wait. If I lost my wife, the entire world was gone bleed until I found the head of that cartel. Motherfuckers didn't want to feel my wrath, but they were about to. She was the good part of me. In that moment, I understood why she wanted us out of this life. This was the part I didn't miss. When the smoke cleared, we had to hope everybody was left standing. My brother knew what I was going through, because he was in this same place with Tank. After sitting down beside me, he didn't say anything, but him being here meant a lot.

Paradise had to make it.

***

After waiting five hours, the doctors finally came back and told us they had been able to remove all the bullets but one. It was too risky right now to retrieve that last one, but she was stable. They had her sedated, but they let us back to see her. We were standing in the room, and I could hear heels coming down the hall. For some reason, the sound was drawing me to it. As I gazed at the door, a woman walked in. She was older and looked like she was Puerto Rican or some shit.

"Hello, Gangsta and Suave. So I get the pleasure of seeing you again," she said.

"Who the fuck are you?" I said. This wasn't the time for games.

"Mary Garzon, head of the Garzon Cartel." She looked at me and waited for me to put it together. This was Paradise's mother. Before I could extend my hand to her and update her on Paradise, she started talking again.

"I take it that you now know who I am. When you killed my husband and all his men, that left me in charge. You know, the head bitch in charge." She was walking around the room like she owned it, and we hung on to every word, trying to see where she was going with this convo. "My mama always said women were smarter than men, and I have proved her right. Using the money I had and my smarts, I was able to expand the cartel and have different factions, but we will get back to that. I see only half of the Hoover Gang is in attendance. I hope everyone is okay." She smirked, and now I was really trying to figure out what this bitch was on. "Blaze and Shadow, you can count out ten million dollars in your sleep, so why wouldn't you just pay the money?"

"Wait, you're the one that Rico owed the money to? I'm confused." Blaze wasn't catching on, but I understood it clearly.

"Blaze, it seems like we have a common enemy. Paradise's mom is the same person your dad owed and the person we have been looking for. She is the head of the faction in Puerto Rico," Suave explained. "What I want to know is, did you know that Paradise was there when you sent your men?" Now this was the answer I wanted to know, and I was glad Suave had asked the question.

She rolled her eyes. "Of course. I was there at Blaze's house when she took out half of my men. It was interesting that one crew I been looking for happened to come help the other crew I was now at war with. I'm able to kill two birds with one stone. You think you were going to use this li'l bitch of mine to kill my husband and get away with it? Didn't she teach your dumb ass anything?"

Before I knew it, I had my hand around her neck and was slamming her head against the wall.

"G, let her go!" Suave yelled. "You can't do this here, or you're going to jail. Gangsta, listen to your big bro. Let her go."

After squeezing one last time, I let her down, and she laughed.

"In due time, gutter rat. We will meet again," she spat.

She tried to turn and walk away, but Blaze ran up on her before she made it out the door. He flicked that Bic, and her hair caught fire fast as hell. She was standing there screaming and trying to put out the flames when this nigga kicked her in the ass. Her and that flaming hair went flying into the hallway. I prayed the bitch hit her head and died. I walked to the door and looked out, and I didn't see any men with her. The nurses grabbed her, and I walked back in Paradise's room.

"We may have taken out most of her crew," I said. "She is going to go home to Puerto Rico or Colombia and regroup. I'll have somebody follow her, and we gone take the war to her old ass. This shit ain't over."

This bitch had to go.

CHAPTER 55

SHADOW

Looking at Gangsta right now, I knew shit was about to go all bad. When Paradise's mother had been talking to us, he had stared at her intently. The minute she had admitted to shooting his girl, his eyes had gone cold. I had never witnessed someone cut their emotions that fast. Even now, he was just standing here, zoned out. When you looked in his eyes, you saw nothing. Realizing now why G was fucking with me, I could actually feel sympathy for him.

Motherfuckers always looked at me as the weak link, because I was the baby. Instead of him making fun of me and just teasing me about it, Gangsta had decided to help me. Now, I would have preferred for him to let me know what the fuck he was doing, but I got it. When I'd watched him in action back at Blaze's house, I hadn't wanted to be in the room. Seeing my brothers stand there and not flinch had shown me there was a lot I needed to learn.

People feared my brothers off their name alone, but motherfuckers feared me only because of my last name. I wanted the same respect that they had. Growing up, everybody had heard stories about Suave and Gangsta. If I had known that was who was at the fucking door when they first showed up, I would have just let the niggas in. A nigga needed his tongue to eat pussy, and that nigga

G known for snatching parts off a motherfucker. That demon that Suave and Gangsta possessed, I didn't have it. Even Blaze had that same sick way about him. Being around my brothers, I had never noticed how I didn't measure up to them, because we had done everything together.

It had taken Gangsta to come and show me my weakness. The good thing was, I was only twenty-two. My ass could learn and adapt. The only problem with that was, now that I wanted to learn to be that ruthless-ass nigga, we were out of the game. Deep in my own thoughts, I realized that so many insecurities I didn't know I possessed had surfaced. My weakness was why the women in my life always walked all over me. Kimmie was different, and I couldn't allow him to hurt her. That was how I knew she was my soul mate. If it had been Shirree's ass, issa funeral. There was no way I would have got in that shit and risked that nigga cutting my hand off.

Now appreciative of the legends that was standing before me, I decided I could work on that shit. No matter what, Shadow wasn't gone be that young, weak nigga no more. It was time for me to step out of my brothers' shadows and man the fuck up. I walked over to G, but I didn't know what to say. Hell, it didn't even seem like the nigga was here. Ain't no telling who this nigga was standing in the room. He liable to kill all our asses. Since I was on my grown-man shit now, I threw caution to the wind and spoke up.

"I'm sorry you going through this, and I just wanted you to know we here. Whatever you need us to do, we got your back."

When that nigga turned to face me, his eyes scared me so bad, a silent fart seeped out. My ass was praying it didn't stank, because the way he was looking, he might kill my ass for it. He turned his head back toward Paradise and didn't address what I had said at all. I looked over at Blaze, and he nodded his head in approval. It was fucked up, because his girl was in this position over our bullshit.

As if Suave could hear what I was thinking, he spoke up.

"A couple of years ago, we were in this same position. He doesn't blame you. Our loyalty is strong, and we knew the risks when we came back. He's blaming hisself for letting her come. I'm not going to tell you it's going to be okay, but know that in this moment, you are dealing with the worst side of him. They just unleashed something he fought so hard to bury. It's not going to be pretty, and he won't stop until they are all dead. We need you to be ready and trained to go. It can go from worse to bad, and we can lose more people along the way, but no matter what, we don't stop until it's done."

"Bro, you know we got you. I stay ready, and we feel the same way. When do we leave?" I said.

"Tomorrow we will go, while she is still weak from losing so many men," Suave replied.

Gangsta finally spoke. "No. We wait for Paradise. No matter how I feel, that is her mother. I didn't kill her father, and I won't kill her mother. The only way we kill that bitch is if she refuses to do it."

"Do you think she will do it?" I asked. If it was me, there was no way I could kill my mom. Blaze's ass would have no problems doing it, though.

"She the one that created Lucifer. She trained me," Gangsta answered.

Nothing else needed to be said. That had just told me that her ass just as crazy as his, or maybe worse, since she

had made him the way he was. As I looked at her lying in
the bed, I was glad she had made it. Now she needed to
get her ass up so we could finish what they had started.

As we walked into the house, we were exhausted. G had
refused to leave the hospital until Paradise had opened
her eyes. Unfortunately for us, that shit had taken two
days. We couldn't have left him there, because we didn't
know if that bitch would return and try to finish off
Paradise. Gangsta had said he was having her followed,
and I hadn't understood why he didn't just have her
killed. The nigga had asked me where the fun was in that.
He was certified crazy.

Kimmie walked up to me, crying, and everybody
looked at us with sadness in their eyes.

"She is okay," I told her. "We came back to take a shower
and change clothes. We will do shifts and take turns
staying with Gangsta until she gets out of there. No one
is to be left alone. If I'm at the hospital, Quick, you are to
stay here. We need precise shooters at both locations at
all times. Tank, if any of the women have to go anywhere,
you and Face will make sure you are with them. Smalls,
can you get your crew to stand guard outside?"

"I'll put them li'l niggas out there. We can take turns
guarding the back," Smalls said.

"How long do we have to do this for?" Drea asked, She
was looking worried.

"Until Paradise comes home," Blaze said. "When she
does, we head to Colombia. Everybody stay on point.
No more playing and no bullshitting around. When all
this is over, I'm going to figure out which one of y'all
did this shit to my eyebrow and its war. My shit was just
growing back."

That was the first time we had laughed in a couple of days.

Kimmie pulled me to the side and held me. "Baby, I'm so scared. This is some real-life movie shit. I just want to go home."

"This is your home for now. If you gone be married to me, then you have to be okay with shit like this. We gone end it as soon as possible. I promise," I told her.

I prayed nobody else got hurt.

CHAPTER 56

BLAZE

Standing there, listening to Paradise's mother, had pissed me off. Who the fuck shot their own fucking child and stood there and bragged about it? By the time she'd turned to walk out the door, I had never wanted to burn somebody so bad in my life. I couldn't imagine what G was feeling right then, but I knew when we got to Colombia, it was gone be all bad. His eyes were so empty that the nigga was giving me goose bumps. A nigga had never been happier to see a motherfucker open their eyes. Paradise scanned the room, looking for G, and as soon as her eyes landed on his, she started crying.

He climbed in the bed with her, and that shit made me feel some type of way. In a sense, it had me realizing what my family had gone through when I fake died.

"Why the fuck would you jump in front of me? Don't ever do that shit again," Gangsta told her.

"I'll do that shit a million times, my nigga. Life without you in it ain't living."

He kissed her, and the shit was so sweet, it made me want to go home and hold my wife. We didn't know how this shit was gone end or if all of us would make it out. No matter what, we had to finish this shit.

Gangsta cleared his throat. "I have something to tell you. The person that we are here to kill is your mom. She is the head of the cartel, and she tried to take you out."

When G said that, she sat up and looked him in the eyes. The bitch ain't even wince from the pain.

"How do you know that?" she asked.

"She came here and bragged about it," he told her.

The room got silent, and I wondered what she was thinking.

Suave broke the silence. "Sis, you know what needs to happen. G wants to give you the respect of doing it yourself. Are you okay with that?"

We all looked at her, and in a split second, her eyes looked like G's had when he was waiting on her to wake up. She looked at Suave with nothing in her eyes.

"Tell me when. The bitch dead to me anyway," was all she said.

Shadow looked at me.

"These motherfuckers crazy," I mouthed to his ass, and we laughed at our silent joke.

"Can we go to the house now? A nigga's balls sticking to my damn thighs," I groused.

"Yeah, but it has to be quick. We have to stay here at the hospital until she gets out. We can rotate," Suave stated as we got ready to leave. "Baby bro, you coming?'

"I'm not leaving until she leaves," Gangsta said.

"Nigga, you gone smell like death and booty. Just know you ain't getting in my car. You better ask my mama how I feel about that funky shit," I muttered.

"Shut your dumb ass up and come on," Suave said. Then he pushed my ass out the door, and we headed to the main house.

Emotions were high there when we walked in, and I knew everybody was scared. Reality had set in that there was a chance all our asses wasn't coming back. Not with me, though. I had died already, so fuck that. It was somebody else's turn. After explaining everything to the entire house, I went up to my room to wash my ass.

Drea followed me upstairs. "Baby, I don't like this shit. What if you don't come back?" she said.

"Your ass better not fuck nobody else for five years. Make sure a nigga really gone this time."

"This is not the time to play," she told me, desperation in her voice. "I'm dead ass. It could have been any one of you laid up in that bed."

"I know that, but one thing is for certain. If we don't go, all of our asses might die. This has to be done. I'm not going nowhere. Just keep our baby girl safe no matter what."

I pulled her into the bathroom with me, and we got in the shower together. They could say what they wanted, but I was about to get this pussy.

It had been a long three weeks, and the shit had been wearing everybody down, but they were finally releasing Paradise from the hospital. A nigga was tired of hospital rooms, and I couldn't wait to get her ass home. Paris was at the house, getting it together, because we were throwing Paradise a welcome home party. This would be the last gathering we had before our asses had to go to Colombia.

The trip was in two days, and I couldn't wait to get this shit over with. Thanks to me, we had been bringing G clothes, and he had showered at the hospital. I couldn't let my man go out of there without getting cleaned up. His ass had been walking around, smelling like peeled lips. After loading Paradise up in the car, we headed to the house. Baby Face had finally healed all the way, and I wondered if Paradise was gone be good to take this trip. If we waited any longer, the old bitch was gone have time to build an entire army. Hoping Paradise was good to go, I pushed those thoughts in the back of my mind and prepared to have a drama-free day. We all needed this shit, and I couldn't wait to get some real food in my fucking system.

Pulling up to the house, I prayed these niggas knew how to take a surprise. They didn't come across as the type that had people jumping out from behind places with the lights off. Fuck around and the entire house could be dead as fuck. That was why I told they ass to just hang banners and everybody just kick it and have a good time. We not doing that surprise bullshit.

As soon as Paradise walked in the door and saw the decorations and shit, her hard demeanor and walls came down. She looked happy as fuck to see everybody, and I was glad. As long as Paradise was happy, G was too. Tank and Suave looked like they were ready to fuck in the front room, and I had to remind they ass I ain't play that shit. Reaching over to them, I flicked that Bic, and Suave put her down.

"Damn, nigga. I get it with your cock-blocking ass. You don't want nobody to get pussy but you," Suave complained.

I shrugged. "Damn right. Now go party."

Face was in the corner, texting, and I walked over.

"Nigga, fuck you doing?" I said.

"This new chick I been dating is trying to see me, and I was debating on whether or not to let her come over here. A nigga need some pussy, but you know we don't bring outsiders to the house."

"With everything that's going on and the war that's coming, let her come. Shid, it might be the last time our ass get to dig in some guts. You think Shay gone be pissed? I saw her ass walking like she had on a ten-dollar pair of heels and them bitches was leaning."

Face shook his head. "She got a nigga, and I don't do drama."

"Cool. Then invite her ass over."

After walking to the dining table, I grabbed me a plate and sat down in the front room to eat. My plate was piled up with baked beans and deviled eggs, and I felt sorry for whoever sat next to my ass. Everything was going smooth, and this was a perfect moment. Until my mama got her nasty ass up and started grinding on the pastor. He was standing his ass there, grinning and shit. When she dropped down to the floor, I was ready to snatch her ass up.

Paris piped up. "Let Mama be great. Y'all been through a lot these last couple of weeks. She need this."

Looking over at Paris, I nodded my head and kept eating. She was right. We had the right to get loose. Once I was done eating, a nigga was gone lay back on and just watch my family have a good time. Shit was going good until my stomach started boiling. When I glanced over at Paris, I saw she was asleep on the couch, and I lifted my leg and passed gas. That shit felt good, but it smelt like horse shit and eggs.

After the third time doing it, I was glad nobody had come my way and smelled this shit. Feeling like I would be good to go if I let loose one last time, I lifted that leg and let it ride. Paris jumped out of her sleep, and her head whipped around so fast, I started laughing before she said anything.

"Blaze, if you open yo' ass one more time, I'ma fuck you up," she snapped.

"My bad. It's them damn beans."

She rolled her eyes and lay back down. I couldn't do shit but laugh. Just then Face walked to the middle of the floor with this fine-ass bitch, and everybody stopped to look.

"Hey, y'all. This my friend Royalty," Face said.

She waved, and we all spoke.

Ma went first. "Who the fuck is this you done brought in our shit? Your ass was ready to throw my dick out the doe, but you come walking in here with some white pussy."

Baby Face threw up his hands. "Ma, she not white."

Ma squinted at Royalty. "Is she black? Then her ass is white. You got a lot of nerve. I should fuck Devon right here on your couch to teach your ass not to fuck with me."

I came to Face's defense. "Ma, for once, can you be normal?"

Her head whipped around, and she glared at me. "For once, can you suck deez nuts? I ain't think so." She walked off, mumbling, and I laughed hard as hell. She had a point, though, but she ain't gotta be so damn ignorant.

Like we were some kids, all the men gathered around Royalty, as if she was a new toy Face had got for Christmas. Smalls walked up with two plates in his hands.

"Am I tripping, or do she look like Journey?" he said.

Gangsta and Suave looked at Paradise and then back at Royalty. They looked at each other, and then both of them pulled their guns on Royalty.

"Party over! Everybody get the fuck out," Gangsta shouted.

Me and my brothers were lost as hell. Who in the fuck was Journey?

CHAPTER 57

SUAVE

When Baby Face introduced Royalty, I hadn't really paid attention to her looks. My bitch was the baddest in the room, if you asked me. When Smalls walked up and said that shit, I actually got a good look at her. Her and Journey looked so much alike, it was creepy. Looking over at Paradise, you could see the resemblance to her as well. Knowing there was no way this shit could be a coincidence, especially since we knew Paradise's mother was behind it, we raised our guns on the bitch.

Blaze and them were looking confused, but they would figure it out soon. As I stared into Royalty's eyes, she tried to keep a straight face, but her eyes changed over. Not to mention, any other bitch would have been scared and screaming. She stood there, saying nothing.

"Party over! Everybody get the fuck out." Gangsta wasn't playing no games, and I wasn't, either.

"Wait, y'all know her?" Baby Face said, looking really confused.

I shook my head. "Naw, we never met the bitch, but we know who she is. Tell him who you are."

The bitch didn't flinch or mumble a word. Waiting until everybody had cleared out of the room, I hit her in the face with my gun, and she passed out and fell to the floor. Paradise walked over and looked at her. Then she reaching in her pocket and pulled out her wallet. She pulled out her ID, then passed it to us. We were right, but I knew that anyway. My gut was never wrong.

"Royalty Garzon. This bitch," I growled.

"We know y'all get it, but help us figure out what the fuck is going on." Baby Face was getting pissed. He didn't like being out of the loop.

"Her name is Paradise Garzon." I paused and waited on them to catch on. Then I continued. "A couple years ago, Paradise's father sent his daughter Journey in to set up G. Nobody knew they were sisters but him. Tank killed her, and we went to war with the Garzon Cartel. The same cartel we are at war with right now. When Smalls said this bitch Royalty looked like Journey, we knew there was no way that shit was a coincidence with everything that's going on."

"I wonder how many kids that old-ass nigga got," Smalls said while he was smacking on some chicken.

I shook my head. "I don't know, but when this bitch wakes up, we gone get everything we need out of her ass. Face, go set up the basement. We need every tool and knife you have in this motherfucker. Shadow, carry her downstairs."

After everything was set up, we waited on her to wake up. When Royalty finally opened her eyes, you could see she knew it was over for her.

Paradise started the questioning off. "Did you know about me?"

"Fuck you." She spit in Paradise's face.

By the looks on the Hoover brothers' faces, I knew they had no idea Paradise was worse than G. They were looking too calm.

Paradise walked over to the table and grabbed a knife, and in one swift motion, she sliced one of Royalty's ears off. "Did you know about me?" she repeated.

Blaze stepped forward and raised his hand, as if he was in class. "Hey, sis. Not to bother you or anything while you in here cutting up bodies, but you did slice her ear off, so how she gone hear you?"

Paradise gave Blaze a death stare, and he laughed and backed up.

"My bad," he said. "You can continue. I'm just saying you mad she ain't responding, but you stepping on her ear."

This wasn't the time to be joking, but I swear, I couldn't stop laughing. It was the truth.

After grabbing a meat tenderizer, Paradise hit Royalty in the face with it, tearing off her skin. "Bitch, your mama sent you here to die. She knew you wouldn't make it out. I'm guessing she didn't tell you about us . . . the stories and how we get down. You gone sit here and protect a motherfucker that set you up to die?"

"Yeah, I knew about you, and I didn't give a fuck. Growing up, all I heard was I needed to be more like Paradise. But look at you. Bitch, you're a fucking mom, and I'm next in line to be the heiress to the Garzon Cartel."

"I'm sure they need a motherfucker that can hear in charge," Blaze quipped.

I looked over at Blaze, and he threw his hands up and laughed.

"Let me talk to her, sis," I told Paradise. She moved back, and I walked over to Royalty. "You don't have to say anything. I just need you to nod. Do you know who I am?"

She shook her head yes.

"Then you know what I am about. I won't sit here and threaten you or raise my voice. You should already know what's coming if you don't answer my questions. How many men does your mom have in Colombia?"

She looked at me but didn't respond.

I pulled a chair up and sat down. "Smalls, go find me a dog," I said.

Smalls scrunched up his face. "Nigga, where am I supposed to go find a dog?"

"I don't care if you have to steal one out somebody's yard. Just come back with a dog for me."

Smalls glared at Royalty. "Sick-ass nigga. Bitch, just answer the damn question. Do you know what he about to do to your ass?"

When she didn't respond, he left.

Never breaking my stare, I waited for Smalls to come back.

Smalls walked in the door with a pit bull on a leash. I stood up, rolled my sleeves up, and walked over to the table. I picked up a butcher knife and headed back to her. Leaning down, I whispered in the dog's ear and then stood up straight.

Baby Face took a step forward. "Suave, you not gone ask her again and give her a chance?"

After turning to Face, I smirked. "I don't give second chances." Before anybody saw it coming, I chopped her arm off at the elbow. I threw it to the dog, but he didn't move. "Eat," I ordered.

The dog started tearing her arm to shreds. Royalty was screaming for dear life, and the shit didn't move me.

"How many men does your mom have?" I asked her again.

"Not many. Y'all took a lot of them out. She is regrouping and plans on coming here in two days. They plan to take your entire family out. Now please, let me go."

I brought the knife down on her other arm, then threw it to the dog. "Eat."

The screams got louder, but she had no idea what was about to happen to her.

"G, you want a part of this before I end her?"

G nodded and picked up a brick. "Come here, Shadow," he said.

The Hoover brothers were looking worried, because they knew baby brother wasn't about this life. But Shadow walked over to Gangsta.

"Take this brick and bash her head in until that shit is removed from her body. You are not allowed to stop until you have a head to give me. Do you understand?" G held out the brick.

"Naw, G, he not ready for that," Baby Face insisted. He wasn't with the shit G was on, but he had to learn at some point.

"Do you understand?" G never took his eyes off Shadow.

Shadow grabbed the brick from Gangsta and kicked her chair back. He slammed the brick down on her head, and he kept hitting her until her head snapped off. Then he picked up the head and threw it at Blaze.

"Nigga, don't play with me. I'll set your asshole on fire," Blaze warned him.

When Shadow walked back over, he had a different look in his eye. He may have had a beast in him all along, and no one knew it.

"Paradise and G, grab a knife. It's time to make her ass disappear," I announced. "Y'all can go upstairs if you don't want to see this. It's about to get messy. We'll put her out back for you to play with, Blaze. Get your lighter ready."

Everybody but Shadow headed out.

"What we gotta do?" he asked.

CHAPTER 58

BABY FACE

"Who the fuck y'all done let in our house? These moth-erfuckers are sick as hell." Quick was trying not to throw up.

"The devil," I said point-blank. "I admit their way of killing is intense, but it's effective. I'm worried about Shadow. I think he is trying to prove to G he ain't a bitch, but he biting off more than he can chew."

"The dog too. How Suave's ass gone make that mutt eat the bitch's arm in her face?" Blaze said with a straight face.

I laughed at Blaze. "Nigga, you know how they get down. I'm surprised you acting shocked."

"Knowing it and seeing it is two different things," Blaze shot back. "I'm just ready to light some shit up. I hope it don't take them long. I'm trying to get some pussy."

"Nigga, you do realize they about to cut that girl's body up and hand it to your ass, right?"

"And I'm gone hand her ass over to hell," Blaze responded.

We laughed at this nigga and walked toward the stairs. He talking about them, but the fact that he didn't see nothing wrong with the shit he did let me know he just as crazy. We rounded the corner, and Juicy was sitting there on the couch. Not moving, I just looked at her. She looked so broken, and I wanted to wrap her in my arms, but I stood still.

Blaze stared at her. "Damn, sis. You must have smelled your dick in jeopardy. Where your ass been? You look bad, girl. Look like your ass been sleeping under the porch."

I punched Blaze in his arm. I needed him to shut the fuck up.

"Can I talk to you, Face?" Juicy said in a small voice.

I hiked my shoulders. "*Now* you want to talk?"

"Please."

Not having the heart to treat her how she had me, I walked over to her. My brothers went toward the kitchen, and I looked at her, waiting for her to speak.

"I'm sorry for the way I was acting. I have PPD."

Blaze went beserk. "Don't bring that shit to my brother with your nasty ass. Face, you better get checked out. Ain't no telling how long she has had that shit. You ain't want me to set you on fire, but you been burning all this time."

I looked over at Blaze. He had eased back into the front room. "Nigga, that mean postpartum depression. Get your dumb ass out of here and let us talk!"

"Wait, so her pussy depressed? Nigga, just fuck her and get your girl back. 'Cause your new bitch getting cut to pieces right now. Her pussy definitely gone be woe."

Running my hand down my face in frustration, I was ready to beat his ass.

Blaze held up his hands and backed away. "A'ight. I'm gone. Niggas never want my opinion and shit. Fuck y'all."

I watched the doorway until he left, and then I turned and faced Juicy again. "Why didn't you tell me?"

The tears started falling down her face. "I didn't know what was wrong with me. All I knew is the baby and you were too much to deal with, so I left. You don't know how many nights I cried myself to sleep, and I just needed to get away. When I tried to kill myself, my mama took me to the hospital, and they told me what was wrong with me. I'm in therapy now, and I would like it if you come with me and we work on our family. If you don't want to, I understand, but I had to come tell you what was going on. I'm sorry, Face. I really do love you."

I grabbed her and pulled her to my chest. "I'll go, but not until I get back."

"You going to see your new bitch?"

"Naw. She down there in the basement, getting eaten up by a dog."

Looking at me like I was crazy, she waited for me to explain.

"Go upstairs and take a shower and lie down. When we done with this shit, I'll tell you everything. I'm glad you're back." Even though she still looked bad, her face brightened up. It was going to be a long road, but I was here for it.

"I'm guessing we done fucking now, since your wife back."

I turned my head, and Shay was standing there in some booty shorts and a sports bra. She was looking fine as fuck, and I needed Tsunami to sit the fuck down.

"Yeah, we gone try to work our shit out. You good, though?" My mouth was saying no, but my dick was saying, "Blow that bitch back out now." She needed to be good, because I ain't want no problems or drama. We had enough shit going on.

She walked over to me and rubbed Tsunami. "At least I know somebody still wants me. If you ever want to hook up again, you know how to get in touch." She slid her tongue in my mouth while she caressed my dick.

When she walked off, I wanted so bad to follow behind her and go for one last ride before I got back on track with my family. Knowing that shit wouldn't be in my best interest, I stayed my ass put. God Himself had to come hold me back, because my dick was trying his best to pull me toward her.

"Damn, nigga, you got three hoes under the same roof. Juicy gone kill your ass," Blaze joked after popping up again.

As I walked toward Blaze to beat his ass, he took off running.

"Nigga, wait until your dick go down first. Your ass wanna wrestle, and your shit looking like it's ready to bust through your pants," Blaze yelled when he looked back.

When I looked down, my shit was at full attention. Laughing, I tried to readjust my shit before Juicy really did beat my ass. Then I walked out in the yard. They had just finished putting all of Royalty's remains in the garbage.

"Go 'head, Blaze. Do your thang," Suave called.

This nigga actually smiled because it was his turn and he got to do the finale. After everything was cleaned up, we walked back in the house.

"We have to leave tomorrow. We can't give her the chance to fully regroup and come here. Smalls, you and your crew should stay behind. That way somebody is here that can protect our family."

Blaze shook his head vigorously. "Hold the fuck up. You know Drea's pussy is friendly. I ain't leaving his ass here to run all through my girl's pussy while I'm over there, trying not to die again."

"Shut up, Blaze," everybody screamed at the same time.

"We leave at six. Everybody go and get some rest. Fuck your girls, love on your kids, and make sure you stay alert. See y'all in the morning."

They all went their separate ways, and I headed upstairs to my room. As I walked down the hall, I heard some noises coming from one of the guest rooms. When

I stuck my head in to make sure everything was good, I found Shay lying on the bed, asshole naked, playing with her pussy. When she realized I was watching, she really got worked up. Her moans had Tsunami back at attention. After watching until she was finished, I walked over to her and slid my hand up her pussy. The shit was so wet, I wanted to dive in so bad. I stuck my finger in her mouth, and she sucked my shit so good, I almost put my dick in it.

"If I wasn't a good nigga, I'd have my dick in your cervix right now. This shit is done, baby girl. It was one night, and it's over. Get some sleep. We got a long day tomorrow." After kissing her on her cheek, I walked out of her room. As I headed to my room with a swollen dick, I knew I was gone be in the shower, beating my meat. Juicy ain't gave me none in forever. When I went in the room, I didn't even attempt to get in the bed with her. I needed to release this nut, so I headed straight to the bathroom.

As soon as the water hit my body, I started stroking my shit. When I felt another hand wrap around my dick, I knew I was about to lose this battle. Shay was determined to get this dick, and I didn't have the restraint to say no anymore. My dick was so hard, the shit was aching. But when I turned around, I came face-to-face with Juicy. I picked her up, then slid her down on my dick fast and hard.

CHAPTER 59

QUICK

All these niggas crazy. Now don't get me wrong. I had no problem laying a nigga down. I'd been killing all my life, but this shit was on a different level. Growing up, I had always thought motherfuckers were exaggerating the stories about G and them. You know how niggas in the hood do, but I had witnessed this shit firsthand, and my ass was sick to my stomach. I had always thought Blaze could get a check for the shit he did and how he didn't mind cooking a nigga. This was a different level–type shit.

Heading upstairs, I needed to gather my thoughts for tomorrow. Seeing Shadow do that shit to ole girl was fucking with my mind. Not the action itself, but how easy it was for G to get him to do it. We had always protected him from the worst part of this street shit. He was the baby, and there was just certain shit we didn't want him doing. Hell, when we were robbing banks, we always left the nigga in the car. I couldn't wait for this shit to be over. It was getting way out of hand, and I just wanted things to get back to normal.

When I walked in the kids' room, I discovered that Zavi was asleep, and I hugged and kissed him. I hated that he had seen another nigga and had looked to him as another daddy. Yeah, I had killed Jason's ass, but my son grieving him pissed me off. I walked out of the room, then headed to my own bedroom. A nigga had too much on his dome and just wanted to take my ass to sleep.

"You okay, Quick?" Ash said when I stepped into the bedroom. She was lying in bed.

"Yeah, Ma, I'm good. Get some rest. When you wake up, I'll be gone. We heading out at six."

The tears started forming in her eyes, and I felt bad. "Please be safe. I can't lose you. We just found our way back to each other."

"It's going to be okay. Once we are done here, we are done for good," I assured her.

"How do you know it won't be somebody else that will pop up and then you have to go to war with them? Is it ever really over? Can a person ever fully retire?"

"I don't know the answer to that, but I will say this. The Hoover Gang is strong enough to handle whatever comes our way. You just gotta have faith in your man and his abilities," I told her. "I'll always protect my family no matter what is thrown our way. We got out the game, but I don't know if someone will try us again. That's what this street life is about. You knew the type of nigga you were marrying, and you have to be strong enough to deal with that."

I went on. "Look at Paradise and Tank. Now, I'm not asking you to be a killer, but they don't question they man or his abilities. They have full trust that they gone handle the shit. I need you to be strong and know that I'm gone be good. Anything can happen, but if it does, you can't break. We have a son, with a baby on the way. They will need you. Do you understand what I am saying to you?"

She nodded her head, and I kissed her.

"A nigga need to take a shower and get some sleep. Come with me. This dick ain't gone suck itself."

Slapping me in the head, she laughed as she got up. Tomorrow would be hell, but tonight I was gone lose myself in this pussy. Ash and the kids were my everything, and I was gone fight like hell to get back to them. Even if I had to cut a bitch's arm off. Laughing at them sick niggas, I closed my eyes as her mouth wrapped around my dick. I definitely had to come back to this shit.

"So what's the plan?" Nobody had said anything about how we were going to handle this.

"Since Paradise know the entire layout of the compound, we are allowing her to take the lead. If any of you see her mother, hold her until she gets there. Nobody is to be left alone, so keep your eyes and your ears open. Quick, you and G are going in the front since you are our most precise shooters. Take down the wall of defense, and we will cover you." Baby Face barked orders, and we all listened.

Baby Face went on. "Tank and her crew will take the back. Blaze, wait . . . What the fuck you doing with that?"

We turned around, and this nigga had his big-ass flamethrower on his back.

"Nigga, it's about to be the Fourth of July in this bitch," Blaze declared. "That li'l-ass lighter wasn't gone do the trick. Y'all cut 'em down. I'm gone light they ass up. Simple. Now hurry up with this long-ass lecture. I swear, you and Suave will have a nigga sitting there for hours for one damn plan. All your ugly ass had to say was, 'Shoot until ain't shit moving.' The end. Let's go shit. Y'all got this nigga Smalls at home with my bitch. If she even thinks my ass dead, issa slip."

"Let's go. This nigga is losing his mind. G, you ready?"
Suave said.

Looking over at Gangsta, I saw this nigga's eyes were
empty as hell. He didn't even respond; nigga just jumped
the gate and started shooting.

"Fuck! Hurry up and get in there. This nigga crazy," I
yelled, agreeing with Suave, as I leaped over him and
covered G. We were laying niggas down, and it wasn't
long before you heard gunfire going off everywhere. I
covered the niggas on the ground while Gangsta took out
the niggas on the roof. When we walked inside the house,
it was too quiet.

"Turn your back to me. You keep that side covered, and
I got this side," G said in a low voice.

Me and G went back to back. As the guards started
pouring in, we laid they asses out. My ass almost pissed
myself when Blaze rounded the corner, shooting fire.
Having a flashback, I got the fuck out of the way before
that shit hit me. Knowing it wouldn't be long before the
house was up in flames, we made our way through
the rest of the big-ass house.

"Damn, how many rooms this bitch got?" Blaze muttered.

Me and Blaze laughed, but G didn't crack a smile. After
we had walked the entire house, G decided to split up.

"I need to find Paradise and this bitch. Y'all go outside
and make sure the others are good," he said.

"You sure?" I asked.

He gave me a look that let me know he was straight.
We walked outside and rounded the compound, and it
was good to see Tank and her crew was good. They had
cleared the entire backyard.

"Where is Shadow, Suave, and Paradise?" I called.

"We don't know. We thought they went in with y'all,"
Tank called back.

I walked off with Blaze, and we peered through a window. I noticed some people in a room. Paradise had her gun pointed at her mom. Me and Blaze noticed some kind of trigger in her hand, and we looked at each other.

"This bitch the real, Blaze. She about to blow all our asses to hell. What the fuck have we gotten ourselves into?"

CHAPTER 60

PARADISE

As soon as the outside was clear, I entered the house. I saw my mama rounding the corner, and I rushed up behind her. She walked into her office and stood by the window behind her desk. I followed her into the room.

She turned and stared at me. "You were always such a disappointment. No matter what you did, I could never get Louis to see you weren't the child he thought you was. He had more faith in you than he had in me, his own fucking wife. Did you know I stood right here in this house and watched you kill your father? He would have given you the world, but it was nothing for you to betray him for that gutter rat."

She went on. "All is well that ends well, though. You saved me from having to do it. He was becoming weak. The enemy was creeping in, taking over, and all he cared about was bringing you back home. He wasn't here for months, and I had to run shit and clean up his mess. You're weak, just like he is, because that low life means more to you than anything else."

"You were always jealous of me, and that's okay," I told her. "I found a family who loves and accepts me just as I am. I killed your husband because he was weak. I killed your bitch-ass daughter because she was weak. Garzons don't do weak. Did you know jealousy is an emotion and emotions are weak? You know what that means, right? It's time to send your bitch ass to your husband."

She shook her head. "I don't think so." She lifted her hand, and I could see she was holding a trigger. "If I put my hand on this button, we all go. Are you willing to kill your low life as well since you just took a bullet for him?" As soon as she said that, G, Suave, and Shadow entered the room.

"Why haven't you killed her yet?" G yelled at me. He was looking at me as if he was unsure I could do the job.

"Because she wants to save your life," my mama told him. She dangled the trigger around. "Now, everybody put their guns down and let me walk out of here. If not, we all go."

We all looked at each other, and I knew we were in a catch-22. If she walked out of here, she would kill us all, and if we didn't put the guns down, we would all die. Not really having a choice, we were getting ready to lower our weapons when a stream of fire came through the window. This nigga Blaze was torching her from outside the window. Quick came right behind him and shot the trigger out of her hand. Wanting to be the one that caused her to take her last breath, I walked up to her burning body and emptied my clip in her head. Then I grabbed the fire extinguisher off the wall and put the fire out. As I looked over at Gangsta, I smiled.

"Hey, G, you want to make a bet?" I said.

CHAPTER 61

BLAZE

We were finally back home, and I couldn't be happier. The shit was done, and my family had made it out one last time on top. When Paradise put the fire out, I was pissed. I wanted to see that bitch's body turn to ashes. She turned to G and was smiling all goofy and shit.

"Hey, G, you want to make a bet?" she said.

When he started smiling back, me and my brothers looked at each other, trying to figure out what the fuck was going on.

"This time, loser has to do everything dealing with Kenya's bad ass for two months. Feeding, cleaning, babysitting, the works," she said.

"Bet," Gangsta said.

"The fuck are you niggas talking about?" I yelled.

Suave pulled us out of the room, laughing. "You don't want to be in there for that. When they first met, they made a bet to see who could cut our parents up the smallest and fastest. Nastiest shit I ever seen. Let's go. Let them have they moment."

"Nigga, and you feeding a bitch to a dog wasn't nasty? All you niggas sick."

We laughed as we waited outside for the nasty-ass couple to finish. Them niggas was made for each other.

As much as we wanted they creepy asses to go back where the fuck they came from, watching them in the foyer with their bags didn't feel right.

"Shadow's birthday is tomorrow. Stay one more day and let us take y'all out to thank y'all."

"One more day, nigga, and we better have fun. I been dodging bullets and killing since I been here," Suave quipped.

Laughing at Suave, we all went upstairs to get ready. Out of everything we been through this month, I was more excited about this than anything. We hadn't been out in a year, and I couldn't wait to party.

After throwing on my all-black Gucci button-up, my black Gucci jeans, and my red high-top Giuseppes, I was ready to go. When we all made it down to the foyer, everybody looked like money. There was almost a billion dollars standing in this foyer, and that right there was enough for me to be happy. Couldn't complain about the life we chose to live or the ups and downs that came with it. At the end of the day, we had come out on top and had lived to tell the story. We jumped in our Phantoms, G riding with me, and Suave with Face.

As soon as we pulled up to Hoover Nights, I started smiling.

"Nigga, what the fuck you smiling at?" G said.

"You have no idea. Watch this shit."

When the first set of headlights went off, the crowd went nuts. G looked at me, all confused.

"What the fuck they screaming for?" he asked me.

Not responding, I just laughed and turned my lights off. After opening our car doors at the same time, me and my brothers stepped out. G and Suave stepped out as well, and we walked to their side. The crowd was going crazy, and people recognized who they were.

"Oh, my God, Lucifer. Can I just touch your hand?" one of the girls screamed from the crowd.

"What kind of place is this?" G said.

Me and my brothers looked at each other and started doing our wave. The crowd joined in and started chanting, "Hoover. Hoover. Hoover."

Suave was laughing, but G's ass had to ruin our moment.

"Y'all aggy as hell," he said. "If y'all don't bring y'all dumb ass on . . . I need a fucking drink, and you out here waving and shit at the crowd like you the queen of England."

Laughing, we all walked in the club. Of course, the crowd went nuts when they saw us.

"Aw shit, the Hoover Gang in the motherfucking building," the DJ announced. "Wait, did these niggas get Suave and Lucifer to come out and party with us? I need everybody to raise they fucking glasses and salute some real niggas. You in the presence of legends."

Everybody raised their cups as our song played.

"I think I'm Big Meech, Larry Hoover. Whipping work, hallelujah. One nation, under God. Real niggas getting money from the fucking start." "B.M.F.," by Rick Ross, played over the speakers as we partied with the crowd.

This was the life, and I wouldn't apologize for nothing we had done. It had made us who we were today, and we some boss-ass niggas with some bad bitches to hold us down. We had more money than we knew what to do with, so how the fuck could you complain behind some shit like that? We had made it, and we had defeated all our enemies. Drea hadn't slipped on anymore dicks, so life was great. We didn't have shit else to worry about, and we could just live life how we wanted.

Shadow came and stood by Gangsta, and I didn't think shit of it until I heard him try to whisper, "G, will you train me?"

The End

Message from the Hoover Gang:

Thank you so much for rocking with us for four books strong. You have made us one of the biggest series this summer. We hate to go, but whenever you're missing a real nigga, just reach in your pocket and flick your Bic.

Everybody good over here. Mama and the pastor getting married, Quick and Ash had they baby girl, and Shadow's dick finally work. Kimmie is pregnant. Blaze still lighting shit up, and Baby Face and Juicy worked out their problems. We go visit Gangsta and Suave often.

We are going to miss you, and we appreciate all your support. Grab you some paperbacks so you can always have a piece of us in your life. We love you.

Keeping up with Latoya Nicole

FB: Latoya Nicole Williams
Ig: Latoyanicole35
Twitter: Latoyanicole35
SC: iamTOYS
Email: latoyanicole@yahoo.com
Join my readers' group on FB: Toy's House of Books.

Check out Amazon for other releases by Latoya Nicole.